Books by Mark Henry

HAPPY HOUR OF THE DAMNED

ROAD TRIP OF THE LIVING DEAD

BATTLE OF THE NETWORK ZOMBIES

Published by Kensington Publishing Corporation

# BATTLE OF THE NETWORK ZOMBIES

# MARK HENRY

KENSINGTON BOOKS

www.kensingtonbooks.com

KENSINGTON BOOKS are published by

Kensington Publishing Corp.
119 West 40th Street
New York, NY 10018

All Kensington titles, imprints, and distributed lines are available at special quantity discounts for bulk purchases for sales promotion, premiums, fund-raising, educational, or institutional use.

Special book excerpts or customized printings can also be created to fit specific needs. For details, write or phone the office of the Kensington Special Sales Manager: Attn. Special Sales Department. Kensington Publishing Corp., 119 West 40th Street, New York, NY 10018. Phone: 1-800-221-2647.

Kensington and the K logo Reg. U.S. Pat. & TM Off.

ISBN-13: 978-0-7582-2527-6
ISBN-10: 0-7582-2527-X

First Kensington Trade Paperback Printing: March 2010
First Kensington Mass Market Printing: August 2011
10 9 8 7 6 5 4 3 2 1

Printed in the United States of America

For Kevin
(on the occasion of taking a joke too far)

# Acknowledgments

Thanks to everyone who supports me and puts up with my bullshit during the course of writing and promoting a book, particularly . . .

. . . my darling Caroline, who not only deals with the snarky mood conjuring up Amanda inevitably brings, but also edits the crap out of my first draft.

. . . Jaye Wells and Leah Sharp Hodge, who wrestled with my writing demons right alongside me, for much of this book.

. . . my agent, Jim McCarthy, and editor, John Scognamiglio, for not calling me a hack every time I turn in a manuscript—or anytime, for that matter.

. . . my lovely and talented beta reader, Stacia Kane, for getting the jokes and giving it to me straight.

. . . the South Sound Algonquins, whose tireless efforts make me a better writer and who listen to the vilest of the vile right out in public.

. . . the members of Team Seattle and The League of Reluctant Adults for making going on book tour, and conference and convention off-hours such a fantastic time.

. . . Todd Thomas, Synde Korman, and Terri Smythe, whose time would probably be better spent not having to deal with the League forum.

. . . all the awesome booksellers and librarians I've met over the past few years—your efforts are much appreciated.

. . . the readers who consistently surprise me with their depravity and hunger for the foul-mouthed undead.

. . . my friends and family who barely see me when

I'm in the home stretch and only give me a little shit about it.

    . . . and, finally, all the online folks, Glamazombies, yahoos, tweeps, and Facebookers—without you, I might actually be more productive.

    Where's the fun in that?

Its official name was the H & C Gentleman's Club—
that's what it said on the tax statement, at least, and in
the phone book—but everyone in Seattle knew it as the
Hooch and Cooch, the Northwest's first hillbilly-
themed titty bar, and it certainly lived up to its backwoods inspirations. The exterior was dilapidated, a
hodgepodge of boards nailed up at weird angles and in-
tervals as siding, while rust from the corrugated-metal
roof striped the building a gritty orange. It clung to the
hillside above Fremont on pilings so rickety, the slightest bump threatened to dump the shack's smutty guts
onto the quiet neighborhood underneath.

I'd applaud the audacity, if the owner weren't Ethel
Ellen Frazier, vampire, mega-bitch and, worst of all,
my mother.

I considered leaving the car idling in the space—a sound getaway plan was looking like my best option—then fished out my cell and hammered in Marithé's number.

"Seriously?" I asked the second she picked up, fondling the address she'd written on the back of my business card.

"What?" My assistant's voice always sounds annoyed, so it's difficult to assess her tone. A good rule of thumb is just to assume I've interrupted something very important like saving time in a bottle, writing the Great American Novel or ending the plague that is zombie crotch rot—more likely, at that hour, she'd be using the Wite-Out to create a budget French manicure.

"The Hooch and Cooch? Since when is one of my mother's strip clubs an appropriate meeting place?" My eyes took in the stories-tall cowgirl on the roof, lit up old school—in lightbulbs rather than neon. Several were burnt out, but most notable were the cowgirl's front teeth. On closer inspection, those seemed to be blacked out on purpose—it's nice to see attention to authentic detail. The ten-foot-tall flashing pink beaver between her legs was a subtle choice, if I do say so.

"He insisted," she said, her voice echoing on the speakerphone.

"Fucking pig."

The pig's name was Johnny Birch and he was famous for three things—crooning jazz standards like that Bublé or Bubble guy or whoever, screwing anything with a hole (including donuts) and doing it all publicly on his own reality show, *Tapping Birch's Syrup* (shown exclusively on Channel SS12). He was also a wood nymph, but even though that's all ethereal and earthy, it's really secondary to the pervert stuff. Apparently he had a proposition, and from the look of the Hooch and Cooch, I had a pretty good idea it wasn't business related.

"Seriously, this better be a for-real deal or I'm gonna be one pissed-off zombie."

"Karkaroff was very specific that this was a *priority* meeting." I could imagine her sitting in the cushy office chair, making air quotes, leaning back with her ankles crossed on the desk, admiring her trophy shoes.

My business partner was already fuming from our recent clusterfuck with Necrophilique. How was I supposed to know the fecal content of the cosmetics? Do I look like a chemist? Still, we needed the money after word spread and the launch tanked. What was the saying, beggars can't be choosers? Not that I was a beggar, by any count, but . . . shit, mama's got bills to pay.

"Fine." I gripped the phone to my ear and started loading my purse with all the important undead accoutrements as she yammered on about her day. Flesh-tone bandages (you never know when you'll get a scratch, and humans are normally surprised when they don't see blood seeping), cigarettes (why the hell not?) and lastly, Altoids, of course, because dragon breath doesn't even begin to describe the smell that escapes up this rotten esophagus.

I did take a moment to wonder if I was dressed appropriately for the venue. The Gucci skirt was definitely fitted and might draw some roving hands, but I could certainly handle those. My big concern was the white silk blouse.

It was Miu Miu, for Christ's sake.

The Hooch and Cooch didn't look like the kind of place that *any* white fabric, let alone designer silk, could escape without a stain.

As if on cue, two drunken slobs slammed out of the swinging doors and scattered out onto the red carpetless cement.[1] One landed on his ass with his legs spread, an expanding dark wetness spread from his crotch outward. His buddy clutched at his stomach in a silent fit of laughter, but then fell against a truck and puked into the open bed. The rest dribbled off his chin and down his loosened tie as he slid to the concrete. I guess that answered my question about fashion choices. Pretty much anything will do if your competition is piss and puke stains, though clearly the blouse was in danger and the stains were much more dubious than I'd imagined.

"Ugh. Christ. Call me in ten minutes. I know I'm going to need an excuse to get out of here."

I stuffed the phone in my Alexander McQueen red patent Novak bag—yes you need to know that, if for no other reason than to understand that I've moved on from the Balenciaga; it's a metaphor for my personal growth—and headed in, stepping over the passed-out figure on the threshold. The urine smell was unbearable. Someone had enjoyed a nutritious meal of asparagus.[2] I shoved the splintery doors into the strip club's lobby and was greeted by a wall of palsied antlers, Molly Hatchet blaring some 70s bullshit and my mother's pasty dead face beaming from behind the hostess stand.

---

[1] No. No paparazzi either. Yeah. I was glad about that.

[2] Don't pretend you don't know what I'm talking about. That piss is rank. Good for getting rid of some quick water weight, though. Just a tip.

"Darling." She crossed the room in three strides, cowboy boots crunching on the peanut shells coating the floor and arms reaching—the effect was more praying mantis than loving mother, I assure you. "You should have called."

I submitted to a hug and, over her shoulder, caught a glimpse of Gil, arms crossed and leaning on the open bed of a Ford F-150 that seemed to have been repurposed as the gift shop—how they got it in there, I have no clue. A pair of those ridiculous metal balls dangled between his legs from the trailer hitch behind him. I couldn't help but giggle. He tipped his Stetson in my direction and winked.

"You're right, Mother. I'll definitely call next time.[3]"

She pulled away, concern spreading across her face. The vamping achieved the kind of freshening a top-dollar Beverly Hills facelift aimed for, but no amount of magic could revive Ethel's sincerity.

"It's just, we haven't had a whole lot of time to sort out this . . . tension between us and I'd like us to be a family, again."

Again. Just like that. Like there'd ever been anything remotely resembling a "family." Unless her definition of family was the people one ridiculed, judged and rejected, then yeah, I guess we had a "family."

I clenched my fists. If blood flowed through my veins rather than thick yellow goo, I might have turned beetred. But instead of appearing angry, I took on a sickly jaundice, which is never cute.

I decided to stuff it and pushed past her to find Johnny Birch. "Sure, Ethel, let's work on that."

"I don't appreciate your sarcasm." She sang the final

---

[3] The authorities, that is, nothing disrupts business like a vice raid.

> ### *Music from the DVD . . .*
>
> *Learn to Strip with the Girls of the
> Hooch and Cooch\**
>
>
>
> *Thin Lizzy • "Jailbreak"
> Foghat • "Slow Ride"
> Heart • "Barracuda"
> Ted Nugent • "Cat Scratch Fever"
> War • "Low Rider"
> Nazareth • "Hair of the Dog"
> The Runaways • "Cherry Bomb"
> Blue Oyster Cult • "Burnin' for You"
> Kansas • "Carry on, Wayward Son"
> Boston • "More than a Feeling"*
>
>
>
> \*for instructional purposes only!

word, as she did when pretending something didn't actually bother her. I grinned, triumphant.

I bounded up to Gil. "How do you put up with that
bitch?" I stabbed a thumb in Ethel's direction.

"Who, your mother? Oh please, she's wonderful to
work for and so funny. . . ."

His voice trailed off, replaced by the twangin' guitar of Southern rock. Mother had obviously brainwashed

Gil to spout this pro-Ethel propaganda and I wasn't about to listen to it. "Yeah. Yeah. Awesome. A real peach."

"A better question is how do I put up with this 70s-ass rock."

The music changed. "Slow Ride" by Foghat. "Seriously. What's the deal?" I asked.

"Part of your mom's plan; it's all she'll play here. She says 70s rock forces guys to buy beer. Something in their genes. Oh . . . and look at this." Gil reached into the truck bed, which was lined with various Hooch and Cooch promo items, T-shirts, CDs, pocket pussies— that sort of thing—and retrieved a DVD. A sleazy, greasy-haired dancer grinned from the cover. One of her front teeth was missing and she wore a wifebeater that didn't do a good job of hiding the fact that her boob job looked like two doorknobs. It read: *Learn to Strip with the Girls of the Hooch and Cooch* (see inset on page 5).

"Jesus. Like one of those Carmen Electra striptease workouts?"

"Yep." He tossed it back in the truck. "Sells like hot-cakes."

"I bet."

I looked past Gil into the club for the first time and witnessed the horrors of uncontrolled testosterone production. A drunken mass of homely men and a few semi-doable ones, surprisingly, crowded around two spotlit islands, shouting obscenities and waving dollar bills. It was nearly impossible to distinguish them as individuals; they'd reverted to some sort of quivering gelatinous state. A few appeared near death, eyes rolling in the back of their heads as though they'd never seen a used-up hooker—I mean nude woman—writhing in a metal wash tub, scrubbing herself with a moldy bath brush and kicking suds off dirty feet at her sweaty admirers. Maybe it's because we were indoors.

Between the two performance spaces—though really I'm being overly generous with that description—was a large shack built into the back of the club complete with everything you'd expect to find in the backwoods of the Ozarks—or in a typical Northwest suburb for that matter—a covered porch, rocking chairs, even a butter churn.[4] Everything, that is, but a little inbred blind kid playing the banjo and showing off the grave-yard of teeth in his mouth.

He must have been on a smoke break.

Booths lined the edges of the room, where hillbilly chicks chatted up customers under the watchful glass eyes of various stuffed animal heads. Fog lights on truck grills jutted from the walls, lighting up the tables and the assorted (or sordid) activities taking place there.

"This place is a regular Rainforest Café. Only instead of cute plastic animals you've got dirty whores."

"Absolutely." Gil crossed his arms and beamed, as proud as a new father—sure, he had a stake in the place, but he was overdoing the satisfaction considering the place reeked of bleach and I'm pretty sure it wasn't emanating from a big load of laundry.[5]

"Pays the bills," he said.

"Listen. I'm supposed to be meeting a guy. Johnny Birch, that fame whore from TV. Have you seen him?"

"Um." He scanned the room. "Totally. What a freak. I think he's just finished up with Kelsey." Gil pointed to a hallway flanked by two columns of chicken coops. A

---

[4] I didn't want to even think what these girls would use *that* for.
[5] It's a curse that my sense of smell is so acute. A curse!

lanky dark-haired man emerged with a jug of moonshine in one hand and a skanky redhead in the other.

"Christ."

The guy was tonguing the girl's ear as I approached.

"Excuse me," I said. "Are you Mr. Birch?"

He spun the girl away like a Frisbee, absolutely no regard for where she might land. She twirled a few times, collapsed in some other perv's lap and started gyrating. Birch measured me in long sweeping stares. Head to toe, lingering on the tits and back to the head. "Sure am." He extended his hand. "And you're Amanda, lovely to meet you."

He pulled at my hand as though planning to pull off a gentlemanly knuckle kiss, but I snatched it back, wishing for a Clorox wipe. "Yeah. Um, you have some sort of business proposition, I've been told. Do you want to talk about that here or do you have a table somewhere? Maybe a private booth they reserve for regulars."

"You mean V.I.P." He winked.

"No." I shook my head. "Just regular."

Birch nodded and chuckled off the jab under his breath.

The next moment, the blaring 70s rock was silenced, an apparent signal for the strippers to make way for the principal dancer in this redneck ballet. They scrabbled off on bruised knees, wet hair dangling in clumps, bulldozing collapsing pyramids of dollar bills in front of them.

Birch pointed toward the shack.

The lights dimmed and a jaundiced glow rose behind the dirty shower curtain covering the front door of the facade. At the edges of the porch, slobbery men set down their jugs and hushed each other as though in reverence to approaching royalty. It became so quiet, I could hear the chickens scratching in their cages and crickets chirping or rubbing their legs together or whatever the fuck they do. Though that last bit was probably being pumped in through the speakers to set the mood. The stage light brightened until columns of dust motes stabbed into the audience from between the rusty metal curtain rings, stretching across the waves of corrugated roofing above and the five o'clock shadows of drooling businessmen below.

And then *she* stalked into silhouette—no . . . shuffled is a better word—to the opening cowbells of Nazareth's "Hair of the Dog"—'cause really, what else would you expect?

"Harry Sue!" I could have sworn someone yelled.

"Harry Sue!" the crowd shouted back in liturgical response.

"*Harry* Sue?" I asked Birch.

"Short for Harriet, maybe?" He shrugged without taking his eyes off the dirty play unfolding.

When the guitar roared in, Harry Sue snatched back the curtain and stomped out onto the porch in Daisy Duke overalls and the most hideous high heels—since when did Jellies make a heel? Her blond hair had been teased and tortured into massive pigtails, hay jutting from the strips of gingham holding them in place. Her face was pretty enough, if you could get past her wild eyes, bee-stung lips and the mass of fake freckles that sadly recalled the broken blood vessels of an alcoholic more than the fresh sun-kissed face of a farm girl.

She didn't tease the crowd of howling men much, making quick work of the denim overalls with two rehearsed snaps at each shoulder; they slid off her bone-thin frame and pooled around her ankles. The ensuing slapstick of Harry wrestling her feet out of the denim mess would have been charming had my eyes not been stuck to her undergarments. Not satisfied with a dirty wifebeater and some holey panties, the stripper wore cut-off Dr. Dentons, complete with the trap door. Of course, in true trashy stripper fashion, Harry Sue wore hers backwards.

The room was filled with redneck boner and there I stood in the middle of it, without a vomit bag, a designer cocktail or a canister of mustard gas. You couldn't move through the room without rotating aroused men like turnstiles and I had no intention of doing that. I did notice that Johnny Birch was standing awful close to me.

Glad to see you, close.

Too close.

"That's my asshole, asshole." I jerked away from his probing fingers.

Johnny grinned in response, totally deserving the punch I threw into his kidneys.

"Ow!" He ran his fingers through his hair, eyes darting nervously at the men around us, as if any of them were looking for anything other than a beaver shot. "Jesus. It's all in good fun."

"Touch me again and we'll see who's having fun."

"Aw." He scowled.

Harry Sue slunk down in one of the rockers and the men whimpered in unison—apparently prepared for what Harry Sue had in store for us. She rocked slowly, pivoting her ass forward on the edge of the chair until the flap was front and center. She toyed with the buttons, tweaking them like nipples.

I glowered. Shot a glance at Birch. Wished I were drinking.

The stripper got my attention when she unbuttoned

one side of the flap, then the other, finally, exposing the biggest 70s bush I'd ever seen.[6] It was massive. Afro-like. Harry Sue needed to be introduced to the wonders of Brazilian waxing, though she'd likely be charged extra. And then it clicked. The men weren't yelling Harry Sue.

They were shouting *Hairy* Sue.

Still. It didn't make sense.

I've read *Cosmo*. I know men prefer shaved to bouffant. Yet they were clearly enthralled by this stripper. I watched more closely.

Hairy (let's just drop the Sue part; it never had any real value anyway) reached for the butter churn and pulled out the plunger, dripping melted butter down the front of her jammies.

She peeked at the mess, frowned, then licked the end of the plunger before returning it to the churn. In one motion, she slipped out of the Dr. Dentons and reached into an aluminum pail next to the rocker and retrieved an ear of corn, which she preceded to shuck, using her teeth. She sprinkled her breasts with corn silk. With the ear she traced circles across her belly, her thighs and then, as though by accident, she dropped the cob on the porch, gasped and then slipped from the chair into a full split, hovering briefly above the ear before nestling it against her buttery crotch.

I shifted from one foot to the other.

There was absolutely nothing sexy about this. These guys were all perverts.

Hairy Sue rose then and bowed to the wild applause and showers of dollar bills. She posed there like she

---

[6] Hey. I've always kept mine neat and trim. Don't go making assumptions.

owned that porch, corncob dripping and a fat smile spread across her face.

The lights dimmed.

"I'd sure like to see *your* bush." Birch again. His lips curled into a lewd smile.

I nearly vomited up my dinner (let's not go into what that might have been, just yet). "Is that some kind of wood-nymph joke? 'Cause I'm done with your poor impulse control."

"Hey." He stepped back, spread his arms and wiggled his fingers. "I can control the trees and stuff."

I let my eyes wander down to the tent in his pants. "But not the wood?"

He sagged.

"Maybe we should just talk." He covered his crotch with cupped hands, a flush rising in his cheeks.

I followed him back to a booth underneath a monstrous moose head, where he laid out the scenario. It was the first time I'd seen his face in full light. He wasn't hideous, though his features were sharp and his nose a bit too thin. The brown of his eyes shimmered with veins of gold and his lips, though pale, were full and unexpectedly alluring. He looked much better on TV but that was probably the makeup.

Mmm. Makeup.

"The calls started coming about three months ago," he said. "At first the caller wouldn't say anything. Just hang up after I'd answered. The phone company said they were always from phone booths. I didn't even know those still existed but they do."

I nodded, though I couldn't remember the last time I'd seen one, either. Still, why do people feel the need to tell me the most random crap? Like I care. I'm dead.

"About a month ago, they started getting threaten-

ing. Not overtly so, just freaky. Like letting me know
that I was being monitored. You're at the Texaco on 1st.
Like that. And then they'd just hang up and I'd be
standing there at the pump, not just worried that my
cell was going to spark and blow me up, but now that
someone was nearby watching. Then a couple of weeks
ago I get the first one."

"First what?"

Johnny reached into a briefcase he must've stored
under the table before his lap dance and pulled out a
plastic shipping envelope, the kind lined with Bubble
Wrap. He placed it on the table between us and leaned
forward, searching the room for observers. Half the
crowd had been culled into the back rooms and the
other half were busy drinking themselves into stupors.

I made eye contact with Gil across the room. He
looked concerned. It must have been my expression of
pure boredom. My eyes dropped back to the envelope.

"I'm not a private detective, Birch. I'm in advertising. Can we get on with this?"

"I know. I know. But, I don't need you for that. I
need you for your celebrity."

Celebrity? I leaned toward him, suddenly more interested. "Go on."

He opened the end of the envelope and pulled out a
thin shingle of wood. Stretched across it, attached with
thick pins, was a creature like none I'd seen, almost
insect-like, with wings that clung to its sides like a ter-
mite. Its flesh was as black as obsidian and shiny from
toe to its segmented abdomen to its horribly humanoid
head. The creature's waxy face was frozen in a torturous silent scream.

"Gross. What the hell is it?" I was unable to look
away from the little body, pinned as it was like a lab

experiment. Better there than flying around, though, or I'd be snatching a fly swatter.

"I don't really know. But it looks like a fucking threat to me. Anyways! I'm going on tour this spring and clearly, with this shit going on . . ." He kicked at the briefcase. "I'm going to need some protection."

"All right. How is my 'celebrity' going to do that? It's not like I'm known for my strength or crime-solving ability." I flicked the edge of the shingle the thing was attached to. It rocked back and forth on the table.

Johnny's finger shot out to stop its movement. He slid it back into the envelope and tossed it into his bag. "It's not. I'm putting together a team of bodyguards and what better way to do it nowadays than with my own fabulous reality contest show? Can you see it? Celebrity judges and weekly death matches. It's exactly what Supernatural TV is aching for. Cameron Hansen would host, of course, and all we'd need is our Paula. You'd be our Simon."

"Simon? I'm too cute and, anyway, you'd be our fucking Paula. What we'd need is a Randy." I reached for my purse and began to scoot out of the booth. The idea was ludicrous.

"Maybe," his voice thundered. "But I'm a nut with financial resources and I'd be willing to pay."

"So you're looking for more than just a guest judge here, then? We're talking about exclusive advertising contract with product placement?"

"That could be arranged."

"Let me think about it." I looked around the Hooch and Cooch and couldn't quite believe that such a gross experience might lead to a potential financial windfall. "All right, let's plan to meet somewhere less . . . disgusting and then we'll talk about it. Sound good?"

"Up to you."

"Well, let's figure it out in the parking lot. I don't think I can stomach this place much longer."

As we stood to leave, a commotion began in the hallway to the private rooms. A steady stream of men was rushing from the exit, most of them screaming and none of them attempting to shield the bulge in their trousers. Following them was a roar that vibrated through the room and a crash as the chicken coops shattered, sending several birds flapping and skittering off toward the door in the shack. Gil and Ethel ran into the room, my friend brandishing a machete, my mother some sort of short club.

"We better get out of here." I turned to Birch, but he'd already darted for the front door. Behind him a massive beast emerged from the tangle of metal cages. Its bulbous head sheared the ceiling as it lurched, creating a groove across the ripples of metal. Its thick muscled arms ended in rake-like claws that shredded the floorboards into mulch with each powerful swipe. It stopped in the center of the room, head twisting wildly from one patron to the next until it found its quarry.

The creature howled with such force, the floor shook under me. Slobber clung to foot-long fangs, like sloppy pennants, flapping in the direction of Johnny Birch, who let out a quivering whimper.

It rushed forward.

Dammit, I thought. There goes the TV show.

Just because I ducked under a table doesn't make me a
coward, I don't care what you say. If a big-ass marauding hulk of meat was charging around your local strip
club (which you didn't want to go to in the first place, I
might add) tossing perverts into the air with the sloppy
abandon of a summer berry picker—raspberry from
the look of the splatter on the walls—what would you
do?

You'd hide, that's what.

It was a pretty good vantage point, despite the cigarette butts, beer bottles and not-so-mysterious wet
spots on the floor—too wet not to have been recent and
too viscous to be anything but some pervert's jizz. And

I was pretty sure *which* pervert. The thought of Birch jerking off under the table while we talked sprang up as a distinct possibility, though, how he could have been aroused in the presence of that shriveled dead creature, is a question for a professional—my diagnoses are more of the armchair variety. I scraped my palm against the seat's piping and gagged only a little bit as goo specked with ash balled up and clung to the bead of vinyl. Composing myself was a process, though it did feel better when I pretended it was beer staining one of my last good skirts, instead of Johnny Birch's gross domestic product.

Just then, Ethel ran past and I shouted after her, "What kind of place you running here, Ethel? There's spunk on the floor!"

She slid to a stop, glowered and hissed under my table, "Prove it!"

As she sped off, I got a better look at the creature. It latched on to one of the poles and spun impressively from a rake-sized fist, clawing several regulars in a single brutal arc and sending the rest backing into the already-clogged log jam at the exit. They stood there, squealing, tongues jiggling in their mouths like cartoons, pushing back into the crowd, punching, jabbing, anything to get farther away.

It dropped off the stripper's island, splinters erupting from a loud crack at its feet and roared, spittle flapping and loosing into the wind of it like streamers off a cruise ship. A dense earthy smell filled the room, part rotten leaves, part dog shit, and all nasty.

"Get those customers out of here!" It was Ethel's voice, and nearby, though I couldn't see her anymore.

Gil I could see.

He tore at the men at the door. Each time he created

a gap it was filled with another flailing idiot, as though they were fish floundering on an open deck. A few of them broke off, attempting to make for the door in the main stage set. Two were caught in either of the mammoth's claws, their screams silenced as it clapped their heads together with the sound and effort of smashing tomatoes. Their skulls splintered, and gray matter oozed between the monster's elongated fingers. It dropped them in a heap around its ankles. The other guy threw himself at the plastic shower curtain hanging in the doorway of the shack, but not before a dank brown stain crept down the back of his white linen trousers.[7]

Ethel rushed back into view, club raised like some cavewoman crammed into a silk suit. The creature turned on her and howled. She slipped past it and swung at it viciously, hammering the thick bat against its pale naked back and thighs. Bruises spread under its skin with each fevered blow. Ethel's face was a wicked mask of glee. She howled back at the thing, spraying its face with blood from the inside of her cheeks. Drops of crimson specked its hairless white belly like chicken pox.

---

[7] White Linen. Like it was the 40s in Johannesburg and he'd planned to attend a garden party. What the fuck? But it does bring to mind a question: what is appropriate strip club attire? Clearly, for dancers it's a no-brainer, just cling wrap a thong to your labia, rouge up your nipples and you're good to get boners twitching. For men, it doesn't seem to matter, they're just as happy to have skanky twat against dirty jeans as they are $1000 suits, or linen trousers, apparently. For me it would have been a question of practicality. Had I known, I would have opted for my vintage Dior swing trench with an Alexander McQueen rubber belt to cinch it, 'cause really, do I look like I need an Empire waist?

Total. Fucking. Maniac.

I wouldn't have expected anything less. Mother was the poster girl for passive aggression and verbal assault all her life, but now that she had a little physical power, it's no wonder she'd revel in the violence.

The vamping had to have been a welcome release. Such pent-up aggression. Such violence in the woman. It explains the massacre at the hospice center, but don't bring that up, or she'll try to dazzle you with her spin. "It was my hour of redemption!" she'd shout. That kind of thing. Never mind that Ethel took out thirty-two terminally-ill cancer patients in one night—like they could fight back at all.

There were two monsters fighting out there.

Do you think it'd be bad if I rooted for the other one? Would you think less of me?[8]

The massive creature spun on her small frame, one paw snatching the bat from her hands and the other closing into a huge fist that connected with Mother's jaw loud enough for a thwack to echo across the room. The smack sent her spinning off into the wall, where a framed shadow box of the Confederate flag slipped from its nail and crashed down onto her head. She eked out a hollow gasp and slipped to the floor, legs splayed and scowling.

Gil finally loosened up the opening enough for the flood of perverts to empty out. The girlish screaming subsided, leaving the monster's marauding the only sounds in the place. The deejay snuck away from his little booth at the far end at some point during the rampage, silencing the barrage of butt rock but leaving the not so subtle shirr of needle against vinyl to provide

[8] Didn't think so.

the white noise for a killing spree. Gil raced along the wall of banquettes, hunching and searching under tables, presumably for me. "Amanda! Where are you?"

"Right here." I reached out into the space, eyes darting between Gil's loping movement and the monster's lumbering rage. It saw the vampire and darted toward him, arms swinging wildly (not unlike Wendy's after a night of clubbing—like an orangutan's, those arms). Gil must have seen me cringe. His head craned toward the approaching thing and a sound like a squeak crept from his open mouth.

He was snatched from his hunch and slammed into the corrugated metal ceiling, which buckled up like a cartoon, and dropped back with a force that would have shattered a human's bones completely.

"Gil!" I screamed and then wished I hadn't.

It turned its whacked-out gaze on me. To say its eyes were googly was being kind. The thing didn't seem capable of focusing, the bloodshot orbs rolled in its head like a slot machine and finally came to rest back on Gil who was crawling—of all places—toward me.

"What the hell are you doing? Lead it the other way." I waved my hands at him, shooing him toward the stage.

He slipped under the table.

"Jesus. That yeti is pissed."

"No shit." I slapped the back of his head. "Where are the fucking reapers?"

"They're not coming." He said the words as if I already knew.

I stared back at him. I think I did one of those ditzy blink things.[9]

---

[9] Purely for effect, you understand. The moment seemed to call for it. Oh, who am I fooling, I was dumbstruck.

"Jesus. Don't you read?"

I shrugged. "Um. That's what you're for. You've been at this supernatural game a lot longer than me. So, what gives?"

"This here . . ." He pointed at the yeti, which stumbled over a serving tray and busily rubbed at its knees. ". . . is a woodland creature and one that's already been exposed."

I shook my head. Not really putting it together. "Exposed?"

"Yeah. Back in the 70s, the Patterson film?"

I nodded, vaguely remembering the lumbering ape-thing trudging through somewhere that didn't have sidewalk sales or wine bars.

"Well, experts were paid quite a bit to report it as a fraud, but in the end, the reapers concluded the damage was done. People believed in them."

As if on cue, the thing in the center of the club began crushing the wooden chairs into kindling with no more effort than you'd snap a matchstick, slamming the furniture into the poles, exploding splinters off into the corners of the room like shrapnel.

"Where's its hair? It's like bald or something."

Gil's eyes sped back at the marauding creature. "That *is* definitely odd . . . and so not a good look."

"Absolutely not. Skin like a morbidly obese whole chicken fryer. It's nothing like *Harry and the Hendersons*."

"You saw that movie?"

I thought a moment, wondered what John Lithgow was up to now, and responded, as though I were offended, "No."

He squeezed in tighter and two things happened.

One. The creature stopped moving, an eerie silence replacing its rampage.

And two. Gil kicked a beer bottle from under the table, off the little dais the booths were built atop and down onto the floor with a clink so loud it could have been a dinner bell.

A roar rumbled through the room like the first slip of a fault line, shaking the floorboards. In the next instant, we were flat on our backs, pressing against a table turned into a great hamburger press. The heels snapped off my shoes and went flying. Gil, who was taking the majority of the weight, started to shake as though nearly ready to collapse. I looked at him. He looked at me, brown eyes sad as a basset hound's and said, "This is the end."

"Yeah, of me!" I yelled. "You'll survive it. The reapers won't be putting my pancaked ass back together. They'll have to bring a spatula."

Gil sucked up into a sour face and nodded a quick agreement as the monster continued to press down in great rocky bounces.

"Yeti!" It was Birch, calling out the creature, who stopped flattening us to follow the voice to its owner.

We set the tabletop to the side. The pole that had been holding it up was bowed and the floor cracked where it was anchored. I pressed myself against the wall and followed it around toward the stage.

Birch stood near the main entrance by the open truck bed. Ethel sagged on the floor behind him a bit, not near as eager to brawl as before. He carried no weapons and his expensive suit certainly wasn't going to shield him from the yeti's claws. But Birch stepped forward with a look of calm on his smarmy face.

The yeti's eyes found their quarry and I swear to God the thing snickered. The snicker turned into a

roaring chortle that shook the pale chicken skin on its
belly like a JELL-O mold.

I took the opportunity to dart to the front of the
truck and slip underneath, pulling myself forward with
my elbows like the soldiers do in those basic training
movies. Was this the correct moment to "serpentine," I
wondered? Seemed not. I stopped moving, just as
Birch advanced into the room. The motion startled me
and I banged my head against the massive metal scrotum dangling off the hitch.

"Dammit!" I patted the spot to check for tearing; that
center stitch in the ball cleavage was terribly realistic . . .
and sharp, I might add. Seemingly intact, and more than
a little impressed I'd bumped into something I might use
as a weapon, I made quick work of disconnecting the sac
and crawled to a vantage point near the tire.

On the far side of the room, peeking from around
the gnarl of chicken cages, Gil waved his hands, as if to
say don't come out any farther. It's like he doesn't
know me at all.

"Duh!" I snapped.

His nonchalant shrug was obscured as the slick-
skinned yeti stomped back into view, crouching as if to
lunge at Birch, its claws spread out and knuckles
cracking with tension.

The wood nymph seemed overly confident, considering he'd fled our conversation at the first hint of trouble. He balanced his weight on one hip, tilted his head
a bit and sang.

Yeah. I said sang.

It didn't seem appropriate to me, either.

Neither did the song, which at first sounded like Mar-
vin Gaye's "Let's Get It On," but turned out to be something else entirely. Johnny peppered the lyrics with a

volley of "*Mmms*" and "*Oh yeahs*." He swiveled his hips seductively at the beast.

I held back the vomit and considered looking away. Johnny's track record of conquests would take up a scroll. Who's to say that this creature wasn't a spurned lover, some backwoods ex come to exact a little *Deliverance* on his ass? Maybe I'd misjudged the entire situation.

It could just be entertainment.

The yeti lunged at the nymph—again, hard to blame it—crossing the floor in three lumbering strides. Birch raised his arms and then his voice. What was once cheesey lounge singing became something different entirely. Even, dare I say, beautiful? The words were gone, or rather, the English was stripped out of the vocalization. What was left was a soothing melody made form that arced and swam in the air. With each note the sound became denser until a swirling mist turned the room and the play into a dream.

The monster stopped dead in its tracks and cocked its head to the side, arms slack and eyes following the streaks of tone.

Birch walked circles around the creature, continuing his song—which, while mesmerizing, wasn't exactly chart-ready. I'll give him this, the notes were otherworldly. I began to understand how the little horndog got laid with such frequency—you couldn't turn on the TV without seeing him slobbering over some flavor of the week as if she were a scoop of dark chocolate chip.[10] I

[10] Yes. That was a jab at the notoriously freckled and obscenely overpaid dancer Marisha Detlove. Word is Birch screwed her out of a very publicly disclosed virginity and a small fortune in Lladro figurines in a bizarre sex-related accident. The news was less than specific, however.

even found myself drawn to the lilting refrain and before I knew it had crawled out from under the truck and stood a few feet away from where both Birch and the creature stood.

Gil left his hiding place, too. His mouth hung open, tongue out and teetering over his bottom lip. I reached up to see if I was doing the same, intent on shoving my lolling tongue back in. Thankfully, I'd managed a modicum of civility.

I slipped in beside him. "Slut."

He looked at me and then down at my hand. "I'm not the one fondling truck balls."

I shrugged, though the weight of the things was likely giving me a totally unattractive hunch.

Birch swept his fingers through the air like a conductor, as though playing the notes he'd already sung.

Nothing happened at first.

Or at least nothing I could see.

Fury burned in the thing's black eyes, lips drawn back from its fangs and quivering. I was pretty sure Birch was gonna end up Yeti Chow, and despite a pretty healthy sense of self-preservation, I couldn't resist the urge to watch the feeding.

But even the yeti's growls were slowed and there was nothing between them but the wood nymph's careful refrain.

Then the air seemed to thicken like fog lazing on glass and that image solidified as a frost, as though the whole scene were trapped in an oil painting. Birch's fingers circled and churned the air, spinning gossamer eddies into the wet mural of the room. The curls stretched and struck the wood floors, where silver sparks jumped and tendrils of new growth shot up from knots. The nymph backed away as sprouts turned into branches that thickened and espaliered around the creature like a cell.

A living cage.

Pine needles sprang from pores in the bark. And all through this Birch sang, his cadence rising and swirling around us like a blanket. To say I was impressed would be an understatement; he'd won me over; I was, in fact, almost a fan.

Which is totally weird for me, I think you know.

It turns out Birch wasn't a complete waste of air.

Damn close.

But not totally.

When he was done, the thing was subdued and totally imprisoned. The singer turned and winked. "Catch you bad-asses later."

"Oh no, you don't." I stepped into his path.

"Ah." He sighed and nodded his head. "You want to come home with me. It's all right. It happens to all the women I touch with my song."

He reached out and slipped his hand across my face, smooshing my lips with a rude ploying thumb. I jerked away.

"You *must* be joking."

He shook his head. "No. And you needn't be embarrassed. I can almost smell your wetness."

"That's not arousal, you idiot. That's rot." I looked around and saw my mother scowl at the comment and purse her lips in heavy judgment.[11] My head swiveled to alert Gil that Ethel was at it again. To prove it. But as is so often the case, the vampire was busy looking at something else entirely. My stomach turned. Gil was assessing the nymph's ass.

---

[11] Seriously. You could feel it hanging in the air.

Birch chuckled at my comment and returned to the destruction of our banquette to collect his bag and the disheveled carcass of the creature that lay nearby.

"Seriously. If you could do all that, why didn't you pull out your magic song when the yeti first attacked." I glanced over at the creature. Its claws clung to the branches, eyes seeking out Birch and following his movement across the room.

"I thought there were more of them—they usually travel in herds, like women at shoe sales. I can handle one yeti." He paused, lost in a memory. "But two and I'd have been so much mulch." He pointed at the pile of torn bodies strewn around the strip club floor.

"I totally get self-preservation, so I'll give you the benefit of the doubt."

"Thank you, madame."

" *'Moiselle!'* Mademoiselle!" Of course, Birch was no longer paying attention. He simply pivoted in his Italian loafers and slunk from the room.

"See you soon," he called behind him.

Gil followed his motion with actual interest.

"What are you lookin' at?" I asked.

"I'm lookin'! He's got a nice can. For fuck sake."

"A can? What is this, the 70s?" I asked, momentarily forgetting that Gil was technically the same age he was in those sexy years of polyester, pet rocks and coke-fueled orgies in artist's lofts.[12]

"Yep." He brushed himself off and we walked over to Ethel, still dazed and spread-eagled on the floor. Gil held out his hand and Mother took it. "Let's get you into something more comfortable."

"Seriously?" I looked back at the cage, half-

---

[12] Was there anyone who wasn't an artist in the 70s?

expecting the yeti to come charging from between broken branches, but it was still inside, hunched down like a big dollop of vanilla pudding.

The prone woman at first waved off Gil's offer with an uncharacteristically pained expression and then yielded to his support with such a sigh I expected the stigmata to appear and squirt blood from her hands like a hose. Gag. Gil hoisted her slim frame into the protection of his underarm and led her around the truck bed and toward a door behind the hostess kiosk.

"Are you going out with Wendy and me?" I called after him.

He spun, jerking Mother around with him, a scowl of judgment plastered on his normally handsome face. "How could you even ask that, with all that your mother's been through?"

I don't know why it surprised me. Really. I should have expected it, but when I turned my eyes in Ethel's direction, she wore a smirk the size of a cantaloupe slice, gushing with her usual hateful gaminess. My fists balled instinctively and I took a step toward her, more as a threat than any real prelude to the beating she deserved.

Gil gasped and looked at Ethel, who instantly put on a pathetic pout for his benefit then curled her lips into a perfect mimicry of a cat's anus when he turned his gaze back to me.

"Really, Amanda, you could work on your empathy a bit," he said.

I'm pretty sure my mouth sagged open like a blowup sex doll, stuck on there like it was permanent. Gil could have probably tossed his entire judgment between my lips without getting any on my cheeks.

I seethed.

"Oh and no. I can't make it," Gil said as he led my mother into the backroom. "I have a blind date."

"A blind date? Who do you even know to set you up beside Wendy and me?"

He nodded his head in Ethel's direction and slammed the door behind them.

I could only imagine the kind of suitor the old witch would pick out for Gil, probably some saccharine vampire accountant who couldn't follow a joke if he had George Carlin's ghost interpreting. It'd be just our luck that Gil would hit it off and the rest of our outings would be soured by the new boyfriend's dead stares and uncomfortable silences.

And that's what I thought about until I turned back to the empty cage and started screaming.

"What y'all screaming about?"

I didn't recognize the voice, but the twang was as southern as chicken on a biscuit, or tea so sweet it makes your teeth ache—both of which, I'd been perseverating on during feedings. Fantasizing is not uncommon for monotonous diets. Looking up, I witnessed a discretely clothed young woman in a tan trench, with her hair pulled back into a tight bun like an actual dancer, though no one would ever mistake Hairy Sue for a ballerina.

I pointed at the cage of branches. "It's empty."

The girl shrugged nonchalantly. "What was in there?"

"It's escaped!" I started to yell and then reined it in lest I draw the thing's attention again.

"What has? What are y'all talkin' about?"

"The yeti! Did it go back there?" I pointed to the stage entrance.

She shook her head, said, "A yeti? Well, Mother Mary in a mock turtleneck you don't see one of those every day."

Now, I've heard a lot of mixed-use religious exclamations in my time, in fact, one of Ethel's favorites, "Jesus Christ on a cracker," popped out of my own mouth from time to time. But this one, invoking a poor clothing choice, really didn't work for me. Maybe a muumuu might be better. Mother Mary in a muumuu. It had a nice irreverent tone.

She continued, "Is that what was making all that racket? I wouldn't know, I've been changin', takin' off all my makeup and stuff after my show. Did you see it?"

"Oh, I saw it." I pictured the thing's chicken skin jiggling on its hairless belly, the rows of nipples, the massive claws. I hoped I wouldn't see it again, though the more the girl talked the less concerned I became. The yeti was too big to just slip past her; it was probably on its way back to the forest, though how it would get there unnoticed was beyond me.

"Did you like it?" Hairy Sue winked, her lips pursed or pouting—I couldn't quite determine the level of suggestiveness she was going for.

"What?"

"My show. Did you like it?"

I grimaced, not sure how to respond. Then opting for the straightforward route, "I gotta ask." I paused. Hairy Sue was nodding already, serious in her consideration. "How did you figure out the whole bush thing? I mean, those guys seemed to be really into it."

"They're creamin' for it, four nights out of seven. I'm not sure why. The longer I let it grow, the more tips I get. Could be somethin' innate. Or maybe them pheromones cling better to the pubes." She shrugged and followed me to the door. "My last show for a while. I'm going to be on a reality show. In fact, I'm packing as soon as I get home."

"Oh yeah?" I muttered absently.

"*American Minions*. You know, with Johnny Birch. He's a regular here."

"Yeah. I figured."

Now I'd seen every inch of the girl and she looked completely human. She smelled like meat with a hint of butter, nothing out of the ordinary and certainly not bodyguard material unless she was a ninja. I figured I'd better not engage with her anymore, professional distance, and all.

"Good luck with that," I said and she bounced off into the parking lot. I swear I heard her pea brain rattle around in the hollow of her skull. It could have been a passing car, I suppose, but the odds were pretty good in my favor.

I followed her out, but oddly enough, wasn't relieved to be out of harm's way, or the clutches of my fiendish mother.

"Oh, come on!" I slapped my purse against my thigh. "Are you serious?"

The man cramming a jimmy down the Volvo window tilted his head up and eyed me vigorously. His hair was scruffy blond and framed his face in that unkempt way that's supposed to be charming, and would have been if the accompanying sneer hadn't stripped away the allure. A cigarette bobbed from between those lips. Smoke curled around his pasty jaw like an arty charcoal and trapped like a fog in the forest of unruly curls. He nodded in my direction and went back to the business of breaking into my car.

Each jarring of the metal shim squealed and echoed, shivering its way up my already-cold frame, mixing with the anger. If I'd been alive the goose flesh would have been visible, even in the shadows.

Haven't I had enough tonight, without having to deal with a thief?[13]

"Hey!" I tromped up to the man. "What the fuck do you think you're doing?"

He shifted the cigarette from his lips to his teeth and mumbled through a clenched jaw. "Vance Ventura, repo artist. You got the keys? That'd make my life a whole lot easier, if you had them. I got a thing later on; don't want to be late. First impressions, and all."

"Well, you're certainly winning *me* over." I made no move for my keys, of course, but scanned the parking lot for witnesses.[14]

"It's Vance." He actually chuckled.

I clearly didn't get the joke.

The "survivors" of the yeti attack huddled around a burn barrel, warming their hands like hobos and no doubt comparing war stories, as though they just fought their way from "the thick of it." Never mind the fact that they screamed like little girls and blocked up the exit like a toilet in a Mexican jail cell. A couple of cars over, a man sat in his car hotboxing a cigarette, his tortured face blinking red with each inhalation. Another

---

[13] Seriously. Haven't I? What the fuck?

[14] For the uninitiated, this is the part where you either skip ahead to avoid the gore or read on slack-jawed as I chomp this bastard.

man steadied himself against a wall at the Daisy Chain motel across the highway, one foot on the ground, the other kicking the wall back—the international pose for street hustlers (and I'm not talking about the kind that throw dice).

Sure.

I know what you're thinking. And yes, it is pretty risky going for a public bite, but can you imagine me without a car? Not in a town like Seattle. For Christ's sake, it rains here. Have you seen what kind of atrocities nature wreaks on high-viscosity rayon?

He had to die.

"Could I talk to you over here for a minute?" I motioned to a gap in the trees and an overlook of the Aurora Bridge beyond, sauntered a bit to get his attention—never underestimate the power of a hip swivel—turned and eyed him over my shoulder. He followed.

I watched a waterfall of ghost suicides plummet from the Aurora Bridge. The reenactments were really quite lyrical, a mid-century oil come to life. A near-constant cascade of amethyst streaked the darkness below the bridge. I suppose it happens during the day, too, but you can't see them as well as the night shift.

Vance Ventura's eyes seemed to focused on the same vista. He cocked his head before speaking, but didn't look at me. "You're wasting your time if you think a blowjob is going to keep me from taking your car tonight."

*Fucker.*

"Wow, you're pretty astute, Vance. I guess I'll have to go with plan B, then."

"Which is?"

I shot a glance through the trees and back into the

lot. Once certain no one was interested in our little liaison—after all, it didn't involve butter churns—I unhinged my jaw. The bones cracked against drying muscle, stretching my mouth wide as a lioness's. I moved for him, twisting quickly to make for his neck, before the shock of the vision subsided and he'd stumble away or scream. But as I pressed him, an arm shot up between us and collided with my breastbone, forcing me backward.

"Mighty big mouth you got there, Grandma. The better to eat me with, right?"

I stumbled a bit and glared. *What did he say?*

"Seriously? A fairy tale reference?" I noted his fingers as they elongated into claws and his eyes flooded crimson like portholes on a sinking ship. I should have seen it coming. He *was* watching the ghosts take swan dives, after all. I dismissed my instinct without even thinking.

*I really am off my game.*

Allowing my mouth to shift back into human form, I kneaded at the ache in my jaw and my pride, of course. Figures I'd run into something inedible while so freaking hungry.

Ventura's lips curled from his teeth in dry jerky slips, revealing not the fine bone of vampire fangs, but hearty, thick canines swathed in a yellowed ruddy calculus—Vance could use a good hygienist. His jaw punched his face outward, the skin loosening to reveal overlapping layers of what looked like scales, but turned out to unravel like rose petals loosening from a bud. They fluttered revealing a clear muzzle. This was no werewolf. Not a shapeshifter at all. The floral aspect seemed to imply something older.

*What's with all the woodland creatures?* I thought. *Three in one night? And so fucking weird, too.*

*I hate nature.*

"So what the hell are you?"

Vance retracted his ability, in a quiver of petals (I guessed), and returned to the same sandy-haired good looks and cocky smile. He shrugged off the question, as though it were none of my business. "Can I get those keys now?"

"You're a real asshole. You knew what I was going to pull. Why didn't you just save me the trouble?" I shoved my hand in my purse and dug. "I don't have another car, you know."

He yawned, twisted his wrist around to get a look at the time. "Thank God for that, I'd probably have to repossess that one too."

"Bastard." I launched the keys at him, hoping to peg him hard enough to leave a dent.

But he snatched them out of the air, denying me even that paltry satisfaction.

"A pleasure doing business with you, Miss Feral." He tossed the keys in the air and caught them again.

"Fuck off."

Gravel ground under his soles and the Volvo's parking lights flashed. He was in and whipping the car from the Hooch and Cooch lot before I even stepped foot onto concrete. I started to dial Marithé, since it was her inability to follow directions that kept me hanging in the Hooch and Cooch in the first place (not really, but it's nice to have someone to blame in these cases). I didn't really want to hear her resounding lack of empathy, so I pounded Wendy's number into my phone.

"Hold on." Wendy picked up mid-conversation. "Make sure to pick up every last bead, I nearly busted my ass on a handful the other day and if I had, it would have been back to Nicaragua with a certain jeweler." She cleared her throat. "Hey girl, what's up?"

"Consuela getting uppity?"

"Her name is Abuelita, like the hot chocolate with peppers or whatever the fuck they put in it."

"Whatever. You gotta come pick me up."

Wendy had decided to further embrace her "undeadness" through a line of supernatural jewelry called Skids. She hooked up with a glorified bead stringer and Nicaraguan immigrant named Abeulita, apparently, through Deadspace dot com, and the two had turned Wendy's apartment into a factory of sorts. It wasn't exactly clear how she paid the little woman, or if she did at all, but I had to hand it to my girl, she was uncharacteristically accommodating, even to the point of gathering down comforters from local thrift stores to make Abuelita comfortable in her special spot next to the oven. And boy, did she need the down. You could see your breath in there since the heat was shut off—well, if you had breath, or if you had breath that wasn't supposed to be visible to begin with, like *moi*.

"Where are you?"

"Hell."

Wendy snickered.

"I'm only half-joking. I'm at the Hooch and Cooch. Had a meeting that turned into a bloodbath."

"Are you sure you're not doing a little moonlighting for Mommy?"

*Always the smartass.* I was in no mood. "Just get

over here. It's too depressing to tell you over the phone. Just get over here."

"Sorry. I can't right now. Abuelita needs me to do a supply run and since I haven't gotten her a bus pass yet, it's all up to me."

"Well then you won't get to hear about the TV show I'll be doing with Johnny Birch." I poked the end button like an eye and speed-dialed Scott, ignoring the near endless call waiting signals.

Poor Wendy, she loved nothing more than gossip.

"I need a ride and I don't want any questions." I bit off the last word.

"Is this some kind of role-playing sex thing?"

"*That* is a question, Scott."

"Yeah, but—"

I shouted the address and tried to press the end button through the back of the phone. What? You act like I don't have reason to be a raving bitch, when I do.

I so do.

Near the motel, a streetlamp pulsed its dying light through clinging mist and the hustler continued trolling for business, bending down as cars slowed and rubbing his thigh for the benefit of leering businessmen. The huddled masses seemed to be tiring of recounting the story to each other and shambled off to spread the story elsewhere. With no reapers to clean up the memories, it was just a fluke that no one had a camera. Of course, it'd just end up on some Discovery Channel exposé a handful of people watch over their uncomfortably silent dinners with the partner they settled with.

I was more interested in my next meal.

I glanced back at the hustler, and weighed the sinking pang in my gut—it burrowed there like a fat parasite—against the odds of becoming someone's hood ornament.[15] Hunger won out. I scanned both directions. The major issue was the cement division separating the traffic. Never one for track and field—I avoided activity like the plague in high school—I didn't think I'd be able to pull off a hurdle, so I needed enough time to stop and crawl over it like the lazy bitch I am.

It was now or never. Scott didn't have the stomach to involve himself with a feeding, so I couldn't wait for him to get there and expect him to be thrilled to wait by some tent city while I darted in for a quick nibble. Nor would I ask—I am a polite girlfriend, after all. We hunted together once and when he saw me dig in, he ended up puking and distant for three sexless days and nights.

That's a record, at least for us.

It turned out I didn't need to make a decision.

"Hey!" the hustler shouted across the highway. He'd waited for a break in the traffic or his irritating yowl would never have had the opportunity to abrade my sensibilities. Jesus Christ on a cracker, it was like feedback. "You got a light?"

"A what?" His words had melted together into a whiny unintelligible "yougawhy."

"A light!" He snatched a cigarette from behind his ear and held it up.

I studied him a moment, while digging for my lighter and a cigarette for myself. He cocked his head to one side and spread his arms in a curt "what," thrust his lower jaw and stared me down like a nemesis. Inter-

---

[15] If I ended up a hood ornament, I'd totally be like one of those painted mermaids on pirate ships, flashing my shit with abandon and pin-up pouting. What kind of hood ornament would you be?

esting. I wasn't aware there were thug whores, especially male ones. It's pretty sad when the opportunities of gang life get so slim, a perfectly good thug ends up skiddin' all the way down to prostitution. Surely there was a car he could jack or a ten-year-old to sell crack to.

Of course, I'd been running on empty myself, so why should this guy be any different.

I pulled the lighter out and he darted into traffic, slowing to avoid a semi, its air brakes tearing the concrete in stereo. He tossed himself onto the divider like a pommel horse and, glancing briefly, scrambled into the traffic, sidestepping a skidding Honda. The driver laid on the horn and screamed obscenities out the window, but didn't stop. Then he was in front of me.

He was about twenty and dark, with skin so coarse it could have borne a *Grown in Florida* label if it weren't for the alternating crop of patchy facial hair and shiny achy pustules in desperate need of a depilatory. He wore a grim pair of Adidas with soles worn thin enough, it was possible his socks were touching sidewalk. The white T-shirt he wore hung nearly to his knees, well past the end of his denim jacket, and his pants were at least three sizes too big, which, while seemingly the uniform of every other gangsta, wanksta and wannabe, probably came in handy for the kind of work that required quick and covert access to the nether regions.

I sparked his smoke.

He nodded, his face glowing red as he took a drag. "I don't chomp no box."

Charming. I would have choked had I any sensitivity left in my esophagus (that was one of the first places to go). But my bulging eyes and gaping mouth must have spoken volumes. He grinned and turned his head to chuckle, as though *that* might be more of a crime than his illicit proposition.

Shaking off the mild shock—really saying something there, as I'm rarely in that particular state—I said, "No? You look the kind that might go in for that."

"I don't do ladies, not normally." He shrugged, rubbing his fist across his mouth and tugging at his loose jeans. He clucked his tongue. "What you got in mind?"

I motioned to the side of the now quiet Hooch and Cooch. Gil and Ethel hadn't left. Gil probably busy heaping unwarranted praises and Mother "debriefing" the girls, or whatever.

The burn barrel let off a soft glow and a flurry of sparks flew like gnats into the still night air and up the side of the building's clapboard exterior. Probably a fire hazard, but after the night's spectacle, I'm not sure I'd even alert Gil if the place caught fire.[16]

The kid nodded and shuffled off in the direction I indicated. When not racing like a madman across a moderately busy freeway, he expressed a slight limp, favoring his right leg explicitly. He lugged the left behind him with a spare hop at the end of each step.

I wish I hadn't seen it.

Those kinds of things make me wish I didn't have to feed the way I do. The thoughts are always fleeting and always my own fault, a hazard of being too observant. Noticing little details of my victims—and they were definitely that, no matter how hard I rationalized—was not helpful. Not. Helpful.

---

[16] What? It's not like it'd kill 'em. Christ, you're so sensitive.

In those moments, when food becomes human, identifiable, I'm more likely to walk away than any other.

Occasionally.

The boy's scent trailed in his wake, dense and meaty.[17] There were sweet hints of maple, smoky bacon. The hustler was a breakfast fan. A lot of street people were, cheap meals done quick and from places that usually kept waitresses long after their expiration date, long after they gave a shit about a kid dining and dashing. Either that or hired them so green they didn't know what to look for.

A quick refresher—if you're late getting on and trying to catch up—when a zombie catches the scent of its prey, it's over. Reason goes out the window, for the most part, and the hunger kicks in like autopilot. When I first turned (after a run-in with a breather and later a misplaced donut box—damn if slick cardboard and concrete don't equal flat on your back dead in a parking garage, at least for a little bit), I had absolutely no control over the process. I'd catch a scent and the next thing I knew I was spitting out a retainer (not mine and not necessarily a kid's, either).[18]

Anyway.

He stalled at the far corner of the Hooch and Cooch, settling into a spot on a rickety picnic table, whose purpose seemed to be only to hold up a massive bloom of cigarette butts sticking out of a spent can of Yuban. He jutted his chin forward, again, lips screwed

---

[17] This is where you lightweights skip ahead. I won't judge. This time.

[18] I don't know why you insist on taking this to a dark place.

up in a sneer, in that defiant way one does when there's nothing to lose or live for. He probably figured if he put that tough face on, I'd be attracted—some women apparently go for the thug type.

He was right. I was definitely into him.

After a quick glance behind me, I shoved my arm through the handles of the McQueen and shrugged it over my shoulder like a pack (shielding it from the spatter, if you must know).

"So whaddup? You getting' on this?" he asked.

I could barely conceal my glee.

I slammed the door and settled my purse in the floor-board, turning to Scott for what I hoped would be the first pleasant moment of the evening—God knows I could use one—but finding a face smeared with enough ugly judgment to guarantee him a slot in the local PTA.

"What?" I asked, agog perhaps and definitely in no mood. 'Cause really, could I pile any more bullshit on my plate?

His disapproving eyes dropped to my cheek. "You've got a little gore on you."

I patted for it, the reduced sensitivity in my extremities not helping me any. "Here?"

"No. A little to the left. More."

We played out the hunt a few moments and then I dropped my hand in my lap and sighed. "You get it. I'm frickin' exhausted."

Scott shook his head and reached across to the glove compartment, retrieving a travel pack of tissue. He balanced them on my leg and turned his head. "I'm going to leave that up to you."

Fucker.

"You know, what you do is worse." I dabbed the tissue around my face until it came back red and spotted with gristle.

"What? How the hell could a few scratches be worse than eating people?"

"Please." I rolled my eyes. "Like leaving them maimed, covered in scars and doomed to a life of unmanageable body hair is a prize." I amped up the mocking. "Do they thank you? I don't know how I've made it this long without juggling dog teeth in my mouth and these extra six nipples. Yeah, you're a real humanitarian."

"Fine. Make fun. It just bothers me a bit."

"Whatever, just drive, I've had a really bad night."

I told him about Birch and his come-ons—he slapped the steering wheel while making threats, which made me smile—the yeti attack and how gross it looked shaved, the weird creatures on the peg boards like junior high biology experiments and the offer to judge on Johnny's show.

"So who wants to kill the fucker this week?" He grinned, lost in some violent fantasy.

I shrugged as we passed the Center, with its mascot the Space Needle towering above us on legs like a modern TV tray. Scott pointed the car toward the high-rise condo district. Streets lined with crappy domestics gave way to Euro-functional Saabs, Volvos and Volks-wagens (mostly Passats, the *nuevo* bugs gone out of favor as quickly as they fluttered back).

"Could be anyone, really," I said. "I'd only known him a few seconds before wanting him dead. There must be a daily tally running. Birch has got to be at the top of the supernatural dead pool."

"How's your mother?" To Scott's credit, he was just about the only one in my life who saw through Ethel's bullshit.

"Still a vampire." I shifted in my seat, drawing one leg up under the other. "You know, she's really twisted Gil around her finger. He's blind to her batshit insane-ness."

"Is that a word?" His eyes crinkled at the joke.

"Shut up. You know what I mean."

"Things change." Two words, and so much behind them I could barely stop myself from jumping out of the car.

I shut down the chatter with a stare.

It didn't matter that I'd just had to fend off an attack from the chicken-skinned beast of morbid obesity, or that my car had been repoed, or that I had to put up with my mother's mindfucks, or even that I was forced to take a job with the seediest wood nymph in reality TV—Scott was clearly moving into an "us" talk.

"Your timing is for shit."

He slouched in the seat, dashboard glow bluing his disappointment like an exclamation point.

"I really like you, Scott. What I'm not too fond of is the insecurity and this clinging to some antiquated idea of commitment. You'd think you'd learn that all this . . ." I waved my hands around (possibly too frantically to ap-

pear serious) ". . . is transient, by now. What are you
expecting to do? Settle down? Get me pregnant? Have
a couple of kids in the suburbs? A fucking Plymouth
Voyager?"

"I *expect* you to warm up a bit. Give a little. Just one
tiny thing that shows that you actually care. You spend
so much time and effort putting this bitch face forward
to everyone you meet, you forget that you don't have to
do it with me."

He sighed, turned his head to gaze out the window.
Leaning forward, I caught the droop of his lids, the corners of his mouth slack with discontent.

*God. I'm an asshole.*[19]

Of course he doesn't think we're going to ever be
normal. Scott was no idiot. He may have been a pretty
boy—and pretty he was. Even then with his blue eyes
sullen and him chewing the inside of his cheek, he was
gorgeous.

The problem was . . . he was just as beautiful inside,
like actually nice, a constant reminder of how much I
wasn't.

But was I cold? I supposed, certainly in that dead
room temperature way, but was I emotionally flat? Distant? Frigid?

Instead of answering, and fucking the situation up
even more, I slipped my hand into his. We drove the
rest of the way to my condo in silence. Occasionally,
he'd squeeze, to let me know we were okay.

I hoped that's what it meant.

\*   \*   \*

[19] Don't you chime in, I'm not trying to hear you right now.

There was a boy on the couch next to Honey, who was sitting far too properly, with her knees pinioned and hands crossed in her lap, to be after anything other than trouble. Her dead brother, the ghost of my dear Mr. Kim, hovered nearby, awash in a disapproving purple aura, his nearly opaque arms crossed vehemently. I didn't have to hear a word to know what was going on.

Both Honey and Mr. Kim lived in the condo, though the ghost had begun wandering farther from me in the past few months, spending time haunting bookstores and movie theaters. Ever since I'd turned Honey zombie, the girl focused almost entirely on boys and relationships and not just for food. Occasionally she'd get the idea she'd found "The One" and bring him home for me to set his lungs with virus. I've never actually given in to her requests, but that didn't stop her from trying.

I really was going to have to sit her down and discuss the whole sexual aspect of having a zombie guy around. Unless they could afford penile implants, unsatisfying doesn't begin to cover that part of a zombie couple's relationship.

This boy was certainly attractive, though, a little emo-banged skater type, younger than Honey by a year, maybe, with a thin nose and zipper-covered parachute pants. They were a striking pair, especially considering Honey's Versace slip dress and blond extensions. The whole scene sprang from a tragically ironic high-fashion editorial spread. I wondered if it were intentional, to throw me off. Honey knew how I loved intentionally posed candids.

The boy eyed me and stood up awkwardly, nearly bowing. "Hello, Ms. Feral. I'm Stoney."

"Stoney?" I glanced at Honey, raising my eyebrow. "Is he a Jonas Brother?"

She smirked, yet held back on her regular witty comeback.

"Honey said you were gorgeous." His eyes were saucers, as though in shock. "But I guess I didn't know what that meant until now. You're amazing."

If I could have blushed, I wouldn't have. I looked back at Scott, who sighed heavily and strolled past into the bedroom.

"Listen, kid," I started.

Honey shot up. "Amanda. Before you say no, listen."

I groaned. "Honey."

"No, dude, seriously. He's totally the guy for me, aren't you, Stoney?"

He rocked from the balls of his feet to his heels, hands anchored into the back pockets of his jeans. Occasionally, he'd shake the bangs out of his face with a neck roll reminiscent of a facial tic.

"Seriously?" I asked. "Looks like a snack."

"No way. We have tons in common."

"Like?"

"Like . . ." Honey stretched the word out, searching for an answer she'd not given quite enough thought to.

"You're taking too long. Don't ask me to do something that's forever, when you're not even sure right now. I'm not turning him. I've never even heard his name before. You could at least try dating them for awhile."

Honey slouched back on the couch.

"Now scram. Scott and I have some talking to do."

"But!"

"No 'buts'—you're getting too old for this bullshit anyway. Goodnight, Stoncy."

Mr. Kim started in as I left the room. "What I tell you. I don't know why you no find nice werewolf boy, like Mr. Scott."


Scott flopped naked across my 1000-thread-count Egyptian cotton sheets from French Quarter in a big X, extremities reaching for the corners, as if I were readying the restraints for a bit of fringe play, which I'm totally not into.[20] He pumped his butt muscles a few times, inched up on his elbows and turned back to see if I was looking.

"Why are we together, Mandy?" He flipped over onto his back, exposing some particularly unmanicured landscaping.

"Ew. Don't call me that unless you've got a sparkly gift. Also, we're going to have to do something about that." I waved my hand over the startling hair mound around his dick. "It's like a forest."

He propped himself up on his elbows. "I'm entering my *au naturel* phase. I'm being serious, though. Why are we?"

"So am I. I'm going to go get the clippers in a minute."

He let out a frustrated grumble.

I spun back around. "Okay." I had to think, usually not a good sign, but I was in no mood for an escalation, so I opted for diplomatic. "Let's see. You are super-hot

[20] So get your mind out of the gutter, pervo.

and completely obsessed with me in an unhealthy way."

Scott's face screwed up quizzically.

"And I really like that sort of thing. Find it completely endearing and adorable. Except for the big 70s bush you're rockin'."

"Oh." He brightened. "I can live with that."

"Good."

I turned to get the clippers. Scott was up and pressed against me in a second. I'd never get used to his speed. But the warmth was unmistakably comforting. He nuzzled the back of my neck and inhaled in long deep lungfuls. I didn't have to imagine the scent, earthy as loam, but could never quite understand the allure. Not that I should question it. Far be it from me to make those kinds of judgments with what I put in my mouth and all. Still, we *right* zombies have a kinship with the shapeshifters in our ability to track by scent, also in our ability to let the power of that scent get away from us and cloud our judgment. Scott's heavy breathing rattled like a snarl.

"Whoa, mister. Careful with those drags."

He huffed and circled my chest in his arms, nestling his hips and obvious arousal against the small of my back, the ruined silk.

I pulled away. "Lemme get this off and hit the shower. The floor of the Hooch and Cooch left some pretty nasty memories on these clothes, plus I could use a brushing before we kiss." I turned to see his eyes flinch, probably recalling of the trickle of prostitute running from the corner of my lip. He let me go, sneering a bit.

"Let it go."

It wasn't a full minute before he abandoned the repellant thoughts and slunk into the cloud of steam billowing from the walk-in shower. "You mind?" Scott dipped past me and reached for the body wash, and snagged the cap on the edge of his teeth and flipped it open, in an attempt to do über sexy gone horribly geeky. Still, it was better than . . .

"I'm gonna slip this all over—"

"Nope." I pressed a finger to his lips. "Remember?"

He nodded, his lips parting a bit. I slid my finger inside and he sucked on it. Goofy fucker.

"Wash my back, lover."

Had to give it up for the guy, as goofy as he came off, he was amenable to change. He started out as the filthiest kind of porno-talking bed buddy and, with the odd bit of backsliding, here and there, had turned into a pretty thoughtful lover. Occasionally. It was hard work weaning him of the habit. A pinch would suffice after a slip like "I'm gonna take you like a six-pack." A hard pinch sure, and it'd leave a bruise, but he healed quick, so . . .

We still had to work on keeping our paranormal selves in check. After all, sex isn't my only need and the smell of hot blood flowing through Scott sparked my hunger to feed, just as much as the adrenaline pumping through him triggered his urge to shift into a big hulking canine. No matter how cute Scott was, human or wolf-like, I had no intention of getting locked up with him and having to call in the reapers to separate us.

'Cause . . . ew. Seriously.

We kept it under control for the most part. It took a lot of focus, but the effort was definitely worth it. Even then, I was reaping the benefits of pushing down my nature.

Scott's soapy fingers danced up either side of my spine, languorously manipulating the tension from my back, kneading their way up to my shoulders and pressuring my neck to release and give in to their command. Snaking around to meet my gaze, he pressed his lips to mine, his tongue darting in playfully before he pulled away and sank slowly to his knees, trailing kisses down my throat, the soft hollow between my breasts. A rare warmth crept from my core and yet I couldn't allow my breath to go unmanaged, no more panting uncontrollably with each wave of sensation, lest the tendrils of viral smoke creep out in search of host.

I pushed the thoughts from my head and focused on Scott's playful nips on my thighs. His hands followed the slim curves of my ass and spread my cheeks playfully, daring, until I tensed and his shoulders shook with a few laughs. He laid a row of kisses down either thigh before narrowing his intent and pressing his tongue against my folds, searching them, lapping at the hot water that streamed there, thumping a gentle rhythm against my engorging clit.

You know that moment when gentleness gives way to animal urges? Where the tide turns from being satisfied with a kiss to needing raw flesh pressed against the whole of your body? It's my experience—and I'm not going to kid myself, I've been around—it's like a switch in men. They get to a point where it's too much to hold back and they surge.

Scott surged then.

He stood up bolt straight, planted his mouth against

mine and lifted me against the wall, urging my legs around his hips. The marble wall was cool despite the steam and I couldn't quite balance but figured he had at least a little control. He arched his back a bit and slipped his cock inside, with none of the gentleness he'd expressed just moments before.

"Slow down, Scott. Make it last."

I looked into his eyes and wondered how I could have missed the fact that he'd moved into a shift. His pupils were blown out to a size not seen this side of a seizure clinic and his canines had split his lower lip. Fresh blood trailed down his chin and neck like hot grease.

I pulled my head as far away as possible, exposing my neck to attack if Scott was completely too far gone, but it had to be done lest I give in to my own carnivorous ways.

"Scott!" I yelled. "Back off!"

His thrusts were rapid and forceful, his thighs grown to haunches, a new crop of fur coating the flesh.

Holy shit, I thought. He's going all the way.

I had to get off.[21]

Scott's transformation could only end in blood. I slapped him, and grabbed him by the ears as I screamed, "Focus!"

And he did, thank God. His teeth receded, and despite a dull pop in my hip, the pounding became much more pleasant.

Much more.

It was as I came, with those welcome waves crashing through the last layers of tension, with me bearing down onto Scott, now mysteriously flat on his back—I

---

[21] Not like that. Jesus.

have no clue how that even happened—covering the drain and creating a hot puddle, both literally and figuratively as his own orgasm washed over him, leaving him slack-jawed. It was that moment when I noticed my left leg jutting from my hip at an odd angle. Knee straight and inanimately disconnected.

"What the fuck?"

"Huh?" Scott lifted up onto his palms and took in the ghastly sight. "Oh shit. That doesn't look good."

"You think?" I glowered and tried to pull myself off Scott's erection. "Still with the hard-on?" I asked.

He shrugged. "I could've probably gone again."

"Oh, no. Jo Jo the dog boy has had his bone for the evening, now he's gonna fix this fucking leg, before I get pissy."

Scott sucked his lips and tried to manage a position where it would even be feasible to extract his protracted boner from an undead invalid. I wondered what it would be like to be found like this. Not pleasant, I imagined. And by who? What would Honey think, particularly now, I thought, with my foundation washed off down the drain along with my dignity. *Jesus, there's Amanda's dead body, naked and busted all to hell. How she ever found a living thing to bone her is nothing short of miraculous. She should be grateful for that, at the very least.* But she probably wouldn't even think that, but run screaming for Wendy, who'd no doubt bring Gil, who'd, of course, gather my mother, a few of her closest whores and anyone else who needed a good laugh to cram into my master bath and witness this complete atrocity.

I groaned. "Come on."

Scott's mouth spread into a silly grin, he snapped his

fingers as though he'd contemplated important strategic scenarios and finally lit on the ultimate tactical response. "You're going to have to lift yourself up a bit and then, I think if I bear down, I can slip out behind you. Easy peasy. How's that sound?"

"I'll give it a shot, but no promises. In the meantime, how about you think about dead kitties or whatever the hell it is that turns off werewolves."

He clenched an eye and bit his lip, pondering playfully.

I leaned in close. "And if I find out you've been sneaking Viagra or Cialis or something, I'm going to kill you."

"Well, if you keep up that kind of talk I'll be flaccid for weeks."

I balanced my torso over my hips and heaved up with my arms, just enough for him to slip out and drag himself, after a minor adjustment, out from underneath me. When I settled back onto the floor of the shower, I heard an eerie pop.

Scott knelt beside me. "You're going to have to straighten out the good leg." His face was serious, stoic even.

"What do you mean?"

"You've said it yourself. You can't afford another reaper bill."

A chill passed through me when I realized what he intended to do, or maybe it was the icy water showering around me. I pointed at the nozzle. Scott twisted it closed and the room quieted to a few sporadic drips and Scott's heartbeat. He waited for me to make a decision.

I couldn't afford it. He was right. Of course, he was

right. I already owed the bitches my first-born child—
or *a* first-born child—whatever the figurative breakdown of forty grand was. Probably triplets.

I slipped my working leg out in front of me and
leaned back on my elbows. "Do it."

Now, I don't know where Scott got his training, but
he knew enough to work quickly. He dropped back
down on his knees, gripped the thigh of my dislocated
leg in one hand and the back of my knee with the other
and popped that fucker right back in place. In another
minute, he had me on my feet and bearing a little
weight.

"Good as new," he said.

I took a few steps and although it was a little sore,
didn't seem any worse for wear. Except for a dark blue
stain that ran from my crotch clear around to my asshole. *Oh, the joys of death.*

I threw my arms around Scott's neck and gave him a
big old sloppy frencher. "You, my gorgeous love slave,
are certainly handy. You'll have to tell me how you
learned to do that trick."

"You mean the one with my tongue?"

"Uh . . . no. But since you went there." My mood
changing in an instant. "What's up with going shifty on
me?"

"I don't know. I just really lost it tonight."

"Well. We're going to have to put a moratorium on
shower sex. How did we even end up on the floor like
that?"

"I don't remember."

"You slipped," a woman's voice said.

My head nearly spun off, jerking toward the sound.
Wendy's head jutted from a crack in the door to the

separate water closet. She teetered forward on the edge of the toilet seat, a vexed grin plastered on her face, and a suitcase at her feet.

"What the fuck?" Scott covered his man bits and scurried from the room, leaving a track of wet footprints and an echo of curse words bouncing off the tumbled marble.

"Wow. Scott's got a real case of winter body, huh?"

"What?" I hobbled over to the towel warmer and snatched one off.

"You know. Pasty. His hair pops against his white skin like a pencil sketch."

Now, it doesn't matter that Wendy's statement was true. Scott could certainly use a tan, but I'm willing to overlook it considering I'd be like the albino being a pigment judger. "What the hell are you doing here, Wendy? I mean other than being a voyeur and pissing off my boyfriend."

"I'm going with you to your reality show gig. I gotta break me off a piece of Johnny Birch."

I gestured to the suitcase. "You act like it's tomorrow or something."

"It's not?"

"Is it?"

"You don't know?"

"I haven't even talked to Karkaroff about any of it, though I'm certain in her mind it's a done deal."

"Well, I just like to be prepared." She patted the suitcase and then her forehead, indicating some level of brilliance I wasn't aware of.

"You're not going, Wendy."

"Oh, no?"

"No."

"Oh, no?"

"Stop that! You can't just keep asking questions and think that'll discombobulate me enough to agree to your crazy plot to screw a wood nymph. Now come here and help me into the bedroom, I'm still a bit wobbly."

"A super-famous and wealthy wood nymph," she corrected, slipping her arm under mine and bracing my weight through the door.

Scott, crammed into his jeans and a tee, busied himself packing spare underwear into his overnight bag. He clomped around the room, snatching his things off the dresser, his face broadcasting his fury.

"So you're not staying?" I asked and shooed Wendy off to the living room. She lingered at the door a bit.

"Get out, Wendy." Scott spat the words like venom.

She scurried away, shutting the door behind her. I imagined her running for a glass to magnify our voices through the door. As it turned out, amplification wouldn't be necessary.

"And no, I'm not staying. In fact, I'm leaving." His eyes bugged, daring me to say something.

"Okay." The word lilted at the end, the beginnings of anger stirring. "Care to tell me why?"[22]

"How's this? You don't value what we have."

"How do you figure?"

Scott stepped around the bed, confronting me directly, using his hands a lot, like wolves do. "You insulate yourself with social engagements. You're so busy being a persona, even when we're alone, you're still 'on.' Or available!" He pointed toward the living room. Toward Wendy. "You're still working."

---

[22] As if I didn't have a clue. Jesus, Wendy.

"It's hard being a celebrity. I thought you were on board."

"You're not really a celebrity, Amanda. You just want to be. You let it cloud your vision. It blinds you to the real important stuff." Scott shook his head slowly, his jaw tightening. "Either way, I'm not a fan, Amanda. I'm your boyfriend."

"I totally value you, Scott."

"Oh yeah? How, exactly?" He waited.

It was one of those moments where your life passes before your eyes. Only these snapshots were select. Ones I'm not particularly proud of. As per usual, they showed up in clear undeniable list format (damn it) . . .

- I left Scott sitting at the Well of Souls to meet Wendy for a photo op at Gangrene, the new slam poetry/art space in Ballard (which is awesome by the way), then totally forgot about him once we started talking to Gilles St. John, who promised to paint me slathered in caviar or some other egg, I couldn't remember just then.
- Or the time he brought home dinner in the form of a recently released sex offender (who was totally against the idea of treatment) and ended up having to sit there putting up with the guy's chronic attempts at masturbation while I mingled on a dinner cruise with Karkaroff and her demonic team of lawyers.
- Then there was the night I picked up the phone, with Scott in mid-thrust. Though, in my defense, it was an important tip on a clandestine red carpet event.

What I remembered most about all of my assaults against our relationship was Scott's response. He accepted them. He didn't complain. Always the one to reach out to me. Which lead me to the following conclusion: I was the asshole.

Damn.

"Okay. So I haven't been very attentive to you."

"That's an understatement." Scott zipped up the tote and charged for the door.

"But you never said anything, Scott. You just let it build up? Why didn't you say anything?"

"I shouldn't have to mention that I'd like to be treated like a person. Like someone you care about." He stormed from the room.

"Have you been reading *Cosmo*?" I called after him, attempting an inappropriate joke. If Ethel taught me anything it was to have absolutely no clue what to say to mend a hurt.

Scott dropped his bag on the couch next to Mr. Kim and turned around. Honey and the Jonas Brother backed into the pantry.

"Yeah," he said, sarcastically. "And they got you nailed, Amanda. Dead to rights. You're a commitment-phobe."

"I am not—"

"You can drop back to your old standby of blaming your mother for all your problems, but at some point you're going to have to take some responsibility for ruining a good thing here."

I think my mouth was open. I couldn't find the words to fight back. And, damn it, Scott was right. But then, before I could agree, he said, "We're done," snatched his overnight bag off the couch and stomped out the door.

Mr. Kim stared at the TV, which didn't happen to be on. Wendy simply shook her head and pointed at me, accusingly, I thought.

"Shut up," I barked.

"No. You've got a . . . thing."

I followed her cringing stare down to my leg. A strip of skin hung off my ankle and trailed across the carpet like a wet streamer, a line of rotting gore snaked from the bedroom. Wendy dug in her purse and extracted a bottle of leather repair kit and a Band-Aid. She heaved her shoulders sympathetically.

"Ugh," I groaned. "Goddamn dew claws."

South Park was one of our favorite breakfast spots, a
small neighborhood south of the city, quiet, if you didn't
mind gunfire, and known for the plentiful and hearty
Mexican food . . . also restaurants, but that's beside the
point.

"What are you going to do now?" Wendy asked.

I glanced up from a totally unsatisfying meal of day
laborer, greeted by Wendy's judgment and a hand
cocked on her hip with a little too much finality for my
taste. Not yet 6:00 A.M. and girlfriend was already on
my last nerve. Not that I blamed Wendy for Scott leaving. I totally take responsibility for my own actions . . .
most of the time.

Seriously though, would it have exploded if she weren't there to prove him right?

See what I'm saying?

I dropped the leg and wiped my chin. "What do you mean? I'm going to finish my meal and then you're going to drive me to the office. Seeing as how you live a life of leisure and all."

"I meant about Scott."

I shrugged and stuffed the remains into the sewer grate. "I'm not hungry."

Wendy sighed. "You know it was only a matter of time."

"I know you're not trying to start an argument with me. Not before I've smelled my first coffee."

"You could get him back." Wendy shrugged, picking at her teeth with a shard from her breakfast.

"I intend to."

"Aw. You're in love."

Was I? "I don't even know what that means, Wendy. You're talking gibberish."

"It means you like him enough to keep him around rather than eating him. Like when I had that Twix bar bronzed to remind me of the progress I've made with my little eating problem."

"But you haven't made any progress."

Wendy looked up from collecting leftover bits of illegal immigrant with a pair of tongs and dropping them into an environmentally sound cloth shopping bag—it said so on the side. "I mean, the progress I'm going to make. It's like when we were alive and had a pair of goal jeans for weight loss." She broke out in a proud grin. "Yeah, it's just like that."

"Scott is my pair of goal jeans?"

"Totally." She crammed the shopping bag into a

Dumpster behind the Taqueria El Soldado and cringed at some goo on her palms. "Do you have any wet naps?"

I dug a packet out of my purse. "What's the goal then?"

"Do I have to clue you in on everything? It's like you don't remember being a human."

"Not true." She pulled out a toothpick and pried a bone shard from between her front teeth. "I just don't recall the love part."

"He's your goal jeans because you need to fit him into your life." She tossed the gore-smudged wipe atop the bin. "And *you* into his."

I raised my brow and nodded in such a way as to indicate Wendy was indeed batshit crazy. No need letting on that she was probably right. That would unlevel the balance of power.

So not happening.

Her theory made sense in an "everything's really simple" Wendy sort of way. Regardless of whether I loved the guy, or not, I knew I liked having Scott around and that was plenty reason to win him back. But, don't go expecting some romance novel bullshit. Cause it ain't happening.[23]

When Elizabeth Karkaroff bought into Feral Inc. as a partner—and by "bought in" I mean "took over"—things changed. You don't go into business with the queen of the underworld and not let her be the boss, now do you? It was her idea to move the offices from the waterfront to the lake—said that Puget Sound reminded her of the Styx. Also, a shudder rolled through

---

[23] Or maybe it will. I do enjoy keeping you people guessing.

her—a crappy endorsement for whatever it was she was talking about.

"The band?" I'd asked, momentarily distracted by the *en suite* bathroom in the office I'd scouted and not particularly interested in her whims at that moment—if I remember correctly, she'd been on a tear about how bad Seattle drivers were, ranting and raving like mad.

"Of course not," she spat.

I shrugged and ran my fingers across the black granite countertop.

"I swear, sometimes you say things just to irritate me," she scowled, flipped her wavy hair over one perfectly styled shoulder (Carolina Herrera sent a new suit for her that very week—must be nice to have a designer on speed dial) and stomped deeper into the offices.

It was only later I'd realized she meant the river.

She had an excuse for being bitchy, of course—and no, it wasn't her time of the month or anything. More like her time of the year. Come every May, the hellhounds start sniffing from their brimstone doghouses, or whatever, for their precious Persephone, goddess of the underworld—Karkaroff, while a gorgeous and powerful attorney in this world, was pretty high up in management downstairs, as it turns out. And time is just as precious there. I've got a pretty good idea which world she'd rather inhabit. Right around the time the cherry blossoms popped open and the cottonwood trees filled the air with so much dander you'd think God was neglecting his dry scalp, the bitch got grumpy.

And by *grumpy*, I mean deadly.

The first year of our partnership, she tore through the marketing department with her bullwhip. Heads really did roll that day and she stomped them into mush. Of course, they were already halfway there, most of them being zombies and all. I had to bite back a comment about the fiscal irresponsibility of impromptu carpet replacement when I saw the stains spreading like a Rorschach.

That said . . .

The benefits totally outweighed the lingering fear of being swallowed up in an inky pit of death and darkness. Really, they did.

Take the swanky new digs. In spite of a potential financial catastrophe courtesy of Necrophilique tanking, we were still living large corporate style, thanks to Karkaroff's sizeable personal accounts.

Wendy dropped me off in front of three stories of glass and chrome in a remodel overlooking Lake Washington, sailboats bobbing in the distance like a fucking Norman Rockwell painting and summer night client cocktail parties on the veranda.

Too bad that last part was history.

"Don't forget the time. We're meeting Gil at 9:00. And I need some time to freshen."

I waved her off. "Just pick me up in an hour. It's just a business meeting, I'll weasel my way out of it somehow."

The mood was remarkably chipper considering the layoffs of the previous week. Those had been exceptionally fun. To be fair, we started with the idea of ditching those hired most recently, but as one of the new guys, Jeff Gorst, was super-hot, we opted to get rid of Rachel Pratchett in accounting. She was a grim little zombie, wore Tevas in the summer and never brought us anything but bad news and even worse breath, unless you consider the questionable and mildly threatening casseroles she'd bring for potluck days an asset. I don't trust zombies that continue to cook food. There's just something wrong with it, like when people who wear leather dusters comment on fashion, or amputees insist on playing soccer. Plus, how many accountants does a business really need? With accounts in the toilet, there's just not that much to count.

There were a handful of others, but Greg Studebaker was the only employee I would miss, and primarily because his presence softened Marithé's often frightening demeanor. Six-foot-three if he was an inch, tan and altogether agreeable, Greg had the kind of hair that stuck up like he'd just rolled in from a night of rough sex. He always had the good sense to wear clothing that stretched across his hips and crotch in such a way, every shift reminded a girl of a thin sheet draped over his naked junk. Marithé was appreciative, to say the least. But since no one could figure out what he actually got paid for, he was one of the first up for the chopping block.

"Congratulations, Amanda!" Marithé looped her forearm through the crook of my elbow and clopped along with me. "Your appearance on *American Minions* and the ad revenue built into that contract is going to turn all this shit around." She gestured to the rows of low-walled cubicles and then to a particularly forlorn employee named Renata. "*And* that."

The woman's head snapped up from a stack of papers, her mouth twisted up like the pucker in a Chinese dumpling.

Marithé continued, "Elizabeth is working on a relaunch of Necrophilique, under a new name and without the excrement, of course."

"Christ, again?"

"Yes, again. Stop being so negative. All Necrophilique needs is pretty people on pretty packaging and the dead will be lining up to smear it on their clammy chops. Besides, it's been two months; there's been plenty of tragedy in the world to keep them occupied. Who'll remember a little shit in their foundation?"

I stopped her as we neared the narrow hall to the executive offices. "Just as long as we don't go the infomercial route, again. I don't want my face attached to another major screw-up. Plus, if I see that Janice Dickinson again, I'll beat her so bad."

"She was a celebrity impersonator."

"Whatever."

The shoot for Necrophilique was wrought with mishaps, general bumbling and a virulent strain of incompetence, none so great as my own, I'm ashamed to say. Despite being accustomed to the camera at local events and club openings and such, I wasn't at all comfortable reading from a script, or memorizing lines or pretending to like things that I don't. That last part must come as no surprise.

The lights hit my makeup like a blowtorch and before I knew it, Dickinson was giggling and pointing and the audience was doubled over laughing as stripes of foundation bled off my face leaving me looking as fresh as a glazed blueberry cake donut. If only I'd had some mustard gas. I could have at least taken out the shapeshifters. No such luck.

"Amanda! Darling!" Elizabeth Karkaroff stomped down the corridor from her office in vintage Chanel bouclé and scooped me up in her arms. "So good to see you!"

I squeezed my stomach in as she continued to tighten her grip, fully expecting my ribs to crack before she let go.

"Nice to see you too, Elizabeth."

"Hmm." She relaxed her arms and stood back a bit, assessing me. "I'm counting on you. And I know you can pull this agency back from the brink."

"It would have been nice to know what I was getting into," I said, thinking again about the death threats on Birch and the yeti attack, rather than my part in the reality show.

"I'd have thought you'd be thrilled." Her voice carried a hint of hurt and her lips pursed.

Marithé crossed her arms and judged, as per usual.

"Well, I certainly don't mind the exposure and I imagine I'll do better just being me."

"Exactly!" Her hands shot forward and clutched my biceps forcefully. A spasm passed through me. "And who doesn't love unbridled Amanda?"

"No one," Marithé added, shaking her head. "Well, maybe soccer moms."

Elizabeth sneered at my assistant.

"What?" she asked, then gestured to me. "I'm talking about her pottymouth."

I supposed they were right. After all, I, myself, love unbridled Amanda.[24]

"Still. It would have been nice to know that Birch has been getting death threats. A yeti attacked us last night. I don't imagine that was part of the pitch he threw you?"

"Oh please." Elizabeth waved off the remark. "Who doesn't want to kill Birch? I can't name a species he hasn't fucked, defrauded or fouled in some way or another. He's a complete Neanderthal and everyone knows

---

[24] And so do you. Right? I'm asking you a question.

it. That the woodland types have turned against him doesn't surprise me in the slightest." She pivoted on her Givenchy stilettos and slinked off into her office, speaking over her shoulder.

Karkaroff had an unhealthy relationship with scale. Her office was long, thin and shiny as a wet birth canal. The perspective was forced as a de Chirico painting; walls slick with subway tile narrowed the full length of the building to just enough space on either side of Karkaroff's desk for the woman to saunter around. The place echoed and was a tad claustrophobic if you ask me, but she didn't.

She never did.

I thought of Birch's voice and the shimmer of sound that filled the room in sensual warmth, brought on by the cold air pumping into the space. "He has his merits."

"Oh, Amanda. Don't tell me you've fallen for his little song and dance."

I shrugged. "Of course not. He has an interesting voice, is all I'm saying. There's a reason why people are drawn to him. It's not his charm, I can tell you that much."

"Like a swarm of locusts stripping a field. Vile sounds from an even more contemptible being." Elizabeth scraped a fresh French manicure across the subway tile; they squeaked and ticked like a needle on a broken record. "I should have . . ." her voice trailed off and the long hall was silent for a moment.

I glanced at Marithé, who mouthed, "What the fuck?"

"Elizabeth?" I asked, stepping toward the woman, the part-time goddess, and the scariest lawyer I knew, not sure whether I was seriously attempting to soothe her, or otherwise bond, in any way. Karkaroff wasn't exactly the bonding type.[25]

"Nothing. Nothing." She spun around, flipping her hair over her shoulder and the remnants of a sad smile from her otherwise stony face. "Shut the door and sit down. We have much to discuss before you leave for the set of *American Minions*."

"And when is that exactly?" I asked checking my watch.

Elizabeth thumbed through a stack of papers on her desk. "Here it is. Principal photography begins . . . tomorrow." She smiled pleasantly.

"Tomorrow?" My mouth dropped open. Wendy's sources were definitely on the ball. Despite it not paying, the gossip blogging thing did produce some interesting and accurate blather.

Marithé joined me on the couch, smoothing her skirt under her ass and sneering at me for monitoring her, presumably. Karkaroff leaned against her desk and continued, shrugging off my horror at the heightened timeline. "I don't need to tell you this agency is on its last leg. The show's going to help, but we'll need to make some cuts to keep us afloat until then." She accentuated the statement with a dramatic scissoring with her fingers.

I spun on Marithé. "We could get rid of your personal assistant."

She smooshed up her face around her nose, as though someone had thrown a turd into the room. Of

---

[25] I know what you're thinking. I'm not either. But you're wrong. I haven't killed Wendy yet, have I? And she's given me plenty of reason, don't act like she hasn't.

course, that'd be me. "Well, I don't see how that would—"

On cue, Cupcake buzzed in like a horsefly to catch a whiff. An ill-proportioned little pixie who favored crocheted berets in odd pastels like creamsicle and puce to anything resembling an actual hat and an unnerving habit of spraying sparkles from her fingertips as she typed—like *that's* useful.

"I have your raspberry-scented oxygen set up for your beauty break, ma'am," she said, eyes batting in adoration of Marithé.

Her boss simply rolled her eyes and seethed, her ability to defend the use of a company employee for her own luxury treatments (not that she could even breathe, so the whole thing was just weird) neutered by the girl's lack of tact.

"You're right," Marithé said and then turned to Cupcake, her hands clasped pleasantly. "Cupcake?"

"Yes?" More eye batting.

"You're fired."

Cupcake's mouth dropped open.

"You heard me. Pack your knitting needles, drawers full of Pez dispensers, office birthday charts and don't forget that row of troll dolls congregating on top of your computer monitor. If I see that you've left them, I'll blowtorch them into a rainbow puddle of plastic and mail it to you with your final paycheck." Marithé scanned her palms, perhaps for her conscience. Finding none, she looked up. "Such as it is."

"But?" A glittery tear slid down Cupcake's cheek.

Marithé reached toward the pixie, and for a second I thought I'd be witnessing a rare moment of tenderness—that is, before she curled her finger under the salty drop and slurped it up like the monster she was.

The monster I created . . . well, with the help of whatever fucked-up childhood she'd been party to. I often imagined Marithé burning down her decrepit orphanage, nuns included, despite the fact that her parents lived in a planned community outside Philadelphia and participated in the weekend farmer's market.

Cupcake burst into a major meltdown, running from the room full-tilt, slamming into the opposite wall as she went, clumsy as a kindergarten tantrum, without the promise of hugs at the end.

I felt for her, I really did. Just not as much as I felt for my wallet.

"Well, that solves one problem," Karkaroff spat. "Couldn't stand that little freak anyway. Did I ever tell you about the time I had to use the toilet after her? She left sparkles all over the front of the seat."

"I wish you would have, we could have made a sign." I said, fiddling a cigarette between my lips.

"How we let you talk us into hiring *it* is a testament to your frighteningness." She thought a moment. "Is that even a word?"

A few more employees trudged through and out the door with their little cardboard boxes full of crap and the same sour faces. It would have been depressing, but really—it's true what they say—misery loves company. If I'm hitting the skids, you better be too.

Of course, the skids never looked so good.

It could have gone on like that all afternoon but I had things to wrap up in my office before getting ready for dinner. Fabulousness is not automatic, no matter what you tell yourself and the only thing that would take my mind off all the crap I'd been enduring was the unstoppable ribbing Gil would receive about his blind date.

Plus we were meeting at Skinshu, a hot new restaurant catering to zombies, or something. The lines were around the block last week when it opened.

"I don't want you to take my bitching about Birch to suggest that I'm unenthusiastic. Quite the contrary. I am excited about the show. The way I see it," I said. "If we can build up enough buzz, the show can be a cash cow. Our own personal cash cow."

Marithé put her bitch face back on, leaning against the couch arm and glowering. "Do you know anything about the contestants? Reality shows only work by catering to the lowest common denominator. The characters have to be freaks, drama queens and prone to irrational outbursts and impromptu fist fighting."

"You say that like it's a bad thing." I winked at Elizabeth, who, I knew, was in love with *Jersey Devil House Party*. And who could blame her? It had everything: skanky trailer-trash nymphos, exceptionally stupid muscleheads in chains, and one bad-ass Jersey Devil that gave the tagline, "You've Been Cut" a whole new meaning.

"Oh, God, no." Marithé kicked off from the edge of the table and fondled the book spines on Karkaroff's shelves as she stalked the room. "I love 'em. When Veronique flashed her patch on *Tapping* and that bottle of cyanide fell out of her snootch . . . well, if I had functioning neurons I would have had a stroke."

We could only be so lucky to get a true trash titan like Veronique. It only takes one breakout. Remember Chastity from *Death Camp 5*? Of course you don't, but I do. *Death Camp* was this show about fat supernaturals struggling to lose weight in this weird Siberian camp setting. It had Nazis and evil nurses—both seemingly essential ingredients of anything entertaining.

Each show concluded with a "Death March," and not of the goose-stepping shoeless wintry variety either. The contestants ran on treadmills cantilevered over a huge meat grinder, the first one to drop, well . . . you can figure it out.

"To answer your question, no. Not a thing. We'll have to wait and see what we're dealing with tomorrow. Now, if you don't mind, I've got some work to do."

"I'm not sure we're done here." Marithé's hand hung on her hip.

"You're right," I said, struggling to come up with a distraction so I could get out of there. "You need to have the commercial spots ready for client review. You should really get on that."

Marithé rolled her eyes and sucked at her teeth like she had a piece of tendon stuck in there.

Karkaroff spun around and caught Marithé's chin in her fingers. The girl jerked as an uncharacteristic fear marred her usually stoic mask. "I need to speak with Amanda. So, yes, Marithé, we're done."

She huffed, collected her files from the small table and stomped out of the room, instantly spitting orders for the benefit of her Bluetooth. "Don't do one fucking thing until I get there, you idiot."

"She's next." Karkaroff grinned.

I giggled a bit, but the thought of firing Marithé scared even me and I'm the one that turned her into a zombie.

"Now. Contingency plan."

"What?"

"If this show doesn't manage to get us clawing out of the grave, I'm afraid I'll have to liquidate to collect my investment. I've lost too much as it is."

I slouched. "It will succeed. I'll see to it."

She glared at me for a moment and I almost thought I could feel her picking her way through my brain, using her abilities to test my resolve. If she was, she came away satisfied.

"See that you do." She pulled out her calculator. "Because the way I figure it, with what the agency is worth right now, even after clearing accounts and selling off the furniture and such, you'll owe me—" Her fingers clicked across the keys, she shook her head and then passed the calculator across the desk.

If I'd had a functioning heart it would have sunk in my chest.

I struggled to keep my Louboutins out of the rat's nest
of fast food wrappers and candy bar detritus heaped in
the floorboard—no small feat with legs as long as mine
and in a space as small as Wendy's new Civic hybrid.
She pointed the trashcan on wheels down Queen Anne
toward the Center and stood on the accelerator. We
caught a little air at the top and when we bottomed out,
the garbage under my calves shifted, revealing another
layer of shame, several empty packages of Depends
and their accompanying sticker strips were balled up
tight as little mysteries.

There's a reason why I always drive.

Or . . . used to.

"You might want to consider cleaning up your binge
evidence."

"Remember, you're not supposed to comment on that," she said, thankfully without looking. Even the slightest distraction could easily turn "barreling" into "careening," and I was in no mood to deal with the police after Wendy mowed down one of Seattle's infamously slow pedestrians.

"Well, Jesus. Don't give me cause. There are at least fifty wrappers in here. It reeks of secret shame."

Wendy shrugged and tugged left on the wheel, rocking me into the car door. "So what's up with this Birch gig?" she asked. "Can I get a ride-along or what?"

First the suitcase, now she wasn't letting it die. I was about to sock her when it dawned on me.

"Oh, my God." I slapped her arm. "You totally have a girl boner for Birch. So gross."

"He's a good singer. You can't deny it."

Couldn't I? Sure his voice was interesting and oddly compelling, at least as far as rampaging yetis go, but was he a "good singer"?

"I guess I never really thought about it. Johnny's other attributes get in the way. Being a fucking pig and all. As for getting you on set, I'm still thinking no."

Wendy clicked her tongue, face souring instantly.

"Karkaroff's on my ass about making this show successful. I can't risk losing ad space, just because you're a star fucker."

"Am not!" Her lips split into a toothy and wholly lascivious grin. "At least not yet."

"Nice. But seriously, I don't think it's gonna work."

"And you do need the cash." She nodded with a sympathetic pout.

Wendy knew about my struggles, as only another accident-prone zombie could. Her reaper bill was one of the primary reasons for her latest foray into retail accessories. In fact, a recent fall had landed her in their clinic for nearly a week. An entire trunkload of Abuelitas, working 'round the clock, wouldn't begin to produce the merchandise required to pay back that debt. Good thing she had the gossip blog ads to keep her in Twix (for what that was worth, I couldn't imagine it was more than a couple of hundred a month), or I'd have to cram another freeloader into my place—two, if you count Abuelita.

"Thank you. Seriously."

She winked. "You know I love you."

"Yeah, now if you could just show it like a good parent. You know how I like to be spoiled."

Outside, every car that passed seemed to be a Volvo SUV. The blue one beside us came equipped with a party girl stippling lip-gloss onto an exaggerated pout. Even the gods were shoving the repo down my throat, mocking my financial problems with a fervor not often seen this side of a political correctness rally.[26]

Wendy pointed the car at a space in front of a three-story brick monstrosity rising out of a sidewalk so broken, its jags and dips lapped against the foundation like frozen waves. A dense hand of dead vines stretched from the side of the building as if the arm of some crumbling giant were holding up the decay. An old, but oddly appropriate theater marquee jutted from the corner, a shiny knife in a vagrant's back. Across the top in

---

[26] Not that anyone actually rallies for political correctness, but whether it's soccer moms for the banishment of the word retard or fashion rejects banding together in white shoes after Labor Day, it just goes to show, there's always something to be offended about.

a scrolling font of lightbulbs read THE GRAND and below that, instead of a film title, GRANTHAM'S RECLAMATION AND RESOURCER—whatever that was.

"Are you sure this is it?" I stepped out of the car and swept my purse off the dash.

Wendy pointed a bit down the street toward a classic Jag—and by "classic" I mean old and funky smelling—centered under a streetlight with the deliberateness of the hopelessly anal. "Does that answer your question?"

Behind the place, down a path of trampled weeds, we found the loading dock, the word SKINSHU scrawled across the rolling shutter door. The edges of the letters dripped down the corrugated metal in a deep rusty brown. If one were to examine it closely, they'd find that it wasn't paint at all, but the dried blood of a good luck sacrifice. For all the good that was worth.

Beside the door, only a small black call box protruded from the brick and not a pack of greedy stalkerazzi, as the news had promised.

"Amanda Feral and guest," I grumbled, pressing the little button embedded in its center; it squished in pleasantly, like a rubber bulb.

"One moment," a mechanized voice responded.

"You know," Wendy breathed. "Just once, I'd like it for you to be the guest."

The door rolled up into the wall, revealing a long rectangle of Japanese garden. A path of grayed boards meandered around serene stones and clumps of black bamboo jutted into the dark heights of the space, their roots coiled in a flooded pebble floor, the walk underlit by the soft glow of stone lanterns. Wendy stalked off ahead and as I stepped onto the boards, the shutter door rolled closed behind me.

Security has become more important these days. Sure, most people wouldn't notice a vampire if they fell on one's dead boner, but theft was up and people were always looking for a score, even in the seedier areas. When thieves start stealing from their own, you know the world's circling the bowl.

I looked at Wendy who shrugged. Her review was a clear, "Eh."

"It's a little obvious, I agree."

"Totally."

Still, my only experience with teppanyaki was a childhood birthday ritual of Benihana onion volcanoes and an awkward inability to catch the goddamn rice ball. But that was a long time ago. And I'd had enough of Ethel for the whole month to even consider going down memory lane just then (but I'm all for blowing out the back door of this bitch with a fat ass appendix).[27]

The zombie hostess was blond and made up like a geisha, except the white makeup wasn't really necessary and I'm pretty sure the red stain on her lips wasn't Shiseido, if you know what I mean. Her ornately embroidered kimono whipped around her as she shuffled (not shambled) toward an arch into the main dining room and the soles of her stocking feet scraped across tumbled marble veiny and blue as British cheese.

Skinshu bore no resemblance to any Benihana I'd ever seen. It didn't even attempt a reasonable facsimile. In fact, that was the best description of the place: unreasonable. Or better yet: fucking unreasonable. And tiny. Also lame.

The closest thing, for comparison's sake, is Me-

---

[27] No shit. See Appendix.

dieval Times. You know, the place where you eat food without utensils and watch heavily costumed men "joust," though really, the whole thing reeks of the gay. Just ask Gil; he had a whole philosophy about guys who do renaissance reenactments. I won't steal his thunder but it has to do with latent tendencies.

He's the expert on that.

If Gil's lonely, you can bet he'll find a closeted, emotionally unavailable werewolf (or something) to fall in love with, help the bastard to come blazing out of the closet to family and friends, only to get his heart broken in some dramatic and often public falling-out. It's his thing. Some women keep reliving abuse, Gil keeps leading the closeted out of denial, like Moses, if he were a top, and he may have been for all we know.[28]

The metal grill tables were there, scattered evenly across a circular balcony and peppered with only a few handfuls of diners, Gil among them. He waved rather unenthusiastically from a table off to our left. This gallery surrounded a frosted glass stage, above which, several eyehooks dangled from clinking chains like giant monocles.

I poked Wendy and pointed. "That's an interesting decorative choice."

She pondered them a moment and then, her eyes brightened in mock surprise, she whispered, "Not if you're a gymnast."

A chill forced its way under my skin, but I played along. "Genius. Maybe it's like a whole French circus thing!"

"With those super fun clowns who like to invade personal space bubbles and speak gibberish."

---

[28] I've not given much thought to Biblical sexual habits. Have you?

"You know how I love that." I didn't. Ever.

"I do." She quivered. Wendy hated those freaks nearly as much as I did—it's one of the many reasons we're friends. Though, if you'll recall, when I first met the bitch, she was wearing a clown mask. And Louboutins, so that kind of cancels it out.

By the time we were led to Gil, he was paler than usual and intent on gouging his eyes out with his knuckles.

"Have you been here long?" I asked, dropping my purse on the seat next to him and scooting in close.

Wendy took his other side and kissed his cheek. "Hi, lover."

He nestled his head against her neck. "Nah. Like fifteen minutes or so."

Gil nodded in the direction of the stage. "I'm guessing Kabuki dinner theater, sake cocktails and sashimi of some young guy. A nice thumping heart. Something nasty and gut-wrenching for you carnivores. Don't mind me, I brought my own." He pulled a flask from his Jil Sander three-quarter trench (unbelted, of course) and took a big swig. "Oh. And check this shit out."

He spread out his palm and hovered over the cooktop embedded in the center of our table. I reached out over it too, and didn't notice anything, but that was normal for us; we don't have a lot of tactile sensations in the extremities.[29] He slapped his palm down. I jumped. Wendy yelped and grabbed at his arm to pull it

[29] Closer to the core and we're hypersensitive, so no cold fish jokes, bitches! And the lubrication problem has cleared up entirely, though the reason for that is so unpleasant, I have no intention of detailing it here. Best leave it to your filthy imaginations. Have I reminded you recently that you make me sick?

back from the heat. But there was no reaction, no sizzle
no smoke. At first. Just a bit of frost creeping across his
pale skin.

"A cold stone?"

"Yep." Gil pulled his hand away and rubbed it
against the leg of his wool trousers.

Wendy's face screwed up quizzically, and then
loosened. "I guess it makes sense. We don't cook our
food, after all."

I leaned around Gil and launched a bemused smirk
at Wendy. "Maybe they'll chop some Twix bar in your
sundae."

Her middle finger snapped up so quickly, I was
surprised her fingernail didn't shoot off the end.

I blew her a kiss and patted Gil on the thigh. "So
how was that date, Slugger? First base? Home run?"

"No comment. How about you? Ready for the big
show?"

"Oh, God. Doesn't much matter if I'm ready or
not. Shooting starts tomorrow."

"I'll be posing as her agent," Wendy said.

"No, she won't."

Wendy shrugged it off and scanned the menu.
"This menu is in Japanese. And not like kanji, either.
English phonetically written Japanese. What good is
it?"

I looked at my own copy and, true enough, they
could be selling turds spread on rotting celery for all
we knew. I turned to Gil. "So, seriously, how was this
blind date?"

Gil's dates were notorious hatchet jobs. In fact, I
can't think of a single guy he's even brought out to
drinks with us. Sure, he's a vamp and he keeps some

taps on hand for draining, but I wouldn't call those relationships, would you?

"Date?" Wendy hunched over the fat straw protruding from her tiki and suckled it like a nipple.

Gil leaned back and stared into the heights of the funnel, sighed, smacked his tongue against his teeth and gave up the ghost. "You know, I was hoping you'd let that slide."

I shook my head rapidly. "Not a chance."

Wendy grinned.

"Didn't think so."


"I'll start at the beginning, because I know that's what you bitches want. Gory details and every bit of my dignity flushed out of me like a wave of painful diarrhea."

"Make it squishy."

"I met the guy through Deadspace dot com.[30, 31]

"I know it's a hook-up site, but Jesus, a guy's got to get some play and I'm not about to go sire a Capitol Hill gymbo just so I don't have to hang out with you two hags every other night. I'm looking for something deeper."

Wendy raised an eyebrow.

---

[30] Damn, that site is getting a lot of play this go round. Social networking's not really my thing. I have a MySpace and I try to Twitter, but it's so easy to forget and if the people reading them aren't available for a late night snacky call then what good are they?

[31] That sharp intake of breath you heard was Wendy and me judging Gil's decision-making. It was done through our teeth and not silently, as you might have observed. It's not good judgment, if there's no whistle. Mark that down in your notebook.

### Interlude of the Bitter and Pathetic

*Part One*

**Gil's Blind Date**

(The Grisly Perils of Dating Karma*)

*the concept, not a person

---

"Now shut up. I'm trying to rock a mood with this." We nodded and let him have the stage.

"The Limelight isn't holding up well," he said, his voice dropping an octave and brow cocking like a pistol hammer. "Don't get me wrong, they still have one of the best vintage blood cellars in town, but if I have a hankering for an Orlando-tapped Tilda Swinton, I'm going to Veinity on 3rd and not some place with banquettes torn up like a ghetto weave. Even the outside has gone to hell. What happened to valet in this town? It's like we're in Tacoma, or something.

"My date definitely distracted me from the shabby hole in the wall. He waited in the rear of the blood bar, blending into the shadows. The first I saw of him was his hand, pale and drifting from the darkness to rub the lip of his bloodglass with slender fingers, the tips alternating and coaxing a thin song from the crystal. Then he revealed himself and I nearly blew it into my boxers."

"Nice," I said, swigging my third sake.

"Yeah, like you don't work blue."

I shrugged and he continued, "Nordic-boned, with ice-blue eyes and blond hair slickcd back like he had Ralph Lauren on speed dial, luckily without any of the hunt club trappings. He wore a black V-neck tee and propped a denim-clad leg up on the cushion. Sexy, for sure, but there was something else there too, like a memory I couldn't quite pull out of my brain.

"'I expect you're Gil.' His words were attenuated and inflected via London, which surprised me a bit. We'd talked quite a bit online, I thought I knew a lot about the guy, but he never mentioned where he was from. I just assumed he was local. He extended his hand and I shook it. Neither of us lingered, that would have been creepy plus I've learned not to.

"Anyways, I said, 'And you're Daniel. Really is great to meet you . . . in person, I mean. How did we not talk about your accent?'

"'Does it bother you?' He motioned to the seat opposite him.

"I slipped in, our knees brushing under the table. I pretended it was the bar holding up the table and left my leg fitted right against his. 'Cause I'm sexy like that and, seriously, I was looking awesome . . . like I'm known to do.

"'Of course not. I like it,' I told him.

"'I took the liberty of ordering us something special.' Daniel turned the bottle of veino so I could read the label.

"'Holy shit. A Lana Turner?'

"'I've been waiting for this for a long time.' Daniel's eyes never waivered, his focus was deliberate and heavy-lidded with a promise.

"I began to wonder what he expected. It's not like I date a lot. Other vampires seem to whore it up with each other but I've never been into the whole blood orgy thing. I really hoped Daniel didn't have that in mind. Though, as I swallowed my first mouthful of Lana, and her warmth and ambition spread through me, I could have been convinced.

"'I hope I don't disappoint,' I said. And then decided it sounded like innuendo. 'I don't mean . . . not sexually, we're not anywhere near that, I'm just ⸺ '

"He shook his head. 'You've already impressed me. The moment you opened up about your experience with Rolf, I felt like I knew you. I've never known anyone to be so brave in his vulnerability. It's really quite refreshing. Especially these days when everyone you meet is closed up tighter than a drum.'

"'Jesus, am I blushing?' I asked.

"Daniel chuckled and leaned in to the table, his hand reaching past his glass to mine. He stroked the hills and valleys of my knuckles. I pulled away—pure reflex—but when he didn't withdraw, merely cocking his head, a slow smile curling onto his lips, I acquiesced, slipping my hand into his.

"'Am I moving too fast, Gil?'

"He totally was, but hey, a vampire has needs and I totally get that, but damn, if this turned into another Rolf situation, I was going to swear off men and buy a Fleshlight. It didn't matter that Rolf disappeared over thirty years ago; you never forget your sire. Like a first love.

"So Daniel talked me into going for a walk on the waterfront, past throngs of tourists mingling with the homeless. He held my hand for a while and we talked about his childhood in England and it turns out we were sired right around the same time. I was surprised at how comfortable I was with the guy. It's really not like me.

"He invited me back to his hotel room and when we got there, I was surprised to see another man sitting on the couch in the suite, a plastic cooler in front of him. I turned to Daniel. 'What's this about?'

"I was thinking we might like a nibble before . . .' his voice trailed off.

"'Before?' I asked.

"Daniel ignored the question. 'This is Chad.'

"The man on the couch stood, taller than both Daniel and I, though no broader. He didn't extend his hand and I made no move in that direction myself, having no desire to clasp the ridges of scars I suspected I'd find there. Chad was more than obviously a tap. He wore the eagerness on his rugged face and in the rouge of his cheek. He dipped into the cooler for a beer, presumably—hard to say exactly because it had no label. I didn't think much of it at the time, because of all the local microbreweries around town. He took a couple of swigs and then stood there, looking back and forth from me to Daniel.

"'So,' he said, voice as gravelly as the two-day scruff on his cheeks. 'Are we going to do this, or what?'

"Daniel gestured for me to go first and the guy offered up his wrist, twisting it enticingly, the veins twisting just underneath the skin, a phlebotomist's dream, so close to the surface and so full. I, of course, couldn't resist. I snatched at him and latched on, drawing the blood in big warm mouthfuls, swallowing greedily. The same feeling hits every time a vamp gets a little life in him. Horny. Daniel knew it, of course. It had been his plan all along.

"I looked up to see him feeding from the tap's throat. He'd torn a small hole there and was lapping at blood pooled in the hollow of Chad's clavicle like a thirsty dog chasing ice cubes in a water bowl. The human moaned. His legs shook, weak and enthralled. One of us, I think it was me, guided him back onto the couch, where he massaged his junk through his jeans, a trail of saliva dribbling in a thin stream down his cheek.

"At some point, I took off my shirt and unzipped my pants, so turned on I could barely contain myself. Daniel had left his meal and was coaxing what little blood Chad still had into his stiffening prick, gripping it through the mouth of the prone tap's fly.

"'You want some?' he asked, shaking the dick in my direction.

"'No.' I shook my head. 'I want you.' "

"Hold on," I interrupted, again. 'Cause I totally had to. What kind of story was this? "Are you about to go all gay erotica on us?"

"Shut up and let him finish." Wendy elbowed me in the side. "It was just getting good."

"You're such a fag hag." I poured the last of the sake and waved the empty container at the waitress.

"You both are, now let me finish. It's seriously gonna get fucked up in a sec."

"It better, I gotta get going soon. Packing and all."

Wendy scowled at the mention of *American Minions*. As much as I'd have loved to have someone on my side on that set, it just didn't seem possible. She'd have to settle for watching me on TV, just like everyone else.

*  *  *

"We left Chad on the couch to recover and hit the bed at a jog, only tripping once, I might add, so my game is getting better, you'll be happy to know. Daniel was lithe and muscular under his clothes. We lay on the bed and I traced the bands of muscle lacing his back and pressed up against him from behind, searching around the flat of his stomach to his chest, where I got a bit of a shock.

"I'm a bit of a nipple guy.

"I like 'em medium-sized and hard as rocks, preferably set off against a backdrop of awesome pecs.

"Daniel's nipples were . . . unexpectedly huge.

"Seriously. I'm talking like a couple of powdered Donettes left over from a sloppy binge. I think my hands spasmed away from the puffy nipple fat, because Daniel asked, 'Is everything okay?'

"'Ya-yeah,' I stuttered, pretty sure I was about to bolt out the door. But just as I began to talk my way out of the sexual nightcap, a cloud of wooziness rolled in, like I'd stood up too quickly and gotten lightheaded. I settled onto the bed and the vampire started massaging my shoulders. He was good at it and  I became more and more relaxed, drifting off to sleep at some point.

"I awoke to a swirl of lights and grunting echoes. Daniel was above me, presumably thrusting into me, or me into him, or some variation of sex that didn't involve pleasure in any way. All I could really see were his nipples, only, in the miasma of color and sound, they'd become actual Donettes, alternating between chocolate and the powdered sugar varieties. They quivered on his pecs precariously, pulsing as though they were breathing and threatening to dislodge themselves and drop on my cheeks in soggy plops.

"If I could have screamed I would have. It felt like a third Donette was trapped in my throat.

"Thankfully, he rolled me over at one point and finished the whole sordid business. He was definitely an active lover. I can still feel him. Unfortunately, I can also feel those fat skin tags dragging across my back."

"Gross." I started to collect my purse.

"I thought you were a top." Wendy eyed Gil suspiciously.

The story was a bit over the top.

Gil's eyes narrowed in scrutiny, daring Wendy to keep going along that line. "I was drugged!"

"Seriously, Gil," I said. "You need to learn to be more succinct. If you're just telling us that you had sex with puffy nipple guy, then good for you, boner boy. But, I really have to go."

He put his hand on my arm. "*Seriously* fucked-up stuff coming real soon."

"Fine," I huffed, pulling out a smoke. Wendy snatched one from my pack and we both lit up.

"At some point, I passed out, and when I woke up, he wasn't in the bed, or the bathroom, or the living room. But Chad was still lying on the couch and white as a ghost and on his way to becoming one, if I didn't do something about it. I ran to the phone to call someone, not sure who. It's not like I could call 911, not with a body drained of blood in a hotel room not even registered to me. Never mind the fact that technically I didn't even exist.

"Sitting next to the phone was a handwritten sign with an arrow pointing toward a flashing 'message' button on the handset. It read:

**Check your messages, Gil.**

There was a little heart dotting the "I." It was with a shaky hand that I pressed the button. And Daniel's voice came over the speaker.

"'Gil, I can't tell you how much I enjoyed tonight. Oh wait, yes I can. Tons. I enjoyed your ass like a fat lady enjoys a turkey leg.' Odd how Daniel's voice slowly lost the accent and took on more slang, I thought. The eerie feeling that came when I first met him rushed back. I must have met Daniel before.

"'You're figuring it out right now, aren't you? It's been thirty-some years, but you remember. Leaving me for dead in my apartment while you had your little tryst with Rolf. Well, *I've* never forgotten. I've thought about that night for years.'

"I dropped back onto the desk chair, shock rolling through me like a chill.

"It was fucking Chase Hollingsworth, date rapist and, apparently, serial dieter, having slimmed down everywhere and everything but his nipples. The last time I'd seen him he weighed three hundred pounds if he weighed an ounce. We'd met on the night of my transformation; he was there, in fact. I think I've already told you about him. He slipped me some drug and blew me on a floral davenport. Gross fucker. Rolf, on the other hand, was far from gross. He was my sire and my longest relationship, until he darted. I hadn't thought about him for years. And blamed Chase for renewing my maudlin feelings about the whole rigma-role.

"Chase continued. 'You and that Rolf. Damn him for making me this way. Do you know how hard it is for a fat vampire? I had to seduce a lot of old women to ferret away the cash for the reaper liposuction. In the end it's made me stronger. My revenge will be my closure. You see, Gil. I've evened the score. I've left you three gifts. I'm not sure you'll like any of them, but you'll have to deal with them. The first is Chad.'

"I looked over at the prone figure. Even now, his lungs sputtered a death rattle.

"'Chad's not going to make it and I've already called the police to report a death in that room. They're on their way now. The second and third gifts, you'll figure out in time.'

"Mortified, I ran to the door and checked the peephole. Chase wasn't lying. There were officers moving down the hall. I looked back at Chad's body and then the windows. We were on the thirteenth floor (or fourteenth depending on your level of superstition) and, as you know, I'm no fan of heights."

Gil continued, "I looked at my watch and of course, it was 5:30 A.M. A mere half-hour till dawn and up shit creek. The police hammered on the door and started shouting.

"I panicked.

"Of course, I'm no stranger to a vamping, but this would be the first time I'd done it for free and to save my own skin. Chad's face was so cold. When I opened his mouth a quiet sigh escaped. There wasn't much time. I bit into the insides of my cheeks and pressed my mouth to his, filling him with a silent blood scream. He gagged and coughed and eventually swallowed and a moment later opened his eyes. I dragged him to the bed and stripped off his pants.

"Just in time for the police to break down the door."

\* \* \*

"Jesus," I said. "What did the police do?"

"Nothing. What could they do? Chad wasn't dead. There were no signs of foul play. They just chalked it up to a crank call and left. Though the judgment was obvious and overly dramatic, I think I smelled closet on one of them."

As he would.

"What did you do with Chad?" I asked.

"He's sleeping off the vamping and whatever drug Chase laced his blood with. I went back over his neck after the police left. He hadn't been opened at all; Chase must have poured some blood in there to make me think Chad was clean. Asshole."

"What are you going to do with him?"

"No idea." Gil sighed, a wry smile dancing on his lips. "He is awfully cute, though."

"Silver lining, maybe?" Wendy asked.

He shrugged. "Doubtful."

"What were the second and third gifts?"

"No idea." Gil looked back at the zombie pit. "And I'm in no hurry to find out."

Gil barely finished telling his tale of woe—if that's what you want to call it (how the hell one gets date-raped twice by the same guy is beyond me, of course we are talking about Gil and he does tend to moon, so . . .)—when the stone-faced hostess shuffled past, an unholy trinity shading her wake like an oil slick. Ashley, Kelley, and Casey weren't top tier reapers but they had the requisite bitchiness and the smallest one did flick a butterfly knife like a baton, so you didn't want to fuck with them.

I shoved Gil forward and slouched into my seat. "Oh, my God. Tell me they didn't see me."

Wendy looked over her shoulder. "The evils incarnate are too busy taunting their chef." She angled away so I could peek around.

The poor guy stood his ground against an onslaught of snapping jaws and drunken catcalls. One of the reapers, Kelley, I think, though they all sort of bleed together—just slap a "y" on the end of a regular name and you've got a reaper—flicked her tongue at the trembling foodie lasciviously.

My understanding is this: they take a regular little girl, presumably some foul little brat—already adept at torturing her parents—and strip away what little humanity she has squirreled away beneath her retainer through rigorous bitch training in the reapers' secret lair, aka The Pretty Princess Party Palace. I'm sure there's more to it than that, but all you need to know is, they've got big teeth, clean up messes faster than a Jean Reno character and twirl their pigtails with razor claws.

Also that one of them was waving at me, nudging her pals and grinning.

"Damn it." I reached for my purse and scooted off the chair. "Grab your shit, we're going."

"What's the hurry, they seem perfectly happy to eat their dinner and leave you be." He patted my wrist and his face was so calm I wanted to believe the words falling out of his mouth.

Our chef arrived with a rolling tray of carving knives, forks and metal shakers like Shinto arches marked with Japanese characters. They could have been spices, though that was unlikely—zombies couldn't eat spices without the inevitable purge hitting. A trio of wine bottles filled with liquids of various darknesses. Blood, to be sure, but bile and what looked like a thick jaundiced mucus.

I glanced at Wendy, whose face said it all.

Gross.

It's one thing to take a whole body, but when you go at it in sections or break a body down into parts like a cut-up fryer, it's somehow less appealing. That's not to say that I wouldn't tear into it, if I were hungry enough. But . . . well, you know.

Across the room, chefs turned away from the diners to face the stage. We did too. A gong rang out behind us and the hostess sauntered in, carrying a tray of cubed beef. She pointed her free hand at a disc in the wall and a door slid down behind her, sealing off the room with a loud clank. As she reached the edge of the stage, the round of metal sunk about a foot and then slid away from us slowly.

We heard the growling first. Low moans and the gurgling rattles of the dead.

It was no stage.

There'd be no floorshow or French circus clowns to terrify us. No gymnasts or ribbon acts or gibberish. Instead, a sunken central staging area revealed itself, crowded, not with living people, as the teppanyaki theme seemed to promise, but with a tangle of fiercely animated and groaning mistakes. The zombies tore at each other in their confinement, ripping deep grooves into green and gray mottled flesh, pressing moldy fingers into old wounds and being generally gross and unappetizing. They sniffed at the air and raised their heads to smell the living amongst the diners and staff. Not humans, but weres and a small contingent of witches at one of the far tables, who sat silently as church mice and took in the spectacle of an actual zombie horde. Most of them had never seen a pack this large. I had, of course, on a number of occasions, but not contained like this. In fact, it was my experience that they could never be contained for long.

As if they heard me, they moved as a single unit to the edge of the barrel, which after a low hum, began to spin like a centrifuge. The zombies were plastered to the walls of the drum, some howling, others mute with horror. I almost felt sorry for them and then remembered they were mindless feeding machines. I felt a little better after that.

Wendy's mouth hung agog, as did Gil's, as did the majority of the crowd's, except for the staff, who scanned their wristwatches and set up their stations, with plates and cloisonné chopsticks and whiter-than-white linens. Waitresses arrived with warm bottles of sake and petite cast iron pots of warm blood that they lifted a couple of feet in the air and poured into china tea cups in thin syrupy streams, the crimson frothing from the aeration, tiny bubbles hugging the surface like rusty caviar.

Another gong sounded and a slew of vampire "handlers" marched in from an arch on the opposite side, the door clanking shut behind them, locks thrown dramatically.

"Why do you suppose they keep making a point to lock those doors?" I asked.

"Maybe it's to show they're being 'safe and sound' with the undead," Gil offered. "Don't want them shambling out into the food supply fucking up our shit."

"It definitely adds to the mystique." Wendy nodded.

Wendy and I both nodded. She played with the choker around her neck absently, as though she understood. The centrifuge slowed to a stop and the zombies dropped to their knees, their equilibrium already compromised simply from being dead—Lord knows it was tricky enough to stay upright in stilettos—add the whole living dead thing and it was near impossible.

They picked at the zombies with lengthy cattle prods and thick poles ending in loops of wire cording. Despite an obvious ability to regenerate and heal, the vampires wore a mesh of armor from head to toe and their faces were shielded by a flap of Plexiglas on a visor, the kind, I thought, they might use in welding. But what do I know? Each was specked with the brown and milky green projectile spit that accompanies a zombie scream. My mistake "cousins" know absolutely nothing about dental hygiene.[32]

Wendy clutched my arm. "Seriously. I'm not sure I'm into whatever this is." She stared out into the hoard of previously human faces. "That one's wearing a Betsey Johnson dress for Christ's sake," she mumbled.

It was true. I'd seen it on a mannequin in the little 5th Avenue store window. Cute. But not with the sash of dried intestines the mistake was sporting—that's never a cute look.

Wendy slapped her hand to her mouth.

Near the edge of the pit, I saw another kimono-clad woman yelling to a muscley vamp in the pit. She was stabbing her finger toward the woman in the Betsey Johnson dress. He nodded and dropped the noose over her head. The mistake clawed at the metal cord, gouging her throat with the few jagged nails still clinging to their loosening beds and sending rivulets of pus down the crimson rose chiffon.[33] He pulled the woman through the throng until she reached the outside of the

---

[32] Or Band-Aids, or prosthetic limbs, or adult diapers, unfortunately. Especially that last one.
[33] Poor Betsey. By the way, they always come in a solid alternative.

circle, attached the end of the pole to one of the many eye hooks dangling from the ceiling and began to crank something below our site level.

The zombie's eyes bulged as she was hoisted off the floor, twitching and kicking. Her toe caught in the empty cheek of another mistake and as she kicked to free herself, the thing's jaw flew off. The nearby waitress snatched it from the air and dropped it onto the shiny metal preparation area. The diners, a curious crew of business-type zombies, not anyone I recognized from the late-night scene, let loose with a round of applause, some cheered.

It hit me then. After all that spectacle, it hit me.

Zombie teppanyaki.

I suppose the place fed into a certain Roman blood lust kind of thing, but, seriously, it was difficult enough to go for live food let alone dead and then chilled on top of that? Cold Stone Butchery?

My mouth hung open as the "Chef" strode from between to Picasso-esque tiki idols (the only thing in the room that was even remotely similar to the original concept). He carried what looked like a cleaver blade, attached to a thin axe handle.

I'd seen enough.

Wendy's mouth hung open wide enough to catch bugs. I reached over and helped her close it. "And you thought sushi was a hard pill to swallow."

Gil was already standing and buttoning his jacket. "I was going to call, but I didn't think you'd believe me."

"You knew?" I asked, momentarily disgusted and then let it slide. "At this point, nothing surprises me."

"Except this," Wendy added.

"Except this."

The reapers got their pick and it was lain across the

cold stone for some rapid fire slicing and dicing. The little girls giggled, cooed and clapped and caught chunks of wriggling zombie in their mouths.

"Disgusting," I said, standing up in a hunch so they wouldn't notice. "I'm outta here. You guys coming?"

Wendy looked green enough to vomit—though in all honesty, it could have been her foundation wearing down to reveal her natural skin tone. I hadn't seen her clean for a few months; there was no telling how much farther she'd deteriorated.

I tipped our discouraged chef and sandwiched between Wendy and Gil. As we approached the closed door to the lobby area the hostess ran up and scolded, in a voice far too loud, "No leaving during teppanyaki, you must take seat now!"

"Shh!" I hushed and looked around her to find the reapers gawking in our direction. The one with copper hair up in pigtails and a herd of freckles grazing on her cheeks whispered to the others in that overexaggerated way they do, "Dammit!"

Kelley—though for our purposes, let's just call her Pippi[34]—plopped off her stool and skipped through the feasting crowd. Considering the rough times, it came as no surprise that most of the people avoided eye contact with the little reaper, instead scanning the rather bland ceiling for distractions or utilizing the entirely ridiculous hand wall.

I simply turned toward the door and dug through my purse for nothing in particular until I felt the inevitable tug on the back of my skirt. I spun around and gave the little devil a sparkling grin. "Why hello, little girl."

---

[34] As in Longstockings.

Wendy slapped her palm across her mouth. Gil gulped audibly.

She looked me dead in the eye as she said, "Can I have a word, Ms. Feral?" Then slunk a short distance from the group and waited, hands on her hips and toe tapping in irritation. When I didn't come immediately, she chastised. "Pick up the pace, I don't have all night."

I grimaced and crouched down next to the little demon.

"You got that money you owe us?" She accentuated the words by brushing pretend crumbs from my shoulder.

"Well . . . no. But I do have a potential jackpot coming my way," I said hopefully. "The money will be flooding into the Pretty Princess Party Palace before you know it. Swear to God or gumdrops or whatever you little bitches swear to."

"Listen." She sighed somberly. "You know, I'm going to have to break something to show that we mean business. We've put up with your poverty act long enough."

I held out my hands. "No. Please. My boyfriend threw my leg out of its socket just last night. Couldn't we just say that you did that and be done with the shake down?"

Kelley covered her mouth and giggled. "Silly," she lisped and then snatched my finger.

Wendy stepped up. "Does it help to know that he's actually her ex-boyfriend and that she just had her car repossessed? It's all very sad."

"No." Kelley's eyes glinted with morbid glee. "Doesn't help her out at all."

My eyes darted between the reaper and my quivering finger pinched off at the base between her pincerlike digits. It would have turned purple if it weren't for my little circulation problem. As I watched, Kelley relaxed a bit and I slacked with relief.

"But nice try." She lurched forward, bending my finger backward until it snapped at the joint; my tendons tore with an audible shirr and coiled up under the loose skin of my hand like a bad carpet job. While I don't feel a whole lot in my extremities, a bone breaking, much like my leg coming out of the socket, can be quite uncomfortable.

So yeah . . . I fucking screamed.

"Dammit!" I shouted and jerked my hand away, cradling it in the other like a crying baby. My finger hung loose and lolled the wrong way, completely disabling my ability to flip people off on the freeway.

She shrugged. "Tell you what I'm going to do. I'm going to give you a week to come up with some cash or we'll come looking for you. And this time, it'll be more than your finger that gets busted."

"So not cool, Kelley," I called after her and she gave a little wave behind her that brought her friends to tearful laughter.

Scott jammed his thumb against the call button, clearly still irritated to be woken hours before his swing shift at one of Ethel's clubs—and yeah, I know, I'd been slowly making progress on getting him to quit and giving the police force another go.[35] The speaker crackled, then fell silent. "The damn thing's busted."

"Thanks for giving me a ride, again." I smiled coyly.

---

[35] You can't have too many "ins" with the cops, what with so much to cover up in this afterlife.

"And this." I raised my bandaged hand. Scott was a miracle worker of impromptu medical attention; a regular Annie Sullivan, except instead of blind deaf mutes, he had to deal with a bitchy dead woman, and he really didn't even have to deal with her.[36]

"Just so you know, we're broken up. You know that right?" He grimaced.

"Of course. Just one friend doing a favor for another. Totally broken up." I winked and looked over my shoulder into the dark neighborhood.

The beefy little Mustang idled in front of wrought iron gates worked to resemble a tangle of thorny rose bushes gone to hips. The stalks scrolled around vertical rods like snakes slithering toward the sharp spires at each peak. Ivy crept in from either side where it took root in the cracks in the brick wall that surrounded the property. Atop the wall, on either side, stone lions kept watch through eyes gone lazy with time.

And shit, did the place ever need watching over and that wall.

Being Seattle, where the estates were often bordered by properties of considerably less value—and by considerably, I mean ghetto—Harcourt Manor stood as a refuge against crackheads, skinny whores and dim real estate speculators. Remodeled craftsman bungalows sat with FOR SALE signs staked in the yards rather than cute topiary and squatters shot up tar in their dirty underwear on the front porch instead of the promised iced-tea-toting thirty-somethings.

So, yeah . . . super desirable locale.

A few burnt out cars, mostly 70s domestics, com-

---

[36] Will someone tell me why I'm talking about myself in the third person.

pleted the overall look. Trendy in that punk, I-refuse-to-shave-my-armpits kind of way, I supposed. I'd have to remember some of the spots we drove through as particularly nutrient-rich hunting grounds. At least I wouldn't have to walk far to get a meal.

See, I'm *brightsiding* sans the stupid little dance that makes me want to run for a gun locker.[37]

"Maybe it's unlocked," I offered.

"Yeah. You go check."

"Just bump it." I motioned for him to drive into the gate.

"Jesus." He rolled up his window and stepped out of the car, leaving the door swinging on the hinge. Rattling the gates did no good, so he started yelling, "Hello? Hello?"

Though, over the rumble of the engine, it sounded more like "yellow yellow." Way too informal for such a grand gate, but when you're trying to re-snare a lover it's best not to be too critical, I find.

When that bore no fruit, Scott turned back to the car, sour as a preserved lemon, and threw his hands up. I always thought that kind of boyish frustration was cute, but with Scott it was adorable. If I'd been out there, I bet I could have heard him huffing.

I leaned over and started honking.

Not a few short bursts, like you might do, I let it blare.

Scott jumped a bit, but in a moment he waved me off the horn and pointed beyond the gate.

---

[37] Joking. If ever there was a trend I'd like to quash it's that little cult of Pollyanna bullshit. Look on the Brightside. Look on the Brightside. Seriously, the dimwits that came up with that can kiss my brownside. At least you have your health, my ass.

A few moments later, the gates swung open and Scott smiled and gestured to someone inside and trotted back to the car.

"Caretaker, or something," he said. "Good thinking with the horn."

"I know." I fluttered my eyelids for him.

He turned away.

Remind me not to pull that move again.

The road took a sharp left inside the wall, bordered by a dense patch of dying rhododendrons, spindly and beaded with an early evening drizzle, and an old growth of evergreens that towered into the night sky, blocking any view of the actual manor house.

Anyone buying into Washington's blatantly misleading state name ("Evergreen") hasn't seen it from eye level. In dense forests, like those surrounding Harcourt, the fir trees only give off their green at the tips. Like a cougar in need of a dye job, the twelve or so feet poking from the roots are dead with graying moss. Beige and unfurling fingers of fern reach from the ground like lazy dead folk—not that we actually do that mind you. The dead don't just crawl from graves to eat your brains, they have to be infected somehow, silly. I suppose if I had a hose and a big drill, maybe. But why? Seriously?

The fog didn't help the mood. It clung to the undergrowth like dust bunnies massing under a couch—no matter how many times you take the vacuum to them there's always more. Always.

"It's kind of spooky, right?" Scott's smile came with a hint of boyish evil, standard, like reclining bucket seats. I waited for him to go on. It was inevitable. "The mist? The fog? An old creepy mansion? Who knows what horrors wait in the shadows."

I yawned. "Um . . . zombies and werewolves, for two." I shifted in my seat to face him. "Have you been reading those adolescent vampire romances again?"

He shrugged.

"You know how they scare you."

A flush broke out on his cheeks like a riot. "Well, it beats those mysteries you pile everywhere. I've yet to see you read one. You're very good at buying and stacking, though."

"I read them," I interjected with a snarl.

"You'd think you get enough drama, as much trouble as you and those two friends of yours get into."

"At least my books are meant for adults."

He clicked his tongue.

The road wound back and forth and descended gently into a glen, where we eventually passed the haggard groundskeeper wrapped up in a damp barn jacket and jeans tucked into rubber boots. He nodded to Scott and hopped over some low ferns into the undergrowth to make way. The brush fell to the sides and the gravel road split a great manicured lawn converted into a parking lot of trailers and tents and beyond that, what had to be Harcourt Manor.

"Um. Is it just me, or does that look like a mental institution?"

Scott nodded. "It's beautiful." He pointed out the window at the people bustling between the tents and trailers. "This, however, looks like a madhouse."

I shrugged.

The architect who crafted the massive two stories with its heavily dormered mansard roof was not satisfied with simply intimidating visitors, he—who else but a man—made centerpieces of eight equidistant and giant phallic chimneys, which sprung from the roof like a giant circle jerk. In the center of the roof, a window-ringed cupola stood watch over the grounds like Karen Black at the end of *Burnt Offerings*.

"It's creepy."

"And awesome."

Scott pulled up to a stone stair and hopped out. "Let's get your shit and make this happen."

He pulled my bags from the trunk and set them on the stairs rather than the damp gravel. It's like he knew I'd have a fit if my Vuitton got wet. Oh, who am I kidding? He did know. I'd bitched at him before about the very same thing. Scott didn't give a crap about material possessions, but he clearly got tired of my demands.

He probably needed this break.

See how I can be positive in the face of adversity? He calls it broken up, I call it a time-out, like when your kid's called you a bitch and you need to teach them a lesson that won't get you locked up.

I swept out of the car and went to kiss him. The kind of kiss he could think about while he jerked off in the shower, or wherever he did it. I clutched at him, ground my hips into his and played with the waist of his jeans, tucking my fingers just past the crimped edge of his boxers. I pulled away a bit to make sure I'd had the desired effect.

His teeth were clenched, his eyes steely. I guessed that meant angry. Not the desired effect, but still, he'd think about that kiss later.

Hopefully.

"Don't do that again." He spat the words like a mouthful of vinegar.

"Sorry." Over his shoulder, figures gathered in various windows. "I think we're being watched."

His neck craned and a grin replaced his glower. "You think I'll get to meet your new boss?"

"He's not my boss."

"Well, whatever he is."

I started up the stairs, rubbing my hip a bit as I climbed. It was only slightly sore, but Scott didn't need to know that.

He grabbed the bags and followed me up to the entryway. The doors swung inward and a robust black woman, no taller than a chest of drawers, with dread-locked hair tied up in braids, beads and strips of cotton, burst out. She clutched my arms, as I reached the next to the last step, so we seemed to be matched in height, and shook them like I was having a breakdown—the kind of shaking that's often accompanied by the demand, "snap out of it." "Amanda Feral, darling!" she barked in a spicy Caribbean accent. "You're more gorgeous than pictures in the tabloids give you credit for—now give Mama Montserrat some love."

I lurched forward as the woman circled me in surprisingly strong arms and squeezed until I was sure my intestines would liquefy and drop out of me in a wholly unattractive way. She smelled of curry powder, Poison (the perfume, not the weapon, though from the creepy house, I can certainly understand your confusion) and, oddly enough, the dense chemical scent of ink. Of course, what I was most interested in was the fact that she reeked of fresh meat. She pushed me back but still held on.

"And who are your two friends?"

Two?

I knew before I turned.

Wendy peeked from around Scott like a nosy neighbor, head tilted and mouth pursed dramatically. She wore her hair in a chignon, like my own (though not nearly as smooth—she needed a lesson, to be sure), a cheap pinstriped banker's suit—one of those you can pick up at Penney's on sale five days out of seven—and carried a small suitcase in one hand and a briefcase in the other.

"This must be your boyfriend?"

"No," Scott grumbled, setting the suitcase at my feet.

"This is Scott." I intentionally ignored Wendy as he stepped forward with his hand extended and was pulled into a grappling hug worthy of a wrestling ring. Mama Montserrat was a bull.

"Nice to meet you," he mumbled into the tunic that covered her breasts and torso.

Wendy stomped forward, dropped her suitcase and handed the buoyant woman a business card so fresh you could see the heat rising off it in waves. "I'm Ms. Feral's agent, Melody Daniels. It's a pleasure."

Where did I know that name?

Mama Montserrat pinched the card between her index finger and thumb as though she were collecting a dirty diaper. "Her agent? I been told there's nothin' left to negotiate and I don't recall no agent bein' involved."

"Ms. Feral will be needing a large suite with enough room for her bags and a small but comfortable salon for me," Wendy said, and then quickly added. "To make business calls, of course."

"Of course." Mama Montserrat's demeanor chilled to sub-zero, the welcoming glow replaced by ashen suspicion.

Scott snorted a bit, shoved his hands in the back pockets of his jeans and gawked at Wendy, shaking his head in disbelief. "You girls have fun," he said as he backed down the stairs. Wendy's eyebrow rose defiantly, daring him to say anything more.

I shrugged. Wendy could have her fun, but from the scowl on Mama's face, she had her hands full with that one.

Scott smiled and nodded to me genially, then bounded down the stairs to the car. The curtness of it hit me hard and I had every intention of calling out to him, until I felt Mama's stubby hand slip into the crook of my arm.

"Follow me, Ms. Feral. We got you a beautiful room right at the top of these stairs." She took the larger of my bags and pulled me inside.

For all its external grandeur and English manor-ness, or whatever, Harcourt's interior was, as is so common in our world, an exercise in overkill. Like the warehouse that housed Skinshu, the mansion was stripped bare and redesigned to resemble some woodland copse. Tree trunks stood in for columns and rose in ashy lengths from a carpet of green moss to a canopy of—you guessed it—leaves. A cobbled path forked to the left and right, dueling staircases arced from a balcony above, clad in stone and patches of loam. A trio of dazzling antler-and-crystal chandeliers dropped from floral medallions in the ceiling; they flooded the space in warmth and a shower of sparkling refractions lit on the foliage like dew.

Identical twin girls hovered against the far edge of the hall like a couple of hookers on a smoke break.[38] They peered silently from around a bust on a pedestal,

---

[38] Which brings to mind the question of whether prostitutes take breaks.

its head fully sprouted into a tangle of clover—this being the only setting where Chia is an acceptable decorating option. Contestants, no doubt—their pale and stony flesh not unlike a vampire's, though that seemed too pedestrian a character for the show's audience. Twins would be the draw, certainly. One guzzled from a bottle of wine, while the other hammered out a text on a little black phone, sneering at us as we entered.

"That's Janice and Eunice," Mama said. She leaned in conspiratorially. "Sirens. So don't let 'em get goin', or they'll sing their little song until you either kill yourself or just wish you were dead. And you know I ain't kiddin'" She added for Wendy's benefit. "You go on ahead though. I'm sure they'll like you."

Wendy sneered.

Voices sprang from an arch in the opposite wall, where shadows danced in firelight and stretched out into the ivy like phantoms. A door opened above us and a tall black woman appeared on the balcony for a moment, waved dramatically and then disappeared down another dark hall.

It occurred to me I didn't really know who Mama Montserrat was, other than her name, obviously. "Mama, I'm sorry to ask this but, what is your role on the *American Minions* show? You seem to know what's up."

"Oh, I definitely know 'what's up.' I'm Johnny Birch's manager and one of the executive producers for this season. Unfortunately, it'll probably be the last." She looked off into the twilight through the open doors. "We kept it going awhile and that's all you can ask the good spirits for. Ain't that right?"

"Or the bad ones, for that matter." It was my attempt at a joke. Now, normally you know they don't fall flat, but Mama just crinkled her eyebrows and stared a moment. Wendy broke through the discomfort with her irritating "agent voice."

"Is there a chance this show could be cancelled? Because if there is, I've got a right to know on my client's behalf. I don't want her taking it up the ass on this one."

Oh. My. God. Wendy's lost her damn mind.

Mama's mouth twisted into a grimace, but to her credit, she ignored the questions and just kept walking. There was really no need to respond, though I certainly shot Wendy an icy stare.

As we reached the top of the stairs, she led us through an arch in the wall and down a darkened hallway. As bright and grand as the stair hall was, this little hallway was its opposite. Shadows clung to the wall as though snagged on the jutting faux Tuscan plaster.

"Listen, little dead girl. Mama Montserrat been around the block long enough to know you're playin' somethin' here. Now, nice Ms. Amanda—"

She dropped my bag in front of a door and turned on Wendy.

I stood behind Mama and mouthed her words in echo at Wendy, who stuck her tongue in her cheek and rolled her eyes.

"Ms. Amanda. She ain't said different and I respect that, on account of she's probably a good friend, but if you make another demand of me, girl, you're gonna find some bad mojo crawlin' up your ass. You hear me?"

Wendy literally gulped.

"I hear."

The woman stomped off down the hall, turning as she neared the top of the stairs. "Ms. Amanda. You got some time to wander before we get started. Have a drink or something, but at 10:00, we're filming the contestants arriving."

"But they're—"

"They're already here, yes, sure enough that's true. But this is entertainment and things don't always go in the order you expect. You just gotta flow with it. Chill da fuck out."

"Chill the fuck out," I repeated and waved as Mama Montserrat turned to leave.

"See—" Wendy started, but I slapped her back, before she could finish agitating, and dragged her into the bedroom.

"What the hell are you doing?"

She pulled her arm away and settled onto a floral matellasse bedspread. "Please. How could I not try to check this out? It's kind of awesome."

I sat down next to her. I wasn't nearly as thrilled. Being in advertising and monitoring commercial shoots and such takes the excitement out of the process. "I suppose it is. And I am glad to have someone to chat with that's not completely freakish."

"Speaking of. Did you see those two bitches downstairs? What the fuck? Like a couple of skanks from the corner. And to think they're contestants."

"Well, I am already judging them."

"Nice skin though. Tender." She shed her fitted but ill-fitting jacket with a shiver. It fell to the floor and stood on its seams, stiff as cardboard; the horror of poorly constructed synthetic fibers. She dropped back on a bed large enough to hold both of us and our choice of twelve suitors and slipped off the skirt, lounging there a moment in the silken chemise she wore underneath—it would have been sexy were it not for the deep blue veins peeking out just above her thigh-high makeup line. Wendy's eyes widened like she'd remembered something and she jumped to her feet and rushed over to her attaché. "I just remembered."

"Hmm?" I sunk into an overstuffed side chair that wrapped me in downy comfort. "Holy crap, this is cushy."

A large console separated the sleeping area from a small receiving room. Atop it were crystal lamps and a bowl of fruit—clearly they didn't know us at all, or it would have been decent and chilled organ meat—and a stuffed polar bear cub (the toy kind, not taxidermy, that would have been wrong). No hooch to speak of— it's like they didn't know me at all.

"Gil gave me something for you. It's from your mother."

A chill coursed through my less-than-warm bones. "Oh yeah? What is it, a bottle of diet pills? An etiquette quiz? Or did she cut out the middleman and go straight for the vague and blurry pictures of my father with his new wife and children?"

Wendy withdrew a paper lunch sack and sat it on the nightstand like some important artifact. "I don't suppose it's a sandwich?" she asked, backing away.

"Who knows?" I dug through my purse for some breath spray—you never can tell when you'll need it and with zombies, a good rule of thumb is every two hours to keep the dank stench of death at bay. Also, it's minty.

"Seriously, you're not interested in what's in that bag?" Wendy stabbed her finger at the crinkled brown lump. "Seriously?"

"Not a bit." Well, okay, a little bit, but I couldn't let

Wendy know that. She'd take it the same way Gil does, as an admission that I wanted some sort of relationship with the leeching hag. And I don't.

I so don't.

I propped my suitcase atop a heavily carved chest and unzipped it. "Now act like an agent and come help me pick out something fantastic to accessorize my gown for the big entrance."

"Can I at least peek?"

"Could I stop you?"

"Nope."

"Well, then."

Wendy tore open the top of the bag. Her eyes fluttered back in her head, while her mouth lolled open like someone had slipped her a magic vibrator. I caught the scent shortly thereafter. It was an organ.

Another whiff and I was certain it was a heart.

Wendy sagged on the bed and pouted. She looked over sheepishly.

"Jesus Christ on a cracker, feel free." I gestured for her to eat up.

Giggling as she withdrew the Ziploc baggy full of gory musculature, Wendy made quick work of it, snapping it clean in two with her already-recovering jaw line. She offered me the other half with all the daintiness of a longshoreman, spattering the carpet with clotted blood.

"Try some. It's delicious."

"I don't want any." I could only imagine the poor soul Ethel had torn it out of probably had to wipe the vomit off the thing on whatever fabric grungy bums prefer for clothing. Flannel, maybe.

"Come on."

"I said no."

"It's not like I shit on it."

"Well, obviously, it would have smelled like chocolate in here."

She squeezed the remaining heart into her maw and swallowed it in two bites, clearly frustrated.

Wendy shrugged and dug in her own suitcase, pulling on a vintage Pucci mini-dress and a wide plastic headband. "Zip me and then we'll figure out your ensemble."

My first appearance on a supernatural-wide broadcast show called for the big guns. Not just my favorite dress, something truly memorable. I opted for a frock by my favorite designer of the moment, Alexander Mc-Queen. He recently wowed a London crowd of bon vivants or fashion victims or the poor or whoever goes to shows in London with a line of avant-garde gowns and separates I simply couldn't resist selling off a bauble for.

The one I chose to unload was a gift.

I'd only known Tom Buchwald—I know, I know, with a name like that, it's amazing I even considered letting him stick anything near me, let alone *in* me—for a few days. It was one of those conference hookups. San Diego, I think, and focused on marketing alcohol to kids and under-targeted ethnic groups, also tobacco, oh . . . and weight loss surgery to those merely bordering on overweight.[39]

The usual.

Tom could banter, wasn't entirely disgusting to look at and as it turned out, knew how to work his hips

---

[39] Might as well cut it off at the pass, right, and if you can smoke a Camel while you're doing it and drink Red Bull and vodka while you recover, then all your friends in Home Ec will think you're all the more tragic and popular. Who doesn't want that?

into a frenzy. He was also good at shoplifting, as a brief jaunt to the local mall proved. But, when the cops stormed the afternoon "What Your Average Ethiopian Doesn't Know Won't Hurt Him" seminar, Buchwald must have slipped the tennis bracelet into my briefcase. I didn't find it until I was back in Seattle.

Now *that's* thoughtful.

I hated to let such a memento go—and I know I could have paid for a few more months of upkeep on the condo—but really, if you think about it, it's an investment in my future.

I pulled the Alexander McQueen smoke print gown out of its envelope of archival tissue and draped it across the club chair.

"Look at it in wonder," I said, reverently, my fingers playing across the satin, the ghostly tendrils of smoke that snaked across the hips in a mottled gray and purple and even a once-vibrant fuchsia, now faded as an old photograph. "Oh, Alex."

"Wonder what? How much you paid?" Wendy was busy squeezing the last of the "*jus*" from the paper bag the heart came in. A few drips lit on her dry thrusting tongue and spread like fractures.

"It is gorgeous, isn't it? Only a little over four grand and worth every penny." I didn't need to turn around to know Wendy was shaking her head, as though her habits weren't just as costly. At least mine didn't strip my bowels out like a bottle of Drano.

The Louis Vuitton heels came out next. Strappy, and violently unreasonable, with more belts and closures than is necessary and high enough to have me looking down at Johnny Birch all night—as if I wouldn't be anyway. I propped them between the asymmetrical drifts of satin and stood back to admire the choice.

"That is definitely a look."

"Right?"

I slipped out of my clothes and stepped into the gown, the satin cascading over my curves and hollows, embracing my form like a desperate lover. I found myself mumbling about the other outfits I snapped up—another from McQueen in a brilliant green was a showstopper. Oh Alex, how do you know me so well?

I worked over my jewelry bag, opting for a pair of pink sapphire and diamond drop earrings to bring out the fuchsia and offset my baby blues (which were, if I'm to be honest, bordering on the color of cumulus clouds, these days), before I even realized Wendy wasn't helping or even responding with polite uh-huhs.

"Are you listening?" I spun around to find her staring intently at her iPhone.

"Mmm-hmm."

"No, you're not."

She looked up, jumped a bit and grinned. "Damn, girl. You're gonna be a star. But not without bigger hair. We gotta rat that shit out."

"I don't want to be a star."

"Please. Like hell you don't. Everyone wants to be a star, Amanda, even if they don't know it yet. But we're not talking about them, we're talking about you and I've yet to see you shy away from a photo op." Her eyes drifted back to the little black slick of plastic in her palm.

"What are you looking at?"

"Nothin'."

I crossed the room and snatched the phone. Abuelita paced Wendy's living room on the small screen. "Abuelita's a webcam girl?"

"Of course not." Wendy stood up and tore the

phone from my hand. Her eyes narrowed, daring me to make a judgment. "I'm monitoring her activities with a nanny cam. You can never be too careful with your employees."

"So you're paying her then? I wondered."

She shrugged. "Not exactly, but if Skids hits like I think it will, then I'll share some profits."

"Really?"

"Uh . . . yeah. Whaddya think, I'm some kind of monster?" she asked and then quickly added, "Don't answer that." She tucked her hair behind her ear and one leg up under her ass as she slunk into the chair, glued to the image.

Her interest sparked my own. I wondered what Scott was doing, whether he was thinking about me. Thinking about that kiss, I hoped. But I feared it was just unrealistic. I couldn't imagine him mourning, either. He was probably leaning against a wall somewhere, looking excruciatingly hot and fending off slutty advances. Or maybe not. Maybe he was hooking up in the alley outside of one of Ethel's clubs. Probably found some girl that'd let him stick it in her ass. Those kind of girls seemed to be Ethel's bread and butter.

*Stop it*, I told myself. *You'll go crazy thinking like that.* It was really a godsend that Wendy showed up to distract me from a complete mental breakdown.

"What's she doing now?" I nestled against the curved back of the chair and watched Abuelita shuffle across the living room and answer the door. Outside stood a swarthy man in a brown shirt and shorts, one hand hanging onto the top of the doorframe, the other offering a package, like a chocolate on a silver tray. The woman took it to the coffee table. Behind her back, the deliveryman smoothed a bushy Magnum, P.I.

'stache, adjusted his junk with a twitch and struck another seductive pose. Abuelita turned toward him, her hips swiveling as she approached. When she got to the door, she seemed to be talking and then she slammed the door in the guy's face.

"Oh for Christ's sake," Wendy said. "Now that's going to drive me crazy. I mean seriously. She didn't even shake it."

"Well, she shook her ass. And he looked like he'd been there before. Did you recognize the guy?"

"Nope. And I would have remembered if I'd ordered something."

"Like a case of Twix?"

"Shut up. She's working an angle. Those people always have an angle." I'm pretty sure she meant immigrants, but I wasn't going to press her on it.

"I think everyone has an angle. It's not the most optimistic theory, but it's how I roll. You know what'd help?"

"Booze?"

"Exactly. Let's go find some."

Shadows seemed to be the principal design aesthetic of the upstairs halls. Where you or I might opt for a sexy little sconce, or even a barrel-shaded lamp on a bureau, whoever had gotten ahold of the place saved money on lighting any space that didn't show up on a camera. Super-convenient, particularly in ankle-breaking heels.

Good call.

I ended up carrying around a lit candle like some pathetic Victorian governess just to maneuver the maze of halls and antechambers that made up Harcourt Manor. Wendy crept behind me muttering on about Abuelita and secret conspiracies. The way I figured it, the woman needed to do something to better herself and anything would be an improvement over slave labor for a self-centered zombie. Had to be. In Wendy's defense, who doesn't shake a package?

Who?

The strains of something vaguely musical floated up a stair landing, not the one we'd come up, of course, that'd be too convenient—and lighted. I looked back at Wendy, who urged me on with a nod. The stairwell was steep and led to a bayed landing that overlooked a vast and formal garden. Strings of lights formed a grid over a patio area where groups of people lounged, drinking, staring absently, chatting.

"Sweet oblivion." Wendy beamed, the light glinting from her teeth and slipping like an aurora across the pale death of her skin.

"No kidding. Let's get a move on."

At the bottom of the stairs, a sign was affixed to the balustrade. It read:

> *The Harcourt Lounge is through the doors on your left. The Grand Hall is back where you came from. Downstairs leads to madness.*
> —The Producers

I shrugged off the last line as melodrama and pushed through the doors into the paneled bar, with its mirrored shelves of booze glistening like Shangri-la. But before we could slink over and order, we were intercepted by a certain smarmy wood nymph.

Having saved my skin once, Birch seemed to think he was owed some leeway in his sexual advances. The hug he greeted me with rapidly progressed to a groping and then kneading of both my ass cheeks.[40]

"Checking me for tumors, doctor?" I scowled a warning.

Birch withdrew his hands with a snap and a smirk, then turned his attention to a much more willing Wendy.

"Melody Daniels!" His arms flew out to surround her. "I've heard so much about you. I feel like I know you. And gorgeous, you are." Stepping back from the lingering embrace, he reached for her hands and spread her arms out like he was admiring her attire, when anyone with eyes and an I.Q. over 80 could tell he was sizing up her tits.

But Wendy, not having a problem with being ogled or objectified, didn't stop the fucker, rather jiggled her goods slyly. Her breasts bounced under the delicate silk.

"It's a Pucci," she said.

"Huh?" Birch's gaze finally met the petite zombie's eyes.

"The dress."

"Oh yes," he coughed. "It's divine." He bent in to whisper the next bit, but must have decided he didn't care what I heard. "You know where that dress would look perfect?"

"Not on me?" Wendy pouted.

"Of course on you." He leaned in again. "Bundled up under your arms while I give you a little bit of Johnny."

"Little?" I asked.

Johnny's normally pale face flushed a vibrant fuch-

---

[40] Because one is never enough, like a Pringle, or a Botox injection. You know what I'm talking about, ladies.

sia matching the print on Wendy's dress. "No. I mean . . . What I mean is."

"What do you mean?" I checked my nail beds. The cuticles were in need of a bleaching—the nails don't grow so much these days, they stop after a while, one of the big lies of death.

He whispered this time, directly into Wendy's ear. Her eyes grew in surprise. "Oh." She played coy, as though this wasn't playing directly into her plan.

"Johnny!" Mama Montserrat stormed into the bar and stabbed her thick paw under Johnny's armpit, dragging him toward the furthest table. "Excuse me, ladies, I'm going to have to interrupt. We've got important business to discuss."

"I wouldn't say you were interrupting," I said.

Wendy sneered at the woman and turned immediately to the bartender, a shifty squat of a guy with a nasty case of carrot top (the hair, not the horrendously ugly comedian poser) and green eyes that swam in his fishbowl glasses like an aquarium. "Two vodka doubles, Chester. Straight up."

"It's Ron." The man's voice crept like the slow hiss of a tire puncture, leaking from his mouth as though he'd used up the last of his will to live squeezing it out.

"Yep. And make it quick." She slapped her palm on the bar, her eyes tracking Birch as they settled in.

Drinks in hand, Wendy led me to a table opposite Mama and Birch, settled in with a clear view of her quarry and started licking the rim of her lowball.

"Subtle," I said, swallowing a fragrant mouthful.

"Men don't get subtlety. They respond to direct visual cues. This—" She stopped to flick her tongue against the glass, while rolling her eyes back in her head. "—implies that I'm a salad-tosser, or, at the very least, I'm not opposed to a little dirty work." She winked.

"Ew. But you are." I gaped at her. "Aren't you?"

She shrugged. "If it's clean, I'll consider it on a case by case basis."

"Jesus! What constitutes clean? I'd have to get Molly Maids in to scour and bleach Scott's hole before I'd even look at it, let alone lick it out like the last bit of sugary Fun Dip from the paper envelope."

"Oh please. Quit being puritanical. Like you've never eaten an asshole before."

"Well. That's different. And in my defense it's not a euphemism when I do it and it's part of a larger array of edibles."

"Whatever. Maybe if you'd been little more experimental, Scott wouldn't have left."

I drained my glass, slammed it on the table loud enough to get the freakish bartender's attention. "You're on thin ice."

"I'm just sayin', all guys want a little finger action." Wendy crooked her middle finger. "Just pop it in and when they're about to go all curly-toed and ugly, just yank that bad boy out of there. It's more effective than chaining them to a wall."

"Which is all the more interesting coming from the zombie who can't seem to get a date." I glanced at Birch and Mama Montserrat.

Their discussion had drifted into secretive whispers, Johnny spending a good portion of it with eyes darting quicker than a peep show patron's—all he needed was a trench coat and a newspaper.

"Your boyfriend's arguing," I whispered.

As we both turned back to watch, Mama stood and

slapped the shit out of Birch's cheek. His head spun toward the wall and saliva sputtered from his lips.

The big woman stomped through the room, floorboards moaning and creaking under her weight. She stopped at the door and turned.

"Yeah. See if I'm joking, Johnny." The words bellowed from her, even as her eyes shrank to slits. "You'll get yours!"

And with that she was gone.

Johnny giggled a bit, noticing the row had garnered the attention of all the assorted lushes in the bar, except for the twins who'd long since passed out in pools of their own slobber. I pitied the dimwitted barman. Johnny sloshed down whatever he was drinking and slid out of the booth. He flashed an uncomfortable grin at both us, the gathered contestants and crew as he sidestepped out the wall of French doors and into the garden.

"Are red rose petals really appropriate?" I whispered into Mama Montserrat's ear. Her eyes followed mine to the path of crimson that led through the forested great hall down the entry stair to the gravel drive, where the first limousine idled—the only one, if I'm going to be honest about the production[41]—cloaked in a cloud of exhaust instead of très gothic fog.

"What you mean, child?" She cocked her head to the side as though legitimately perplexed. Could she

---

[41] And why wouldn't I be? It's not like I'd intentionally cram all nine contestants into an old Lincoln stretch, for Christ's sake, it wasn't even black. If it showed up on your doorstep to take you to the airport, gleaming white like a smile, you'd send that shit back to the white trash wedding it came from.

really not know? What woman doesn't know the symbolic nature of roses? Hell, Valentine's Day is built on the assumption.

"Well, it's not really a dating show. I suppose yellow petals could be an option, but red? It's not like anyone's coming here to find love."

"Don't be a dumbass now. With Johnny Birch, every show is a dating show," she clucked, shook her head and then shot a grimace over her other shoulder.

I craned around her to eye Birch, who was busy admiring himself in a hand mirror, smoothing his eyebrows down. Satisfied, he flexed his lips into a kiss and smoldered a bit. I'd seen the smolder before, though I believe it was patented by a romance author I met once at a convention in Pittsburgh. Could be wrong. Johnny tossed the mirror behind him, where a vine uncoiled, snatching it from the air.

The whole "living" room concept could have been no one's idea but Birch's. The mossy lilting dips and hills were even thicker now than when we first arrived, covered with a perennial thickness of ivy. It crept around the barked columns and out the door, wedging them permanently open. The space creeped me out nearly as much as the decorator, and not just because an open door was an invitation for a home invasion—Johnny's "talents" were just plain weird.

The vine dragged the nymph's discarded mirror up the wall behind us to whereabouts unknown.

"Can you not do that?" I asked.

"What?" He blinked as mechanically as a porcelain doll.

"Make the greenery do your bidding? It's a bit unnerving."

"I'll try." The words were clipped, noncommittal.

More reason to hate the guy. I wished I'd brought a hedge clipper, or pruning shears or total vegetation killer.

Oh shit. That one even cracked me up. I suppressed a giggle.

Wendy's head poked out from behind a tree trunk like a demented stalker squirrel after a nut, or a nutjob, in this case. I would have waved but she was squarely focused on Birch.

I tapped my pen, straightened my score pad and sighed. "What's the holdup?"

"Shh." Mama Montserrat tossed her beaded dreads as she spun on me. They settled around her head like a macramé plant holder. "It's starting."

I lazed back in my chair a bit to get a better angle on the front door. Cameron Hansen stood on the outer steps, oddly an easy foot taller than his normal five-foot, two-inch frame. I suspected some radical reaper treatment until my eyes lit on his shoes. Massive platforms nestled under his suit pant cuffs. Not since Frankenstein had footwear been so horrific. The effect was not unlike hooves.

He turned and raised his hand in a little salute, at first I thought for my benefit, but then I sensed Birch's leering nod to my left. By the time I turned to look, he'd taken to considering some lint on the table. Mama stared past Cameron blankly.

Despite spending quite a bit of time with the celeb, as the fiancé of my friend Liesl, I'd never taken to the guy. His smarmy charms reminded me of his conquests and his night job as an incubus. Sure, Liesl was no saint, she'd delivered countless devil spawn into the world, those mewling little worms, cute in a bizarre trendy cuddle toy sort of way. A succubus's work is thankless, though, all the big-ups go to the forked cocks the "Inkies" swing.

And Cameron made sure to feature his in the tightest flat front trousers known to man, or devil.

I waved to the douchebag, to be polite, but he'd already turned to mug for a cameraman.

"The limos are pulling up and nine lucky contestants are about to gain entrance to this fantastic mansion and a chance of a lifetime. A chance to compete for a singularly fantastic opportunity. To protect one of the most famous and influential celebrities in all of supernaturalness."

That's not a word, I thought.

"Through these doors, the contestants will meet our judges and be judged . . . harshly," he said as he strode across the carpet of rose petals toward our ivy-covered dais. "First up, she's the gorgeous and mysterious woman who's captured the imagination of undead everywhere—"

I grinned. Nodding, but only slightly, as he went on to describe how my face had graced the cover of everything from magazines to Mojo powder. That last one I didn't recall posing for, but I smiled and politely took the compliment, figuring he knew what he was talking about. Whatever it was couldn't be any worse than Necrophilique.

"A star that outshines the night sky," he hopped onto the raised platform and held his hand out to . . . "Mama Montserrat, ladies and gentlemen."

Canned applause filled the room and if I could have, I'd have turned red as baboon ass. Thank God for low blood pressure.[42]

---

[42] The lowest. None.

Mama Montserrat didn't say a word. She pulled out an ivory pipe, stuck it into her mouth like she was stabbing a pincushion and sparked it up with one of those lighters crackheads use. You know, the kind that looks like flames from a jet engine. I imagine they're sold wherever you go to pick up Mad Dog 20/20 or a "40" of "Old E." The smoke coiled around her head like a snake darkening at the head, which refuse to dissipate. Finally, she acknowledged the camera with a blunt nod— no pun intended—without once looking at Cameron, who merely shrugged and continued.

"Next on our panel is none other than the undead socialite herself, that party girl extraordinaire, not often seen without a Big Gulp of booze and clothes you wouldn't be caught dead in . . ."

At least they didn't corral a real audience to provide the snickering that snuck out the speakers.

"Oh, wait . . . except she *is* dead . . . and she's wearing it anyway, ladies and gentlemen!" Cameron broke out in a fit of laughter, never once taking his eyes off me. The fucker relished my discomfort. Always had.

More laughter poured into the room, big rocking guffaws. I had to force myself to shut my mouth. He really couldn't be talking about my McQueen. Not unless he had a death wish.

"It's Amanda Feral, everybody!"

I put on my biggest smile and gave a tidy wave. "Thanks, Cam, looking dashing as ever."

"Why, thank you," he said and then for the camera's benefit, "I clean up pretty well, if I do say so."

"You certainly do. That suit is beautiful."

Cameron brushed his hands down the lapels of his jacket.

"But those shoes!" I hunched over the table to gawk.

His hands hovered around his waist, the smile deflating on his face.

"Now, those are really spectacular. In fact, I haven't seen platforms so high since the Olympics. Are you training?"

Cameron blushed, but deflected with a little spin that brought him directly in front of the man of the hour. "Johnny Birch is a bona fide star of stage, screen and countless recording triumphs," he chanted. "His celebrity is such that he's become the target of many crazed female fans, and some male." Cameron gestured as though he'd asked a question.

Birch nodded.

"Each clamoring for a second of his precious time, a private serenade or possibly his head on a stick for their home altar!" Cam shouted.

Johnny's eyes bulged.

Mama rolled hers.

I felt a headache coming on.

"Ladies and gentlemen . . . Johnny Birch!"

"Thank you for that . . ." the wood nymph stood and searched for the word and didn't find it. "Introduction," he finally said.

I'd have inserted a few adjectives, like insane.

He rounded the table and came to a stop next to Cameron, resting his hand on the host's shoulder like they were old pals. "I'm excited about the prospects of this show. As you know, I've yet to find the love I so desperately deserve on my fantastically popular and, if I do say so myself, romantic television series, *Tapping Birch's Syrup*. That's right America, I've yet to be tapped."

Chuckles and a smattering of applause echoed

from hidden speakers, as opposed to the gagging I'd have introduced.

"Bullshit," I coughed and struggled with my purse until I landed the little flask of whiskey, unscrewed the cap unceremoniously and took a long drag. Cheap shit nowadays, but it packed a punch and flooded my weak veins with some welcome warmth—Lord knows I wouldn't get any from this crowd.

Birch swiveled toward me, "That one's gonna be trouble . . . and I love it."

"Meow," Cameron added with what he wrongly assumed was the requisite cat's paw mimicry. On a child it'd be cute, on him it looked retarded, just like the shoes.

Jesus, I thought. This gamble better pay off.

Meanwhile, Johnny beamed for the camera, sucking in his cheeks and rocking his head on his shoulders in what must have seemed to him to be a saucy seductive move. Turns out, he just looked drunk. I'd have to remember to tell him later.

"Are you ready to meet the first contestant?" Cameron motioned for Johnny to sit down, but he just stood there, mugging and stabbing the air with his arrogant chin.

"He means, sit your ass down, Birch!" I yelled and the camera spun on me, its oculus tightening in. I couldn't resist a smirk. Who could?

Birch huffed his way through a fiendish scowl, presumably for the benefit of the invisible audience, as it clearly had no effect on me, and pointed a twiggish finger in my direction—a threat—then darted around to reclaim his seat. Once settled in, he leaned back in his chair.

"Good stuff," he said. "Keep up the false antago-nism, it can be our shtick."

"Who says it's false?"

"You kidder. I knew you'd work out great."

"Listen, Birch. I'm just around to buy some time and exposure for my company and to see you get mur-dered. Get any more suspicious packages in the mail?" I winked and then glanced at the camera mischievously, hoping they'd caught the exchange but doubtful the wendigo working the damn thing gave a shit about any-thing other than waxing his antler.[43]

He waved off the words.

Mama Montserrat puffed a cloud of smoke that hung around her head like a phantom. "You two shouldn't joke about those threats. Someone sendin' dead things is serious bad juju. Means they serious." Her face poked out of the gray cloud like an Eskimo emerging from a dirty parka. "Serious as a heart at-tack."

Cameron's voice interrupted her by proclaiming, "Welcome! To *American Minions*!"

He led in the first victim, a vinegary, rat-faced woman with bleached-blond hair as crispy as chow mein noodles, a pale pink blouse that fit as loosely as sausage casing and thoroughly eco-conscious and ut-terly beige slip-on hikers. I scanned the atrocity be-tween my fingers—there's nothing more offensive than unchecked fashion don'ts—they do produce maga-zines for that very problem, you know? Her skin was nearly as gray as Mama's pot smoke and veins webbed her face—much like mine when I don't expect anyone

---

[43] Yes, that was both a euphemism and a critique of his supremely shiny rack.

to stop by the condo. Most likely a zombie, though I really hated to acknowledge our kinship.

Is it really so hard to slap some makeup on the dead? Really?

"*Je m'appelle* Absinthe," she spat. "I'm Belgian."

"Like Poirot?" I asked. The fact that I was reading *Evil under the Sun* seemed overly coincidental; never mind that I'd likely abandon it for the DVD.

The woman soured further—I know it doesn't seem possible[44]—and began to speak in that decidedly French way that features hairball coughing in every other word. "Hercule Poirot is a fictional character. I don't see how I merit ze comparison. I'm here, aren't I? I exist, *oui?*"

"Of course you exist, Absinthe." Cameron patted the woman on her back. "At least until someone knocks you out in an elimination round."

"What. You zink a ghoul can't prevail? Well you are most wrong, Monsieur Hansen. I've learned a variété of techniques to—"

"Lovely to meet you!" Cameron shouted, cutting off her rant. "Please wait for your competition in the study." He swung his arm around her and sped her toward the door in the rear of the forested lobby.

A commotion bustled at the entryway, as Tanesha thrust herself between the twins who'd been politely waiting their turn and stomped across the tangle of vines snaking across the floor.

"What the hell is all this shit anyhow, sugar?" She steadied herself against Cameron as if he were a small stool and kicked up the tallest stiletto I'd ever seen to pick out some stray threads of ivy from a hollow under

---

[44] Turns out it was.

the pad. "I better not trip up in here or y'all bitches are gonna hear from a lawyer." She scanned the judges and ended on Cameron. "A good one. You got it?"

"I do," he said. "Ladies and gentlemen, our next contestant is Tanesha Jones, drag wolf."

"With a 'u'," she added.

"Drag wulf with a 'u'." Cameron raised a note card. "It says here, Tanesha is an expert in the ancient martial art of transformational glamour, a regular Mac-Gyver with cosmetics who can also, and I quote, vogue the hell out of some bustas."

"Oh, hell yeah," I shouted, checking my co-judgers reactions.[45] Mama continued to puff away nonplussed, while Johnny leaned forward with an odd look on his face. I wasn't sure he was entirely aware of what he was looking at so lasciviously. Tanesha struck a seductive pose and Birch's eyes followed her form from those deadly-ass shoes up her sleek chocolate gams to a body-hugging red halter dress that accentuated her plump ass. She must have been wearing a bullet bra as her breasts protruded like weapons.

"That's right, sugar," she called out to me and winked saucily.

Cameron ushered her to the study and joined the twins in the center of the room.

"Hurry up with those two, Cam." Johnny propped his hands behind his head. "Don't want them to get bored and start singing, we'll end up washed up on the rocks." He howled with laughter.

I stared at him. "That would have been hilarious, if it were a joke."

"You can do better, I suppose."

---

[45] Let's just go with "judgers." It's what I'm comfortable with.

"Of course." I dug a cigarette out of my purse and lit up. As far as I could tell the show was a solid piece of crap. The only thing to do was play up the camp.[46] "Now get me an ashtray, fairy boy."

"You—" Johnny was definitely riled. He slid his chair back like he'd attack.

"Shh!" I interrupted. "The ladies don't like 'em abusive." I thought about that for a moment. "Except for the ones that do. Oh, forget it."

Birch mumbled a curse under his breath and a swath of ivy turned brown behind him, like he'd cut some magical fart.

"Nice," I said, and then pointed out the cameras.

Cameron escorted in the alcoholic twins—escorted being the appropriate word, since they still looked like hookers—skirts hiked up to their poons and eyes glazed over with the sort of intoxication reserved for twenty-first birthday celebrations or amateur porn shoots.[47] "Janice and Eunice are sirens from Lake Ontario who spend their time lounging on the misty rocks of Niagara Falls coercing receptive men[48] into ill-fated barrel rides. God love 'em." He slipped in between the two, wrapping his arms around their shoulders like he was about to give them some much needed advice— not that he knew any. The twins shook their hair, cooed and fluttered their vocal chords. Cameron's face slack-

---

[46] Which is the solution to so many uncomfortable situations. Bored. Camp or vamp it up, throw in an accent, make a little fun, at the very least you'll be entertained. And isn't that all that matters?

[47] I'd put money on the latter. Not then, but at some point in their lives. No question, they've taken it in the rear for money. You know the look. Don't tell me you don't.

[48] Aren't they all?

ened and his mouth drooped like a naughty kitten cuffed by its mother.

"Simmer down girls, he's the host, not your quarry." Mama Montserrat tapped her pipe on the edge of the table, sprinkling the cloth with red sparks and black char and eyed the girls ominously. "What good are you to the legendary Johnny Birch, if you can't control your venom? No good, that's what."

Janice and Eunice scowled, one scuffed her bare (and dirty, I might add) feet in a tangle of clover, while the other batted her pale lashes at Cameron, himself slowly coming back from wherever it is sirens send their victims.

As the girls stumbled their way to wherever Mama and the other producers—assuming there were others—designated as the green room, probably the bar, Cameron and the rest of us turned toward the door just in time to watch a billow of fog roll across the ivy and rose petals and swirl about the host's stilt-like shoes like a hurricane in miniature. The smoky substance grayed as it formed snaking tendrils; they coiled up his body dragging the cloud behind until Cameron was co-cooned in its murky roil.

He began coughing and in that moment, the smoke instantly receded to his left, becoming columnar and dense. A pair of badgers scampered in, dragging a large piece of silk behind them. They darted up the column and wrapped the smoke in a silky kimono, seconds before the haze turned to flesh, then huddled together behind one of the "trees."

Before us stood a beautiful Japanese woman, black hair draped around her bare shoulders like a shawl. She clutched the robe closed with one hand and reached out to Cameron with the other. I glanced at Johnny. He needed a napkin for the gush of drool spilling from his gaping mouth.

"Japanese smoke ghosts, or Enenri, are rare in this part of the world and as you can see, both dangerous and beautiful." Cameron stopped to hack up a little more lung and then continued. "Maiko hails from Osaka and easily wins the farthest travelled to compete on *American Minions*. Welcome, Maiko. Aren't you something?"

The woman eyed him suspiciously, shrugged and then turned toward us and bowed. I gave her a polite nod, which she seemed to scrutinize and make me regret even acknowledging her.

Try to do something nice.

She shuffled toward the doors, whistling for her badgers to follow, which they did after a fit of hissing and scratching each other.

When the next contestant entered, I wasn't exactly shocked, though I couldn't imagine what sort of supernatural creature she might be.

It was Hairy Sue, clad in a plaid shirt, tied off above the belly button, and a pair of Daisy Dukes. Cameron swung his arm around her shoulders as she kicked out a cowboy boot and rested it on its heel, swaying the toe back and forth like one of those little pageant girls.

"This here's Hairy Sue." Cameron took on a southern accent that faltered at every other word, making him sound like he was gargling. "She's got her some special talents, don't you darlin'?"

"I do, Mr. Hansen. But y'all will have to wait longer than St. Peter on a poker to see 'em." She giggled.

There it was again, another weird religious statement that didn't mean anything. Something was definitely off with Ms. Hairy Sue . . . other than her big old bush, I mean. I didn't care for her cute little accent, either. Creeped me out.

"Our last contestant is another unique Asian beauty, a manangal, but this one has only had to travel from up the street at Mr. Wally's Pho-tastic Noodle and Nail! Welcome, Angie!"

A petite Filipina strode in wearing a pair of milc-high cork wedges and a bright smile, massive waves of black hair piled atop her little frame like a troll doll . . . only cute.

"Now what's your story, Angie?" Cameron took on a chummy tone with the little brunette.

"Well, let's see. I'm a nail tech like you said, I like Chinese food, romantic comedies and . . . oh yeah. I can do this." She bent her head forward and a slithering sound emanated from her body. The next thing we knew, a dripping tentacle was tapping Cameron on the shoulder.

He spun away from her and spasmed as though he'd been forced to touch a tarantula or something. The tentacle was nothing alien as it turned out, but a prehensile entrail from inside her body, more flapped around the hole in the back of her neck like a collar of sea anemone. Gross, yes, but more than that, impractical.

"So." Cameron chuckled uncomfortably. "And on top of that, you're also a vampire?"

"And I do a great acrylic and fills at very competitive prices. Also mighty mean beef broth."

"Good to know!" Cameron's knowledge of supernatural species was only slightly more advanced than mine, which is to say, I've got very little interest in anything that doesn't effect me directly. Basically, I lump them all into two categories. Cute and not cute. Werewolves? Cute. Vampires? Also cute. Yetis? Obviously not. Angie was one of the rare species that didn't fit neatly into my system. Sure she was cute in her skinny jeans and off-the-shoulder disco blouse, but the blood and bile draining down her back was a deal breaker. Nothing kills "cute" like gore. This, I know from firsthand experience.

I leaned over to Mama and whispered, "Weren't there supposed to be nine contestants? What happened to the other two?"

The big woman took another toke and said, "Well, we had a charming chupacabra named Shirl and a were-maltese who looked like that Dee Wallace Stone in *The Howling* but the manangal got thirsty and, I'm afraid, the limo was woefully undersupplied in the blood department. Don't worry, child. It'll all come out in da wash."

Cameron hopped up on the dais again. "So you've seen the contestants. Quite a pool, if you ask me, but let's get the opinion of our judges." He stabbed his hand in my direction. "Whaddya say, Amanda. Any frontrunners?"

"Um . . . no, dumbass. We just met them, how could I—"

He cut me off with, "You're definitely a firecracker." He whipped around to ask Mama the same question.

"I'm partial to a big puff a smoke now and then, in case you ain't notice. That Maiko, child gonna be somet'in' to watch. Mind you."

"Well, I'm buying whatever Tanesha's selling," Johnny added. "That girl could bite a batwing off a buttercup."

"Okay now," I said. "You people are just making those phrases up to get on my nerves."

"What's that supposed to mean?" Birch sneered.

"There's no such phrase. It doesn't make any more sense than Hairy Sue's bullshit chattering."

"Ahem." Cameron must have sensed I was about to explode, as he interjected, "So. We've got some varied opinions and some dark horses, all of them, in fact. It's bound to be a rollicking good time on this season of . . ."

The camera pulled back to the far corner. The contestants were herded back in and urged to stand in either threatening or seductive poses, provocative at the very least. Cam stood in the center of the indoor meadow, amidst the vinca and morning glory and spread his arms with the gusto of a musical theater major—only slightly less effeminate. Unfortunately the pan was wide enough to also catch Wendy spying on her intended victim, Johnny.

Cameron shouted, "*American Minions*!" at the same time someone screamed, "Cut! Some old cooze is clogging up my shot!"

Wendy rushed from the room backwards, kowtowing in Johnny's direction. So embarrassing. Mama Montserrat hissed quietly beside me, while Birch chuckled in his self-satisfied manner.

There was really little else to report.

After they wrangled Wendy outside, Cameron went on to describe the various trials and tribulations the contestants would endure and the frequent "cuts" that sounded both threatening and, frankly, sub-par in the reality show world. I wasn't feeling great about the future of the show, when so little work had been put into the premise. It's like the producers had never seen *Shrunken Heads* or the even more famous *Ichi Ni San*, which despite some mishaps in the first series—I'm sure no one meant to eat the host—is undeniably the most cutthroat challenge-oriented reality show out there.

At least in my opinion.

I fully expected some Hollywood style afterparty to mingle with the contestants in some congenial and closely monitored way—replete with flattering lighting and security guards for us celebrity types. So you can imagine my surprise when the crew rudely darkened the room and skulked outside to their trailers to begin drinking beer around metal fire barrels and jerking off into sweat socks, or whatever it is they did on their free time.

Wendy was busy being inconspicuous and attempting to tail Johnny from room to room as he chatted away on his cell phone. So I was left with no recourse but to swipe a bottle of 151 from behind the bar and let Wendy know I'd be drinking my way to a pink blush in our room—alcohol being the next best thing to a functioning circulatory system.

Opposite the bed was a door to a small balcony with a cell of black wrought iron for a railing. I slumped into a cushy deck chair, tossed the cap and went to it, the warmth flooding through me like only the Bacardis know how—thank you, above average alcohol content. In a few minutes, I heard Wendy slam the door behind her and flop onto the bed, sighing discontentedly.

"You okay, honey?"

"Fine," she huffed, clearly grumpy, but my bottle wasn't going to drink itself so I opted for selfish and continued guzzling.

A few moments later—I'd moved on to contemplating the ever-expansive nature of the universe, also picking out which stars were actually plane lights[49]—I heard a commotion below me in the garden, followed by voices.

One of them, I'm pretty sure it was Johnny, was denying something vehemently and in hushed tones (always an indicator something's eavesdrop-worthy).

"I gave you nothing. Whatever it is you think you have, you got from somewhere else. I'm clean."

"It came from you, Johnny!" Another man's voice, this one thick with what could have been a South African accent, itself a hodgepodge of so many nationalities, it was impossible to keep track of. "Where you got it is the question."

Is that how guys argue, I wondered? One supervague question after the next? Poor things, it's like their communications skills never quite developed past playground shoulder punches. If only Scott were so simple. But then again, if he were, would I have connected with him the way I did?

I scrambled off the chair and onto my knees, mindful of my hip, and crawled to the edge of the balcony, hoping to get a look at Johnny's accuser—of what, I

---

[49] It's amazing what you can convince yourself of in the middle of the night and after a fifth. Those flashing plane lights? UFOs or at the very least dying stars. When I was alive, I might have chalked them up to aneurysms, but again, I'm not a doctor, also I'm dead so that diagnosis doesn't really work anymore. Though I am still thinking so I suppose it's possible a neuron or something could explode up there.

had no clue—but all I could see was the wood nymph. The other man was beneath my line of sight, somewhere below

"Well, here's your answer." Johnny raised his fist and lunged for the guy, landing an audible blow and grunting like the caveman he was. They scrambled through the overgrown bushes, rolling out beneath me into the arcade outside the bar. I could hear things breaking, glass shattering—ashtrays probably, and with that thought a fresh cigarette found its magical way into my mouth, no small feat lying there on my side, either—before the mysterious stranger broke away and stumbled through the darkened garden, tumbling over the rose bushes and yelping in the process.

Birch didn't give chase, so I imagined him battered and bruised below, hugging his legs to his chest and rocking to ease the physical and emotional trauma of the beating, a single tear trailing down his cheek.

It made me smile.[50]

---

[50] I find it's important to take pleasure in the little things, cute puppies, a bargain at a designer trunk sale and well-deserved assaults. Just a tip.

A scream tore through the calm veil of night, or rather, interrupted my reading. I'd been lounging in a silky chemise by Natori—I do love her shit—perusing my pristine copy of *Evil under the Sun*, my leg slung over the arm of my chair airing out the lady bits—like one does. Wendy had been terribly busy practicing her bored sighs and irritating me, so when the shriek filled the room, we perked up quicker than a couple of dry drunks at a wine tasting.[51]

I tore the door open and skidded into the hall on pink dressing mules. Wendy blasted out of the gap be-

---

[51] Just when the DTs were setting in, too.

hind me and collided with my sore hip, like I'd hesitate to beat her dead ass. A fresh ache spread through my torso.

"Watch it!"

"What?" Wendy shrugged innocently, but quickly gave way to a needling smirk that spread across her lips like a venereal disease. "It's not my fault you're into bestiality."

Before I could chastise, she looped her wrist around my elbow and pulled me behind her toward the ruckus at the far end of the hall. A clutch of yammering girls posed before the tangle of vines and branches concealing the darkened wing, home to Birch and Mama Montserrat's quarters. We reached them at the same time as Tanesha Jones, Drag Wulf, who shuffled from her room in a darling pink terry robe, fluffy slippers and her massive weave held back from her face by a sleeping mask pushed up into a makeshift hair band.

"Adorable," I remarked, and gave her the old up and down.

"You too, bitch. I'd kill for this little thing you're wearin'." She flipped her mane over her shoulder and reached a single airbrushed claw to flip up the hem of my kimono. "Of course, on me it'd be hiked up to my waist and show off my candy." She winked lasciviously. "I'd still work that shit."

"Don't I know it? I've seen you work."

Wendy stepped up and stood on her tiptoes trying to get a look through the deadlock and into the hall. "So what's going on back there?"

The rest of the contestants, and a couple of camera guys trying but not succeeding in blending into the background, turned around and stared dimly.

"No one's even looked, have they?" I asked, foot beginning to tap out my irritation.

They all shook their heads.

"Well, then which one of you screamed?" I looked from the twins, their matching raccoon eyes smeared with mascara and eyeliner, to Angie, who rubbed her neck, sneered and rubbed her neck, like a threat—the last thing I wanted to deal with was the manangal's entrail tentacles painting everything they touched with gore[52]—to Absinthe, who true to her name was drinking something green from an etched juice glass (was it too much to hope that it was a household cleanser?). Nothing. Not a spark of knowledge on their sleepy, drunken faces. Maiko and Hairy Sue were nowhere to be seen.

"Jesus. Get out of the way." I pushed past, Wendy and Tanesha in my wake. The contestants parted like sides of beef on hooks, bumping into each other and stumbling. Fucking retards. How we'd possibly find a better candidate than Ms. Jones, I had no idea. Nor did I plan on looking very hard. Johnny was already smitten with the trannie's "impressive thighs" anyway. That he didn't know the carpet *really* didn't match the drapes was his problem and his alone.

A couple of shakes loosened the vines enough to make an opening, revealing a hall coated with the same greenery. Leaves rustled and the whole place stank of rich earth and old carpet. The walls swelled and re-

---

[52] Seriously, what kind of a vampire flies around like that. It just wasn't right, or cute, at all. Wait till I told Gil, he'd puke up his Fran Drescher, or whatever celeb vintage he was chugging nowadays.

ceded like the heaving of a sore throat, the vines lacing the walls, a thick green sputum.

The hall grew darker the deeper we stalked. Shadows stretched into inky black pools that flooded across the barely visible Orientals and washed up the walls in waves. There was no telling what lurked beneath the cords of vine and leafy clumps. Rats were my first thought. If I listened intently enough I could hear their maniacal scrabbling—though I'd be forcing it. The ceiling was dark as midnight, no telling what might hang there—besides the cameras, of course, their red eyes blinking on lifelessly. To the left a door opened a crack, tugging against the web of ivy and tendrils drilling into the wood. I heard a garbled stream of curses, before the door gave a few inches more.

A slice of Mama Montserrat's face crept into view.

"What's going on? Who screamed?" Her voice shook.

"It wasn't you?" I pulled at the vines, enlisting the help of Wendy and Tanesha, until we'd freed the woman and created a pile of living debris, the broken vines snaked off and wove into the net covering the floor.

"Fuck no, wadn't me, child. Why'd I scream like a mad banshee?" Her head swiveled toward the far end of the hall, eyes narrowed with suspicion. "Johnny?"

I followed her gaze. "Johnny," I agreed. Though, frankly, I was more than a little surprised that he'd dragged his ass back upstairs after the beating he took—though the one in my head could have been far more brutal than the reality. If he'd indeed even taken a beating. In my mind it was heinous violence. The guy probably socked him in the shoulder.

Wendy's hand curled around my upper arm as we

progressed, tightening with each step until I'd had to reach up and swat at it. Tanesha urged me forward from the other side, nodding and pointing in the direction of Johnny's suite with her chin. Mama trailed behind us, kicking at the tangles beneath us.

A charred smell filtered down the hall, the remnants of a barbecue or a chimney fire—perhaps the crew pulled together an impromptu cookout after tonight's soiree. Smoke and rotten meat tossed into a blender for the ultimate in odd perfumery. Next up from Chanel: Creosote #5, charbroil the fantasy. The image of Carole Bouquet lying seductively across a smoldering grill popped into my head, but only for a moment, long enough to solidify the idea that we were about to find a body and not a tasty burger.

Johnny's door wasn't covered with ivy the way Mama's had been. In fact, it was marvelously free of the creeping plants. The doorknob even glinted in the low light, daring me forward. I felt something slither across the top of my foot and stiffened. Wendy grabbed me from behind, attempting to lift herself out of the bramble.

"Jesus, Wendy. Get off!"

Tanesha prodded my arm, forcing my palm around the doorknob, a brass monkey paw. It didn't budge.

"Well?" Tanesha asked. "Are you gonna go in there or what?"

"It's locked." I twisted the knob again, and was met with the same curt denial. "We're going to have to bust in."

"Like kick it down?" Tanesha stepped back into some martial arts pose so twisted her robe began to open at the waist, revealing a blue satin demi-bra and a slick pair of bulging satin panties, ill-prepared for both the drag queen's penis and his oddly hairless scrotum, which hung out the seam and clung to his inner thigh like sap running down a tree trunk.

Wendy's eyes bugged at the spectacle, her mouth gaped.

"Yeah . . . no." I stepped in between them. "And you might want to just tighten up the belt on that, before you get an admirer you don't want." I tilted my head in Wendy's direction. "Like you didn't know."

"Oh." Tanesha inhaled sharply and wrapped herself tightly and stepped away from Wendy. "Sorry, hon. Thought I was done for the night so I took the tape off."

I quickly put my fingers up to the drag queen's lips. "I don't even want to hear anymore."

Tanesha shrugged, smiled at me and continued to edge away from Wendy, who continued to stare at the drag queen. She wore an expression halfway between a grin and a question.

I tore the vines away from a nearby bureau, and opened the top drawer, candles, a few boxes of matches and a candle bell—its handle too thick to fit in the slim break—clattered inside. Nothing useful.

"I've got a credit card in my purse," Tanesha offered.

"Does that even work?" Wendy asked.

"It works on TV, so . . ."

I nodded and Tanesha stumbled back down the hall, leaving Wendy and me staring at Mama Montserrat. Her saucer eyes darted back and forth between us, as sweat beaded on her brow in such an obvious fashion, I couldn't help but elbow Wendy and point it out.

"Mama looks nervous," I said.

"Of course, I'm nervous." Her eyes edged back to

the door. "Who knows what we'll find inside? What if he's been hurt? Or worse, what if he's dead?"

I shrugged. I wouldn't be weeping, that's for sure.

Mama's eyes narrowed in scrutiny, her palms moving naturally to a spot just above her hips. "If he's dead, we don't have a show."

And if we don't have a show, I thought. I'm screwed. "Oh." Scratch that earlier comment, I'd be bawlin' like a fucking baby.

"He's not dead." Wendy pressed herself against the door, clawing at the frame dramatically. "He can't be."

"Jesus, Wendy. Dignity isn't just a designer fragrance."

Tanesha plodded up behind me and pressed a Visa into my palm. I shoved the drama that is Wendy out of the way and went to work on the lock. It was old, so I figured it wouldn't be any problem triggering the mechanism. Lucky for me, I had experience busting into places I shouldn't. Thanks to Ethel's insufferable need to hide her sweets.

I maneuvered the card into place, got the perfect angle on it and the moment it connected with the latch, lost my grip and watched as it slipped away into the dark gap.

"Dammit!" I spun around, daring the others to say a word. "I'm gonna need another one."

Tanesha's claws descended into her open purse. Her long, thin claws. Snatching at her wrist, I pulled her hand close to the door

"Just loosen up your fingers. Lemme work with 'em."

"All right. But you better not mess up my manicure. It took three hours to have Usher airbrushed in various states of undress. See."

She fanned out her nails, they lifted and fell in a gentle cascade and sure enough, from pinkie to pinkie, Usher went from full dress to nude and—clearly—aroused.

"Nice work. I promise to take care of all of Usher's parts."

Tanesha closed her eyes and relented.

She followed directions well, and in a few moments, I managed to work one of her nails into position, scraping the back end of the latch and shimmying it into its space in the door. A quick push and the door opened into a motionless suite.

"Nice work," the werewolf said.

"It's a handy little skill I picked up in childhood."

"Sweet." A knowing smile played on Wendy's lips. "Amanda was the model for those Precious Moments knickknacks."

From the second the door opened, there was no question the burning smell emanated from within Birch's darkened quarters. Smoke still curled in dissipating clouds in the corners of the room like dream snakes or migraine worms.

I was hesitant to cross that particular threshold, probably even more so than if I'd known Birch were alive and in there doing God knows what.[53] But I crept in anyway, watching my feet, lest I trip over a dead wood nymph.

The room glowed a dim green from a glass banker's lamp in the corner. The bulk of its light blossomed outward in a column, spotlighting a pile of steaming ash on the floor. The other side of the room

---

[53] And by God knows what, I think you know, I mean whittling. And by whittling, I mean jerking off.

flickered from the light of a silent television, a woman busy pleasuring two men at the same time; let's just say she'd welcomed them through both doors. I grimaced as my mind conjured images of six-pack rings. I suppose I should have been impressed that it wasn't some freaky Swedish scat show. I wouldn't have put it past Johnny to be into some extreme kink.

Mama spoke from the doorway, "It's in Johnny's talent rider."

"What? Porn?"

"He says he's like an athlete. When he's not actually competin' he still has to train that thing out."

My eyes spotted a stack of tissue boxes on the dresser. "Gross. Don't touch any used tissues, ladies, this area is a biohazard."

As I stepped past a comfortable sitting area, I noticed the pile of ashes had a specific shape. Very specific.

A human shape.

"Johnny," I whispered. The sound was more of a squeak than anything resembling a real word. Then, "That had to hurt."

As much as I didn't like the guy, I certainly didn't wish that kind of fate on him or anyone for that matter—except maybe Ethel, but she's an evil of another sort entirely. Johnny had his faults but no more than any other sleazy horndog.

Wendy stepped in behind me and gasped. "Shit. Is that Johnny?"

"I think so."

"Well, there goes that idea." She shook her head, her interest already waning along with a prospective sugar daddy. "What the hell did that?"

"Did what?" Cameron barged past Tanesha with a cameraman in tow. "What's going on?"

He looked at the pile of Johnny-shaped ashes, glanced briefly at the porn still flickering on the TV and put it together. "Ah, shit."

"Before being so rudely interrupted by little man's disease, Wendy was asking what did that." I pointed at the remains. "The answer is, of course, how the fuck should I know." I glanced around the room looking for an answer, though I didn't expect one to be forthcoming.

On the desk, beside a tall bottle of scotch wrapped in grosgrain ribbon and beneath a gallery of stuffed animals lay two shipping envelopes, identical to the one Johnny showed me at the Hooch and Cooch. I turned the top one over. The same handwriting littered the paper, though this one was addressed to the Minions mansion. Sure enough, the one below that was the very same I'd seen before. Underneath them, glossy and black as an oil slick, another of the insect-like creatures lay paralyzed in a scream, this one a bit longer in the leg, its wings open, heavily veined and sheer as long dead leaves.

"Johnny showed me this exact thing the first time we met." I turned to Wendy and Mama shoving the carcass in their direction. They winced at the sight of the disfigured insect crucifixion. I pulled the second one from its envelope. "See?"

"Girl, I don't know what the hell I'm lookin' at, but I sure as shit see it." Tanesha flopped down on the bed, picked up one of the porno cases from the nightstand and pinched her face in judgment, as you do—regardless of whether you're actually offended—when people are watching.

"Said it was a death threat. From what or who, I

don't know. Though the yeti at the club seemed to have it in for him." I thought about it for a moment. I wasn't actually sure the monster was after Johnny. Sometimes a rampage is just a rampage. I mean, don't we all want to go on a good rampage from time to time?

"How do you know?" Wendy peered over my shoulder.

"How do I know what?"

"How do you know it's the same one he showed you?"

I turned the envelope over in my hand. "I guess I don't, but that's beside the point. This time clearly they followed through on the threat." I tossed the thing on the desk and collapsed into the side chair, defeated and glaring at the pile of Johnny. "Well. That's the end of the fucking show. Guess I'll have to get a job at Jack in the Box with the blue balls crowd."

Cameron puffed out his chest. "It's no secret Johnny'd received death threats, why else would we be doing a hunt for a bodyguard?" He pressed the toe of his platforms into the ash leaving a gray print. "Anyway. I'm outta here. This just stopped looking like a paying gig and I don't do camera time without serious bones, let alone none." Cameron stomped out of the room.

The cameraman, a bald zombie with a face full of scruff dark enough it could double for a bad shoe polish job, tossed his equipment off his shoulder onto the bed, where it clanked and ruffled the brocade duvet. He snarled and flipped us all off before storming out, his big fists balled up at the ends of his stiffened arms like hams.

A few moments later, a chorus of shouts rose in the mansion followed by the rumble of footfalls as the predominantly zombie crew flooded out into the drive.

The four of us crowded into the window to watch the production crew abandon ship like the undead rats they were. They kicked over garbage cans and porta-pottys, flooding the grass with chemical bile. The entire lawn cleared out in a spray of mud and grass clumps, brown tracks criss-crossing the once lush green like crappy argyle. From the far side of the manor a familiar Civic hybrid zipped through the gravel and followed the train of mutineers.

I was about to say, "Isn't that your car?" But when I turned to look at Wendy, her face, screwed up tighter than a baby's first taste of lemon, gave me my answer.

"Motherfucker!" she screamed, fists pumping at her side.

"We could call the police, maybe?" I asked, trying to offer some solution. I hated to see Wendy so upset, especially when I was dealing with some pretty heavy shit myself, like the end of a clothes-buying era. It was kind of rude, if you ask me.

Her head lolled back on her shoulders. "Don't bother. That'd be like calling a retard stupid. Redundant."

"What do you mean?"

She looked me square in the eyes. "Times are tough for other people besides you, Amanda. I stole that shit off one of my meals a month ago."

"Ooh. Sorry. You really shouldn't take those kinds of risks though. I'm not sure you could handle a night in jail, with our diet of homeless vagrants, drug addicts and criminals, it'd be like a bulimic hanging out in the refrigerator."

She threw her head back, tongue pressed to the roof of her mouth. "Yes, please. Tell me how to live,

Ms. 'I Just Got My Car Repoed and Can't Keep A Man.' "

"Cold." I could feel my lips pursing.

"Shut up, you two!" Mama backed away from the window. "Don't you rotters know this is the end of us?"

I thought about the implications of the production closing down and had a little montage moment.

A foreclosure notice hung on the condo door, rolling out a sleeping bag next to Abuelita, Marithé carrying a box of her personal things (a pen case and an iPod) from the defunct offices of Feral Inc. and then the horrific finishing blow, my mother waiting with open arms as I carried my suitcases up to her little house in Magnolia.

*Dear God.*

I could feel my knees giving out. And then I glanced from the abandoned camera to the body, a plan congealing in my undeniably gorgeous head like a Waldorf salad of brilliance—actually I don't care for that simile—let's just say . . . with the intricate and deranged beauty of a Hieronymus Bosch painting and call it good. 'Cause it was.

"Like hell it is." I grinned at Mama Montserrat. "I say we keep on filming."

"What?" The trio stared back at me blankly.

"Yeah! We just change up the format. Go with this." I jabbed a thumb in the direction of the steaming pile of Birch. "Make it a mystery reality show rather than the competition we had planned. Lord knows we have plenty of suspects."

"Who?" Wendy asked. "Those girls probably never met Johnny before *American Minions*. There's no motive."

"Oh, come on. I knew him for three days and I would have shanked him if I could have. But, since you're probably right, we can script it a little bit, if we have to, no one needs to know any different."

"And who's our star?" Mama asked, but her wheels were already turning. She saw the kind of potential I did.

"Me, of course." I gave them my signature starlet pose.[54]

"I'm not sure you can be a sympathetic lead, Amanda," Wendy said.

I spun on Wendy. "Seriously? You're thinking you might be a better option? You haven't even had any screen time."

"Maybe Tanesha would make a better detective."

"Mmm-hmm," Tanesha hummed.

I shook off Wendy's comments. "We don't have time to argue about this. I've been reading lots of mysteries lately and what we have here is a classic locked-door murder. There's bound to be clues all over this shithole."

"She's right." Wendy finally came in for some back-up.

"Well, sure, you'd be behind your client."

"Client?" Tanesha asked, swiveling around to glare at Wendy. "That bitch is her friend. I kicked her bony ass out of a club once."

Wendy scowled and Mama Montserrat's eye's

---

[54] Perfected after more mirror time than I care to admit. Beauty is work, people. The days of a little mascara and some lipstick are over.

scrunched up in hatred. She shook her charm bracelet of dried animal parts at her, mumbling something vaguely threatening.

"All I'm saying is," Wendy continued, blowing off what was clearly a curse. "It's just like that Robert Altman movie where they gathered every British actor who'd ever done work in a period flick and shoved them in a spooky mansion."

"*Gosford Park*?" I offered.

"Exactly! And then the host is mysteriously murdered."

"Didn't see it." Tanesha yawned.

"Besides," I said. "It can't be like that movie. Too boring. Plus, we're short one Kristin Scott Thomas."

I fully expected to be corrected and told that *I* was the Kristin Scott Thomas.

Instead I got . . .

"You're kind of like Maggie Smith, if that helps." Wendy was scanning her iPhone again, unconscious of the sharpness of her barb. My jaw was tightening like I'd been cut open with a rusty can lid instead of Scott's aggressive dew clawing, tetanus making a home of hatred in my dead veins. I glanced at the fine beads of leather repair gel holding the strip of skin back into place. The top had begun to curl away, revealing a divot of gore gone green with mold.

Damn humidity.

But that's beside the point!

*Maggie Smith!* Why don't I have any other friends? Nice ones.

The blonde looked up, grinning. "I mean because of your dry wit, of course."

*Bitch*.

"Get the camera." I stabbed a thumb in the direction of the bed.

Wendy blinked.

"We're going to film this gonzo style. On the fly. None of us can afford to have this show go tits up, can we?" My eyes darted to Mama Montserrat.

"She's right. We've got to do something," Mama said.

"So grab the camera and we'll reshoot this whole thing, like we were just finding the body. And this time . . ." I pointed at each of the women and the drag queen in a dramatic show of deliberation. "With feeling."

The trio, sufficiently enthusiastic about my brilliant scheme, rushed into the hall to take their places.

I lagged.

It might help things if I knew what the hell I was doing.

After three reasonably threatening voicemails went
unanswered—and figuring Scott was still mad over our
little fight—I conned an East Indian cabbie named Raj
into picking me up and driving me past Smitty's Diner,
an all-night shithole Scott frequented for comfort food.
I met the taxi in the neighborhood outside the manor,
pretending to be a resident of a particularly disheveled
Victorian, the landlord of which owes me a favor for
cleaning up his squatter infestation, thank you.

I'm not a fan of cabs. They're often older model domestics, for one. And with old cars, or used cars in

general, there's always a chance you'll run into the ghost of a heart attack victim or, God forbid, the non-corporeal result of a fatality crash—particularly bitter entities and to be avoided at all costs. Unfortunately, limo services were a bit out of my reach, these days.

Scooting in next to a pair of sour purple apparitions, I kept my face forward, intentionally avoiding their scrutiny.

"Smitty's Diner by Safeco," I said, and settled back into the seat.

Raj grumbled, set the meter and pulled away, grabbing for his phone all in one fluid movement. The next moment, a mixed stream of Indian and English spat from his mouth at someone named Baljeet, who wasn't taking any shit.

"You listen to me, mister high-and-mighty, I get all the girls I want, don't need to go to school or make anything real of my life, Raj. I make the rules around here and if you want to keep dragging your sorry butt around Seattle in one of my cabs—yes, you heard me, my cabs—you'll pick up my things from the Vindaloo Mart. I'm not joking here brother. Not joking."

Raj sighed, cheeks flushed from the verbal beating. Our eyes met in the rearview mirror and I could have sworn his narrowed, as though he'd just lumped me in with bitches like his sister. I had to bite my tongue from correcting him. We all know I'm a bitch of a different sort, entirely.

"Do you need me to tell you what to get again?"

"No."

"Well, just don't forget our mother's incontinence pads, or do you want to clean up her poop again? Is that it, you like to clean it up?"

"No." His answer was as clipped as you'd expect,

full of that adolescent hurt that echoes its way through an adult psyche.

"Hmm. And turmeric. I'm out. Get the one in the bag not in the jar no matter what Mitesh tries to sell you."

"Fine." Raj's knuckles were white; his hands kneading at the loose steering wheel cover viciously. He reached for the knob on the radio.

"Don't think of turning off the radio. This isn't your last call you know?"

I couldn't bring myself to look in the rearview mirror again, which was just as well, because the ghosts were shifting around a bit to chat about me like a couple of schoolgirls.

"She's a harsh looking one," one of the ghosts said. His tone was haughty, the words measured.

"Dark and disturbeded, be my guess," said the other in a grumbly stutter.

"Why do you suppose she's going down to the tracks at this hour?"

"Prolly lookin' to meet up wit' a man."

I kept my focus on the window, clouding with a fresh drizzle that pooled in dots and drew lines in the wind as straight as mattress ticking. The houses gave way to aging strip malls hawking Vietnamese noodles, dry cleaning and Super Mega Hot Nails, Low Low Price for Fill. I considered my own nails, thick and sharp as talons. The French manicure covered up the monstrousness, but only from a distance.

"She looks lonely."

"I agree completely."

Bastards.

"Doesn't have the propinquity for relationships. She's too hard."

"Too cold."

"Frigid. Probably take a can of bacon grease to loosen her up."

My head spun at that, glowering at the ghost nearest me, then the other. "Am not," I hissed. Though really . . . I was guilty on most of those counts, but I'd be damned if they were going to talk shit.

Raj glanced back over the seat, not skipping a beat in his chastisement of his sister. He nodded and opened his eyes wide under the folds of a sagging turban. I shook my head.

"Just talking to myself," I said.

Raj went back to his argument.

"I knew it." The ghost furthest crossed his arms, a burly man in a pinstriped suit with round glasses and hair greased tight to his obviously lumpy skull. "I could smell dead meat the second we pulled up to that joint."

The other nodded a face as round as a pie-hole, lips smashed up into his nose like he'd stumbled on a garbage scow. "Definitely. Dead meat," he repeated and scooted closer to his friend, his aura fading into a calm blue—ridicule, apparently, is like ghost Xanax.

"So what *are* you doing out at this hour?" Lumpy leaned around Pie-hole to judge me more directly.

"That'd be none of your damn business, spook," I whispered, glancing at Raj, who either hadn't heard or was too busy arguing to care. "Can't you two hang out on the roof or something?"

"It's raining." Pie-hole pointed at the streaks on the window, sheepishly.

"Besides," Lumpy added. "We don't get to talk to zombies every day."

I sighed.

Raj turned at the intersection between Safeco and the new hotel I can never remember the name of. Smitty's appeared on the right, a spot of chrome growing out of a wet parking lot like a prosthetic.

"Pull up slowly."

"Ooh! Surveillance!" Pie-hole's head jutted in next to mine. Lumpy's took up the opposite side.

"What are we looking for?"

I'd been confident in Scott's predictability and sure enough, his tussled mop of blond hair marked his favorite spot behind an otherwise sweaty window. Probably nibbling on a tall stack with butter pecan syrup, sausage patty on the side. I didn't have to think twice to know he was wearing his favorite pair of jeans, worn nearly threadbare on the back pocket and the left knee.

I loved those jeans. And the way he filled them out.

The cabbie slowed to a crawl and Scott's preternatural senses must have kicked in. He swiped a clean streak from the window and peered out, forcing me to duck down onto the filthy felt seats; I didn't need him seeing me before I had a chance to ditch Raj and his spectral passengers. Lumpy and Pie-hole ducked too, purely for effect.

"See! She is on a man-hunt."

"Yeah. But you meant the other kind."

"Wait. What kind are we talking about?"

I'd almost gotten out of the cab just to get away from the yammering and then remembered I didn't have a dime. Raj would be plenty pissed when I stiffed him.[55] It's situations like these where a dysfunctional moral compass really comes in handy.

---

[55] That's "when" not "if."

"Keep driving." I punched the passenger seat. "I need smokes."

The cabbie grunted and pulled us away from Scott's line of sight. He stood in the window, goggling his hands to see out into the dark. I straightened, pointing a finger in the direction of an all-night convenience store. "There. The Stoppe and Shoppe. Pull in."

"There are very bad men hanging around this area," Raj warned.

"That's true," Pie-hole agreed.

"Drunks and rapists." Lumpy raised an eyebrow, to show he was serious, I presumed.

"Sexual perverts," Pie-hole said. "And Salvation Army nuns."

That last one was kind of scary, I had to admit. Though did they even exist anymore?

"You must be very careful inside." Raj reached for the meter.

"No no no." I reached for his hand. "You wait for me here. I've got another errand to run after this."

For a moment, I thought he'd argue. He did take another look at the ticking numbers, settling in at $26, before picking up his cell and yelling at Baljeet again. Maybe that'd be enough of a distraction. I slipped out of the car and stepped into the convenience store making a point of not looking back.

"See you in a minute," Pie-hole called after.

"Not if I can help it," I mumbled.

"Oh, buddy. She's tryin' to stiff the old man," he told Lumpy. "She'll have to fake her own death to get away from him."

"She's already dead, dumbass."

I figured I'd let them work it out.

The Stoppe and Shoppe was worn to near ruin,

linoleum curled up in spots and chipped away entirely in others. Where it was still smooth, sooty scuffmarks tagged it like talentless graffiti. A bank of refrigerator cases, dark except for one that flickered like a strobe light, lined the back wall, making the rows of shelves stand out like atolls of cleanliness amidst the smudged décor. Most of the shelves were empty except for off-brand potato chips, generic mouthwash and, oddly enough, a thoroughly stocked toilet paper display. The homeless apparently weren't willing to skimp on anal cleanliness.

I saw the clerk's feet first. Dingy white socks propped up on the counter next to an open container of pepperoni sticks so desiccated they resembled twigs. He was reading a car magazine with a girl on the cover massaging the hood of some sports car like it was a muscled chest.

"Hey," I said, opting not to prod his gross foot to get his attention.

He swung his feet down and stood up lazily, his greasy hair hung in strips. His eyes were bruised and his nose taped, the victim of a beating or a sloppy surgeon. More likely a robbery. "Yeah?"

"Um. Do you have a back door?"

"What?"

"A back door?"

He twisted his head quizzically. I'm not sure why I expected him to be anything other than an idiot. Maybe I figured the black eyes were earned. Like he was a smartass or something. Sadly nothing like that, just dim.

"I need to get away from that guy out there." I pointed at the cab. "He's been following me. Stopping and flicking his tongue between his fingers."

He made a peace sign with his fingers and lifted them to his face. "Like this—" he began.

"You don't have to." I waved my hands hopefully.

The clerk flicked his tongue in the webbing.

"Really?" I shook my head. "Listen, fucktard. Is there a back door?"

He pointed to a hallway even darker than the rest of the store. I looked out the front door. Lumpy stood on the cab hood, a mischievous smile at play on his shadow lips. Pie-hole sat in the passenger seat facing Raj, his mouth working pretty fast for a ghost no human could hear.

*What are you up to?* I thought.

Then, Raj bolted out of his side and charged the door, screaming in that same unintelligible way. Fucking ghosts were learning new tricks every damn day. It seems like just yesterday, Mr. Kim walked away from my Volvo, like he'd never been chained to it in the first place.

Now they can be informants? It's like there's no fucking rules.

I darted down the hallway, slamming myself into the door, somehow expecting it to just pop open easy as a ten dollar hooker, but luck wasn't playing fair. Never did.

The door was locked. I bounced off it and spun around as Raj reached out for me, fists pumping with anger.

I hissed and ratcheted my jaw open fully, snapping at the air in front of him. I lurched forward, doing my best impression of a shambling mistake. My nails were dragging the walls as I went for him. Raj opened his mouth and let out an honest-to-God "ieeee" before clutching at his chest, twitching a bit and then dropping to the floor in a heap. I closed my mouth with a snap and a second later—as luck would have it—the clerk was hovering over the body.

"What happened?" The kid knelt beside Raj and dug through the layers of clothes to feel for a pulse.

"He had a heart attack, I think." My jaw still ached from the threat of chowing down on some Indian food. I, of course, had no intention of eating Raj. First off, I don't know if you've ever noticed, but they tend to wear a lot of clothes around these parts. Sure, it's cold compared to Mumbai or wherever, but really . . . parkas? Two, he'd taken at least fifteen radio calls since he picked me up, including a heated argument with Baljeet, whoever that was, over spices or some shit—I wasn't really listening, though he made it clear after he clicked off that she was "full of spite and cruelty." Plus I was kind of full, so I'd have to purge at some point. Try and explain regurgitating a partially digested corpse—they don't flush well—I know, I've tried.

Finally—Hello—Witness!

"Well he's dead, now." The kid pulled back his hand like he'd accidentally touched a fresh turd. He even stared at his fingers, a look of actual horror in his eyes.

An odd feeling took hold of me. Something not unfamiliar, but latent, missed.

It was envy.

I opted not to disrupt his epiphany and instead said, "Wow. Life really is fragile."

The kid nodded, still examining the body.

"Okay, then. I gotta go." I rushed for the front door.

"But wait. What about the—"

"Bye!"

"—police?"

Pie-hole and Lumpy sat on the front bumper of the idling cab applauding. What's the sound of two spectral hands clapping? You guessed it. Nothing.

"I'm afraid you two are going to need to get a new driver. Sorry."

I sallied off down the sidewalk toward Smitty's; behind me I could hear the two ghosts commiserating.

"Must have been all the ghee."

"I've heard lentils are actually dried roundworms."

"That's ridiculous."

"I hope that guy turns off the car, or we really will be here all night."

A thought stopped me in my tracks.

I parked the cab in the alley behind Smitty's, tucked it right in between a Dumpster overflowing with flattened cardboard and a drunk passed out in a puddle of his own sick. Oh yeah, I'm awesome at parallel parking. I didn't even clip the fucker's feet. Pie-hole and Lumpy were suitably impressed.

"Nice job."

"Thanks."

"Could you turn off the radio before you go? Baljeet will be calling every ten minutes, screaming about Raj's laziness." Lumpy paused. "Of course, he just got a whole lot lazier."

I reached for the knob and found it had been snapped off, probably by Baljeet, herself. As if on cue, the squelch of the radio kicked in again.

"Raj, you soppy pile of baboon shit, where are you? Raaaj!"

"Sorry." I shrugged.

The two ghosts looked at each other, Pie-hole through the nearly opaque hands that covered his face.

Ancient grease clung to the warm air or the waitress with the blue-washed bouffant smelled like an order of onion rings—and if that's the case, she was definitely my ideal meal. I rounded the bar and spotted Scott dunking fries into a salad bowl full of tartar sauce. He shoved them into his waiting maw three at a time and swallowed with an economy of chomping.

He looked up, deep-fried content turning into a wholly unnecessary scowl.

"Jesus, Amanda. What are you doin' here?" he asked, dropping his face into his palms and groaning. "I thought you were on location?"

I slid into the booth next to him. "I figured you'd be moping, so I swung by to cheer you up with my sparkling personality."

"Is that what you're calling it?" He eyed me suspiciously.

"Um . . . yeah." I beamed, aiming for wide-eyed innocence, but may have overshot into babydoll, a dangerous misstep as evidenced by . . .

Scott slid away down the seat, putting a few more inches between us and pulling his fries along protectively. "Well, thanks, but just so we're clear, when I break up with someone, I usually don't talk to them again."

"Hold on. Is that what happened?"

He responded with a narrow stare, a sadness slogging in the creases on his forehead. "Amanda, come on."

What I said was, "I'm totally going to respect your need for space and I own that it was all my fault and

I'm an asshole and all that. You're a great guy, Scott, and I want all the best for you." What I meant was: you're totally mine. Don't even try to run, 'cause I'll hobble your ass.[56]

He angled a wary eyebrow.

"Fine," I said. "Don't believe me."

"All right." He passed me a fry to sniff. "We'll try out the friend thing."

"Deal." I beamed at him and he actually cracked a smile, while I snorted the hell out of that fry. "While I've got you here . . ."

"Yes?"

"Those people making threats against Johnny Birch?"

"Mmm-hmm? Oh, I dug up something about that, yeah."

"Wait. What I was going to say is, they acted on their threats. He's dead. We found what's left of his body a few hours ago, burnt down to cinders in his room. That wood nymph went up like kindling. Must not have used moisturizer."

Scott inhaled sharply. "Rough!"

"I'm just glad enough time has passed where we can laugh about it. Oh! And get this! The door was locked."

"Suicide?"

"I don't think so. He had another one of those creatures on his desk—this one apparently had been delivered to the mansion."

"Was there anything else in the room?"

"A large collection of porn. His clothes. Nothing that didn't seem normal for Birch."

"Hmm. So what now? Did the reapers come?"

"Jesus no. There weren't any humans about so they

---

[56] Yeah. Like you didn't know I'd be possessive. Keep up. Seriously.

didn't sense an issue and I sure as shit didn't call them. In case you don't remember, they're not exactly happy with my debt to them."

"Doesn't this mean the end of the show?"

"Absolutely not. I talked it over with the producer and we're going to continue the show, only with Johnny's murder as the premise. It's gonna be huge." I looked away. *Or tank completely*, I thought, *leaving me penniless and mooching off my friends*.

"But? You look worried."

"I need to be sure what I'm doing. I'm going to be the 'sleuth' and all I have to go on is a handful of mystery novels—none of which involve people as nasty as the yetis—and the handful of real life crap I keep falling into."

"Oh, about that." He perked up. "I did find out that there's been a little tiff going on between the nymphs and the yeti, which used to be called sasquatch but they took offense at being categorized by the humans and took back the previously derogatory Asian moniker. Also, don't call them 'abominable' if you want to live to tell about it."

"That's all very interesting. What does it have to do with Birch?"

"Well. The yeti have been launching frequent attacks on wood nymph strongholds, which aren't, like you'd think, made of old rotty bark and twigs but actual cities out there in the woods."

"Creepy."

"So apparently, there's talk of the yeti taking out a very visible member of the wood nymph constabulary."

"Johnny."

"Exactly."

"It's all very sci-fi channel, don't you think? Too easy? Territorial bullshit is so kindergarten."

"I thought that too, but when you take into account the threats and now this obvious statement being made with the method of his murder, it kind of makes sense."

"It does. Except for one thing. No one mentioned seeing or hearing a yeti rampaging through the mansion."

"Ah. But they're very good at concealing themselves."

"Well, not the one—" I stopped myself. Maybe the yeti at the Hooch and Cooch hadn't left the cage at all, maybe it'd gone chameleon or some shit. "So maybe the yeti was in the hallway, hiding in the leaves or something?"

"Leaves?"

"Yeah, Johnny had a boner for interior decorating. He overdid it with the ivy."

Scott called over the waitress. She dropped a plate of toast in front of some homeless teens counting change on the counter and slunk over.

"Two coffees, please."

She nodded, collecting his empty plate and tartar sauce and trudged off.

"I'm gonna need, at the very least, a conspirator. Someone in that house that knew it was going down."

"Listen to you with your lingo." Scott grinned, playfully, eyes crinkling at the corners. "What you really need is to get in there and pore over that room. Look under the bed, in the closets, drawers. Everywhere."

"That's not going to be must-see-television."

Scott shrugged and took the mug from the waitress, dumping a pile of sugar so large it floated on the surface for a moment before drowning in the brackish brew. Not having thought to bring a mutsuki, I greedily inhaled the heady aroma curling off my own mug. I stuck my tongue in, swirled it a bit.

Scott's brow arched.

While I've kept some secrets, the zombie versus food issue has been all over the supernatural news lately. So much so, that I'd learned a new trick. I grabbed my napkin and circled my tongue with it, blotting off the offending liquid.

"That's damn good coffee," I said.

Frankly, if I'd known how much fun investigating was going to be, I'd have opened a private detective agency, just to experience more easy banter with Scott. I totally took the guy for granted. He knew his shit. Add to that his ability to all but overlook my eating issue and drive me to bowel-churning orgasms almost every time we went at it, and the regret started to really sink in. Still, the healing had begun, as one of my previous therapists would have said.[57]

Or at least I hope it had.

"So, start interrogating people," he said. "Get the bastards alone. See where they were when he died. Do you even know when he died?"

"Well he screamed around 1:30, so I'm guessing right about then."

"Find out where people were. Also, if they knew Johnny before the show. Find out their motives."

I nodded. It made sense, and I totally would have done all those things eventually, but it never hurt to dot your "ıs" and cross your "ᴛs". Plus, if I was ever going

---

[57] Had I not devoured him in a parking garage.

to be able to snare the were-hunky ex-cop again, it would be by showing him I have the capacity to change. And the first step was valuing him.

"Thanks, so much." I put out my hand to shake and his fell right into my palm (said the spider to the fly). "I don't know what I'd have done without you."

I slid out of the banquette.

"Call me if you need anything else," he offered.

I smiled, already making an extensive list of things I "needed."

Just because things went well with Scott, don't go thinking I started shooting stars and moonbeams out my ass—we are, after all, talking about . . . me. How I rose to the top of karma's shit list was still a mystery. Another one. I mean, seriously, don't I play my part in alleviating the homeless crisis? Aren't you happy not to have to put up with a herd of patchouli-smelling hippies picketing your favorite boutiques? Haven't I improved the general aesthetic of the supernatural scene?

I'm going with yes.

I'm a fucking giver. I don't care what you say.

So stashing Raj's full-sized cab on the grounds of Harcourt Manor should have been way easier.

It's not like I could just pull it up to the door, Baljeet

hollering on and on in that ugly mish-mash of words—the damn radio must have some magical power supply for the beating she put it through. It was bound to draw attention—maybe less so than out in the ghetto neighborhood surrounding the Minions Mansion, where it would either be stripped or used as a shooting gallery, or worse, a toilet—especially with the phone number tattooed across it twenty million times, as if anyone has ever tried to call a cab that just passed them. Come back! No. Doesn't happen. But one of the bitches up in the mansion might just respond to Baljeet's call, just to be spiteful. With the slew of threats the woman had vomited during the drive back, I just couldn't risk it. Apparently she's fond of both eviscerations and amputations, to hear her tell it.

Old Mister Withers, let's call him, the caretaker, shambled up to the gate in a rain slicker, torrents streaming down the folds. He tugged at the lock a few times, finally slamming his fist down on it to get the mechanism going. Fifteen minutes, people. To think he didn't get the finger as we blew past him. Lumpy chastising Pie-hole for an impromptu b-a, an affront to only two people and the intended victim wasn't one of them.

"Get your hairy ass out of my face!" he yelled, causing the dwarf to just shake his wide haunches all the more, ass jiggling like a rap video dancer. Lumpy's aura turned bright red, his face seethed with anger. "Knock it off!"

He swung at Pie-hole and, to my surprise, made contact, doubling the ghost over.

"Jeez. Cool it, I was just fuckin' around."

"Fuck around over there." He pointed to the opposite side of the car. "Or on the roof. Nowhere near my face or I'll do you worse next time."

I curved past Withers's cabin and pointed the cab into a gap in the undergrowth. A squeal echoed as branches dragged their sharp nails against the body and the windshield was showered in pine needles. They wriggled in rainy rivulets like teeming maggots.

"Jesus!" Pie-hole yelled. "That sound is nearly as painful as Baljeet's screeching."

With that, Baljeet let loose with another stream of curses.

"Whoever you are, know this. I'm coming for you with my khukuri! You're a dead woman. Oh yes, you are. So dead I can hardly keep from laughing. You hear me? You hear me?"

There was one last squelch and then an ominous silence.

Two questions. How does she know I'm a woman?

And.

What the hell's a khukuri?


I threw open the double doors of the grand hall dramatically and posed there for a moment, the wind whipping hair around my determined face.[58] The storm followed me inside, the space exploding in a whirlwind of dry leaves and whipping vines. With Johnny gone, the ivy withered and died back to woody creepers. It swayed from the ceiling like hangman's nooses and coiled limply around the bottom of columns.

---

[58] There's something to be said about a stylish entrance, don't you think?

It would have made an awesome opening shot.

Would have.

Neither the camera nor Wendy were there to catch the melodrama.

"Wendy!" I barked and stomped across the wasteland and through the doors into the main hall.

What I saw there filled me with an unnatural glee. Flattened against the wall, terror bouncing around her slim featured face, was my best friend. Leaning in and trapping Wendy between her wanton and frighteningly thick forearms, Absinthe's eye twinkled lasciviously in the dim light. If I could have peed myself, I probably would have.

Instead, I did what any reasonable best friend would do. I dove into my bag for my cell phone to capture the entire event on a surprise video.[59]

"So, uh." Absinthe growled when she spoke. This was her sexy voice, I presumed, though she sounded exactly like a French waiter I'd had once—and I don't mean that in a dirty way. "Are you and your girl, how do you say . . . close?"

"I don't know what you mean." Wendy flinched.

"Oh come on, *cherie*. I mean, why don't we take zis quiet time, go upstairs to my room, and I'll fuck you like you've never had it before. Fuck you square."

Wendy's mouth dropped open and I must have giggled because Belgium's own lezzie ghoul's head snapped in my direction.

"Well, hello, Amanda. I've just been chatting up your girl here."

I put the cell phone to my ear and pretended to end a very important call. Wendy pleaded with her eyes. If

---

[59] What? Like you wouldn't.

I'd had time, I might have played with this situation, but we needed to get the opening shot before the wind died down.

I swept in between them and wrapped up Wendy in a tight hug. "This one is all mine, Butch."

Wendy's lip curled back in horror.

"Aren't you, baby?" I asked.

"Um."

"No need to put on a show *pour moi*. I could tell you two were . . . family." Absinthe wrapped the words in an exaggerated set of air quotes. "Just wish I'd known yesterday. I might have talked you two into heading down to ze Boar's Snout for a couple of beers and darts with a few of my girls."

"*That*," I said, "would have been fuckin' awesome. Huh, doll baby?"

Wendy glowered.

"Well, Absinthe, we'll be chatting with you later. Got a TV show to salvage. We didn't put our balls in this basket just to get 'em smashed, now did we?"

"Hell no."

I led Wendy out by the hand.

"She was going to eat me alive. Dead or not, I could tell."

"Oh yeah. She was lookin' to eat something." I stuck my tongue out and flicked it.

"Gross. You're getting dirtier, the more you rot."

Chuckling, I pointed out the room and how creepy it looked. Wendy got it. Another reason we're friends: we have that whole sync thing going on. I told her about Scott and my successful first steps to winning him back as we blocked out the scene.

\*   \*   \*

Don't ask me how she managed it—half the time I don't understand the mechanics of the world I inhabit, like it's piecemealed together from the whims of some unseen madman[60]—but the manangal, Angie, had turned her meager quarters into a full-blown nail salon, complete with paying customers and a mix of Top-40 chart-toppers bleating. I had to give it to the girl—she definitely capitalized on her assets.

Janice and Eunice sat at repurposed writing desks, their hands being worked over by the deftly nimble filing of a pair of Angie's tentacle-like innards stretched across the room from a gaping gash in the back of her neck. More stringy gore slithered down the back of her smock and washed brushes in a little basin, soapy bubbles stained pink in the effort.

Do I need to mention that my stomach turned at the sight?[61]

Tanesha lounged in the comfort of a massaging pedi-bath, a copy of *Hello Underworld* spread across one palm. The claws on the werewolf's other hand appeared massive and threatening threaded through Angie's delicately massaging hands.

Angie looked up from her work. "You two want mani-pedi?"

I scanned my nails. They were a little ragged from the torture I'd wreaked on them at the Stoppe and Shoppe, but not totally fucked. Wendy was doing the same, the camera drifting to her side with the effort. I

---

[60] Ahem.

[61] Didn't think so. I put up with an awful lot of gore in this afterlife, but manangals took the splatterfest to a whole other level. Just thinking about it makes me want to run for a bottle of Pepto and some therapy.

gave her a quick elbowing. "No, thank you," I said. "We have some questions." I spun toward the camera. "For Tanesha Jones."

"Drag wulf," Wendy added.

"Yes," I agreed.

The glamorous shapeshifter glanced up from her magazine, eyelashes batting violently. "Do you realize that every year in this God-forsaken country, werewolves go hungry because of supernatural job discrimination? Makes me want to vomit."

"I was not aware of that, no. Now—"

"Well, it's true." Her eyes returned to the article, her index claw tracing a punctuating line as she read, "Janice Dickinson, for one, is appalled. It says here, the 'world's first supermodel' and recent werewolf transformee is leading the charge against werewolf inequality next month in a campaign she's calling . . . 'Claws across America.' "

"Wow, she's like a saint. Saint Janice." Angie moved on to cutting away at the cuticles that curled around Tanesha's nail beds like seawalls.

"That's quite magnanimous of her," I said. Note to self: contact Ms. Dickinson for possible ad placement. "Now, Tanesha. I have some questions as to your connection to the death of one Johnny Birch."

"I was with you."

"Well, yeah, but before that?"

She sighed heavily and folded the magazine, slipping it between her hip and the arm of the lounge chair. "I was in my room. Getting ready for bed, untaping my candy, which can always be a bit of a chore. Need to soften up the adhesive—"

"It won't be necessary to go into—"

"Or else," Tanesha spoke louder, daring me to interrupt her again. "When I pull it off, a little bit of me comes with it. Or a whole lot of me, if you know what I'm sayin'." She tossed her weave over her shoulder and winked saucily at Angie, who cackled.

"Ooh girl, you so bad."

"Bad ain't the half of it, catch one of the boys wrong and the maid'll be cleaning balls off the lampshade and Tanesha dies childless."

Janice and Eunice chortled.

These questions were going nowhere. It was time to pull out the big guns and I think you know I mean lying. Nothing will get someone to tell you the truth quicker than a big fat lie.[62]

"Isn't it true you hated Johnny Birch?" I peeked at Wendy. Confusion marred her pretty face.

"Hate's an ugly word, Ms. Amanda." Tanesha's tone turned haughtier than a Kiera Knightley character. "I don't hate anyone."

"But you didn't like him."

"That ain't true at all." She moaned. "Oh Johnny!"

I shot a wide-eyed glance at the camera. Wendy licked her lips in anticipation. We love the gossip, you could probably tell—I suspect you do as well, or you wouldn't have stuck with us for the long haul. Again, if I'd known this was part of the detective thing, I'd have started long ago. Long ago.

"There was a time we were very much in love, Johnny and me. He swept me off my feet, so to speak. Or rather I wrapped him in a gossamer cocoon of my charms. I'm talking about a croquembouche."

"The French wedding cake?" Wendy suggested.

I shot her a suspicious look. Leave it to the Twix

[62] Try it today!

fiend to have an encyclopedic knowledge of international desserts.

"They're my specialty. I surround the cream puffs in a golden nest of spun sugar. Johnny Birch was entranced." She stood up and stepped out of the footbath, pacing the room and speaking with broad extravagant gestures. "It was years ago, but I remember it like yesterday.

"Johnny was a guest at the wedding of Gloria Gaslight, the famous performance artist and her life partner Cuddles, which happened to be a blow-up doll with black electrical tape over its gaping mouth and eyes— also its butthole, but I didn't ask why. The two of us were standing in the back of the hall, me behind the cake in my black beaded flapper dress with the feather trim and my hair up in a blisteringly stylish Mohawk. That's right, it was delicious."

"Sounds like it," I said.

"And Johnny leaning against the wall in his tight little tuxedo pants, making roses grow from the cheap 70s paneling. He plucked one out of the wall and tossed it to me." Tanesha leaned in to whisper, "That's not all he tossed that night."

"See, now I thought Johnny was straight."

"Oh, he was. Most definitely."

"How do you figure, doll? I mean no disrespect, Tanesha. You are a gorgeous and powerful woman, but let's not kid ourselves about—"

"About my candy? Oh honey, I'm not sure if he ever got a good look at it. I'm very good at finding flattering lighting."

"Still," I pressed. "The sex."

"Now Amanda, I don't have to tell you about the three options, now do I?"

"I guess not."

"Besides, Johnny was not what you'd call a gentle lover, he was unskilled labor, despite a healthy roster of conquests, as I'm sure you're aware."

"So how did this affair end? Badly, I'm assuming?" Tanesha crossed her arms, her jaw tightened.

"There was another woman. Greedy and cruel. With an unusual accent. Fat old island woman."

I gasped. "Mama Montserrat?"

Wendy nodded, as if she'd known all along.

"Twisted old bitch wouldn't leave us alone. She'd call at all hours of the night and day. She's a nasty thing with pejohos in her fapuna."

"What?"

"Never mind. But I'll tell you this, even after we separated, she stalked Johnny."

"But she's his agent. The producer of his shows. How could the gossip columns have missed such an odd pairing. It doesn't make any sense."

"It makes sense all right. She had him under her spell and I'm not talking about beguiling him with her sex. She doesn't have that in her. I'm saying she cast out some dark magic and lured him in. Johnny didn't have a chance and in the end, neither did our love." Tanesha crossed the room in three long strides and dropped onto the window seat tragically.

Montserrat's room was identical to ours. A small seat-
ing area was set apart from the bed by a bureau holding
up a pair of crystal lamps, a stuffed mink or ferret leaning up against one. In our room, the space between the
lamps contained a large bowl of fruit—I suspected this
was some sort of joke. Like we could just reach out and
eat a mango. Someone was an asshole. Mama had
something else in that spot.

"Look at this shit right here." I waved Wendy over.
"Get a good shot of this."

The voodoo woman turned the bureau into a makeshift altar to her love. Johnny Birch's photo sat dead
center, surrounded by candles of various lengths, a
wooden bowl with what looked like a raw egg in

tomato sauce—though it totally could have been blood—
a garland of chicken bones and various little statues,
and linen bags tied off with thin cords.

"Crazy." Wendy sang the word, eyes wide with mock
peril.

"Absolutely. But it must have some purpose."

"Well, those are called gris-gris bags. I saw them in a
movie."

"Oh yeah? Which one?" I pressed.

"I don't know, something with Kate Hudson and lots
of humidity."

I skimmed the surface of the altar with my fingertips. They came back red. The belly of her welcome
harp seal was likewise rouged. I went to the door and
knelt down next to a line of the same chalky substance
drawn in front of Mama Montserrat's door.

I rushed to Birch's suite, Wendy hot on my heels.

"What are we looking for?"

"Anything that could help us figure this out. Scott
told me I need to really tear the place apart because
there's bound to be something there. Has to be. If you
totally throw away the idea that the door was locked."

"It's true. That's a big problem. I haven't stopped
thinking that he killed himself. But then you throw in
the envelope and the way he died. It's just too weird."

"Too weird," I repeated. Kneeling on the floor in
front of the open door. "Look."

Wendy knelt next to me the camera focusing in on
another line of the red powder. This one was broken in
two spots, like someone had cut across it with their fingers.

"What do you think it means?"

"Well, it's on both of their thresholds, so either

something that bonds them, or protects them, or binds them, maybe."

"That narrows it down."

I ignored her sarcasm and stepped inside the room, intent on discovering something this time, some for real clue that might lead us to an answer. Mama Montserrat for sure played a part, but why? Why would she kill the star of her show? Didn't make sense.

I rummaged through drawers of underwear and socks. Johnny seemed to be stocking up for the apocalypse. Either that, or he shit himself with regularity. The closet held his clothes, nothing in the pockets. The nightstand didn't even have an alarm clock on it. I scanned through the porn titles.

*Jacked Up 2*, *Double Fisted*, *Frosty Fuckers 5: Ice Orgy*, *Pooper Scooper*. Each movie seemed more perverse than the last. The only thing the films—and I use that term very loosely—had in common were an absence of anything that seemed like normal sex. Not that it was surprising in the slightest that Johnny was into kink. The opposite, in fact. I'd almost half-expected even more disgusting stuff, though the pictures on the scat DVD did make my evening quarry back up into my mouth a bit.

"What are we missing?"

Wendy shook her head. She panned the camera over all the surfaces, before returning to center me in the frame.

I knelt beside the heaps of ash, hesitating a moment before slipping my fingers into the remains. Sure, I'm not the most sensitive sort, but I did know the guy and it seemed weird to disturb his ashes. That said, it kind of reminded me of spa scrub, granular and gritty. Occasionally, I'd come across larger pieces, like finding sea glass in sand. As I ran my fingers through what would have been Johnny's waist, I found a little lump.

Once extracted and brushed off, it was clear that Mama had been involved in the murder. How else could the little thing have survived the fire and completely unmarred? I held it out to Wendy.

"Look what I found."

"A gris-gris," she whispered.

"It's the clencher."

"Now we just have to find her. She was talking about Ether the other night."

A stretch, since everyone was talking about Ether, Ricardo's newest engineering marvel slash night spot, but what were our options, really?


I pulled the cab out the front gate and turned left toward the main artery back into downtown. Thankfully the rain stopped its torrent and the radio was blissfully silent. Baljeet's final curse, may have been just that. One could hope.

"Um, Amanda?" Wendy asked, not looking away from the screen on her iPhone.

"Yes?"

"Who are those guys in the backseat?"

I glimpsed their reflections in the rearview mirror, one straightening his tie hopefully, the other digging in his nose for some spectral booger. "I'm calling them Lumpy and Pie-hole."

"Those aren't our names," Lumpy grunted.

Wendy just nodded, her interest transferred to the image on her little screen. "Abuelita's opening the box!"

"Ooh." I'm not saying I'm a bad driver, but I did watch the entire scene unfold. I'm a talented multitasker, in case you weren't aware.

The two ghosts pushed through the back of the seat to get a better look, faces nestling in next to Wendy's cheeks. Her blond pigtails hung into the center of their transparent skulls like handles on a bizarre pair of Harijuku girl handbags. Lumpy and Pie-hole's eyes narrowed with interest, then confusion.

"What the hell is she doing?" Wendy enlarged the image as much as she could.

The bead stringer sat on the couch, pensively pulling what looked like a metal paint can from the UPS box. She sat it on the coffee table and disposed of the box, returning with a soupspoon and prying open the tin lid. Abuelita chewed her nails and stared into the opening, sinking back onto the couch. It seemed to be emitting a pulsing glow.

"Wha's in there, an asteroid?" Pie-hole mimicked the immigrant's nervous habit and stuck his phantom nails between his equally ineffective teeth.

She leaned over the can, held the spoon like a prison shank and stabbed it inside, withdrawing a massive glob of glowing white paste and plopping it into her mouth. There were a couple of close calls where Abuelita seemed to be heaving, but ultimately she choked down the mouthful.

"It's like toothpaste, or something."

"I think it's gravy."

"Nah," I said. "Too thick."

She dropped the spoon on the table and leaned back on the couch, rubbing her stomach, kneading at it like dough. Her movements slowed until, finally, her head rocked to the side, her mouth open and drooling.

"Okay, that was weird," I said, returning my attention to the road.

Where Ranier Avenue escapes the sea of crack houses, whores working out of shadowy bus shelters and gang-infested Vietnamese billiard halls and turns into Boren Avenue, an equally shady area of public housing and under maintained rentals, I started noticing the headlights of a car, weaving into oncoming traffic and then darting back into the lane behind me.

As we crossed the intersection, the car revved up beside me, the passenger window descended and the driver—a middle-aged Indian woman, bendi maniacally applied above her right eyebrow and mouth slashed into a growl—shook her fist in my direction.

"I lojacked you, bitch!" she shouted as I rolled down the cab's window.

"Oh shit!" Lumpy and Pie-hole screamed in unison.

"Baljeet?" The name shook loose from my lips like a sob.

"Damn right, you white devil. I told you Baljeet's coming to kill you. You misunderestimate Baljeet." She lifted a long curved machete, fatter at the tip than the rest of the blade. To accentuate her threat, the psychotic dispatcher twisted her wheel and slammed her car into the side of ours.

The impact sent my hip colliding with the doorframe—yep, that hip. I heard it pop before I lost balance in my hips. Clinging to the steering wheel, I hit the gas and pressed past Baljeet's swerving deathmobile, Wendy and the boys screaming in terror like virgins at a sacrifice—not that any of them would have to worry about that.[63]

---

[63] Well maybe Pie-hole.

Baljeet escalated and as we rounded Madison, she slammed into the back bumper. The cab spun in the intersection, my leg ground in the socket. Pain sluiced straight up my spine and I screamed, more than a little bit.

I regained my sense of surroundings to the tune of Wendy yelling, "Go! Go! Go!"

Baljeet's car barreled toward us, the woman ranting madly inside as though we could hear her. I floored the accelerator and we barreled over Capitol Hill, toward the freeway overpass. The two ghosts faced out the back window.

"Is she still coming?" I asked.

The cars and buildings were blurring around us. I looked down at the speedometer and hit the brake. Sixty downtown was a death wish. Baljeet's car clipped us as she sped past to prove my point—the car shimmied as paint and metal grated. The other cab swerved a bit, and I thought she might just ease past the garbage truck idling at the stoplight. But without braking at all, Baljeet plowed into the mass of steel at full speed. The cab collapsed on itself. Glass shattered across the street in all directions and the cab's trunk drove straight through to the engine, coming to rest underneath the hulking truck's bumper. The top of the cab crimped like a used soda can.

"Holy crap. Look at that, would ya?" Lumpy slipped through the front seat and onto the hood of the taxi. "Cut her right in two."

I inched forward. Lumpy was right. Baljeet's torso, severed just below the breastbone, jettisoned through the windshield and slid down the closed bin of the truck, arms twitching and leaving a brownish smear.

The ghosts didn't take the presence of viscera well

at all. Pie-hole hung out the window, spewing great big mouthfuls of ectoplasm onto the street. Lumpy moaned and covered his eyes, threatening to puke himself.

I glanced over at Wendy, who simply shrugged and went back to her surveillance of Abuelita.

"I guess I don't have to worry about Baljeet anymore." Nor did she look particularly appetizing amidst the Hefty bags, though you probably weren't interested in hearing that.[64] There is something to be said about presentation—you eat with your eyes, after all.

I wriggled my pelvis around and somewhere in the melee, my leg popped back into place, thank God. Still it was sore as fuck. I dreaded the inevitable limp, made all the more obvious when amplified by a pair of peek-toe stilettos.

"I'm gonna need a little help when we get out at Ether," I said.

"Why, did you poop yourself?"

Pie-hole and Lumpy let loose with an explosion of laughter, the dwarf sniffing the air and the other holding his nose dramatically, each laughing riotously at the other's mockery.

"No. I didn't poop myself; that's your modus operandi. I just have a little issue with my hip."

Ether filled an empty space between new construction on 1st Avenue. On the left, some high-end boutique hotel sat atop a churrascaria, on the right, shops with clearance signs in the windows instead of merchandise held up a new—and completely unoccupied—condo complex.

---

[64] Sorry. But if you are primarily interested in the thoughts of vampires or werewolves, I'm sure your local bookseller could hook your ass up.

When I say *empty space,* I mean it.

Ricardo enlisted the help of some psychotic banshee architect to design the place, a tribute to the club owner's love of breezy minimalism, modern furniture and the shoegazing music of the 90s. Ether was neither visible, nor accessible to anyone, not without a guide. The bouncer, as it were, lounged on a bench tapping fat ashes directly into a smoldering trashcan, smoke drifting from it in thin curls of accusation. A crumpled fedora cast a mysterious shadow, hanging like a veil to a spot just past his nose. He wore a long wool coat, wrapped around him like a robe, and his legs were casually crossed at the ankle.

Wendy helped me hobble over.

"Are you the guy?" I asked.

The cigar shifted from one side of his mouth to the other. "The guy?" The man's voice was as graveled and pained as bare feet on aggregate. He sniffed in our direction. "Somethin' smells wrong."

A growl muffled inside Wendy.

"Of course that ain't the guy!" An androgynous creature in an odd combination of hotpants and combat boots sashayed in from a darkened alley. A moment later, a businessman squirreled his way out of the same place, buttoning up his shirt, head darting side to side pathetically. "I'm the guy, dolls!"

The fairy—I'm making an assumption here, based on both his highly effete aura, and slight elfish nature—flopped down next to the gruff gentleman like a rag doll, draping his arm around the other's shoulders congenially. "The name's Max, but I go by Maxey." The man struggled to pull away, a look of disgust revealed as his fedora fell.

Maxey giggled at his response, reached over and

flicked his ear like you would your little brother. I expected some sort of violent retaliation. After all, if someone flicked my ear, I'd at the very least sock them in the head—after I picked up my ear and forced Wendy to glue it back on, of course.[65] Instead, his face sagged and his body went slack like the flick sent a stream of heroin straight to his brain.

"That's better." He lifted his hips and slipped one of his legs underneath him in a single hop. "Grumpy can just sit there and think about his mean behavior, while we talk about fun stuff."

"Like Ether?"

"Exactly like Ether. What could be more fun to talk about. Have you been? Oh my God, it's so awesome. And the cover's only twenty-five bucks each, can you believe it?"

I turned to Wendy and blinked innocently.

"Don't look at me," she said and pointed the camera at me. "I'm the crew. Remember?"

"Here's the thing, Maxey."

"Mmm-hmm." He clasped his hands and brought both index fingers to a point, playing with his lower lip while he listened.

"We're filming segments for the new Johnny Birch reality show and I'm certain Ricardo would just adore having Ether featured. Plus, we know him really well. He even created this fabulous zombie you see here." I gestured to Wendy, who did a quick pose, twirling a pigtail like she was winding up a clockwork.

"Gorgeousness!" He clapped his hands rapidly then stopped short. "But I'm still gonna need a fitty to take you in. It's my fee."

[65] Damn decomposition!

"Isn't there a password or something we can try for?" Wendy pouted.

"You could try, but since there isn't one, it would really just be for my entertainment."

I slipped onto the bench next to him. "What if I could offer you a guarantee that you'd be on TV?"

Maxey's face brightened, and I do mean actually glowed. "Keep talkin'."

"We could film the entire exchange once we're inside. You take us to Ricardo and we all talk about what a sensation you are."

"Okay. But I'm still gonna need my fifty dollars."

"What if we owed you?" Wendy asked.

"Are you serious?" He grinned. "You want to be beholden to me?" He shrugged. "Okay, let's do this."

Maxey bounded from his spot between the grump and me and reached out his hand to Wendy. "Just say, I'm beholden to you and we'll be good as gold."

The blonde frowned then, looked at his delicately constructed hand like it might hold a trick buzzer, then to me. I heaved my shoulders, probably not the best person to seek advice from, since I only cared about getting in. She took his hand and spoke the words.

A visible shiver passed over the fairy's frame and he chuckled like Wendy just let loose with an inappropriate joke. He skipped a short distance away and planted his hands on his hips. "Well. Come on then."

Maxey flitted to a nearby concrete planter—despite his
lack of wings, his ability to rock some airtime was
quite impressive—and motioned for us to follow.
Wendy boosted me up and stuck close as we balanced
the thin ledge behind the fairy, his hips swiveling care-
lessly as a hula skirt.[66]

The gap between the buildings gave way to steep
stairs carved into the hillside and running at least a
hundred feet down to Western Avenue, where most of
the supernatural clubs hid amidst the warehouses of
home furnishing stores. I held on to a maple branch, as

---

[66] This might be a good time to discuss the word fairy. I've seen it
written in a number of ways, fae, faerie, faery, even phaer-e (but
that was the name of an alternative band that ended up joining a religious cult in Venezuela or somewhere).

we peered out over the Seattle harbor. A massive cruise ship churned in the distance.

"So where is it?" I asked.

Maxey pointed toward the horizon. He squinted a bit and our eyes followed his. "See that?"

Literally, it was a dot of light, as difficult to find as a white guy at a Blood or Crip function.

"What are we looking at, exactly?" Wendy asked.

"That's the keyhole."

I looked at Wendy, who was clearly as confused as I. "So . . ."

"Yeah, yeah," Maxey said. "It just looks far. That's why you need a guide to get to it. Can't just put out a doormat for any Tom, Dick or Normal to wander through, now can we. Besides, if not for this, where would I get to use my fantastic people skills?"

"Well, there is your side job." I tossed a thumb at the alley where we'd first seen Maxey appear.

"Oh, that." He snickered. "I don't think of it as work."

Wendy and I just stared.

"Now just follow me and watch your feet. There's a walkway here, you just can't see it and it changes weekly so don't think you can just walk on in for free next time. Got it?"

Maxey stepped off the concrete and onto either some really clean glass or a bridge of some sort. His steps were measured and accompanied by a verbal count. We shuffled behind him.

"Try not to look down," I suggested to Wendy, who glanced back thoroughly unconcerned.

Sure. I might have been projecting a little, but you try traversing an invisible bridge in the middle of the night with a bum leg and see how you do.

A couple of sidesteps and a near-fall and we all but fell into Ether.

The door swung open into a wide arcing hall filled with the usual suspects of the club scene, like Gretchen de Bellefour in a fur they must have stripped off a mammoth to cloak her in—the reapers have their magic, but they can't change eating habits.

Ricardo stood at his usual spot, behind the bar, shining glasses and smiling like he knew the person on the other side. Ricardo Amandine was good at making people feel comfortable, a compelling trait in a bartender and a deadly one in a flesh-eating zombie. He waved us over.

I shifted my weight to Maxey, and motioned for Wendy to get to taping. I waited for the little red light before heading over.

"Ready for your close-up?" I whispered to the fairy, who blushed a bit, more out of excitement than any nervousness, I imagined.

"Mr. Amandine. These, um . . . ladies, have some questions or something." Maxey's delivery was stiff, measured, like he'd been rehearsing it in his head during the walk.

"Thank you, Maxey. I'll take them from here."

The fairy bowed a little, winked at Wendy and then swished off toward the dance floor, where people moped to the sounds of My Bloody Valentine and could quite possibly commit suicide at any moment. To call it music was an exaggeration—the vibrating and/or swirling guitar strains and muted vocal gibberish were best suited to shifting your weight and hanging your head in shame than to anything resembling real dancing. Why Ricardo enjoyed the music was beyond me. At least he'd given the brooding dancers something to look at while they

### *Soundtrack for Mopey Potheads*

*(Shoegazing at Ether)*

*Lali Puna• "Left Handed"*
*My Bloody Valentine • "Only Shallow"*
*The High Violets • "Chinese Letter"*
*Lush • "Undertow"*
*Cocteau Twins • "Orange Appled"*
*Slowdive • "Souvlaki Space Station"*
*Silversun Pickups • "Rusted Wheel"*
*Chapterhouse • "Pearl"*
*Swervedriver • "Duel"*
*Loop • "Breathe Into Me"*
*Jesus and Mary Chain • "Just Like Honey"*
*The Raveonettes • "Aly, Walk With Me"*

shambled like a horde of mistakes fresh from death—the floor was made of Lucite, clear as day—or night—and hovering, unbelievably, hundreds of feet over Western Avenue. The perfect vantage point to watch zombies, vampires, werewolves, hell, even, lizard people if you watch long enough, spill out of clubs like the Well of Souls and Convent and onto the street, falling down drunk or looking for some swollen shadow to plow a conquest.

"Are you loving the place?"

I took a moment to scan the predominantly white room. It had a Grecian feel—blessedly lacking the pretentiousness of columns—white, but not in a glossy, new-house kind of way. It was as though every surface was smudged with a lack of color, dusted in a light powder. Even the couches and chairs were barely delineated, edges fuzzy as peaches. Panels of sheer fabric drifted inward from arched windows, undulating gossamer tents beneath a cloud of ceiling that could have actually been clouds for all my understanding of the place.

It really is fantastic, Ricardo. You've outdone yourself, though—"

"Though?" he asked, concern arcing his dark brow and sliding a Hendricks in front of me.

I sipped at it, stirred the concoction with a thin polished bone. "Where is everybody? Your clubs are normally packed at this hour."

A fat smile spread across those fit lips.

I'll take a moment here to admire the majesty that is Ricardo, the only zombie I know able to maintain a naturally blemish-free olive complexion seemingly without several layers of makeup. Crotch achingly hot, the entrepreneur is at the top of his game and stalked by nearly every female he comes into contact with (and several males). Wendy drools for the guy—I'd certainly give him a go, if it weren't for Scott—but he somehow allowed himself to be ensnared by Marithé, whose intentions were about as wholesome as a Tijuana donkey show. I happen to know—and this is totally between us—that my assistant, Ricardo's loving partner, talked him into an experimental virility treatment at great cost, physically and financially.[67]

"The vast majority of the guests are otherwise preoccupied in the anesthesia lounges."

The gin blew out of my nose like liquid fire. "Anesthesia?" I managed, glancing at Wendy, who, of course, nailed that shot at what would prove to be the most unflattering angle imaginable.

Bitch.

"It's the latest in supernatural party favors—when alcohol just won't get you there. When was the last time you even caught a buzz, Amanda?"

I drained the gin and set the glass on the bar. "Long time, lover. Are you telling me, you've got some gas that'll reach beyond the grave up in here?"

"Oh, hell yeah. Good stuff, too. I even have to have it professionally administered."

My heart would have skipped a beat. As it was my stomach clinched up tighter than a clergy coffer, or an altar boy's ass, for that matter.[68] It was the word "administered" that frightened me, sounding very much like a job for a certain evil Girl Scout troop. I started looking for the exit.

"Relax." Ricardo sensed my fear somehow. I didn't have to think on it very long to figure out Marithé had some loose lips when it came to our relationship (probably hers with Ricardo too, but that's not what I'm talking about). "I had to contract some people to watch the amounts. Apparently, abovegrounders have a tendency

---

[67] But you didn't hear that from me.
[68] Might as well. I mean, as long I'm stickin' it to the Catlickers. That's "Catholics" for you slow fuckers. Note to self, send memoirs to the Moral Majority.

to lose consciousness . . . permanently, if they take too much."

"Jesus," Wendy whispered.

"We've got it under control. Now it's just an easy comfortable trip."

Back to the situation at hand—there was no telling how long the camera battery would last[69]—I said, "Is one of tonight's trippers a certain zaftig Jamaican voodoo woman?"

"Mama Montserrat? Of course! She loves a little hit. Been coming religiously since we opened. Made us a little protection charm. Very sweet. She gets our mildest dose, being technically human and all."

I told him about the murder and to keep it quiet for now. Ricardo, luckily, could be trusted to keep his mouth shut. I suspected the news wouldn't even reach Marithé.

We followed Ricardo from room to room—the place was cavernous—scanning the intoxicated faces of both wealthy and influential figures of supernatural society. Ricardo led us to one on the right. Inside, Mama Montserrat reclined in a state of drizzled intoxication, her head lolling atop a thick fold of chin fat wrangled loose from the neck of her sweater, revealing a small tattoo of a rooster like a label on her fleshy travel pillow. A thin stream of spit stretched to a wet spot on her shoulder.

Ricardo knelt beside the prone figure and shook her gently by the shoulder, while he dabbed the corner of her mouth with a tissue. "Mama? Mama? It's time to wake up."

[69] Does anyone ever know?

She groaned, her eyes creeping open over a lopsided grin. "Nom?"

"No. We don't have any food." I took Ricardo's place and motioned for Wendy to get a close up. "We're here to ask you questions about you and Johnny."

"Dad," she muttered, her lids fluttering.

"He was your father?" Wendy gasped.

I spun so she could see me rolling my eyes.[70] "She said 'dead,' not 'dad.' Jesus." I turned back to Mama, pressed the back of my hand against her cheek. "We just need to know about your relationship with Johnny."

She batted her eyes.

"Your *sexual* relationship with Johnny."

"Noneya." She slapped at my hand. "Cold," she spat, pouting.

Wendy nudged me. "She's so wasted. You should ask her the big question. Quick. Before she comes out of it."

"Or maybe we could just order up another round, or twilight dose, or whatever. Right, Ricardo?"

Ricardo smiled, dropped onto the lounge and settling into a casual slouch. "That's funny."

"What is?" Over my shoulder, Wendy had a needy looking snarl plastered on her mouth, like she'd bite into the guy if she got another chance.[71]

"Twilight *is* what it's called, because it's kind of light and ineffectual, perfect for the undecided and easily swayed. Pretty benign stuff, though, I'm not going

---

[70] 'Cause, really. What's the point of it, if no one knows your judging. It's like that saying, if a tree falls in the woods and no one's there to hear it, does it even judge?

[71] But that's a story for another time.

to test a second dose, just in case it has an adverse reaction, so you better ask your questions quick."

Mama eyed me curiously, a lazy finger stretching toward my cheek when I looked back at her. "Cheek," she said poking.

I pulled away. "Now Mama. You didn't kill Johnny did you?"

"What?"

"Did you kill Johnny?"

"Course not. Ask that bitch."

"What?"

"The bitch he been fuckin'."

"Who?"

Mama's head lolled on her shoulders, drifting out of consciousness. "Hairy!" she barked and then she was gone.

I looked into the camera. "Hairy, ladies and gentlemen. I think we all know who she's just fingered."

Wendy giggled, followed shortly thereafter by the unfettered guffaws of Ricardo. He pointed at me and then to my cheek.

"Oh shit," I said. "There's a dent, isn't there?"


As we arrived back at the Minions Mansion, a brawl of epically coiffed proportions spilled into the grand hall from, presumably, the bar, as so many brawls do. Of course, the nature of the melee was far more dangerous than a paltry busted bottle fight outside your local dive. I mean, it's not like a flying Filipino vampire head shows up because some jerk insults your friend. Just doesn't happen.

At the center of the dispute stood a haggard Hairy

Sue, her usually stringy hair a matted ball atop her pale head. She spun around, fending off aerial attacks from the disgustingly tentacled Angie, her intestines spattering the floor like a maniacal, and decidedly monochrome, Jackson Pollock, and ground assaults from Absinthe, her jaw snapping with the conviction. The stripper held the ghoul at bay with a garbage can lid she wielded like a shield.

Maiko slunk in from the main hallway, her little badgers quarreling around her heels. She nodded to us and yawned.

"They've been at it ever since we found them." Tanesha descended the stairs regally in skinny jeans and a purple peasant blouse, arms dripping in gold bangles.

"Found who?" I asked.

"You two better follow me and keep that camera rollin'—you're not gonna wanna miss a second of this."

"Well, that got my attention."

As we were heading up the stairs, I glanced at Wendy just as she recoiled in horror from an image playing out between the girls below. I spun toward the scene, but nothing seemed overly frightening or shocking.

"What?" I asked her.

"Hairy Sue," she said. "She sort of, well . . ." Wendy blew air into her cheeks and spread her arms as though she were growing. "Puffed up. Swelled."

I looked back. Absinthe had joined Maiko, chatting quietly at her, since the Asian beauty was busy just then sneering. Angie was nowhere to be seen, presumably floating back to the empty husk of her body. Hairy

Sue backed away toward the now-busted dais, holding a torn scrap of fabric over her breasts—surely more covering than she was used to five nights a week, so the need for modesty seemed a tad dramatic.

"What do you mean, swelled?" I asked as we passed into the hall toward Johnny's suite, dry dead vines crunching beneath us.

"I mean she got big. Just puffed out everywhere. Like a monster."

"Well, swelled sounds like an erection."

"Ahem." Tanesha stood in front of the scene of the crime, one hand on her hip, the other on the knob, lips pursed in frustration. "Are you two even remotely interested in this?"

I nodded, scolding Wendy with a stern finger.

Tanesha pushed open the door and stepped back.

At first glance, I thought Janice and Eunice were passed out drunk, splayed out on the oriental carpet like a pair of broken dolls—ones that split a bottle of expensive scotch and enjoyed sticking bows on their foreheads. After all, it wouldn't be the first time. In fact, I wondered if I'd ever seen the two of them sober. But their flat dry eyes and the blood crusting their mouths gave away the reality.

Dead.

Poisoned, by the look of their mouths and, from the battle waged downstairs, I guessed probably not from the alcohol. Or not *just* from the alcohol.

What the hell is going on? First Johnny gets burnt alive and now the sirens drink themselves into a literal oblivion. How could *that* be connected? It didn't make any sense. Well, killing Johnny makes sense on a purely practical level, of course. I mean, one less asshole in the world is a blessing no matter how you slice it. I'm sure Hairy Sue had good cause. But a pair of mute sirens with really bad pool hair?

"What kind of madman kills the disabled?" I said.

Tanesha clicked her tongue. "The girls are certain it was Sue."

"I'm not convinced. You?"

"All I know, is you gotta be a crazy bitch to do your bad business in private. If I'm after you, people gonna know it. I'll do you out in the open. Quick." She swiped her claws through the air with a whistle.

"But you were brought up right," I noted.

"Mmm-hmm. Someone here ain't been, tho.[72]"

---

[72] I suspect that's the correct spelling in this context.

"House meeting, bitches!" I screamed, stomping down
the stairs like I was heading for the catwalk—I made a
quick stop to change because confrontations are best
done in green Alexander McQueen dresses.[73]

Maiko and Angie sat on the bottom riser, glowering
at beer-swilling Absinthe, who didn't get the memo
about green and opted for a "Belgians do it better with
Frites" muscle tee—whatever that means—and torn
jeans. To give her credit, she had spiked her T.L.D. with
some actual product this time.[74] So kudos.

---

[73] Shut up.
[74] T.L.D.: Traditional Lesbian 'Do, as in, short for hairdo. Keep up,
please.

Wendy rushed past to get the shot from a better angle.

"So I've just seen the bodies and while I can't lie and say I was fond of either of them, I'm fairly certain I didn't kill them."

Wendy coughed from behind the camera.

I nodded. "Wendy either. We're kind of members of the clean plate club. So." I spun around dramatically. "Why do you suspect Hairy Sue?" I scanned the room. "And where has she gotten off to, now?"

"She darted while you were making wit ze love . . . avec le caméra vidéo," the Belgian ghoul slurred.

"She took her bags, too," Angie added.

"Fleeing the scene of the crime, huh?" I paced the grand hall. "That doesn't look good."

Maiko stepped forward, her perfect black hair cascading off her shoulder in midnight waves, "It's just like in Moriko Harikama's *Glass Tower Shoebox*."

"What the hell's that?" Wendy asked.

"A movie, of course. In it, Hoku Yabukawa, the very handsome and muscular actor, plays a man who finds the body of a yakuza assassin and instead of reporting it to the authorities, he covers his presence at the scene and sneaks out. Only there's a witness to his cowardice, the gorgeous Akiko who reports his actions not to the police, but to the mafia."

"What does that have to do with Janice and Eunice?"

She shrugged, pointing to Angie. "Angie saw her leave Johnny's room right before we found the twins."

"It's true. I saw her leaving that room. Rushing away is how I'd describe." Angie crossed her arms. "Plus she doesn't have mani/pedi. I can't trust a person that doesn't respect nail hygiene."

All but Absinthe nodded. Angie's silent scrutiny swung to the Belgian's hands and feet.

"I sink it's just like zat Hercule Poirot movie, *Murder on ze Orient Express*." It was just like a Belgian to toss the British author under the bus. "You all did it. Took turns stabbing ze bitches."

"They were poisoned," I interrupted, but then something dawned on me. I stalked to the center of the room. "The ribbons," I said.

Wendy spun around me in a wide arc. "I'm going for arty drama. Keep going."

"I'd seen that bottle of scotch before on Johnny's bureau. He hadn't even opened it and it was covered in ribbons. I contemplated taking it, myself. A gift! You know what this means?" I asked the remaining contestants.

Tanesha stepped forward. "That Johnny was the target, not those garble-voiced bitches. Their death was an accident!"

"That doesn't clear Hairy Sue." Angie snarled, head jarring to the side as though it could fly off at any second. And no one wanted to see that again, least of all me.

"No, it doesn't. Nor any of you," I said and winked for the camera, but my zeal was short lived.

"Or you," Maiko added. "Or little friend. I don't trust zombie."

Angie silently nodded her agreement, eying Absinthe.

"Absinthe. Let's go somewhere and talk. Get to the bottom of things. And before you start looking smug, Angie, know that you're next."

The nail tech mugged defiantly.

* * *

Absinthe's room was blessedly free of Belgian paraphernalia, not that I'd know what that was exactly. She had added a rainbow triangle throw pillow to her bed, which, while being very festive and out, is never an attractive decorating accessory.[75] Neither was the stuffed anteater perched on her bureau—Johnny's gift-giving was pretty random.

The butch ghoul dumped herself onto the loveseat.

I took the chair opposite. "Okay. Let's start with how you felt about our deceased host."

"Did you say 'diseased' host?"

"That too—how'd you feel about Johnny Birch?"

"He was a pig. I hated ze way he treated ze women on his show. Like cattle. Like farm animal. But, zis was a paycheck, no?"

"So you didn't come here to kill the bastard?" I figured it was best to get right to the agitation cycle, how else do you get someone to come clean? "Because, I heard you did?"

The ghoul didn't flinch or even glance away. "No. It's not true. I need ze money, zis is all."

"Okay. Say I believe you, perhaps you've seen something here that could help in my investigation?"

"Well." Absinthe leaned back on the couch, exposing two pits so fluffy with hair, you'd think she was smuggling rabbits under there. I nearly heaved.

Can we take a moment and discuss body hair?

---

[75] A note for my gays: please limit your pride accessories to rainbow windsocks and a single modest car sticker. Those stick figure families with my two dads? Those are like zombie menus, you don't get a free out from death, just because you're marginalized. Sorry.

I know quite a few razor-free lesbians, Europeans, and Seattle has its share of the hippie crowd. I've been known to be in the presence of men, as you know. But seriously, I can't handle looking at a huge hairy armpit. Even Hairy Sue's shocking pubic puff doesn't compare. It's about the dewy sweat that makes it glisten. It's a body odor issue and though you may enjoy funk, don't expect the rest of us to revel in your freedom to be natural.

I decided to keep the sermon inside and gulped. "Well?"

"Yes. I witness a blond man leaving ze house while I was outside smoking my Gitanes."

"When was this?" I wished I'd thought to bring a notepad.

"It was after we all left ze bar. He came from around ze side of ze house where ze garden is."

I thought back to the argument I heard from the balcony. Johnny and another man. Could this have been the same guy? It seems likely. The timing was right. "What did he look like exactly?"

"Well, it was dark, but I could tell he was tall and, how you say, willowy?"

"Willowy?"

"Yes."

"Anything else you can think of?"

She shook her head. "I can zink of ozer zings." Absinthe planted a determined eye up at the camera and Wendy. "Lots of ozer zings."

Wendy dropped the camera to her side. "We're done here."


*   *   *

"I didn't see anything. I was doing my nails," Angie said.

"You were doing your nails for the past three days?" I asked.

"Look." She pressed her pinkies together and lined up each of her intricately painted nails to reveal a completed image. Da Vinci's *The Last Supper* rendered on a canvas of acrylic tips. The job was masterful, the dips and valleys across the nails had been corrected through clever perspective and Jesus' eyes were tiny little crystals.

"Brilliant," I said. Thinking that kind of detail was alibi enough, we left the Filipino vamp to apply another layer of clear coat. Never say I don't promote the arts.

Wendy rapped her knuckles softly on Maiko's door and immediately jumped to the side as though expecting a shotgun blast.

"Jesus, Wendy, this isn't an episode of *Cops*." I stepped up and hammered.

She shrugged, fiddling with the camera.

"You need to put that focus on automatic, I don't trust your eye."

"What? I have a great eye."

My eyes trailed down to Wendy's outfit. I could see her inspiration was firmly rooted in the 70s, but if you're going to pay homage to that decade, do it with satin dancing pants, not super-short exercise shorts, knee-high striped sweat socks and high-heeled tennis shoes.

"That's never gonna be a look again, girl," I said.

When I got back to her mouth it was screwed up as tight as—you guessed it—a cat's anus.[76] Her eyes were giving off that tried and true purveyor of seething anger: Stank.

The beautiful Asian opened the door in a shimmery kimono, obsidian koi swam against a current of aubergine, filigreed as a Van Gogh sky, the only thing identifying her as anything other than human were the swirling trails of smoke that lagged behind the movement of her hands, her footsteps. Her dark hair piled up loosely and smoke curled from her blood-red lips, though she held no cigarette, cigar or joint. Her mouth was like a smoking gun, I thought, and made a mental note, with more than a little pride.

"Maiko," I said.

"Yes? That's my name, as you know."

"We're here to ask some questions."

"I'm aware of that. You announced it downstairs." Her tone was all business. She swept an arm toward her sitting area. She snapped her fingers and one of the creatures she called Tanuki shifted into a black teakettle, and the other lugged it away to the attached bath. A moment later, the sounds of water running drifted from the open door.

"I hope that's not for us."

"Of course not, I'm not an idiot. I can't offer you a mutsuki.[77]"

---

[76] An expression Wendy's been perfecting for as long as I've known her.

[77] Mutsuki: a Japanese diaper. I only know this because, I refused to call them diapers on the few occasions I'd surfed the brown waves of food intake. The word I chose, mutsuki.

I giggled a bit.

"I'll tell you that I had nothing to do with Johnny Birch's death. How could I? My intention was to win this competition, and I would have, and protected the wood nymph full-time. It doesn't make sense that I'd be suspected."

"What did you think of Mr. Birch?"

"I thought very little about him at all. He's a job." The tanuki kettle whistled from the bathroom, followed shortly thereafter by the other badger-like creature's return carrying a small porcelain cup.

Wendy's fearful gaze glazed with boredom.

"Arigato gozaimasu Tanukisan." She sipped at her tea. "What I know is this. At about one in morning I hear doorbell ring. I go to the balcony, overlooking hall and see Hairy Sue accept an envelope, from whom I do not know. I could not see delivery person."

Maiko took another sip and set the cup down on her bureau, next to another badger, this one stuffed. Without turning around to face us, she continued, "She then took envelope to Birch's room."

"So." I stood, Wendy following suit. "That is totally helpful, Maiko. Do you remember anything else?"

"No. Nothing. Goodbye." She bowed, excusing us and retreating to her bath.

"I guess we're done here," I said.

"I guess," Wendy muttered. "Kind of a bitch."

Maiko coughed loudly.


Back in our suite, I made a clandestine phone call.

"H & C Gentleman's Club." The voice was uncharacteristically gracious.

"This is Detective Marshall," I growled, having been dreading the call from the moment it came to me. The only two people I knew having actual history with the stripper were her employer and the bouncer at the club. Too bad Gil's phone was off. He never could remember to charge the battery.

"Ah, Amanda. Lovely to hear from you, your calls are so dear to me." She paused and then added, "Also infrequent."

A chill ran through me. I dropped the fake accent. "Mother, I need to know some things about Hairy Sue."

"Darling. I can't very well reveal personal information about one of my employees. What kind of a person do you think I am?"

"I'm going to assume that's a rhetorical question and get to the gist of this, okay?"

"Fine with me."

"Johnny Birch has been murdered and there's reason to believe Hairy Sue may have been the culprit or at least knows who did it."

"Hmm. That is upsetting. She's one of my best girls, you know?"

"I do. That's why I've opted to leave the reapers out of this little situation."

"Why, that is kind of you." There was an underlying tension in Ethel's voice. I was certain she was holding something back. Not about her dancer, but about me. Gil must have confided in her. Damn it.

"I'm trying to be civil here, for the sake of finding out who killed this guy. You're going to help me, right?"

"Of course, I'll help my only daughter."

We were both silent a moment. Her response was

loaded with what sounded like regret, which if you're not familiar with it, sounds a bit like drifting into a memory. Either way, it's not good and you know it. Particularly in regard to our relationship.

*Must not respond*, I told myself.

Ethel started speaking without further prompting. "Hairy Sue hasn't been here for a few days. I expected her to dance tonight. She called in earlier and said she'd be coming by for her paycheck and I believe to make a little extra cash. Tips and such."

On the word "such" my mind flashed to the back room. I imagined Sue could make a pretty penny grinding that bush on some pervert's leg, being a unique and oddly desirable commodity and all.

"Have there ever been any scenes between her and Birch?"

"He was a client, I believe."

"Just a client?"

"Well . . . no. I suspected a relationship of some sort. She was always spending time with him at his table, without getting him to order drinks and . . ."

"And?"

"And he didn't tip. That's the giveaway."

"Do you know anything else about her, specifically?"

"She comes from a little town in the mountains. Sky-komish, up near Steven's Pass. Pretty isolated, amidst the forest and all."

"Thank you, Mother. That's been very helpful."

"Well, you know I aim to pl—"

I clicked off. Woodland creatures. Could that be the real relationship between the two? Both of them nymphs?

"Hey." I turned to Wendy. "Do you know where Birch was from? Like where he grew up?"

"Of course. I do my research." She pulled out a little notepad and flipped through the pages, lighting on the correct one with a grin. "Skykomish."

"Well I'll be damned. I think Hairy Sue and Johnny Birch are kissin' cousins."

"Gross."

I made a couple more phone calls, the first to Scott to
keep him updated—and me on his mind—and the second to Ricardo. Mama Montserrat was lucid and on
her way back to the mansion in a cab. I figured it would
be important to keep track of all the players, since
three of them were already dead. Also, we totally forgot to ask Mama about the gris-gris bag.

"Well, there's nothing we can do about Hairy Sue
just yet. Since we have no clue where she is. But we
can certainly take a look around here and see if some
poison turns up."

"Good idea. But first." Wendy pulled out her iPhone

and connected to her camera. A moment later she yelled, "Whoa!"

"Jesus, what?" I ran to her side.

The image was certainly unsettling. Wendy's apartment was the scene of a rather large gathering of vampires, fangs exposed and circling Abuelita like a bunch of pilgrims at Mecca. They tightened their proximity, brushing against her with bare arms and then sloughing away so their friends could push in and do the same. Others, the taller vamps, reached across the heads of those nearest to brush her cheek with a gentle hand.

"What the fuck?" Wendy's mouth dropped open.

"Seriously," I agreed.

The crowd diminished as vampires left the circle to lean dreamily against walls or simply slide down them to loll on the carpet. One particularly amorous bloodsucker took to rubbing his face in the bead stringer's exposed cleavage. He came away dazed and stumbling, his eyes black as tar.

"Cloud."

"What?" Wendy asked.

"I think it might be some kind of cloud party."

"The drug? But they usually just put it on from a tube."

"It might be something new. She was eating all that paste earlier. Remember?"

"How could I forget?"

"They pretty much look the same as a cloudhead. It just goes to reason."

"Ugh." Wendy clicked out of the image and tossed her phone onto the bed. "I'm pretty sure I didn't need to see that ever." She dropped onto the bed, face first.

"It's not so bad. At least she's making friends."

Wendy held her face and kicked her feet a bit.

Speaking of controlled substances got me thinking about poison. Whether Hairy Sue was Birch's murderer or lover or cousin, or all of the above, didn't change the fact that someone different had killed the siren sisters. The methods were too different.

Johnny's burnt body was the biggest clue to that fact. A body scorched down to ash and bone meal? The fire would have to have been blistering, yet nothing else in the room was charred. There wasn't even enough smoke to set off the detectors.

There's only one thing that can be responsible for that.

Magic.

Not that I know a ton about the dark stuff, but enough to know that there's a big difference between someone who can pull off a trick like that and one who'll taint a good scotch with rat poison or whatever.

Absinthe, Maiko and Angie didn't have any real motive. I didn't do it. For Wendy's purposes Birch needed to have at least a little life left in him. So that left Mama Montserrat and Hairy Sue. One lover spurned, the other a secret.

"How about you stay here and figure this out, while I do a little looking around?" I picked up the camera. Wendy didn't respond.

Hairy Sue'd stripped her room bare, the bed sheets wadded in a ball on the floor and dirty footprints all over the hardwoods. She'd wrestled the couch cushions out to a small balcony where she must have been sleeping. The assorted detritus of her slumber—she'd cut open a pillow and dumped its contents into her "bed" along with some leaves from Johnny's redecorating—reeked of farm animal, pig trough and Pabst Blue Ribbon. In the corner, cans were stacked in a pyramid the stripper was probably proud of.

Somehow, that didn't surprise me.

The medicine cabinet was empty as well. Despite being filthy, Hairy Sue cleaned that room out, damn well.

Mama Montserrat was less fastidious.

Her things were crammed in every drawer, cubby and cabinet. Weird things too, chicken heads, finger bones and charcoal. It was like she carried her own special voodoo pharmacy with her wherever she went. I found more of the gris-gris bags and a jar of the red powder. On the outside, written on masking tape, it read: Protection.

That made sense. Why else would the stuff border her threshold, as well as Johnny's.

After about twenty minutes of digging, I got a little frustrated and tossed one of Mama's suitcases at a wall—like you do—only this time, instead of just making me feel better, a loud pop sounded in the room, followed by a clanking roll like dice shaking in a cup. When I opened the case again, a false bottom had broken free and three glass bottles rolled around in the hollow. I picked up the first one.

The label read:

***Fae Away***
**A Multipurpose Pest Killer**

*Good for eliminating the most
frustrating flits, garden
gnomes, gulley trolls, water
sprites, and wood nymphs and
all the yeti varieties.*

**Directions:**
*Two to eight drops in the pest's
water supply and you'll be free
of fae.*

The bottle was empty. It looked like Mama Montserrat wanted to be certain to eliminate her particular pest.

At that moment, off the suite's small balcony, I heard a loud scream followed by a thud. I crept out the door to peer into the rear garden and saw nothing at first. Just the regular twists and turns of the hedge maze, the rows of hybrid roses and a man lurking in the shadows or the willows. Oh . . . wait. That last one shouldn't be there.

Could this be the guy who'd met up with Johnny the night before his death?

I rushed to the rear stair and slipped out under the arbor, hiding behind the thick wisteria-wound columns and searching the ground for some sort of weapon. The camera's low-light lens came in handy. I found a loose brick and held it tight as I padded lightly across the gravel toward the last spot I'd seen the man crouching.

He was quiet now. I couldn't hear him breathing and the only scent rose earthy with manure from the sodden soil. Either whatever had caused him to scream was gone or he was simply gone. I relaxed a bit at the thought and crept around the edge of the maze, glancing back toward the house in time to see the shadow figure creeping between the roses.

I froze.

What exactly was I thinking of doing? It's like I was in the thrall of the video camera. If the Fae Away would make good television, imagine an assault in a dark garden. I'd lost my fucking mind.

I'd just begun to back up, looking around to see how far I'd come, when the gravel nearby crunched under the sole of a heavy shoe. I darted, turning once to toss the brick, and then charged full speed toward the back door, screaming at the top of my lungs, "Wendy!"

"Jesus, Amanda." The voice was distant, familiar.

I stalled with my hand on the doorknob and pivoted. "Gil?"

## *Interlude of the Bitter and Pathetic*

### *Part Two*

### **Gil Opens His Gifts***

*or at least two of them

"This morning, after my blind date?" Gil's eyes were downcast, ashamed was my guess, though that could be any day of the week with Gil.

"Yes?" We both asked, glancing at each other.

"I went home and crawled into my bed and everything was all comfy and cozy and high thread countie but when I woke up, I . . ." his voice trailed off.

"For Christ's sake, what?" I yelled.

"I woke up with a mouthful of balls." Gil looked away.

"Like Whoppers?" Wendy's eyes lit up at the thought of malted milk balls.

Gil shook his head.

"Something a little more salty is my guess," I said.

"I made a decision to let Chad stay with me. That was my first mistake. Apparently he's a bit needy." Gil tightened the windbreaker he wore, closing it around his chest like a security blanket.

I could think of another needy vampire, but it didn't seem like a good time to bring up Gil's sire, Rolf, nor his desperate escape from Gil's constant attentions.

"So, I told him he could take the spare bed in the office and crash there as long as he needed until he could sort things out with his own place. Lightproof the bedroom. That kind of thing.

"'Do you think I could stay in your room,' he asked, sliding his hand seductively up my thigh.

"Now, at this point, I'm pretty sure I'm into Lars and while we're by no means an item and I would have been totally fine screwing Chad—I think I've told you, he's beastly hot, in a longshoreman with a metal lunchbox kind of way—there was just something not right about him.

"I couldn't have known how not right. Couldn't have.

"We sat around a bit and chatted about all the stuff you do when you're recently vamped and he took notes, but when it came time for questions, he'd say, 'Do you want me to give you a back rub?'

"I declined and got him a bottle of blood, figuring if he were vein drunk, maybe I'd feel more comfortable. I was already regretting my offer to let him stay by that point.

" 'How about we drink this together and I'll blow your bloodhard?'

"I had to shut him down at that point. It was just getting creepy. So I told him to go to his room and settle in and not come out until dusk.

"But, when dusk rolled around, he was straddling my shoulders and dunking his testicles into my mouth."

"Ew!" Wendy screamed.

"What did you do?" I asked.

"I fucked him." He threw his hands up. "But I got rid of him right after. He seemed to be okay with it, too. Something about thanking me for giving him what he's always wanted."

"Teabagging?" Wendy winced, knowing full well that wasn't the case.

"No! To be turned. You're so mean, make me say shit."

"Well, he's gone and you've got this Lars guy and that's great, I'm really glad your love life is turning around. Really."

"But . . ." He rung his hands.

"But what?"

"That's not the worst part. I think Chase gave me something." Gil dabbed the little wound on his forehead with a damp washcloth, and the blood came away nearly black.

"Like a present?" I slid the McDonald's straw out of my mouth—there are times when a flask draws too much attention, so I carry a stack of new fast food cups/lids/straws wherever I go. Well, they get to be a habit after a while and for some reason the glass of vodka seemed to warrant one. After the help left, I figured washing the glasses wasn't on the top of the contestants' to-do lists.

Anyway.

The damn thing caught on my lip and flicked a fat globber of alcohol-laced spittle over the coffee table, past a derelict glass with blood curdling in its base, finally splatting against Gil's retro aviators.

"Oops."

Gil didn't appreciate my modern art, sneering.

"No, not like a present!" he roared. "Like a venereal disease. Christ, you old lush—" He snatched the cup from my hand and tossed it into the room's waste can. "Will you pay attention? I'm serious."

"Okay. Jesus, no need to get testy."

Wendy dropped onto the couch next to Gil. "She's right. It's Chase's second gift to you. The one that keeps on giving."

I nodded for him to follow along. "It's true."

He glared, jerking the lavender silk pocket square from his jacket and rubbing the spit from his glasses with the intensity of a five-year-old foot-stomping tantrum. "You're probably right. But see how pleasant *you* are when you're dribbling blood out of your snatch like a Depends model."

I screwed my face up. "Ick. Really?"

"Yeah, *really*. I've got to pee all the time." He accented the last word by clutching his crotch and wrestling himself into a new position; a slow deep groan accompanying the exercise. "It's new. Something's wrong. I haven't taken a piss since the seventies. If that weren't inconvenient enough, the blood is so curdled, I've got to flush like six times, just to clear the bowl."

I whistled. "I'm impressed by your dedication to sanitation." I allowed a sparse giggle to accompany my rhyme, but the vampire's face curled up around his nose all threatening. I held up my hands. "Okay. Sorry. Have you been to a doctor?"

"What do you think?" His words were hissed, clipped.

I shrugged.

"I ran into your friendly neighborhood reapers and they are on a collections tear. Refused to see me at all until I forced you to pay them."

"Jesus."

Besides the reapers, there were three witch doctors in town. Achebe Ababe ran a quaint necropathy clinic out of a restored Victorian mansion on Queen Anne. Though reportedly fluent, he refused to speak English, preferring to dictate prescriptives through a series of quarrelsome tongue clicks and clucks understood only by his steadfast and towheaded nurse, Sojourn. Many suspected that the foul little albino was the actual doctor in the scenario, using Ababe as a ploy for undead cred.

Grant Coolidge was a snappily dressed aurapuncturist and noted venal-chakra surgeon, known for making house calls in his black Maserati and making time with his clients. Lawsuits plagued the man like, well . . . plagues, though he deflected them with a flourish of rattlesnake tail and the services of Anton Snell, esquire of the fifth borough of Hell.

The last one, Elliot Wasserstein, was known as much for his soft windblown hair—not often seen this side of the eighties—as he was for restoring humanity to werewolves and the occasional vampire (these claims have come under scrutiny by the *Undead Science Monitor* in no fewer than four separate articles). The doctor was in a practice with the famed voodoo priestess, Beth Liebowitz, who'd be no help curing a supernatural urinary tract infection, as her specialty was curing fashion disasters through the channeling of Erdu. Whatever that meant.

The problem was Gil had slept with all three.[78]

"I'm sorry. Really." I patted his knee. "What are you going to do?"

"Well, I'm certainly not going to tell Lars." He repositioned himself with some discomfort.

"Who?" Wendy asked.

"Lars. He's the guy your mother set me up with. Turns out he's a pretty decent guy, though a little woody."

"Is that a fae joke?" I asked, more than a little tired of our woodland neighbors.

"Yeah. Seriously hot. Very blue collar and kind of scruffy."

"Yummy," Wendy growled. "Are you totally in love with him?"

This was sounding a little familiar, a little too Vance Ventura, Repo Artist. I interjected, "Blond hair?"

"Yeah." Gil's brow furrowed.

"What does he do for a living, this Lars?"

---

[78] Yet only Coolidge was gay. Funny how that happens.

"He's in maintenance, I think. You sound like you know him."

"No. Just sounds like the guy that repossessed my fucking car."

"I don't think so."

"I don't know. He totally could have lied to me about his name. This could be my guy."

"Well he was driving a Volvo SUV."

I slammed my fist on the chair arm. "Shut the fuck up."

"No. I'm kidding."

"Jesus. I'm sorry. I'm just really paranoid. First all the crap with my finances, the job, and now this murder mystery business."

"What?" He perked up.

Wendy and I traded on and off telling him the story of the deaths at the Minions Mansion, our little road race with the Psychocabbie of Mumbai and Ricardo's new club.

"So you've been filming everything?" he asked.

"Yep," Wendy added.

"That's not all she's filming," I pointed to the cell phone on the bed. "Show him."

"Oh yeah." Wendy bounded for the phone and clicked it on and then off again, face curdled with disappointment. "It looks like someone's knocked the camera down. All I can see is the floor molding."

"Oh. Too bad."

"Gil," she said dropping back down next to him. "I need you to do me a favor and go over to my apartment. Abuelita is throwing some weird vampire frotteurism party."

"Okay." A crooked smile starting on his mouth. "I'll get right on that."

"Whatever you do, don't touch her. She's full of cloud."

"What?" He shook his head like he didn't hear her correctly.

"Like a Carpathian drug mule," I said.

"Is that a little joke?" Wendy asked, suddenly confrontational. "I don't see the humor in it."

"Come on, it's pretty funny," I countered.

"It is pretty funny." Gil agreed and reached for his empty glass. "What are we going to do about this?"

I slurped the remaining vodka from my own glass. "Bar!"

There wasn't a whole lot left in the Minions bar liquor cabinet, but at least the fat-headed bartender had enough sense to lock it up. I busted out the glass with my shoe and pulled out a bottle of tequila and a dusty Perry Como for Gil.

We were just sitting down for a drink when Mama stumbled in, soberish and ready for some real questioning.

"Care for a drink, Mama?" I asked.

Gil took a seat nearby, while Wendy ran for the camera.

"Line 'em up, child. 'Cause I got woes to kill, somethin' fierce."

I poured her a shot and she threw it back, slamming the glass back onto the bar and tapping the rim. "One more to show you like the Mama."

I poured it out and she threw it back again.

"Now, let's get to talkin'."

Wendy sped in with the camera up and ready, as Mama told us again that Hairy Sue and Johnny had been seeing each other for some time and despite her protestations, Johnny ensured the stripper a spot on both his last *Tapping Birch's Syrup* season and *American Minions*. Rather than listen to stuff we already knew, I decided to force the issue—as I'm wont to do.

"I have to tell you something, Mama." I leaned against the bar and looked her in the eye. "The sirens were found dead in Johnny's room."

"Oh, lord, no," she wailed.

"They drank the scotch."

Mama's wailing stopped dead.

"I'm going to ask you again. Did you kill Johnny?"

Mama spat a fat loogie onto the bar.

"I wasn't trying to poison Johnny. Are you insane? Look at what we had to lose in his death. No. I was trying to get rid of that pig Hairy Sue. Johnny never could resist trailer trash. He felt like they'd give up the stink quicker than a girl with breeding. Most men are fascinated with the ass, dontcha find?"

"I do find," Wendy agreed, giving me that, "told you so" look.

"So why poison the scotch and put it in Johnny's room?"

"Johnny doesn't drink scotch, you see. Never touches the stuff. Wood nymphs are sensitive to alcohol, so I was sure he wouldn't touch it. Now Sue. That bitch could drink her weight in alcohol, probably started in her baby bottle. The gift, I assure you, was for her." She stood and looked out the window. "I'm only sorry those poor girls were such raging alcoholics that they couldn't leave well enough alone."

"And how did they know it was even in there?"

"That's a good question, child." She reached for her purse. "While you're figuring it out, I'm going to find

Hairy Sue. If that bitch didn't kill my Johnny then no one did. Hell, I even saw her drop that envelope off in his room. She didn't see me though. Not too bright that one."

I placed my hand on her forearm. "One more question." I pulled the Fae Away out of my pocket. "This is what you used, right?"

She nodded.

"So clear something up for me. Hairy Sue is like a nymph or something?"

"Hell no. Nothin' that dainty." Mama laughed as she staggered from the room, keys jingling.

"I think she's right. It's gotta be Hairy Sue. Wendy?"

Wendy looked up from the camera screen. "Yeah."

"One last thing before we get out of here. Follow me."


Everything was right where it should be. Pile of ashes half on, half off the oriental carpet on one end, two dead girls with over-processed hair on the other. Scotch bottle. Pornos. And Johnny's envelopes.

"Wait a minute. Do these look right? Were they both closed like this?"

Wendy shook her head. "I don't remember."

I looked at the first one again. The same one he'd shown me at the Hooch and Cooch. I slid the thin plank of board out and the creature lay pinned there, screaming, just like it always had. The damn things gave me the chills. I opened the second envelope, the one addressed to the mansion. I pulled out the plank and dropped it to the floor.

It was lacking a certain something.

A certain creepy creature. I didn't even want to

think of where it could have gone. Maybe they weren't even dead. The pins just kept them trapped or something.

Wendy looked down at the empty board and a small squeak issued from her mouth, she started backing toward the door. "Where is it?"

I looked under the desk and started for the edge of the bed before losing my nerve entirely and running for the door.

We caught up to Mama Montserrat straddling the two
center lanes down the old Highway 99. The tequila
shots were kicking her ass. Gil held the Jag back a bit,
making sure we'd be around, in case the voodoo
woman turned her beater's nose into the divider or
sideswiped a young couple, their new baby and super-
cute Jack Russell terrier and sent them careening off
the top of an overpass onto a school bus or something
equally as tragic, and worse, newsworthy. After seeing
Baljeet bite it, I was more than a little sensitive about
psycho drivers.

My phone vibrated inside the Novak bag.

"Scott," I said aloud and answered. "Hey, hon."

"Watch that. We're buds now, right?"

"Right. Absolutely."

"I found out some shit on your yeti problem."

"Great, I'm gonna put you on speaker, okay?" I clicked the button and held the camera up to the phone. No sense in having to do a voiceover if we could help it.

"So I tracked down an expert on the woodland and in between being bored to tears, found out a little known fact about the yeti. They're basically human with a bit of a twist. It seems their cells expand when they're emotionally agitated."

"Like when you eat carbs," Wendy added.

Gil sighed and looked at Wendy like she was a dumbass.

"Sort of. But this is all of their cells. They can get really big, like the one at the Hooch and Cooch."

I thought back to the rampaging creature and the havoc it wreaked on the club. If it weren't intentionally designed to look like a dump, Ethel would have had to do a major remodel for all the damage the yeti caused.

"You mean Hairy Sue?" Gil asked, his wrist draped casually over the steering wheel.

"What?" I stared at him in the rearview mirror, fingers digging into the leather headrest and anger threatening to actually flush my deathly pale skin—if only it could.[79] "You knew?"

"Of course. I hired her." He shrugged.

"But you acted like it was going to kill us. Like we were really in danger."

"We totally were. Sue gets really pissy from time to time, usually on payday but manages not to kill any customers."

Wendy slapped the dash and spun around. "That's

---

[79] Also, how the hell did I get stuck in the backseat? Unforgiveable is what that is.

what I meant when I said she puffed up. It was like really quick and then she shrunk back up like she'd tried to hold in a fart or something and finally let it out. It was some Looney Toons shit."

"They can do that," Scott said. "Reel it back in. She's probably had some anger management classes."

"Yeah. Court-ordered. I can't imagine that thing at the club being able to control anything. Hell, Birch had to cage it up. You're telling me, that's normal? What have you and Ethel done in the past to deal with your star dancer's demented rampages?"

"Ethel has an epi-pen of Thorazine somewhere. She's used it a couple of times, but, for the most part, Sue can pull it back together on her own."

"God, I'm such an idiot."

"No. How could you know?" Scott's nurturing voice flooded the car, deep and parental. He always could soothe me. I missed him all the more. He's my epi-pen.

"It's just absolutely ridiculous, I didn't put this together. I mean, could there have been more clues pointing to the fact?"

"It probably speaks to our lifestyle that these kind of things are so normalized, we accept them without much thought." Wendy examined her nails, while she spoke. "I really need to go see Angie."

I slouched back into the seat and clicked the phone off of speaker. "You are such an intellectual. We're off speaker."

"Jesus, I've gotta pee," Gil said as we curved onto Suicide Bridge, where hundreds of ghosts mingled before taking their dives.

"It's like a freakin' block party up here." Wendy rolled down her window, stuck out a pair of eager rock fists and screamed. "Fuck yeah!"

A group of surly looking specters shot us the finger.

I tuned out the mayhem and settled into the conversation.

"Seriously, Amanda. You've got a lot on your mind," Scott said. "What with the business and the condo and all. Then this." He paused. "I probably didn't help with all my pushing toward a real commitment. I apologize."

What? I perked up. What was happening here?

"No. It was all me. You are so great and I'm just lucky to have you in my life at all, even as a friend."

"Um . . . about that—" Scott started.

"What the hell is she doing?" Gil pulled the car into the Hooch and Cooch lot. Mama Montserrat was miraculously on her feet and stumbling around the outside, pouring powder out of black bags and waving her hands in front of the side exit doors, before chalking a big "x" on each, then moving around to the rear of the building.

"Hey, Scott. I'll call you back, okay? We're going to confront Hairy Sue."

"What? No way. You can't."

"Talk soon. Bye."

I dropped the phone back into my purse and darted from the car as Mama came back around and headed for the front door. Wendy's feet pounded the pavement behind me.

"Come on!" I shouted back to Gil, who was too busy relieving himself behind the shelter of the open car door. A puddle of blood spattered at his feet.

"It burns!" he screamed.

I pushed through the doors a moment after they swung closed and already the inside of the club had erupted into anarchy. The strippers were crowded on the stage just behind a topless and infuriated Hairy Sue, her hands balled into fists and one of those curled tightly around the butter churning bat. Mama Montserrat faced her adversary from the floor, shaking the bones dangling from her wrists and chanting. Surrounding her was a crowd of booing perverts freshly cut off from their fix of beaver pelt, the steam not yet evaporated from glasses, bulges still tenting from their Sansabelts.

Ethel stormed in from backstage. "What the fuck is this?" She yelled and called for the deejay to nix the music with a scowl and quick finger slash across her throat. The room was quiet for a moment. And then the waller and din of the crowd erupted again.

I stepped in behind Mama and put a tentative hand on her shoulder. "Mama?" I asked. "Maybe we should—"

The woman reeled toward me, eyes black and coursing with hate magic. "Leave!" she bellowed in a voice not quite her own. Deeper. Darker.

"Holy crap!" Wendy barked from beside me, her camera hand drifting sideways. "What the hell's got into her?"

"I think that's exactly what's in her now. Hell." I backed away from the woman and took her in. Her feet were planted sturdily despite the wild gyrations of her hips. Mama's tongue flicked and she shouted a garbled mishmash of sounds and words in both Spanish and French. Nothing I understood, but the meaning was clear.

She was calling for something.

I noticed movement on the dais. Hairy Sue stepped forward, her face twitching, her teeth clenched. "Get out of here, Mama."

"Like hell, I will. You took my Johnny!"

"He was never yours!" the stripper spat back.

*Oh, shit.*

I glanced at Wendy. Her face wore the unmistakable grimace of identifying with Mama Montserrat's pain. "We better move away, someone's gonna cut a bitch."

Even Ethel had shrugged and given up trying to control the situation. She squeezed herself into the truck, next to Gil, who seemed to be holding himself and rocking.

As we pushed through the crowd, I noticed some of the men were hovering around the exit, throwing themselves at the doors, trying to bust out. Even the front door, which bore the same chalk marks Mama applied outside, must have been enchanted to keep us inside, a spell activated by the voodoo priestess's venom, possibly, though I know as much about voodoo and black magic as you do.

Wendy and I took up a position on the opposite side of the truck. It seemed a good idea to put some metal between us and the action taking place in the center of the room. Occasionally, I have good ideas. Not as good as Gil and Ethel, who seemed a hell of a lot safer inside the truck.

"Shit." Wendy pointed at Mama, or a space just behind her. "Look at that."

The floor cracked open and a gray smoke rose out of it, encircling the men nearby, who dropped to the ground in heaps as it clouded their heads. A poison, perhaps. Tendrils of the fog tentacled through the room, seeking out mouths, noses, even stabbing into ears, yet slithering right past Wendy and me with all the haughtiness of a back-handed compliment at a country club function.

It didn't occur to me what we were witnessing until movement inside the truck cab drew my attention. Gil and Ethel cranked the windows closed feverishly and closed the vents as best they could. I couldn't make out anything from their muffled shouts but their eyes were pleading. A wisp of smoke snaked from the floorboard up into the cab and Gil slapped his hand over his mouth and nose and the other over his left ear. He nodded for Ethel to follow suit and then preceded to press their exposed ears together.

I would have chuckled at the ludicrous position, if I hadn't realized what was happening. Vampires can't handle the zombie virus, it fills their dead lungs and veins to the point of embolism. I know. I've killed someone with the breath. I joke that it's the breath of life, but it isn't really. It's just more death.

More and more and more.

Whatever *this* smoke was seemed to be a bit more powerful, both delivering the virus and killing its target with a single infection. Potent.

There must have been at least fifty of them that rose, gray-skinned and eyes white with cataracts, the smoke blistering through them like the steam off a meth lab, stripping the life out of them and cauterizing the wounds on the way out.

The yetis didn't seem to be effected. I followed the edges of the misty haze. It seemed to stop in an even line parallel with Mama Montserrat. There were even a few men huddled behind the deejay booth, eyes struck wide with fear and, likely, insanity.

"Get behind me, children!" Mama Montserrat called and swung her arms to her sides for her forces to gather there. They shuffled forward, lining up like trained soldiers, albeit less disciplined. They clawed at each other's flesh and chewed off neighboring fingers and cheeks.

"Oh, no you didn't." Hairy Sue stripped off the

chaps and her panties, standing naked before the mass of groaning dead.

"Yes. I did."

Mama Montserrat raised her hand in the air as though collecting the zombies' attention, but before she could utter a word, the lead stripper stepped forward, opened her mouth wide and roared. The voice was deeper than you'd imagine, gravelly and torturous; it shook the waddle under Mama's chin and heralded Hairy Sue's transformation.

The flesh of her legs, arms and torso puffed—just like Wendy'd said—to at least three times its size, folding over on itself in great voluminous fatty rolls. Her feet and fingers cracked as they stretched, elongating into those same rake-like claws that tore through the beams and dented the ceiling only days prior. As the yeti's head grew fat and bulbous, Hairy Sue's long stringy backwoods locks seemed to recede into the follicles, though it was much more likely that the fat and skin cells were growing out past the follicles and the hair was simply enveloped by its girth, much like the way a fat man's dick turtles inward as his pooch gets fatter—a scene I've witnessed only once, and, thankfully, for only about the three seconds it took me to grab my coat and scurry away from my horrifying inappropriate blind date.

Hairy Sue roared again. Fully transformed, her claws reaching out on either side in a massive span.

It was then I noticed the other strippers.

They inched forward on their purposefully dirty feet, gathering around the yeti like a shield. I wondered what was in it for them. Why protect the yeti and so fearlessly to boot? Didn't make sense.

And then they changed too.

The walls vibrated from the intensity of all the roaring and Wendy slapped her palms over her ears. Ethel and Gil had hired an entire girl gang of yeti strippers. I had half a mind to rip open the doors of the truck and blow in some more zombie virus. Dumbasses.

Mama was furious, but as she turned to deliver orders to the throng of zombies, Hairy Sue reached out— I thought to just snap the voodoo woman's head clean off with the ease of a child popping a candy dot off a paper strip—but instead she smacked her upside her head. The woman's body collapsed to the floor, but before she even hit, the zombies behind her surged forward.

"Damn." I huddled in closer to Wendy and pointed for the gap underneath the truck as a safer option. We crept under slowly, trying desperately not to attract attention from either the yetis or the zombies, newly released from their contract to Mama.

I didn't have to worry. The guys hiding with the deejay began to scream and were swarmed. The yetis weren't faring much better, despite their distinct size advantage. The mistakes tore through the bar for fresh meat like a line of termites through dry rot. Blood streamed in great crimson arcs across the walls and ceiling. A yeti stumbled out into the open, four zombies chewing at her knees and arms. The left leg went first and the creature toppled, valiantly tearing apart a pair of zombies in road crew overalls on the way down—the sounds of their spines stretching and snapping one after the other filled the room for a second and then they were tossed into the air like confetti.

Writhing confetti.

There had been six yetis, including Hairy Sue, at

the start of the battle. So when I peeked out from under the truck and saw that there were only four, yet at least thirty of the supercharged zombies still battling, my thoughts started to shift toward escape. Then, the deejay staggered out from behind his wheels of steel, his jaw twisted at an odd angle and bloody tongue lolling out of a mouth split open at the sides like an amateur episiotomy. Five more freshly revived corpses trailed him out. One lurched forward, juggling his loose bowels, while another crawled behind him snapping greedily at what could have been a shoulder blade or a nice shank.

I do enjoy a nice shank, from time to time.

Mama's zombies travelled in packs. They separated the remaining yetis and circled them, attacking from all sides and gnawing with ferocity and numbers, the supernatural equivalent of piranha. Two more of Hairy Sue's peers dropped without taking out a single mistake.

"These fuckers are organized," I whispered to Wendy.

She stopped filming and stared, her face paler than usual. "We gotta get the fuck outta here."

"Agreed. And before they're done with the soft-skinned woodland folk."

"No doubt. I almost feel sorry for them." Her voice was distant, almost dreamy—probably all the meat scent hanging in the air. She twisted toward me. "But how? Mama's blocked all the exits."

"Maybe that spell ended when she died, just like her control over the mistakes. Stay here. I'm going to check in with the other undead."

I patted the undercarriage of the truck, an idea already forming, and pushed myself back out, curling up slowly to avoid the attentions of some hungry perv's cadaver. Gil and my mother were in the same position, frozen like that in fear.

I opened the door and crept my head in. "I think the smoke has dissipated, but if you're comfy like that I can fill up the cab with some more."

"Mow," Gil mumbled underneath his undoubtedly clammy palm. His head shook slightly, as he pulled his hand away from his ear and then let the other one fall. Ethel followed suit.

"Does this bad boy have keys?" I asked.

Ethel nodded. "They're in the office."

I looked past the tailgate toward the hostess station and knew that just beyond that was the door. There were a couple of the less stable zombies bumping into each other and bitching in that groany way of theirs. I looked back at Gil—his face was green with whatever Chase screwed into him. Useless.

That only left Ethel.

I glanced her way to find her staring intently at me, seemingly ready to act. I could smell the violence on her, just below the surface, and I knew I needed it.

"All right, Mom. I guess it's you and me."

She grinned.

"Gil, get Wendy up in here—she's underneath us—and shut the door. And, sweet baby Jesus, don't slam it. Got it?" He nodded. One of his hands crept to his crotch, kneading some shame away, his faced more pained than usual.

"You ready?" I asked Ethel.

"Damn straight I am, let's kill us some creepy crawlers." She squeezed herself over Gil and bounded out of the car, crouching and heading forward with much more stealth than I'd have given her credit for. I followed and watched her extract the metal testicles from the hitch and send them sailing through the air and straight through one of the shambler's heads.

Leaving two.

I slid in behind her and whispered, "We don't need to kill them unless they notice us, and since we don't smell like food, they're less likely to . . ."

"Oh, I get you."

We put our backs to the wall and inched around the corner behind the little hostess podium. The papers on its top were spattered with blood. As we reached the door, a zombie lurched towards us, fingers atrophied into perilous-looking claws. I opened the door and before the zombie could moan a single, "brains"[80] Ethel reached out for its claws and jerked it into the club's tiny office.

"Shut the door," she hissed, drilling her thumbs into the thing's eyes. It spasmed, as Ethel helped it onto its back, rolling up an issue of *Sunset* and driving that down into the eyehole.

"I think you got it."

"You never can tell," she said, standing up daintily and brushing her hands off on a neat wool skirt. Her eyes searched the room, a question on her face before she spoke. "Where are those g.d. keys?"

I opened the top drawer of an old filing cabinet, pharmacy green and heavy with sin. The employee files. "A whole horde of stripper yetis," I said. "Who'd have ever believed that back in Rapid City?"

"I know it. I'd never even thought of such a thing. Or even believed they could exist at all. Oh." Her face brightened. "I remember."

---

[80] Which they totally don't. But it's funny to think about.

Ethel scooted up next to me and opened the next drawer down. A set of keys hung inside on a little hook.

"You know, honey. We're going to make it out of this."

I cringed. The nurturing made me want to vomit, especially coming from her. "Let's just go. And don't jingle those out there. You'll draw attention to us."

When I opened the door, I realized the keys were the least of our problems. A swarm of the zombies must have been hunting us and they stood outside two deep, ten in all, snarling and teeth snapping. I shut the door as they collided with it.

"Well, that's not good," Ethel said.

"Get the chair and slide it underneath this knob. Won't keep 'em out long, but maybe long enough." I tapped my fingers against the wall. "Is this hollow?"

"Um. I think so. Drywall probably, maybe a little insulation. It's still loud as hell in here when the girls are dancin'."

I picked up a pair of scissors from her desk and stabbed it straight through.

It was probably the first time I'd smiled at my mother that didn't involve me trying to get something from her. "This is how we're getting out of here then."

Ethel joined me at my side and drew her fist back.

I snatched her hand. "Aim for the spot I stabbed through. Vampire strength or not, if you hit a stud it's gonna take a while to heal your busted hand."

She nodded and punched straight through to the inside of the club. The sound of struggle grew as she kicked and knocked out a ragged opening between two studs. It was nearly completed when the door behind us came off its hinges and several of the dead men scrambled in, luckily stumbling over the chair and creating a ridiculous pile-up.

I pushed Ethel through the gap, screaming, "Suck it in." And just as I moved to go out myself, one of the zombies reached out and sunk his fingers into my shoulder, digging through Alexander McQueen's sumptuous fabric with such frenzy that my skin tore beneath it. A black stain spread across the side of my dress and I turned, so furious that he'd ruined one of the last great pieces of clothing I owned, I jabbed the point of the scissors through the base of his nose and into his brain. I pushed his quickly fading body at the approaching zombies and squeezed through and out into the gap between the truck and the wall.

The door was open and I dove in, slamming it behind me.

"Jesus. They got you." Wendy poked at my shoulder.

"It's not so bad," I said. "You should see the other guy."

We chuckled for a moment, then realized it hadn't been funny in years and stopped.

"So when I crank the engine, we're going to draw a lot of attention."

"Absolutely." Gil nodded.

Through the passenger window, I could see what looked like Hairy Sue fighting off ten of Mama's voodoo zombies, snapping off heads and cannoning them toward other approaching ghouls.

"You all ready to get out of here?" I asked.

"Is that even a real question?" Wendy sneered.

I cranked the engine and three things happened.

One, Ms. Hairy Sue's head twisted in our direction

and she barreled through zombies at breakneck speed, tossing them off left and right[81] until she dove into the bed of the truck, just as, two, I dropped the transmission into drive instead of reverse and stood on the gas pedal. And three, the tires squealed against the wood floors for a second and then we were speeding toward the back wall of the Hooch and Cooch.

"Wait!" Wendy, Gil, Ethel and even Hairy Sue screamed in unison. "Wrong way!"

And then we were all screaming as the truck barreled through the wall and out into the air over Ballard. We skidded off a steeply pitched roof in the next moment, banked off the side of a bridge piling and then finally found the ground again, though barely. The angle was too steep to do anything but keep us from going end over front.

Or at least I thought so—it was hard to think about anything when you're busy screaming.

We flipped and tumbled—and do you think any of us had managed to remember a seatbelt? Not a chance. The four of us bounced inside the cab like corn in an air popper.

The truck finally settled into a gulley behind three stories of brick and wrought iron with clothes strung up on lines between a pair of fire escapes.

Thank God. I started to speak but realized my neck was broken, twisted nearly all the way around and facing something even more upsetting.

The truck was pointed back up from where we came and the Hooch and Cooch, never the most stable of buildings, was quickly losing its battle with gravity.

[81] Heheh.

Creaking timbers gave way to the screams of splitting pilings and the loud shirring of corrugated aluminum roofing. In a matter of seconds, too quick for any of us to make a decision to run, crouch or do anything other than scream—not that we could have for all the broken and dislodged bones poking out everywhere—the building crumbled from the cliff and pummeled us with falling foundation, beams and assorted dead things.

My last thought was: *I hope my face will be recognizable enough for an open casket.*

I really love sleeping.

I miss it.

You never understand the value of those comatose hours disconnected from reality until you die and lose them forever. I suppose insomniacs get it, those long hours of agonizing wakefulness, images racing behind their eyelids, replay of the crappy-ass moments of their day on a seemingly endless loop, not to mention the 2 A.M. refrigerator assaults and misguided masturbation that ends up getting their hearts so jacked they have to watch infomercials about hermetic sealers to calm down.

It's all so terribly boring.

The daydreams and fantasies help, but it makes for a

horrendously long existence, especially considering my distinct difficulty, rotting. Though I have a few fantasies that I indulge in quite frequently like not cramping up and exploding after a donut binge, blushing—rouge only goes so far—or making friends without the hidden motive of eating them later. I imagine myself without dark veins and the little areas of sag. Smooth. Resilient.

Wendy's body seems to be going a little quicker than my own. I've noticed loose spots in need of fills and bruising that doesn't seem to ever subside.

A quick trip to the reapers could cure that for sure, but that costs money.

My eyes snapped open at the thought.

Hillary gawked at me, lashes batting and blond hair hanging in perfect ringlets from underneath a paper nurse cap, like the many coils of a snake pit fat and swollen with babies.

It had to be the blond one.

"Wakey-wakey, Amanda!" The words rolled off her tongue in a grating singsong rhythm, interspersed with smack off her Hubba Bubba. "You've had yourself a wittle accident, now haven't you?"

It took a moment to gather up the fragments of my memory and make sense of a truck crashing through a wall, careening off a steep embankment and the loud crashing din of an entire collapsed building being tossed atop the wreck like the final grave dirt. Must have been all the screaming that threw me.

"Christ," I muttered, though it hurt to even speak. "How am I even here? How am I anywhere?"

"Well, we used shovels." She blew a big pink bubble, poked it down and then stretched the gum out to an irrational degree. "*We* didn't. The lowly werepeople we recruited to help certainly did. Nice folks, we found them on the side of the road with signs."

"Cheap labor. That's great." I lurched up on my elbows.

"The cheapest. Worked for clinic credit which is always a great help to us in these deeply troubling financial times."

I ignored her hint toward my bill. "You couldn't just wave it all clean? Make it like it was?"

Her mood changed in an instant, as was common with this particular reaper. Hot one minute, cold the next, or rather, various degrees of cold. She snapped. "Listen, you dead bitch, if I'd had my way, I wouldn't be talking to you right now. We'd have let the city churn you up with the rest of the debris and haul you off to the dump where *your* kind of trash belongs."

"Jesus," I groaned. "Harsh."

"It seems you and your motley crew have some friends."

My "motley crew." I assumed Britney—or whatever the little shit's name was—didn't mean the band. And I hoped to hell she meant Gil and Wendy, but I really hoped she didn't mean . . .

"Your mother has been asking about you."

"Oh, God."

The demon in the little girl suit cackled and skipped off.

If I were that kid's mom she'd be so grounded.[82] I watched her flick the files of each hospital bed she passed, startling Mama Montserrat, in particular, mirac-

---

[82] And by grounded, I do mean buried alive. I'm playing hardball. Children beware.

ulously free of bite trauma and cocooned up tight like Travolta in *The Boy in the Plastic Bubble*. Across the aisle, Hairy Sue, shrinky-dinked down to a size 0, convalesced on her back—a position with which I'm certain she's quite familiar, although I imagine her knees get more of a workout—both legs stuck straight out, casted and lassoed in traction cables.

When I twisted to my left, I nearly jumped out of the bed in horror. Wendy lay prone on the hospital pinks—notice a pattern—her tits and snootch covered by a pair of thin throws of fabric (also pink). In the few spots her pale flesh wasn't marred by puffy purplish bruises, a thick pus pooled around each of the hundreds of needles stabbing into jaundiced sores, painfully—maybe not for her, but it was certainly painful to look at, even more so than one of her woefully tragic outfits. A Tesla device hung from the ceiling, arcing electricity to each of the vile protuberances. They hopped and vibrated with each jolt.

What's worse?

Wendy's paralyzed Cheshire smile, that's what. Toothless, except for her two front teeth, she beamed at me, eyes wide and seemingly waiting for something.

"What the fuck are you grinning at?"

The grin turned into a smirk.

"What?" Wendy is frustrating, sure, but this was hitting new levels. It's not enough that we were broken and nearly killed; she was getting some weird joy out of it.

I tore my eyes away and laid back into the less than sumptuous pillow. That's when I noticed my very own matching Tesla coil, humming and sparking and dripping electricity into my needled flesh. The sensation wasn't entirely unpleasant, just gentle jolts followed by the odd pulsing of flesh. The worst bit was the expulsion of fluids from the needle prick. It glugged like fresh crude, only yellow and rank with a fetid rottenness that hung around me like a cloud.

And. It was ugly.

Pig-fuckingly ugly.

Passing out would have been a welcome relief. Especially since I suspected the reaping bitches added this little part of the treatment for their own pleasure, rather than any real curative properties.

"Hillary!" I screamed. "Hillary! I want out of here."

Wendy chuckled.

"Shut up," I hissed, from the side of my mouth. "Hillary!"

Whether I was in their back pocket or not, I fully intended on wiping the floor with the little cooze for this insult.

Another of the reapers bounded up to the bed. "Hillary's taking a very important phone call and can't be disturbed just now. I'm Britney." I craned my head to look past her down the ward. Sure enough, the little blond midget chattered into her cell, twisting her hair casually with her free hand. When she noticed me glowering, she shot me the finger and a wide grin.

"Bitch!" I turned to Britney and smiled, I hoped sweetly, though really that would be a stretch. "Hi, Britney. Can you gather up some of your dear friends and get these needles out of me and my . . . friend?" Also a stretch, at this point.

"Oh, no. I couldn't do that. The little shocks you're getting help move all the healy goodness through your dead flesh. Kind of like vitamins. Just think of it that way. Pretty blue vitamins. Okay?"

I snatched at the lapel of her pink uniform and

pulled her close. Her carefully constructed smile gave way to the evil underneath her skin. Britney's lips pulled back to reveal rows of tiny shark teeth. Her tongue played on the sharp peaks. "Yes?" she growled. "You have a question?"

I released her and smoothed the front of her smock. "No, I don't suppose I do. Just thank you. That's what I wanted to say."

"Mmm-hmm." Britney pulled out a little plastic remote and pointed it at the Tesla ball. "How about this, you don't ever touch me again and then I won't ever be forced to do this to you."

"What?" My eyes drifted from her hand to the humming globe above me. The arcs jumped in broad sweeping curves down into the needles and before I could even contemplate what that could mean, my body was jumping on the mattress like a demon possession.

Britney released the button and I dropped back into the bed, only seconds later to have the entire scene replayed, this time to the tune of several little girls clapping and giggling.

Monsters.

She leaned in close to my ear and whispered, "Besides, Hillary told me to tell you we've still got the matter of your bill to settle. You're not leaving here until we get our money." With that, she planted a kiss on my cheek, started to scamper away, twisted around cheerleader style and zapped me again.

"God, y'all. Really?" a male voice chastised, instantly recognizable as my friendly neighborhood collection artist, Vance Ventura. He probably drove to the reaper clinic in my Volvo, spitting chaw on the floorboard, or whatever it is men do on the rare occasion they don't give a shit about a car.

Britney giggled and strode up to him, hips wiggling seductively.

Now.

I know the reapers look like little girls, no matter how old they get, and that this one was probably older than me, but it doesn't change the fact that it's unnerving to witness a child attempt to seduce a full grown man even when that man is technically a bug or twig or something. Still, I'd have rather taken another humiliating shock than endure Britney rubbing Vance's thigh.

Grossed out doesn't even begin to cover it.

"Ew," Wendy muttered.

The look on Vance's face implied agreement. He soured and brushed her hands away, a shiver rolling through him with such violence you'd think someone took a metal rake to a chalkboard.

Britney shrugged her shoulders and cooed. "You silly. I'll just leave you to your visit." She turned and shook her finger at me sternly.

Crap. Here we go, I thought. Not conscious five minutes and already I'd been treated to a litany of my failures. Apparently, it's not enough humiliation to be shocked to the point of bowel release—no, I didn't, I'm just sayin'.

What did the guy need to repo now, anyway? My soul?[83]

He pulled up a metal folding chair and crossed his leg far more elegantly than I expected from a glorified

---

[83] If he could find it. Probably rolling around in my body somewhere like a chunk of coal and not the cute candy kind you shove in your kid's stocking as a joke.

car thief. "Ms. Feral. I'm glad to see they've been so fastidious with your care. Hillary assures me you'll be good as new within the hour."

I scanned the rows of needles piercing my body and wondered how she figured. "Oh yeah. They've been lifesavers."

"Literally," he added.

"Though, I suspect they're scouring their dungeons for even more inventively torturous treatment modalities, as we speak."

"They do enjoy their humiliation, but you can't deny the results are nothing short of miraculous. You should have seen your bodies when they brought you in. Your friend there was like a pile of ground beef laced with satin ribbons." He jerked a thumb in Wendy's direction.

"Ground sirloin." She propped herself up on her elbows behind him, drool pooling in her mouth, I'm sure.

"So what is it now, Vance. Do you need my teeth or something?"

He slapped his knee, chuckling. "No, no, nothing like that. In fact, I've been running some numbers and if you sign over your condo to the reaper clinic, that'll cover your bill, and get you out of here pronto."

"You can't be serious?"

"Oh, yeah." The excitement spread across his face like a rash. He pulled a spreadsheet printout from his briefcase and pointed out various strings of numbers. "If you'll notice here . . ." Vance continued jacking his jaw about equity and figures and so on, but all I could think about was how far I'd fallen. It seemed like just a few days ago I was living the high life. Expensive shoes, bags, gowns, an awesome boyfriend, who sparkled on my arm like antique Bulgari.

Living the dream.

Vance's scruffily handsome face was bright with the kind of hopeful glee I wanted to slap clean off.

"If I do that it'll cover all of it. I won't owe those bitches another dime?"

"Well, most of it, there'll be some charges for today, but I'm going to take care of that for you with my collections commission."

"And why is it that you'd help me, Mr. Ventura? Did your last porn tape go platinum or something?"

As if on cue, Gil strode into the ward, Ethel following close behind him, chattering on about insurance payouts. I thought I'd be miserable seeing Mother again, but instead there was an odd tinge of regret. After all, she'd lost her business, as I was surely about to lose mine.[84] Then there was Gil. His attitude always cheered me up.

So you can imagine my displeasure when my best friend, and first supernatural I met after my zombification, ran into Vance's arms for a deep kiss and a quick butt grope.

"Seriously?" I looked to Wendy for some support.

She shook her head. "It doesn't seem right."

Gil turned towards my bed, arm slung around Vance's waist. "You've met Lars, then. Doesn't he glitter like new money?"

To Vance's credit, he cringed at being shown off like a trophy wife, but his easy smile in Gil's direction

---

[84] But don't think I'm going soft on the old bitch. She's still got it comin' to her. In spades or however that saying goes. You know what I mean. Lots.

loosened some of those coals in my dead heart. "I know him as Vance, and yeah . . . he's cute."

"That's his work name."

"Don't make many friends in my line, so I keep it up, like a stage name."

"Yeah. I figured." Though I figured something entirely different.

Ethel squeezed past the happy couple and sat next to me on the bed. She grimaced at the needles and attempted to feel my forehead with the back of her hand. "Ew. Cold." She withdrew her hand with a snap.

"Yeah. It goes with the whole zombie thing. And it's actually room temperature, so . . ."

"Well, darling. I know the delightful Mr. Ventura has spelled out your options and I just wanted to offer up a spot in my guest room. It's small but I have clean sheets and towels and a basement for you to keep your victims if you like a late-night snack. I don't know exactly how it is you . . . creatures deal with that kind of thing."

"Or," I suggested, head snapping in Wendy's direction, waiting for her to make an offer.

She stared at me blankly. "Or?" she asked.

"Or I could stay at your place for a while."

"Yeah. The thing about that is, I've got this whole Abuelita thing going on. And so, until I get that dealt with . . ."

"I could just roll out a sleeping bag next to the stove."

She shook her head, nose crinkling.

My mouth hung open.

I turned to Gil. "Gil?"

"Your mom's is a really nice place and it's only for a little while, until you get on your feet again." He shot

an uneasy grin at Ethel, who was nodding conspiratorially.

I glanced at the papers sitting on the side table,
next to a small tray of what looked like false teeth,
though they weren't set into any acrylic gums. They lay
loose like charms, only instead of a loop each root
ended in a long nail head. I was reminded of Wendy's
broken grin and shuddered to imagine what the reapers
had in store for her dental needs, also secretly glad that
she'd be getting a healthy dose of pain for what she was
willing to put me through.

"Fine!" I snatched up the papers and Vance/Lars
rushed over with a pen.

"Here and here and here." He pointed out little
exes and I scribbled my name next to each one, stabbing the pen at the paper with rage.

"I hope you know I'll be bringing Honey and Mr.
Kim. They go wherever I go." I glared at Ethel.

"Well, I'll just run on home and set up a spot for
the dear girl right now." She leaned over with vampire
speed, or else I would have pushed her away, and
kissed my forehead. I went to rub it off and then
stopped myself. Gil already thought I was childish in
my interaction with Mother—I'd be damned before I
gave him more ammo. Ethel gave each of the men a
quick hug and then clopped off down the hall with the
kind of spring in her step that could only come with the
knowledge that I'd be in her evil clutches once again.

Gil and Vance left shortly after.

I was numb.

"You know," Wendy said. "There's always the
show. If that hits big, you might be able to buy the
condo back."

A little glimmer of hope shined into my pre-suicidal

mind. The show. Absolutely. All we needed to do was solve the mystery, compile all the footage in a fresh and stylish way and I'd be rollin' in it again. I'd probably be able to keep the business too.

"Thanks, Wendy. That actually helps."

"You're welcome."

"And at least we have the camera."

"Oh, thank God. You do have it. I've been lying here wondering." Wendy whistled in relief.

I sat up and scanned the little table next to the bed, reached down and opened the drawers, nothing but gauze and little jars filled with spiders—undoubtedly considered medically necessary by the Marquises de Sade of the candystriper set.

"What? You don't have it?"

"Hello? I was kind of falling off a cliff and being crushed by a building. Didn't have time to worry about the Amanda Feral Show."

My stomach flipped.

The camera was gone.

Of course it was. Even inanimate objects got the memo. Must fuck Amanda Feral. Kick her while she's down.

What's next, karma? World destruction?

"Well, I'm not going to sit here and take this lying down."

"Huh?" Wendy looked up as I started plucking the needles from my pores.

"Reapers! Bandage me the fuck up, I'm getting out of here." Britney stomped down the hall toward our beds. I stabbed a thumb in Wendy's direction. "And this one, too. I'm putting her back to work."

"Well, aren't you demanding?"

"You bet your ass."

I pulled on a pair of jeans—Gil rustled up some clothes
for us at a nearby Urban Outfitters—and shoved a pair
of borrowed twenties into the front pocket. I'd owe
Ethel back for the cash in blood, but I'd rather that than
be beholden to the woman, especially with her so glib
over her apparent victory.

We hailed a cab and slipped into the back.

"Where are we going," Wendy asked, picking at the
bandages on her arms.

I slapped her hands away. "Don't pick." I gave
Wendy's address to the cabbie—I wondered if he knew
Baljeet and Raj—and we were off.

"What's at my place?" Her face dipped into griev-
ance. "Other than a cracked-out vamp whore?"

"Your camera, the one you've been spying on Abuelita

with. Once we get it, you can keep filming me as I search for the real camera. This shit is going to make for some intense TV."

She lifted her phone. "Couldn't I just film you on here?"

"Well, yeah. But then we wouldn't know what the hell's going on at your place."

Wendy's eyes narrowed. "True."

She lived in a turn-of-the-century walk-up on Queen Anne. The peek-a-boo view of the sound added five hundred a month and was worth every penny, though the vampires littering the living room floor brought down the property value dramatically. Abuelita, passed out on the couch and pasty as a glazed donut, grunted as we entered.

"Wake up." Wendy kicked the woman's foot.

"Hmm?" Her eyes opened with a snap. "Oh! Missus Wendy. I can explain."

"I save your ass from a life of wearing poorly constructed sandals, beading handbags no one wants and pushing Chiclet saleschildren out of your snatch and you repay me by throwing wild drug parties in my home? You're damn right you've got some explaining to do."

I scanned the mass of vampire flesh. Most were spooning in pairs or trios. A few curled up, fetal as babies. I nudged one of them I knew from the clubs. George, I thought, or Gio. He smiled up at me dumbly, pulling his arm out from under another passed-out vamp, this one totally fug and wearing a ratty thrift store sweater. I gave him a wink and helped him to his feet. "You better get your friends and get into the hall. Wendy's pissed. She's likely to chew her table into enough wooden stakes to finish all of you."

George or Gio scrambled to his feet, kicking his buddies and rushing for the door. Threats are particularly effective with cloudheads. Even the smallest gesture gets blown out of proportion in their drug-addled brains. In a matter of seconds, the vampires cleared out, leaving the floor a mess of blood stains and dried pools of drool.

"I need to make moneys to bring my family to the States. You no pay me, so I make moneys the way I know how." She reached for the empty paint can and held it to her chest like a Teddy.

"Moneys?" I asked, stepping up beside Wendy. "How much moneys?"

Wendy's head jerked toward me. "What are you doing?"

"Just chill." I petted Wendy's hair, then to Abuelita I said, "How much money are we talking about here?"

"Five hundred for each gringovamp." She opened the canister and pulled out a fat roll of twenties.

Now if I were an ethical zombie with designs on simple brain eating and shambling around, I couldn't very well sustain your interest. I require a certain level of income to keep up my stylish demeanor. It ain't free. Fabulousness costs.

Big.

And no. I had no intention of eating the little mule.

I'm not in the business of burning bridges, in case you haven't noticed. I looped my arm through Wendy's and led her into the kitchen for a chat. "Okay. So this is going to sound bad. I know you feel violated and betrayed and all that, but I counted at least twenty bloodsuckers up in this cuddle party. At five hundred a head, that's ten grand."

Wendy's face was stolid.

"How much do you expect to make with your jewelry line? A couple extra hundred a week?"

She shrugged, clearly irritated at my direction.

"I'm just sayin'."

Abuelita had followed us to the doorway and caught on, agreeable to the unspoken idea, probably out of fear of being eaten than anything else. "Sí, Missus Wendy, we go into business together. I have connections for the clouds and you know lots of the vampires, *sí?*"

"Well, yeah."

"I'm gonna go downstairs and wait while y'all make a decision. Don't forget the camera."

Wendy glared at me.

The vampires hadn't made it very far, taking my suggestion of going to the hall quite literally. The hallway was lined with the addicts and no fewer than three of them were snoring at top volume, forcing me out to the fire escape at the end of the hall to call Scott.

"I need your help."

It was more than that. I've never needed help from a man before, I've always been able to manage on my own. It wasn't help I needed. It wasn't little tips or clues or direction on how to solve a mystery—one I wasn't even sure I cared enough to figure out. No. It was Scott.

I needed Scott.

"I was just thinking about you." His voice was husky and deep.

"You were?" Did the words sound desperate?

"I was," he said.

"Well, you needed to be. I almost died last night."

"What?" he barked. There was a sudden urgency to it that thrilled me.

I told him about the accident at the Hooch and Cooch and gave him general directions to the site of the collapse, clicked off and promptly screamed. Holy crap. Did he say he was thinking about me? Oh yeah. I climbed down the ladder and sat on the hood of someone's car, drumming my fingers hopefully.

Wendy blasted out of the back door of her building, a pair of car keys jingling and a bit of a smirk on. She didn't say a word until we pulled out onto the street.

"Well?" I asked.

She nodded. "I'm a drug dealer."

"Awesome." I slapped her thigh. "What are the keys to? I was pretty sure you were carless."

"Let's see." She punched the alarm button on the ring and a sporty little red Mazda flashed and honked like a game show prize. "We have a winner."

"Let's go get famous."

It took a little while to find the spot, since we'd only ever seen it for an instant and then only from the vantage point of the rear of the building, but it wasn't too difficult once we found the spot on the ridge where the Hooch and Cooch should have been. It would have been way easier to spot from the bridge, but who wants to put up with all those ghosts on a beautiful sunny afternoon?

Wendy paralleled and pulled a pink stuffed rabbit out of her bag, shoved her hand up a tear in its ass and pulled out her video camera, then tossed the violated animal into my lap. I was reminded of the tiger Johnny had left in my room to welcome me to the set and actually felt sort of sad at the thought of him cut down in his prime. Or in my prime, to be more accurate.

"Nanny cam?"

"Hell yeah. Clandestine is the way to go. I watch *To Catch a Predator*. I know what it takes to get the footage."

"Clearly."

Scott arrived at the collapse before us and was knee-deep in debris by the time we rounded the corner of the Chinook Apartments, battling the mushy grass in my stilettos.

"Why the hell don't they have a sidewalk around here like regular people?" I asked.

"Maybe if you'd told them you'd be crashing here, they could have accommodated your shoe needs." Scott wiggled his eyebrows.

"Funny. Are you having any luck?"

Scott threw up his arms. "Been at it for a half hour now and no sign of anything that even looked like a camera. Found a pair of trailer hitch testicles, though. You want 'em?"

"Pass."

"I really don't see how it's possible that it survived though. Know you don't want to hear that, but."

"Well, I'll just make all the suspects reenact our interrogations. They should get a real kick out of that."

Scott slid his arm around my shoulders congenially—and I'd know if it were anything else, I'd been examining his every move since I saw him. Looking for an opening.

"I'm sure you'll figure something out," he said. "You are the most creative and ambitious woman I know."

"Ooh!" Wendy yelled, darting to a spot at the top of the rubble. "Say that again, I need a more dramatic angle for your romantic reentanglement."

"Jesus, Wendy," I spat.

"Reentanglement?" Scott chuckled. "Is that even a word?" His eyes met mine, blue with what I hoped was longing. Though I'd settle for obsession.

I turned to see Wendy teetering on a beam precariously. "Why don't you head on home to your new business partner. I'll catch a ride with Scott."

She hopped down and backed toward the side of the building. "No prob. I'm going to throw your bag in his car and get out of here. Talk to you later."

"Bye." I turned to Scott and found his gaze so welcoming, I rushed into his arms tilted my face toward his and waited.

His lips were on mine in an instant. Our kiss was passionate with regret. We'd lost something. Hopefully two things. My self-absorption—at least in terms of Scott—and his unwillingness to share his concerns.

"I should have told you what I was thinking. I won't dwell anymore, I'll just let you have it. Lord knows you're strong enough to hear it."

"Yeah. And I'm not taking you for granted. If I do, I expect you to tell me right then, hell, beat me over the head with your discontent. I deserve it for what I've put you through. I'm shocked that you're even around."

His hands played with mine, fingers threading and then pulling away, tickling circles into my palms. "Oh, I'm around. I ran, is what I did. Pathetic. It's not going to happen again. You can count on it."

He wrapped me in his arms again and pulled me toward the opposite corner of the building. The side with the walkway, if I'd only looked for it.

"I need you."

"You have me"

"No. I need you right now." He shrugged, like a little boy who had to go pee. Like it was simple as that.

Actually, it probably was. Simple as it could ever be between a wolf in street clothes and a dead woman in borrowed jeans.

"Right here?" I looked at the gap between the buildings. Paint chipped away from the clapboard like checkerboard and the cement was cracked in a single centerline, from the back patio out past the front of the building.

"Can't wait. I'm 'onna fuckin' explode." Scott groaned, his lips against my throat, muffling the words into quiet murmurs, a deep humming that vibrated across the surface of my skin like a memory.

His hand found mine and guided it to the full hardness in his jeans, then slipped up under the thin cotton of my shirt gently kneading my breasts, pushing my nipples up over the top of the bra's cups. His rough fingers teased them thick as his mouth went to work on my earlobes, the curve of my jaw, the shallow cleft of my shoulders.

I rubbed at him slowly, methodically. Wrapped my leg around him to press my pussy up as close to him as I could. The seams of our jeans met, snagged and slid deliciously, sending jolts of pleasure up inside me, up my spine.

He fumbled with the buttons on my shirt, opening it from the waist up and unfastening my bra with a deft flick of his fingers. Not a second later and his tongue curled around one swollen bud, then the other, sucking them into his mouth with soft smacking sounds.

I found the top button of his jeans, then his zipper, and slid my hand inside the band of his boxers, across the soft mound of pubic hair—trimmed, I'll have you know. I followed the length of his shaft, lingering on the silken underside, tracing circles with my fingertip.

Scott moaned into my ear, a wanton beseeching sound. His face turned skyward and he ground his teeth as I stroked his cock, pressing down the front of his jeans and underwear with the other, releasing him. I licked the palm of my hand sodden as he watched me, heavy-lidded with desire. His eyes followed my hand down to encircle him, twist his length, toy with his head.

Both of them.

"You're making me fucking crazy," he sighed, nearly breathless.

"Oh, yeah?" I whispered, stroking him faster.

"Yeah." His voice hopped a bit, as though I'd brushed up against his pain threshold. I released him and let him pull my shoes and jeans off. He lingered at my toes, sucking at them, lapping at the hollow of flesh at my inner ankle, before working his way up to my thighs, his fingers kneading the curve of my ass as he crept toward my pussy in a trail of soft nibbles.

He threw one leg up onto his shoulder and then he was there, tongue lapping between my folds, sending shivers through me that for a moment made me feel alive, more than alive.

Electrified.

He kept his eyes intent on my face while he tongued me and stopped only once, to dip his index and middle fingers into his wet mouth, before rushing back to tease my clit with unyielding thumps of his tongue. I felt those wet fingers trace the line of my taunt and I clenched a bit as Scott played with the taut pucker of my anus, slipping his fingertip inside only briefly while he swirled his tongue masterfully around my engorged clit.

There's something to be said about a lover with no

boundaries. Ladies, you know what I'm talking about. Every moment with Scott feels like it could go in any number of directions, from the last time where he lost control and shifted partway through—by the way, thanks for asking about the hip, it feels fine now, you insensitive assholes—to moments like this where he'd happily take me to the edge over and over again. Teasing me with the promise of an orgasm and then making me wait until I imagine I'll shatter. Of course, there are the other times, when he'll ask for something he's not going to get, but I won't sully this, our reunion make-up sex, with tales of anal gone awry.[85]

I clawed at the clapboard behind me as his effort brought me close. Near to that place where I knew I'd explode. I reached down and clutched at my lover's neck, pushing his mouth tighter against me.

His nose whistled against my thin patch of pubic hair as he pressed even closer, his head twisting from side to side. He broke free only once to gulp at the air before diving back in with a maniacal glee.

"Oh, fuck." My body seized with the beginnings, that moment that threatens death before the pleasure rolls in like a tsunami. But he stopped, just before, like he had me on a timer. "You fucker!" I screamed.

Scott chuckled and stood up, steadied himself on bent knees, grabbed his cock and slipped his full length into me, filling me. "Yeah. I'm a fucker."

I held him tight and crossed my ankles behind his ass, as he held me up with one strong hand, his other cradling the back of my head.

His face wet with saliva and a faint scent of my own juices (I'm never quite as human as on release day

---

[85] 'Cuz that just wouldn't be sexy.

from the reaper clinic—and for that Hillary gets one free pass in that dark alley beatdown I owe her). I kissed him deep, sucking at his tongue as he thrust up into me. I gasped as Scott pulled all the way out before driving his cock in deep, pounding hard into me before shifting his weight and thrusting shallow, caressing the grooved nub of my g-spot with the head of his cock.

"Oh, slow," I moaned, the words stretching out like a sob.

Scott leaned his head in close. "I love you," he said.

And before I could process it, disconnect it from the pleasure he was giving me and figure out what to say, it came out, "I love you, too." And then again, with more conviction. "I love you."

He grinned and laughed and thrust with greater rhythm, his breath hot on my face.

The orgasm hit like a seismic slip.

I screamed as wave after wave of pleasure rolled through me, threatening to spill out the top of my head. I shook from my core.

Scott came next, grunting in that sexy way of his, teeth clenched and lip quivering. He shook his head and I ran my palm across his face, wiping the sweat from his brow, the back of his neck.

It's a testament to our passion that I didn't notice the adolescent kid masturbating in the neighboring apartment until after Scott and I had sunk to the ground, him breathless and going flaccid inside my still-swollen cunt and me sated and more than a little worn from cumming as hard as I did—swear to God I thought I'd have an aneurysm, if that's even possible. He was about fifteen and tan as a handbag, floppy brown hair and a sunken chest, the head of his waning erection plastered in wet toilet paper. I flipped the kid off as he picked at the tissue, smirking the entire time.[86] Thankfully he, finally, shut his blinds and I was able to hold Scott a bit and make out some more.

"You, sir," I told him, "are going to have to do me up like that several more times before the night is through."

"Is that right?" He grinned, though there was a thought playing in his eyes, a tinge I thought I recognized.

"Yes," I said. "I love you. You're mine and I've been the biggest asshole in the world. I'll do anything to keep you, just ask. And don't ever stop asking."

He kissed me and I him and vice versa, until a familiar swelling flared up again.

"We better get out of here."


I wrapped myself in the chenille throw I'd bought Scott on his birthday, sage green with chocolate stripes, though honestly it was for me—there's nothing cute about a girl saronged in a pilled-up Target blanket. Just doesn't work. Plus, what's softer than chenille? Baby ass maybe, but you can't get away with a baby ass blanket. Not these days.

Scott kept a bottle of Jameson's on top of his fridge. I dragged a chair from the Formica dinette and snatched it and a dusty lowball from the cabinet. Rinsed and two-fingered, I slouched at the cluttered table, books and notepads stacked next to bags of bulk cereal and two liters of regular Coke.

[86] How is it kids nowadays aren't embarrassed by a thing like that? I would have been mortified to be caught flicking my switch.

The first book I dragged off the pile, a leather-bound number heavy as an anvil with an equally hefty title, *The Greenwood Obscura*. I drained the whiskey and poured a second. Heaving my bag off the back of the chair—a big hobo monstrosity the reapers dug up for what little of my effects could be salvaged—I dug through it for my smokes and instead pulled out Wendy's big pink bunny. I sat it on the table and propped its ears up. My cigarettes were, of course, at the very bottom.

*The Greenwood Obscura* was an encyclopedia. Full-page color photos of all sorts of woodland fae accompanied a written history of each. I flipped through the pages, admiring the coloring on the creatures wings—much like the Versace Spring Collezione—until I landed on one in particular. I almost didn't see it set against the blackened bark of a burnt-out fir tree, but as I shifted the page to turn it, the angle brought all the bug's wretched attributes into focus. It was the very same type of creepy crawly the killer sent Birch as a threat.

I read the entry, fully expecting to find that the creature was a harbinger, a warning, but finding something else entirely.

Scott shuffled into the room, yawning, hair sticking straight out on one side and a hand down the front of his boxers massaging his sore balls. "Wow, that was quite a workout. I might need to ice these up before we give it another go."

"Pig." I gave him a quick smile and he leaned down and pressed his lips into mine, humming his pleasure. I kissed him back and reached for an ass pinch. "Well, then rehab those puppies, 'cause I'm gonna need some celebration lovin' after tonight."

"Ow!" Scott jumped and backed away. "You're dangerous."

"True enough. Oh. I was gonna ask, what are all these books for?"

He filled the coffee pot with water and grounds and set it to brewing. "Just some research for your yeti problem, though it seems that's hit a bit of a snag."

"Oh, I don't know."

"What's tonight?" he asked, filling the sugar bowl from a Rubbermaid container.

I turned the book in his direction, pointing out the picture. "I've got a show to finish."

I glanced at the stuffed rabbit and grinned.[87]

---

[87] Don't you just hate it when I keep secrets from you? Well, tough. Secrets are a part of life. Besides, you don't want me to be totally honest with you, or to tell you everything—if I did then you'd have to hear the reason I no longer mention vaginal lubrication. And no one wants the details on that. I just tell myself it's natural and think of soothing ocean waves and jungle waterfalls. Now let it go and keep reading. I'm sure there'll be something else to offend you coming up shortly. Move along.

**CHANNEL 20**
**Tuesday**
10:00 P.M.–12:00 A.M.
*The Mrs. Deadly Mysteries*

Mrs. Eudora Deadly (Ramona Rachek) takes a holiday, she thinks, and ends up investigating the case of a missing werewolf bride at an isolated seaside resort. With a kidnapper at large, will her faithful manservant Burtleby be next?

If you ask me, the best part of any Agatha Christie novel (or movie adaptation, for that matter) is the big-ass parlor reveal. No question. You know, that moment, right after the detective—in most cases the rotund and hilariously egotistical Hercule Poirot—figures out all the clues and puts together the blueprint of the crime for the gathered suspects, who in turn are either mooneyed with admiration, mortified at the wrongdoing or exposed as the bad-ass killers themselves. Either way, the conclusion is always the same and I bet you think you know the answer.

But, no, it's not the conclusion of the mystery that happens in that moment, because anyone paying attention to the clues can figure out what's happened. No, it's something far more valuable.

It gives the detective the floor.

The star of the show gets the spotlight.

That'd be me.

I greeted each of the players into Harcourt Manor like the happy hostess, Wendy filming from one side, Scott the other. I wasn't about to fuck this up, not considering the work I'd done to put it all together.

The first to arrive was Tanesha, weave surrounding her face like a lion's mane and the Lycra catsuit to match. The wide 80s belt was a stroke of genius. She planted a peck on my cheek as she passed. "Shorty, you a Hot Tamale on Ice Cream tonight. Dayum."

"Thanks. I try." I did a little turn. I haven't brought out the big guns in a while, and the Azzedine Alaia gown cinched me bullet-casing tight. If there'd been a stray patch of flab the designer's flair for working in tight stretch fabrics would have taken care of it quicker than a plastic surgeon's vacuum. Luckily, I didn't have to worry about that, being hot and all. And still bearing a hint of blush from the reaper rejuvenation—they do have their merits.[88] My hair fell in soft silent-screen-actress waves and I wore a single pendant monocle, in case I was inspired to judge at exceptionally close range—though with the pores on these people, there was fat chance of that.

"Make me wanna bump donuts." She thrust her hips forward with a high-pitched, "Bump."

"Oh my God, Tanesha, you're gonna kill me."

"Wouldn't want to do that, girl." She sashayed off for the bar. "Gots to get me a tasty beverage."

---

[88] Midget bitches.

"I know that's right."

What is it about sassy black girls that makes you want to talk like them? Even ones that are technically men, and wolves? I don't know, but I love it.

Maiko and Angie came together, neither particularly pleased to be attending, but still thankful for the opportunity for some more screentime, or at least that's what they said. Maiko continued with her trend of dressing in stereotypical Hollywood fashion. I'd tried to tempt her with some exceptionally avante-garde Issey Miyake, but she hissed a stream of smoke at me, and if it were anything like what I could expel from my lungs . . . Let's just say I knew to take it as a warning.

"Your nails are gorgeous."

"Angie is so good at it."

The little Filipino shrugged her shoulders and beamed. "Thanks!"

Absinthe arrived shortly before Hairy Sue, wearing a dusty leather biker vest over a pair of Big Mac overalls.[89] Absinthe winked at Wendy as she passed and shook my hand brutally before passing into the manor. I glanced at Wendy. Her face fouled by the green grimace of a curdled stomach. "Are you gonna be okay?"

She waved off my concern.[90]

Hairy Sue required a ramp and though it seemed she was really struggling to propel her wheelchair, neither Wendy nor I offered any assistance. She was, after all, the principal suspect and I needed to keep her on her toes, even if they were covered in casts. She gave us the

[89] Where do you even buy those anymore? It's not like she's a farmer.
[90] For the best really, since it was just the set-up for a brutal ribbing.

finger as she passed, sweat congealing on her brow like lemon curd.

"Nice look," I shot. "Very meth addict."

Mama was the most difficult attendee to manage. Apparently, because she was human, her treatment was a little more traditional. The bitchy blond reaper—I'm calling her *Hell*ary now—accompanied her with a big ogre of an orderly she called Spew—the only thing more noticeable on the creature than his curled antelope horns was the blue-black toupee teetering atop his head like a coarse black bear pelt.

Spew rolled the voodoo priestess's plastic infection bubble into the bar on a gurney. It jarred violently crossing the ridge of the threshold. Mama screamed bloody murder and shook her bone bracelets at the orderly, cursing his "bastard birth." I really had to question the sterility of the infection bubble, 'cause . . . bone bracelets? How hygienic could they be?

I told Gil he could bring Vance to watch the spectacle, like a real date, because this one had witnesses. "Sit in the shadows, though," I told them. "You don't belong in the shots, okay." The way their hands scrutinized each other's bodies, there'd be a bigger risk of horny grunting showing up in the final edit. I added, "And keep it down, I don't want your dirtiness caught on tape."

They chuckled and slipped into the booth farthest from the group.

Seated, the women eyed each other suspiciously. Maiko, Angie and Tanesha scowled at Absinthe like she'd taken a dump in their pedi-baths, while Absinthe trimmed her nails to the quick into the crystal ashtray on her table and grinned at Angie, who in turn cringed dramatically and flicked her tongue in the webbed vee of her fingers. Mama glowered at Hairy Sue through plastic, Hellary reclined in the booth behind her read-ing—*In Touch* magazine—finding out exactly how pa-thetic and lonely Jennifer Aniston was this week, as opposed to last—while Spew picked his teeth with a splinter he'd pulled off the underside of the table. Hairy Sue shot Mama the finger and crammed an un-coiled wire hanger inside her cast to get to a particu-larly evasive itch.

"So you're probably all wondering why I called you back here."

They were quiet a moment. Hellary yawned. Why I expected them to cooperate was the real mystery. Maiko broke the silence . . . unfortunately.

"Isn't it obvious?" She pulled out an excruciatingly long cigarette holder and started puffing away, no ciga-rette necessary. "You think you've solved mystery and want to torture us with long-winded reveal, no doubt implicating each one of us in order to celebrate your own brilliance as you unveil actual killer with theatri-cal flourish."

Bitch.

"It isn't the Maiko show. So why don't you just sit there and drink your Tanuki piss or fold paper birds or whatever the hell you do and shut the fuck up."

"Mee-yow." Tanesha could always be counted on for smart commentary.

Maiko scowled and puffed fat rings of smoke into my path as I paced the room. I waved at them to break them up a bit, but some of the smoke clung to the back of my hands like Styrofoam packing peanuts. I rubbed it off on a table edge.

"Now," I continued. "I'd like to call your attention to the premise of *American Minions*: the fact that Mr.

Birch was in need of a bodyguard. Oddly enough, it wasn't just for the show, as you'd imagine it would be. We met only two days prior to shooting to discuss several death threats he'd been receiving over the phone and through the mail. Including some quite disturbing dead things, which were really more gross than frightening and kinda stunk, but that's beside the point. Johnny was certain that someone was plotting to kill him and, clearly, as he *is* apparently deceased, that must have been the case."

Angie leaned forward, head threatening to teeter from her neck. "Why do you say 'apparently'?"

"I'll get to that." I slipped behind the bar and poured myself a gin. "From the first night at the mansion, I was aware of tensions between Johnny and his agent, the show's producer, Mama Montserrat."

Mama gasped for air in her tent. "Oh child, you don't mean to suggest . . ."

"I mean to suggest just that. The two of you were seen arguing in this very bar. Do you care to tell us what that argument was about?"

Mama's mouth clamped shut for a moment, then, "There were problems with the crew, nothing more. No doubt you saw how quickly they abandoned the project, well, they'd been threatening that before the production began. We've had some financial difficulties as a result of a rapid decline in the ratings of the last season of *Tapping Birch's Syrup*. It's as simple as that. A financial argument."

"Fine. Believable, I suppose. You didn't quarrel about your sexual relationship with Johnny at all? Not a word?"

Mama's mouth hung open, and she whispered something to Hellary, who waved her off summarily, in favor of the *In Touch* crossword on celebrity drunks.[91] Mama huffed and crossed her arms.

"Now, on the night of the murder, if that's what it was."

"Why do you keep saying zat?" Absinthe asked. "Do you mean Johnny wasn't killed. Zat he committed ze suicide?"

"I'm getting to that. Just relax." I took a swallow of the gin and slammed the glass down on the bar for effect. Wendy gave me the thumbs-up and I continued. "Well, first off, we can only speculate what happened behind Johnny's closed and very locked door. What we do know is that he was visited in his room just prior to our discovery by Hairy Sue, who brought him an envelope delivered by a courier, who just so happens to deliver at one o'clock in the morning, like anyone's ever heard of a delivery that late."

"So, the envelope busts this shit right open, right?" Tanesha fanned herself. "Is it gettin' hot up in here? Anyone?"

"In a sense. But let me finish. When we got the door open, we found several things. Johnny's extensive porn collection, a bottle of expensive scotch, two envelopes, both containing gross dead things, a herd of stuffed animals and a pile of ashes in the shape of one Johnny Birch. We each got stuffed animals in our room, so that doesn't seem terribly dubious, or does it?"

"Does it?" Angie asked.

I shrugged. "The pile of ashes was definitely that, ashes, and after a little checking through the porn it

---

[91] I knew this because occasionally, she'd blurt out, "six letters, third letter is a 'D,' Lindsay's definitely a lush," or "Judy Garland could knock 'em back with the best of them. Twelve down."

didn't appear that anyone here was sidelining as a scat queen or a fist-fucking enthusiast so that just left the scotch, the envelopes and the two dead carcasses.

"This is where things got interesting. We started interviewing you all and found that you each either had a motive to kill Birch or would have if you knew he planned to film your romantic escapades with his nanny cams." I lifted up a stuffed animal, set it on a nearby table and patted it on the head.

Angie and Maiko gasped.

"I'm not saying we've collected any hardcore footage, I'm just sayin' we might."

Maiko scowled.

"It's unlikely either of you knew you were on NannyCam, so you're not high on my list of suspects. After all, neither of you were jilted as was the case with one . . ." I spun around and fingered the beautiful drag artist. "Tanesha Jones."

"Drag Wulf," she added, nonplussed.

The other women gasped, right on cue. The night was going exactly as planned, at least in my mind. I glanced at Scott, who nodded proudly—or maybe I'm projecting.

"It's true," Tanesha said. "I'd had a brief and tumultuous affair with Johnny that ended rather badly."

"Wait a minute," Mama Montserrat growled. "Are you trying to say that Johnny was gay? I don't buy it for a second."

"Like I done told Amanda, Johnny was certainly not gay and he never treated me like anythin' but a lady."

"But it was sexual?" Maiko's eyes narrowed.

"Definitely."

"Then how did he not know?" Mama hissed.

"Some secrets I'll take to my fuckin' grave, if you don't mind, bitch." Tanesha stood up, her claws snapping, crackling and popping into the long daggers of a werewolf, while the rest of her remained all lady . . . ish.

Scott's eyebrows raised in admiration. That kind of control over specific body part transformations was the work of a highly controlled shifter. I'd only known one other and she was quite dead, or wished she was, living out an afterlife sentence in the bowels of the underworld courtesy of one Elizabeth Karkaroff, my boss, if you'll recall.[92]

"Calm down, girl." I stepped between her and Mama.

"I'll pop her. Don't think I won't." She reached an exceptionally long index claw at the voodoo priestess's oxygen tent.

I stretched to put my hand on Tanesha's arm. "I know you could, but I also know you'd feel bad about it, later."

She lowered her claws and sighed. "It's true. I'm sorry, Mama."

"Well, I'm not!" she shouted from her bubble. "I know your kind, tried to change him didn't you?"

I needed to rein it in before the tensions exploded. "If that's the case then it didn't work, did it, Mama? After all, Johnny started up a sexual relationship with you shortly after and you're not hiding any tackle under that girth of yours, are you?

---

[92] And if you don't, might I suggest buying my previous memoir *Happy Hour of the Damned*: on sale now, wherever it is pretty people buy books.

She scowled and Tanesha chuckled, relaxing back into her chair.

"But never mind that, I'm certain that you're not Johnny's killer. But you are *a* killer."

Hellary glanced up from her rag for that one. "What?"

"That was an accident," Mama spat. "And you know it, we've been over this."

"You see, ladies, that expensive bottle of scotch wasn't meant for Johnny. He doesn't drink, never touches the stuff. But his lover did. Like a fish, though I'd have pegged her for a Mad Dog 20/20 grape wine kind of girl. I'm talking about, of course, Hairy Sue!"

The stripper broke her beer bottle on the edge of her table and started wheeling furiously at Mama Montserrat. "You tried to kill me twice, bitch? I'll cut open that voodoo snow globe of yours and show you who's gonna kill who."

I stepped forward and planted a Louboutin on the front of Hairy Sue's chair, kicking her back in the opposite direction. "True enough," I said. "But she didn't. She did, however, inadvertently dispatch Janice and Eunice." Figuring we'd fit in some sort of photomontage of the crispy-haired sirens, I looked directly into the camera. "God bless their souls."

"Okay," Tanesha said. "That takes care of the booze, but you said the envelopes were the real clue."

"And they were. Not so much because they were there. I'd already seen the first envelope at the Hooch and Cooch where I met Johnny."

"You met him at a strip club? That's kind of tacky." Hellary peeked over her reading glasses.

I sighed. "We're totally going to edit you out of the show, I hope you know that."

"Whatever." Her head rocked from side to side as she sing-sang the word.

"The real clue came when we searched Johnny's room a second time and only one of the carcasses was present. I didn't know what it meant at the time, but my impression was that the creepy bug-thing had come back to life. Having a bit of experience with that kind of thing myself, you can see how I'd make the jump to that conclusion. So we tore out of there."

Hairy Sue glared at me venomously.

I slunk toward her.

"I've got you. The envelope you delivered was empty, wasn't it?"

She didn't even blink.

"It was a couple of days later that I found a photograph of one of those creatures in a book." I crouched next to the frothy stripper, rage seething behind her gritted teeth. "Sue, would you like to tell the crowd what those little creatures are?"

Her head jerked away and she folded her arms across her chest.

"No? Didn't think so." I stood and took a spot in the center of the room.

Wendy and Scott took their places to get the reaction shots. Mouths were already open in anticipation. Tanesha even licked her lips.

"They were wood nymphs."

Silence. Stares even.

Apparently I'd confused the gathering, but not Hairy Sue who was backing away silently into the shadows.

"You see. I wasn't aware—and how could I be, really, it's not like I study woodland creatures, that'd be bor-ing—that when wood nymphs aren't walking among us in human form, their natural state is this odd-looking twig-like insect. When threatened, they can and do go into a state of paralysis mimicking death. Some of them can even achieve this state through dehydration and exhaustion."

"Are you saying that—" Tanesha began, but was cut off by a familiar voice.

"She's saying that I poured out the ashes, transformed myself and slipped myself inside the empty envelope that Sue delivered and then snuck out while you bitches tried to claw each other's eyes out."

I twisted toward the voice and came face to face with the barrel of a gun.

Johnny Birch lurched out of the shadows wearing a dinner jacket, an ascot and a smarmy grin.

"Terribly mediocre Poirot impersonation, Amanda.
Maybe you ought to spend a little more time reading
Agatha Christie and a little less time getting your skin
to sag like her corpse."

I offered my coldest stare, jutting both my jaw and
hip violently.[93]

"Oh girl, I know you ain't gonna let that twig-dicked
motherfucker talk to your ass like that." Tanesha stood
up menacingly . . . and sat back down once Johnny
aimed the gun at her.

"That's right, love, just sit your pretty butt in that
chair and be quiet." Johnny sidestepped behind Hairy

---

[93] It's what I have instead of heavy artillery. Some might say it IS
heavy artillery.

Sue's wheelchair and laid a reassuring hand on her shoulder. "Everything will be fine, darling."

"Like hell it will!" Mama Montserrat rolled over and pushed up on her knees, snatching at a pendant around her throat until it released, revealing a thin sliver of bone she wielded like a prison shank.

But before she could cut her way out of the bubble, Spew stood up and shook the entire contraption like a snow globe. Mama slipped around inside and settled on her back, winded and humiliated.

Johnny chuckled, but continued caressing Hairy Sue as he talked. "I've gotta say, I'm impressed with your perseverance, Amanda. I wouldn't have believed you'd take this crazy show idea of yours and run with it."

"What else could I do? We all need this to work. Well, maybe not the contestants, since I'm guessing prize money is out of the question."

"What?" The word rose up from four different points in the room, though it wasn't so much a question as a threat. Tanesha's jaw shook, Maiko's hands turned a translucent gray and were stretching across the table, Absinthe's jaw started cracking and popping (and we all know what that means), while Angie simply glowered.

"I think you better explain yourself. You might be able to take out a couple of them, but it's doubtful you'll make it out of here alive after coming between a girl and her money."

"I'm not explaining shit, rotter." He stepped forward and pressed the muzzle of the gun to my forehead, much to the delight of Hellary, who clapped her hands excitedly.

Scott growled through shifting vocal cords. I didn't have to turn to know that the pops and shredding I heard was his shirt coming apart at the seams and buttons bouncing off the walls; likewise, Wendy's jaw echoed with the ratcheting of bone and sinew, her mouth stretching open for a brutal feeding.

"Saint Francis on a fuckin' fritter!" Hairy Sue screamed, her eyes wide with fear and warning. "Johnny, watch out!"

Johnny inched backward, glancing sideways and quickly ducking as Hairy Sue's casts blew out in a massive blast of chalky powder and chunks, her legs thick as tree trunks and clothes dangling in strips off her waist and neck. The wheelchair blasted away behind her, crashing into the wall and busting a table clean in half.

She roared, also, but that was really just overkill.

Scott jumped into her path. He was smaller than the yeti, but only by a hair and lean with muscle rather than the bulbous pouches of fat covering Hairy Sue's gargantuan frame.

"Now now," Johnny said, trying to soothe his lover. "We don't want any trouble, do we, Sue?"

"I think she wants trouble." I peered around Scott and took note of the blood pooling in the corners of the yeti's eyes. "I'm pretty sure."

"So do I." A man I'd never seen before marched into the room with a gun in one hand and nose spray in the other.

Gil gasped and stood up, slamming one fist on the table—he might have managed both, for added effect, had he not been nursing a rather large goblet of the red stuff.[94] "Chase. You motherfucker."

---

[94] And I don't mean Pinot Noir. Though if you need to believe that to make it through the night, then run with it.

Johnny spun on the newcomer, biting his lip with schoolgirl glee. "Chase."

"Don't 'Chase' me, I've been tracking you for days." Chase squinted, searching the depths of the bar for the other voice. "Jesus, is that Gil?"

"Uh, yeah." Gil pursed his lips, reached down and brushed Vance's (or whatever his name is) face gently with the back of his hand. "And this is my new boyfriend."

Chase shrugged and rolled his eyes. Gil sneered.

"Zat's him!" Absinthe pointed at Chase. "Zat's ze guy I saw come from around ze side of the house."

Hairy Sue's head swung from Johnny to Chase, thin ribbons of spittle dangling from her fangs. She shifted from one leg to the other, anxious for violence, ready to pounce—or possibly needing to pee. Either way, I wished I had an Uzi and some training.

I kept my distance, but not my mouth shut.[95] "I smell love triangle."

"Shut up!" Johnny yelled. "You don't know."

"She knows," Chase advanced. "She's figuring it out, just like everyone else is."

I wasn't really, but who's gonna argue? I mean really, they both have guns and looked pretty edgy, maybe they'd take care of each other.

Hairy Sue stopped growling and cocked her head, eyes narrowing to slits.

Gil stepped out of the shadows. "Are you here to tell Johnny about the venereal disease you gave him, too?"

"Gave *him!*" Chase barked. "Try the other way around."

Hairy Sue roared and spun on Birch, snatching him

---

[95] As if I ever could.

up by his throat before he could cast his bluesy magic. His legs kicked out from under him and he hung for a moment, gagging, clawing at Hairy Sue's enormous fist with one hand as his face turned a nasty shade of Violet Beauregarde blue.[96]

"Oh shit, someone else besides Mama gots the pejohos in their fapuna!" Tanesha was nothing if not colorful, but if she was trying to turn that into a trendy saying, I was afraid she was facing an uphill battle.

"She means," I interpreted for the slow. "Someone else received the gift that keeps on giving."

I'd nearly expected it to be the end of the show. Wendy was already advancing for a close-up when Johnny brought the gun up to the yeti's head and, without the slightest hesitation or change in his stoic demeanor, fired. The blast plastered both the ceiling and the portrait of Samuel Harcourt with Hairy Sue's brains and shards of bloody skull—it dripped from the patriarch's teeth like sloppy summer watermelon.[97] Her body slammed to the floor, splintering the hardwood. Cracks radiated through the room.

Chase moved toward Birch, cocking the pistol, even as he snorted nasal spray from his other hand with a great heave.

The wood nymph jerked toward the vampire and flickered, light dancing off his skin like the crackling projection of old film. He threw back his head and spread his arms out wide, releasing some kind of plea to the wood.

---

[96] Yeah. That was a *Charlie and the Chocolate Factory* (and not a *Willy Wonka and the Chocolate Factory*) reference. I don't care how much you drip for Johnny Depp, that remake was an assault on childhoods everywhere.

[97] And if Samuel loved anything it was a shard-spitting contest.

His song craned to a high pitch at the same time as the
stench of dank mildew filled the room—I guessed from
his ass. But jokes aside, you know I was moving away.

Vines sprung from every wooden surface, slow curling sprouts giving way to thick tangles that jutted into
the room ramrod straight and sharp at the point, knots
piercing the room with barked lances.

One of the branches sprang up between Johnny and
Chase, knocking the vampire off his feet. He fired the
gun ineffectually into the ceiling and when he scrambled to his feet, the bar was a jungle of whipping creepers and deadly spines.

I didn't notice Johnny disappear and I don't suspect
he did, probably shrinking down to his insect form, but
Mama must have known that for sure. She threw herself at the side of the plastic bubble with a shriek. It
rolled off the gurney with a muffled thud, crushing a
Medusan shrub overrun with snaking vines before she
hamster-rolled it toward the last place he was visible.

"He was here! I saw him!"

"Aren't you going to do something about this?" I
asked Hellary, who rolled her magazine up, slipped it
under her arm like a dad on the way to his morning
constitutional and strode out of the bar, coughing
"losers," from the doorway.

"Real mature, Hellary!" I crouched next to Mama,
her eyes wild and hands pounding the floor of the bubble.

"If he under there, he gotta be dead, right?"

She reared back and the bubble lifted off the
crushed vines and twigs, revealing a crack in the floor
wide enough to lose a heel in. If this show didn't pan
out, I had a feeling an exercise DVD for yeti might just

make some money. There was a population that could benefit from some exercise. I glanced at Hairy Sue's body, expecting it to have returned to human form in her death and not the pile of pocked chicken skin that lay before me. But why would it? The big lumpy thing was its natural state.

"He's in the basement!" Chase yelled and wove his way through the flora and fauna toward the main hall door.

"Make sure to take some swag on your way out!" I called.

He stooped a bit in mid-trot and snatched a small gold bag out of the basket at the door. The contents were mostly shit, a few drink tickets to the Well of Souls, VIP status at Convent, that sort of thing. What was most important was the tiny package of earplugs. I couldn't have been certain that Johnny would show up at the big finale, but I wasn't planning on taking any chances. And, since I kind of liked some of these people, particularly the most fantastic drag queen I'd ever met, I figured I'd make sure we all had a defense against Johnny's vocal power.

Tanesha, Maiko and Absinthe darted out after him, Angie sort of floated—well, part of her did—her entrails curling around the branches and propelling her disembodied head forward. Wendy, however, stood at the bar draining a bottle of Tarantula in greedy mouthfuls.

"Really?" I asked, snatching it from her hand and draining it dry.

Scott lurched forward after her, the claws on his hind paws scrabbling on the floor. Gil and Vance were behind him, my friend grumbling the whole way about chewing Chase a new asshole. I guess it was supposed to sound threatening but came off a tad gross considering the context.

Spew coughed and I turned to see him lounging in his booth, hands behind his sizeable head as his toupee slipped back to reveal a high forehead pasty as floured marble.

"Care to get in on this?" I asked.

He shook his head without meeting my gaze. "I'm opposed to violence. Have fun though."

"Are you ready?" Wendy asked, eyes skittering toward the dark doorway.

I nodded and crept toward it. Wendy tiptoed behind me, so close, had she been able to breathe, I'd have felt it on the back of my neck. She did run into me a few times, blaming the camera for her lack of perspective, or something to that effect.

I checked the full length of the hallway before stepping out into the melee—a girl can never be too careful, plus it's always advantageous to be the last one at a fight—either it's been resolved by the time you get there, or the players are so exhausted I can pick them off easily with a few carefully placed bites (and by carefully, I mean making sure to get the head)—but I took too long to get moving as Mama's bubble rolled over my foot as she barreled past. The bubble bumped and bounced against the walls of the hallway like a pinball, finally slowing to a crawl about halfway to the rear staircase—that it didn't occur to her to simply cut a hole through the damn thing amazed me. Mama's prone figure lay curled at the bottom, worn out.

The stairwell, dark even during the day, was veiled in the kind of shadows even childhood monsters fear, black and inky as midnight on skid row and twice as dangerous. I looked at Wendy, hopeful she'd take the lead. She glowered and shook her head with finality. I clung to the railing for support—the last thing I needed was a fall and a new reaper bill.

"Watch yourself, I don't want you tripping on top of me."

I could hear shouting and the thuds of furious combat below. At one point, a scream rang out, a woman's voice, only graveled and husky.

"Absinthe," Wendy breathed.

I nodded.

At the bottom, a welcome glow calmed me somewhat. The light came from the source of the ruckus, a doorway about halfway down the hall, and spotlit the crumpled figure of the Belgian ghoul, headless and nude, her flesh stitched in black vine like a homemade rag doll. Focused on the atrocity and not my footing, I caught on a tangle of growth, dense and covered in yellow flowers—St. John's wort, I thought. A fairly common ground cover for the area. Trudging through the stuff was no easy task and the tiny buckles all over my stilettos didn't help matters any. But about halfway down the corridor, I caught on something heavy and toppled over it and onto my knees with an aching crack.

"Oh shit." Wendy's face was white with terror—or whiter, pale being our natural state, and all.

I reached for the object, a mound only slightly higher than the rest of the brush, and retrieved what seemed to be a wet bundle of leaves.

Too heavy for that, I thought, and drew it toward me, realizing I didn't really want to know and probably would have been better off just trudging on, but couldn't stop myself. I pulled some of the greenery away and then dropped it.

It was Absinthe's missing head, threaded with vines, mouth gaping in a silent scream.

Johnny's hobby was not so cute anymore. Apparently redecorating wasn't limited to just rooms.

We pressed on, and reaching the open doorway, heard another scream. Wendy nudged me forward and I pointed out a sign on our right. "The Hungry Desert. What do you think that means?"

"No clue. I'm sure it's something horrendous. That would figure, right about now," Wendy whispered.

"The challenges were meant to be held down here, but since Johnny died first, I never knew anything about what they were."

The light emanated from an overhead bulb hanging ominously from a black cord in the ceiling. It cast a triangle of light onto the far wall, decorated with the harsh edges of two words, painted from floor to ceiling: HUNGRY DESERT. The edge of a door was visible just left of the first "R" and obscured that letter as though it were simply a crease in paper.

I, for one, wasn't looking forward to this. But Johnny'd played his cards and it was time to play mine, if I can use a poker reference. And I can, because, hey, it's my book. Plus, what's a reality show without a big finale. A flop, that's what.

Over my dead body.

Deadish, even.

We pushed into the first room, a vast space filled with sand that rolled out like seaside dunes. The ceiling was higher than feasible and reflected a moving sky of fluffy cumulus and cerulean blue. In the distance a rectangle of black ruined the illusion of nature.

"There's the door," I said, pointing for both the camera and Wendy's benefit. I started to move through the sand and nearly fell over backward as my heels sunk deep into the surprising cool depths.

"I wouldn't if I were you." The voice came from our right. A girl's voice. My stomach tensed.

Hellary.

I rolled my eyes even as I turned—it was refreshing not owing the bitch money.

She'd stripped off her Mary Janes and tights and hiked up her jumper to the crotch of her panties and lay in the sand sunning. "They all went through there. Some of them made it."

"Some?" Wendy's horror gave the word three syllables.

"Yeah. I think." The reaper fluttered her eyes. "Or maybe they all did, I wasn't really paying attention. Sorry."

"Made what?" I asked. "There's nothing in here."

"Oh." Hellary smiled. "There's something in here, it's just not visible."

"I don't suppose you care to tell us what?"

"Nope." She waved me aside. "You bitches can find out on your own. Now get out of the way, you're casting a mighty fat shadow."

I scanned the hills and valleys of the desert landscape and at first saw nothing—I did make a note to only vacay near the ocean, somewhere cute with palapas, poolboys and drinks with umbrellas in them—then noticed patches of green interrupting the sea of beige. I walked slowly to the nearest sprout. White pentacle-shaped flowers snaked from the leaves. Morning glories. I figured they were either a sign of Johnny having been there or moisture or something.

I was about to test my theory and follow them like a path when Wendy came running up behind me carrying Absinthe's head like a football. She reared back and lobbed it in a high arc, dropping it at the crest of one of the taller dunes.

"Nice one." Hellary held her hand over her eyes like a visor.

"Getting your aggression out?" I asked.

"I just figured we ought to see what's out there, that's all."

As we watched, the green globe of leaves and gore sunk into the sand and out of sight. Not the object of some dragon's snapping hunger, it just simply sunk and disappeared.

"Quicksand?" I suggested.

Wendy nodded.

I went back to my original plan. I could have been completely wrong, but I was pretty sure that the spots of morning glory grew in Johnny's footprints. It just made sense. Plus the crooked seam of them led straight to the open door on the opposite side.

"Stay behind me and if I start to sink, for Christ's sake, get it on film."

I slipped off my shoes and stepped across to the first patch and the ground felt firm enough, I mean, as far as sand goes. Wendy followed a few paces behind. My next few steps were a little shaky. I felt the sand shifting under my bare feet and had to leap to the next patch of plant life before I slipped into whatever the hell quicksand was. I had an image of that cheesey 80s horror flick *Blood Beach* and the monster that sucked up bad actresses and the steroid junkies that loved them later spitting them out in a spray of blood. I was pretty sure we weren't dealing with that kind of thing.

Though I could've been wrong.

That's why this next part is a little sketchy on the integrity side. Don't get me wrong, I love Wendy. She's my best friend and I wouldn't trade her in for anything. But when I saw the gap between the last two patches of morning glory, there was nothing else I could do.

"Wendy?"

"Yes?" She held on to my arm and looked around my shoulder. "Wow. That's a long way. Good luck with that one."

"Why don't you lay down between them and I'll just tip-toe across? Easy as can be?"

"What?" She glared. "Are you fucking nuts?"

I shrugged. "It's not like you're going to die. You might sink a little bit but really it's nothing more than a nice salt scrub. Your face will look as fresh as a five-year-old's. Swear to God."

I knew nothing of the sort, of course. But I figured that even if she sank to the bottom, we could always come back and dig her out after it was all over. It's not like she had to breathe, and I could probably do my own camera work.

She grimaced at the expanse of sand. "And you'll pull me right out?"

"The second I get across. No shit."

She crouched down to her knees and eyed me suspiciously. "Right out?"

I snatched the camera from her hand. "Absolutely. But let's do it quick so you won't sink very far."

Her eyes widened and she stiffened. I couldn't let her ruin this chance, so I did something I'm not proud of. I pushed her over. She fell with a muffled thud onto her face buried in a pillowy hillock. It was really sort of amusing as long as you weren't Wendy.

Before she could react, I padded as softly and quickly as I could once onto her ass and then—God help me—the back of her head, forcing her face back into the sand. When I reached the final patch of morning glories, Wendy was thrashing atop the sand, not having sunk an inch. Hellary howled with laughter, doubled over and wheezing.

I reached down and pulled my friend—no, scratch that—my best friend, to her feet.

"You're a hero," I said.

Her face was scrunched in anger.

"You're *my* hero," I emphasized, nodding my head aggressively. "Saved my life, and I'll tell everyone so."

Wendy stood in the very spot I'd pushed her down into. She stomped her feet, just to show me how firm it was, as if the scratches on her face weren't clue enough. I figured it probably wasn't a good time to tell her about those and was lucky not to have to as another scream broke the silence between us.

The door led to a balcony overlooking the heart of the house, the boiler, a large metal cylinder, orange with rust, and pipes protruding from it to feed the house. But the steam it produced didn't make the scream.

That was all Johnny.

And, to his credit, it could have sounded a lot more effeminate, considering Angie had him in a great big gory tentacle hug and was alternating between vicious bites at his cheek and lapping at the blood—or whatever—that splashed from the wound.

"Back off!" Chase approached the struggling pair. He pointed his gun at Angie.

"Watch out!" Maiko shouted.

Tanesha and Scott fought against the vines binding them to the far wall. Both howled in frustration. This was the only time I'd seen them side-by-side in their supernatural form.

Tanesha was only slightly taller than Scott's seven werewolf feet due to her fabulous weave; it didn't transform—something about it not being natural. I wondered what would happen if the drag queen ever got breast implants, the idea of silicone double DS bouncing around under all that fur made me want to vomit . . . and pursue advertising geared toward the altered were.[98]

"Stay back or I'll shoot it in the head."

Angie's entrails slackened, leaving trails of gore and other bodily fluids in their wake. Her large intestine snaked around his throat a bit before finally giving way.

"Her," Maiko spat.

"Well she bloody well don't look like a her." Chase kept the gun pointed at Angie and moved to stand next to the wood nymph.

"He's not even British," Gil spat. "And he used to be so fucking fat you could start a soap company with the weight he carried. Jesus, haven't you seen his nipples?" Gil shook violently and leaned into Vance's

---

[98] Because I'm sensitive to the needs of today's trannie shapeshifter as well as the cosmetically altered. It's not going away, people. I might as well make some money. Lord knows I could use some.

comforting embrace, the drama hanging like a cloud around them.

Johnny wiped at his cheek with the front of his shirt, eyes pinioned on Chase's approach.

"Nah gaw shoo you. Promise." His accent slipping into a bad Brit flick cockney.

"Oh okay, then," Johnny said. "Like you didn't fire off a round upstairs. What was that, fucking foreplay?"

"No, seriously, I forgive you." His accent gone totally American now, the bland speech of a Pacific Northwesterner.

"Mmm-hmm. Come here then." Johnny held open his arms as though to hug the vampire but when he was close enough—and really, who didn't see this coming—Chase turned the gun on Johnny and blasted a hole through his shoulder.

The wood nymph fell back on his ass and gawped up at Chase, already aiming for another shot. "I knew you'd do that."

"No, you didn't."

"I did too."

Chase began to shake his head, but a pair of vines struck his wrists from above, sending the gun skittering off under the boiler. They coiled around his throat, leafy and thick as a feather boa and lifted him several feet above the floor, where he kicked and gurgled.

I glanced at Gil, who smirked a bit.

Johnny knelt on the floor, his face a study in hatred. Vines shot out of the beams and walls, targeting Chase and drilling through his convulsing frame. Congealed blood and bone meal dropped to the floor in clumps and even Gil couldn't smile through the torture his rapist endured. Though he should have.

He's way nicer than me, as if you couldn't tell. But

even I flinched as the body was torn apart, quadrants dropping onto the floor in big wet plops.

"Gross," I said aloud.

Maiko was next to act, rushing forward and evaporating into tendrils of gray smoke mere seconds before Johnny blasted two shots in her direction. Her ghost form swirled around Johnny's head and contracted, tightening in like a helmet of toxic gas.

The wood nymph batted at the haze and ran from the room. I helped free the rest from the vines and we followed easily, traversing the desert and up and out of the hellacious basement.

We found them in the Grand Hall.

Johnny stumbled out of Maiko's smoky cloud, gasping for air and lurching for the front door, one foot broken and flopping. When that happened was hard to tell, though I didn't much care either way, just as long as Wendy was capturing it.

"One last thing, Johnny." I stepped up to the battered nymph and tipped my head in what I hoped was a welcoming gesture, or at least comforting. "Why'd you do it?"

"Why?" he croaked. "I'll tell you why . . ."

A loud scraping sounded through the hall and all heads turned to see the plastic infection bubble roll into the main hall.

Mama, pathetically exhausted and stumbling to keep up the momentum, limped toward Johnny. The woman was on her last legs, literally. Anger and revenge fueling her motion, she fumbled at her throat for the polished sliver of bone, tearing it free and holding it awkwardly in one hand while she clawed at her chest with the other. With the last of her life, Mama Montserrat stabbed the shank high up on the bubble. She teetered a moment, the bubble squealing against the marble floor and then slumped forward. The ball moved slowly toward Johnny and me.

His bloodied lip curled into a grin at the woman's fallen form.

What happened next couldn't be helped.

The story needed an ending.

I owed the viewers something, didn't I? What could I do? It's not like I didn't just do the same thing to my best friend.

I pushed Johnny over.

The wood nymph fell flat on his back, a yowling scream stretched out of him as Mama's steamrolling coffin crushed his legs, then his lousy balls, his heaving chest and finally, ever so slowly, the bone dagger curved around and drove deep into Johnny Birch's skull.

The scream silenced instantly.

Blood pooled around the body as the ball rocked back and forth on its deadly anchor.

*"That,"* I said, pointing at Johnny, "took too fucking long. I'd totally fast forward through it if I were watching it at home."

It's hard to know where to end the story. Do you leave
it on a high note, full of hope and warm fuzzies, a
happily-ever-after, if you will? Or do you tell the truth
and follow the denouement straight into the toilet bowl,
taking the reader on that last spin down into the sewer?

I wouldn't expect anyone to believe I'd somehow hit
the rainbow jackpot, not with my luck—that would be
too big a leap of faith. So here's the reality (or realities,
since they tend to come in spades—a whole deck of
them). . . .

It took some begging and pleading and, finally, offering to be Karkaroff's errand girl for a month—no
small sacrifice considering her requests were never
quite as simple as scrounging up a coffee, and often-

times required actual sacrifices—but I got Karkaroff to spring for a clothing budget for the *American Minions* promo junket.[99] I managed to snag the only Elie Saab cashmere tulip dress in town—quite a coup when that town is Seattle. It should come as no surprise in the land of downy-armed vegans, a fox skirt would have a target on it, even with yummy guipure flowers adorning the fur. The PETA crowd, had they known, would've stroked out on the sidewalk in front of Zero, the boutique owned by former supermodel/zombie Gialla and her business partner-cum-lover, Skitchy, a sculptor with a penchant for Sears overalls and stolen prosthetic limbs as her medium of choice.

"It's stunning, dahling," Gialla'd said, dabbing a small sore above her eye with a dainty silk handkerchief. "It's both contemptible and elegant."

I spun in front of the mirror. "What do you think, Wendy?"

"I think you're gonna be late."

Wendy swiveled around on the leather puff in the center of the dressing room, her press pass stuck between her front teeth. She snapped it out and flicked off the leftovers from last night's meal. "Mmm. Sexy. Is that what you're going for?"

"Sure. Why wouldn't I be?"

"I'm just wondering if that's the right message to be sending out, now that you've snared your werewolf again."

"He's fully aware of the importance of my public persona."

"Whatever you say."

---

[99] And no, I don't expect you to bemoan my fashion budget. We're not at the crappy part yet.

\* \* \*

Duncan Donut was the chunky werebear host of the hottest supernatural talk show in town, *Live from Les Toilettes*.[100] Everyone watched it to catch the latest gossip and celebrity skewering by Donut and his panel of snark stylists. I'd often thought I'd be perfect on the show, but Mink and Bibi, the host's constant werecub companions, weren't going anywhere until they gave up the hidden camera video of Duncan caught with his pants around the ankles of a high school football player, or at least that's what I've heard. So I'd have to resign myself to a spot in the "hotseat," which in this case was a stainless steel toilet with a see-through plastic cushion over the seat—it's not for "us" to get the joke, apparently, because it's never explained why the host and his lackeys giggle every time someone sits on the thing.

"Our guest tonight is the lovely party-hopping naughty, Amanda Feral. She's the star of the insanely popular *Who Killed Johnny Birch* right here on Supernatural Satellite and its been getting rave reviews and climbing up the ratings chart. Welcome to *Live!*" Duncan reached across the gap with fingers plump as breakfast sausages, which actually complimented his complexion—a jaundiced skin tone always reminds me of egg yolks for some reason. I squeezed his hand lightly to be polite, worried they'd be greasy and not at all surprised to be right.

---

[100] No. Unfortunately the name is not an ode to the fabulous breakfast treat establishment, but rather Donut's particular sexual proclivity. One I'd rather leave to your own imagination. Oh . . . who am I kidding? He's a chipper, a food fetishist. The kind that likes to dip (or dunk, if you will) their edibles into a fancy stretched-out ass (or donut). Gross, right? I blame you for making me tell.

"Glad to be here. You have a wonderful audience, for a bunch of chubby chasers," I snarled as the audience booed, several shifting into bears of various types, though the single polar bear in the front row couldn't have been more yellowed from the waist down if the entire audience had relieved themselves on him.

Now, before you get all huffy about it—abrasive was de rigueur on *Live.* To come on and be polite was both frowned upon and vehemently shunned to the harshest degree. Obviously, I didn't have a problem with that.

Duncan chuckled, his man-boobs jiggling with the effort. About three hundred pounds, with a close-cropped white beard and eyebrows that needed a serious trim, Donut was a shoo-in to play Santa at whatever passed as a Christmas pageant at Les Toilettes, though I expect the flip of white hair he kept at just above shoulder length would prove irresistible to the golden showers crowd said to frequent the club.

"Ooh, swarthy!" Duncan squealed. "I like it. Now tell me, who did kill Johnny Birch, we're all dying to know." He leaned forward, steepled his fingers and pressed them to his lips.

"Like I'd tell you, you fat fuck. You'll have to wait until the season finale just like everyone else." I leaned back on the toilet and crossed my legs. "Now, can someone get me a drink?" I thought a moment, then added. "Nothing yellow though, I'm on to your games."

The crowd roared with laughter while a skinny carrot-topped boy in leather lederhosen ran over from the bar with a martini glass. He shook a bit as he passed it into my hand.

"The reason I ask—" Duncan paused, grinning mischievously for the camera. "We have reason to believe that the show has run into some financial difficulties."

I spit a mouthful of vodka at the frightened waiter, who skittered off like a bug.

What the hell, I thought. I should have known I'd get lambasted publicly the minute Marithé came to me with the offer to appear on *Live*. She probably played a part in whatever Donut was about to spew. I flicked the olive into the crowd, threw back the rest of the martini and tossed the glass. It shattered nearby faintly under the din of the excited crowd.

"Yeah?" I asked, steeling myself. "What might those be?"

"Absolutely. In fact, we have someone here, who'll sort the whole matter out."

A suited man stood from the bleachers and approached the little stage, opening a briefcase on Duncan's desk and withdrawing a handful of papers, which he forced in my direction. I didn't move. If the fucker was going to serve me then he'd have to be ugly about it on TV.

Apparently that wasn't a problem for him. He tossed them and they hit my chest before cascading to the floor.

"You've been served," he said and shut his briefcase. His face was thin, pinched around the nose and mouth and his eyes were as beady as you'd expect from a guy in his line of work. He smelled like human, but I suspected demon. Most lawyers and their ilk were hellspawn somewhere in their heritage.[101]

I glared at him, them, the cameras, everyone. Things were just starting to look up. After Mama's untimely death, Feral Inc. took on the show and worked with the network and advertisers to secure a good time slot and

---

[101] That should come as no surprise to any of you.

such—you have to understand that technology among supernaturals is still relatively new, and is still shunned by purists who view TV as a virus of our own food supply. It was a relatively easy process—the stations were all small and privately owned and SS12 was more than willing to take us on. Advertisers fell into place as soon as they heard what we'd been able to capture between the handheld camera and the nanny cams in each of the rooms. The major tragedy would have been the loss of the footage at the Hooch and Cooch, but, after considerable digging, Ethel was able to recover her security footage.

When I watched it, I was surprised at the clarity and even more shocked at the chemistry between Ethel and me. The scene in her office made for damn fine television and for once, the woman seemed genuinely concerned for my wellbeing. So much so, I was worried we'd be offered our own show and I'd have to spend more time with the bitch. Luckily, I hadn't had to turn anyone down.

"So what's all this?" I pointed at the papers around me.

"Feral Inc. is being sued by both the estates of Samuel Harcourt and the recently deceased Mama Montserrat and Johnny Birch."

"Awesome." I looked him dead in the eye. "Bring it."

"Ooh. The kitten's got some fight left in her," Duncan said. The process server plodded off and the host continued. "Now Amanda, we've heard that prior to the show's success you'd hit the skids a bit. Can you tell us about your struggles with poverty?"

If you think I'm the type to buckle under at a moment like this, then three books have taught you nothing. I had no intention of being victimized on network television, or anywhere else.

"Well, Duncan, if by Skids you mean the fantastic line of jewelry my friend Wendy just launched then yes, it's true, I'm all over the Skids. In fact!" I shook my bracelet, a dazzling crimson number, resembling three stitched slashes across my right wrist. "As for poverty, I wouldn't say I struggle with the poor, I merely eat them." I shrugged, smiling broadly.

"Aren't you concerned about these lawsuits?" he asked, befuddled. Clearly this wasn't turning out to be the hatchet job he'd planned.

"Not in the slightest," I yawned, gesturing at the papers. "These things have a way of working themselves out."

"Well, then." Duncan Donut sneered. Bibi and Mink mimicked his expression.

"Well, then," I agreed.

"Well, then, let's take a caller." Duncan reached down with his fat finger and stabbed one of the six flashing buttons on his phone. "You're Live at Les Toilettes!"

"Is this Duncan Donut?" The voice was too measured. Too familiar.

"Yes, it is. Do you have a question for our fantabulous guest, Ms. Amanda Feral?"

"I sure do. Amanda, this is your mother. I've got your room ready and waiting for you. Do you have any idea what your timeline is for moving in, because I've got your Aunt Rachel coming in for a few days and I don't want to have to move you out to the couch when you could just hold off until I've had my nice visit. Though, come to think of it, she's almost blind so she probably won't be able to tell you're dead, except she has quite the nose and . . ." she paused. "We both know there are days when you're not so—"

I groaned and reached across Duncan, picked up the receiver and slammed it back down ending the call.

I met up with Wendy after the show to grab a snack before coffee with the guys. It was odd to think that Gil was part of a functional couple after all these months of sad sacking, but sure enough, Vance (or whatever he was calling himself) was still around and seemed to be genuinely enamored of our guy.

Wendy held out what looked like a piece of heart— never my favorite organ, too chewy if you ask me. "Oh my God, Amanda. You've got to try this, it's awesome."

"That's okay." I waved her off and went back to my dinner of crude construction worker who wouldn't leave well enough alone.[102] I wasn't really in the mood to talk about the lawsuit either and luckily for her, Wendy could take a hint. About some things.

"No, seriously. Taste it."

"I don't want any. Really." I pulled away from her jutting hand.

"Come on." Wendy's face scrunched up. "It's not like I shit on it."

After dinner we stood in front of the spot where Wendy parked the car. I could have sworn I saw it piggy-backing on a tow truck.

"Um," was her only response.

We hailed a cab at the corner of Western and 3rd and that's when things got ugly, and by ugly I mean crazy bendi-dot Indian-ghost ugly. I noticed something was wrong before Wendy even pulled the door closed behind us.

---

[102] I know. I know. Fast food is bad for you.

First off, Pie-hole and Lumpy were back and staring me down like I'd shit on their firstborn. If they weren't bad enough, Raj, fresh from the dead, grimaced from the front seat, eyes fidgeting toward the driver. I winced. Somehow—and these days I don't even bother to ask—Baljeet had managed to drag her dead ass out of that garbage truck and track down the cab.

Yep.

You guessed it. Ghost. But how she managed to drive a car was beyond me. The stuff the spectral can do these days. Progress, I guess.

"Oh, don't you sure look fresh and lively, Ms. Amanda Feral," Baljeet said, sneering. "Not a hair out of place and don't look any deader than when I last saw you. Son of a bitching murderous, is what you are, I ought to drive us all right over a cliff."

I sighed.

There wasn't anywhere this could go but wrong. I tried to ignore the din of voices. Pie-hole and Lumpy complaining about an eternity listening to Baljeet bitch and complain about "this or that or the other thing."

I pointed at Raj. "How was I supposed to know he had a bad heart? I'm not a fucking doctor."

"Did you think to ask before you went screeching at him in your terrifying 'I'll eat anything that walks' American-entitled-zombie way?" Baljeet punctuated her attack by curling her fingers into claws and glowering like she imagined I had.

"I apologize, Raj." I nodded in his direction. He shrugged.

"A bit late for that! Now, he's bound to this cab forever and by Krishna will never give our parents the grandsons they so desperately deserve. Can you apologize for that?"

Wendy leaned forward and looked Baljeet in the eye. "Well, I didn't do shit to Raj or you and I'd like to get to the Starbucks on Cap Hill. Or is this not a real cab anymore?"

Baljeet scoffed and put the cab into gear, pulling away from the curb, tires squealing. We both dropped back into the seats with enough force to wind me, sending a curl of viral breath into the cab. I didn't bother to suck it back in, considering my traveling companions.

"Hey, Baljeet?" I asked hesitantly as the ghost somehow maneuvered the cab down toward the waterfront. I watched her gauzy hands play across the vinyl of the steering wheel. It turned under some supernatural pressure beneath her phantom grasp.

"What do you want? I won't answer just any of your stupid questions, devil."

I leaned forward. "I was just wondering where you were going."

Baljeet chuckled and even her laugh was accented. It rose and lilted with a humid timbre, not tropical exactly—it lacked the sweet and sticky undertones. Baljeet's laugh masked the intentions of a killer, scimitar raised high and ready to slash.

Raj squirmed in the co-pilot's seat. Eyes darting nervously to his left, fearful of his sister even in death.

We scraped bottom as we careened through the first intersection, the car bouncing on stressed shocks and launching out into the air at the next hill. Seattle streets follow a suicidal slope toward Puget Sound. It feels a bit like San Francisco, without any of the associated romance.

It was even more clearly unromantic in a dirty cab, surrounded by the dead and facing down another car crash. I was beginning to think walking was a palatable option, but who am I kidding, I just needed to get a fucking car.

At the speed we were travelling it took me a moment to realize where we were headed. I elbowed Wendy. "The Harbor Steps."

She grimaced and frantically fumbled with the seatbelts. I followed suit, pressing half into Pie-hole, who grinned as though I'd touched his ghost package. Maybe I had. I pulled the belt around and tried to find the buckle, squeezing my fingers into the crevasse between the cushions and coming up empty.

When I glanced up, we were crossing 1st Ave. I braced myself against the seatback and closed my eyes as we jumped the curb and launched out into the space above the steps. My insides shifted in that weightless moment and I felt like I would spew, but in the next second the cab collided with something hard enough to send me tumbling over the seats and out the front window.

I must have passed out.

Sort of a welcome event.

Sort of.

"Amanda." Hands on my shoulders, rocking me. "Amanda."

I peeked out of the corner of my eye and saw Ricardo's concerned face hovering over mine. "Wow. Is that your prosthetic digging into my hip?"

He might have flushed but instead just smirked. "No." He stretched out the word, like he wasn't aware Marithé had let the cat out of the bag. Or the boner, as the case may be. I decided to let it go.

"Can you sit up?"

I pushed myself up on my elbows and stared at the

wreckage of the cab. Twisted metal and shattered glass marred poor Ricardo's minimal atmosphere. A big hole in the wall overlooked the well-dressed human patrons of the nearby churrascaria, while tanks of anesthesia spun uncontrollably, filling the room with a scraping metallic noise and sputtering clouds of the Ether's life juice. Baljeet planted herself atop the heap, her arms folded and a scowl severe enough to create instant wrinkles carved into her face. Raj and the boys wandered nearby. A single arm snaked out of a dark gap, waving frantically.

I sighed, scanning my body, which miraculously appeared unscathed. I probably should have been happy just to be alive and moving. I really was blessed.

The arm retracted into the wreck. A grumbling echoed inside the hulk, Wendy curling around inside like a turtle.

You know what I could have really gone for just then?

The arm shot straight out, dangling from between the zombie's delicate fingers, a pristine cigarette.

"Get her out of there!" I screamed.

Maxey popped in through the hole and snapped his fingers, a spark rolling off them like he'd tossed a die. It popped up off the floor and bounced across the cab, leaving a thin bead of molten metal in its wake. The crumpled car split in two and Wendy emerged wholly unscathed.

She grinned at the little fae.

"That's two you owe me."

Ricardo frowned and shook his head. And I ran up and snatched the cigarette from her hand, and as I was lighting up I whispered, "You look good."

\* \* \*

"If you order a fresh-baked cookie you get a song." The barista grinned broadly and cocked her head. I half-expected to hear a hollow "tink" as her pea brain rolled from one side to the other.

"Well, in that case," I said. "We'll just have the two espressos."

Mortimer, as her nametag suggested, soured up real quick and stabbed the keys on her cash register even as her face twisted like a camera shutter. I shoved some cash across the counter and joined Wendy at the opposite side of the Buick-sized espresso machine.

"I'm sorry about the lawsuits, I know that can't be good for business or your finances. I want you to know I wouldn't seriously force you to live with Ethel. Hell. You'd murder her within twenty-four hours."

"No doubt." I shuffled my Ferragamos. These sorts of emotional and genuine discussions were pretty rare in our circles and I'd learned to let them happen and not make fun—as is my nature (not telling you anything you don't know).

"You can stay with Abuelita and me," she said, putting her hand on my shoulder, which was really a bit much, but again my instincts aren't always right, so.

"Thanks." I brightened. "I don't think that'll be necessary though. Things with Scott and me are going really well. I've got a place to stay . . . if it comes to that."

"Still, Karkaroff is going to be hot when she gets back and gets word of this."

I imagined she would, but that was three months away and her partners at her law firm would be all over it long before then, just to see her name listed on the court documents. "She's the most frightening attorney I know," I said, reaching for the tiny paper cups of espresso. "If anyone is prepared to deal with it, she is."

We took our spots on the veranda beside the drive-thru. The only thing we'd changed about our daily ritual was the time of day, or night as it were.

"So when's Seattle's most adorable drug dealer premiering her opium den?" Gil flopped down next to Wendy, slipped one arm around her shoulder and tickled her side with the other.

She batted his hand away. "Stop it! You're going to pinch off some skin. And anyways, it's not an opium den, it's more like a Tupperware party, only with frotteurists and pretty models instead of cranky housewives and burping seals. I'm still figuring out the business. Abuelita's teaching me the ropes. Getting some 'ins' with the distributors. Gotta isolate my niche, you know?"

"The whole fetish angle has got to be cookies and cream for kinky vamps." I sniffed the steam coming off the dark shot. Heaven is a memory for me. The crema crept up the sides of the little paper cup like snowdrifts. Dirty snow drifts. Oh crap . . . you know what I mean.

Gil narrowed his eyes. "Were you looking at me when you said that?"

I smiled and joined in the weird cloud comparisons. "It's like a *Home Interiors* party only instead of sniffing eucalyptus candles, guests get to dry hump and pass out in a pool of their own sick."

"Exactly."

Vance came whistling out of the café, hefting a massive blended coffee concoction and pulled a chair up behind Gil, resting his head between his boyfriend's shoulders as he slurped.

"So here's a question." Wendy took a big shocking gulp of her espresso and slunk back in her seat, propping her feet up on the edge of the table.[103] "Why'd he even try to fake his own death?"

"Who, Johnny?" Vance asked, a dollop of whipped cream on his nose. Gil kissed it off lightly and their cuteness made me want to run screaming into the night to do something horrible like eat a preschool or mix batteries in with the recycling.

"Who the fuck else would we be talking about?" I snorted the steam off my espresso.

He ignored my irritation. "That's simple. He knew the yeti were gunning for him. Would have crucified his ass, too, had they gotten the chance."

Somewhere I knew that, from Scott, but it got lost in the money matters. Also because I was secretly hoping that it'd happen. I guess the appearance of the creatures in his mail threw me off, thinking it was part of his plan.

"What about the wood nymph carcass?"

"What are you talking about?"

"Johnny's hate mail. It included a wood nymph carcass pinned to a cedar shake."

"That doesn't sound yeti to me. Too weird. Unnatural. They're much more straightforward. Like if they catch you they kill you. That kind of thing."

"Well, that really doesn't explain Hairy Sue then." Wendy smirked, like she'd blown the conversation wide open.

I cleared my throat and dug in my purse for a smoke and my cell. "Yeah, but she was a whore in addition to a yeti, so . . ."

---

[103] She'd be cursing herself later.

"The yetis targeted Johnny a year ago. They needed someone high-profile enough to make their bloody point and he certainly would have fit the bill. I'm probably moving to the top of their list now." Vance chuckled a bit and then stopped, face souring.

I scooted my chair closer to Gil, puffing away and scrolling through my videos for the perfect entertainment. "Have I ever shown you this?"

I pulled up the clip of Absinthe working Wendy like a leather chew toy.

"Ew." He shivered.

Vance winced.

"Nice, Amanda. I swear to God, you think you'd be worried about karma or something." Wendy picked a piece of coffee grounds off her tongue.

"I'm through worrying."

Gil patted my leg. "What'll you do now?"

I looked at him, suddenly confused.

"Now that the money's probably going to be tied up with lawyers and such." He nodded, like that would help me understand what he was saying. "The money from the show?"

"That's not necessarily true," I defended.

He shrugged. "You should write a book."

"Maybe I will."

"Do."

"I will."

The End . . . except for . . .

# Appendix
## (Even better, an Adolescent Appendix[*])
## Let's call it . . .
### *Amanda Shutter, Juvenile Delinquent*

[*]You didn't think I'd miss a chance to veer dramatically from the actual story line, did you? Remember? I promised a fat-ass appendix, so here you go.

This one time—I think it was my thirteenth birthday, but I could be wrong—Ethel and the guy she was hot-boxing that week, Burt Friendly, of Friendly AC and Heating Supply Superstore, decided it would be nice for the three of us to celebrate my birthday without the pesky annoyance of friends or gifts. So thoughtful. We got stuck at Benihana, at a table with two drunken marines—one of them wore a scar like a permanent part in his hairline, the other was missing his front teeth[104]— and a tight-assed married couple. At the farthest edge of the grill table sat the couple's son. About my age, probably a couple of years older, but all you really need to know is this: he was hot, in that grungy, patched-army-jacket, eyelids-heavy-with-too-much-sexual-knowledge, kind of way.[105]

[104] Well, to be honest, I'm not sure he missed them. He sure had fun darting his tongue in and out of the gap.
[105] Or he was good at his act. Either way.

It was the kind of grouping that could only end badly . . . and in front of a strange Japanese chef with sharp spatulas.

Burt Friendly introduced himself and gave everyone his card, not the one for his business, but his special "swinger" card, because "you folk look like you enjoy a good time." The marines examined it and laughed, but the kid's parents were wide-eyed with shock, staring at the card as though Burt had handed over some hard-core scat porn. I glanced at my mother, attempting to shame him and put a stop to this horror, but she simply lit up a cigarette and used it as a sizzling baton to motion the waitress over.

"I'll have one of those tiki jobbies," she demanded. "And make it strong, I know how you nippers like to cheat the round eyes."

I sunk in my chair and dug up the courage to sneak a glance at the sexy hoodlum. His eyes smoldered in my direction, shoulders shaking in silent laughter. Whether it was at my mother's remark—I hoped not—or his parents' discomfort was arguable. Then he did the unthinkable, he parted his lips a bit and winked.

It was a quick wink, more of a flutter really, and even though I wasn't sure it had actually happened, I looked away and pretended to be interested as the chef lit shit up and chopped a shrimp into eight little tasters with maniacal abandon. I figured the longer I averted my gaze, the more he might think I'd missed his first volley.

I was wrong.

The boy was still ogling me.

He winked again, the way an old man might, mouth agape and tongue probing the corner. The only thing he missed was the newspaper to peep around and an overcoat hiding his pasty nakedness. Now, I thought, he's just trying to gross me out.

I mouthed, "Are you high?"

He shrugged, picked up his bowl of miso soup and darted his tongue in and out of the salty broth like he was the second coming of Burt Friendly.[106]

"You can take your card back, sir!" his mother shouted with venom, breaking the moment.[107] Her hair didn't move a centimeter as she whipped her head around, the whole thing encased in a web of Aqua Net so thick I thought I could see the strands. "We're not interested in your filthy disgusting godless lifestyle." Her head whipped toward her bug-eyed husband, busy slicking back a spike with freakishly long fingers. "Are we, Harold?"

He shook his head and looked at his son.

"Speak for yourselves." The boy's grin was punctuated by a circle of spring onion, stuck to his front tooth like a scarlet letter—"O" for "obnoxious," or maybe "O" for "Oh my God, what a dickhead."

I didn't point it out.

Burt snapped the card back with a shrug and passed it instead to the marines with a wink. "There's an extra for you, then."

They launched into fits of drunken laughter at the undoubtedly vulgar words. Ethel slapped Burt's arm as if to chastise him, but then whispered something in his ear, stood up and swaggered in the direction of the restrooms.

The man leaned back, hands slipping across the yoke of his sailing shirt and drummed his chest as he

---

[106] Or second cumming, for that matter.
[107] If you could call it that. I'd call it an eternity.

eyed my mother's ass, which, of course, kneaded under the thin silk skirt with all the tasteless freedom a lack of panties provides.

"I think the little lady needs a hand with her powder puff, if you catch my drift." He pushed away from the table and followed.

I might have blushed just then, if I hadn't seen it coming. In thirteen years of birthdays, Christmases, Halloweens, and Memorial Days (especially Memorial Days—mother loved uniforms), Ethel had yet to let an occasion pass that didn't somehow involve her getting her rocks off. That she'd do it at the risk of my public embarrassment seemed to be a parental requirement, though where she got her advice on the matter was less Dr. Spock than *Penthouse Forum*. Instead, I reached for the closest tiki cup and drained the sweet red brew. It went down smooth, like Hawaiian Punch or something, only warmer.

I glanced back at the boy. His face changed; his mouth agape, as if it were even possible to shock such a little perv. Our eyes met briefly and I thought he flinched, until he brought his hand up to his mouth and imitated a blowjob, his tongue working a pulsing bulge in the opposite cheek.

"Bastard," I mouthed.

His parents grimaced, but not the two crewcuts. They were ribbing each other and whispering. The one with the scar got up shortly after and followed Burt through the gap between the sizzling tables. A moment later, Toothless Grin stumbled behind him, excusing himself slovenly.

The woman's face scrunched up in disgust once more, as though someone had dropped a dog turd in her sukiyaki. She shifted her chair toward Harold's and focused on the chef, who'd begun the ritual rice ball toss.

The boy was first and as expected, he snapped it out of the air like a great white shark on a seal. Harold opened his maw wide and the gluten-o-fun plopped right in there with a wet thunk. The woman declined politely and refused to make eye contact with the chef.

I hadn't really paid much attention to the tall chef. He was younger than I expected, maybe twenty-two, with a chiseled jaw and a twitch of mischief in his dark eyes. His mouth curled at the ends as he juggled the last rice ball on the end of his spatulas.

"You next." He nodded in that shy way I'd never thought was sexy before that moment.

And then he did it too.

He winked.

I must have gasped because the next thing I remember, the rice had clogged the back of my throat and I was shaking in my seat, struggling for air, with tears streaming down my birthday cheeks. It was the sexy chef that Heimliched me. Three strong pumps and the rice launched across the table and stuck to the boy's forehead like a mucus-covered bendi.

He held me for a minute more, hands lingering beneath my breasts. I closed my eyes and felt his breath against my neck. It would have been an actual "moment" if the combination of the tiki drink, the miso and the abdominal assault hadn't made me so queasy.

In the next second, three things happened.

One, the waitress, who really should have had us kicked out after Ethel's racist comment, dropped a bowl of green tea ice cream in front of me with a candle sticking out of it. She smiled wanly and bowed, as behind her a gathering of Japanese in kimonos began tò sing their version of the birthday song, with all the extra syllables they could fit in, it seemed.

Two, Burt Friendly burst from the women's bathroom with his pants hula-hooping around one ankle like a field day activity. With each pass, he maneuvered the cotton hazard with an awkward little hop and shuffle, his rosy prick bouncing amidst a mass of gray pubic hair like a festive Christmas homage.[108] The act made all the more perversely ridiculous by the fact that he had hold of Toothless Grin's throat the whole while, screaming about courtesy and recognizing receptive holes. They toppled over each other in a mangle I hesitate to refer to as "homo-erotic" as it was neither manly nor sexy, unless you count the moment where Toothless caught Burt's scrotum in the snaggle of his teeth and bore down.[109]

Ethel prowled out behind them, straightening her skirt and barely registering the scandalous actions of her "boyfriend." Scarhead loped in her wake, a dim grin spread across his mouth like melted butter. He followed close enough that I thought maybe my mother had found a replacement for Burt. No big loss there.[110]

Three, I puked my guts out all over the teppanyaki griddle—a lot. It sputtered and popped like water in a grease fire, specking the boy, his parents, the cute chef and the choir of waitresses and busboys with scalding puke. They pushed away from the table en masse, some

---

[108] Oh yes I did just make a Kris Kringle nose reference.

[109] And if you do count that, I have the number for a therapist I'd recommend. Yes, there are a few left, I haven't eaten. I don't know why you have to get smart with me.

[110] And I mean no BIG loss.

vomiting themselves, others bumping into other diners, smearing them with the mix of bile and bean sprouts. Screams and bilious retching vied for loudest expression. The family stalked out of the room, presumably to find the manager. Only the boy lingered, slipping his hand into his pocket and jotting down a note, which he jogged back and delivered into my palm with another wink.

Come to think of it. Not that bad of a birthday.

Burt Friendly leaned against the doorframe, his house shoe dangling from his raised foot like a scuba flipper and his bulk blocking my way from the bathroom. His robe was open around his chest and the untrimmed thatch of hair grew wild and gray. Old growth. He reached up and closed his robe a bit, mostly, I'm sure, to note that he'd seen my gaze linger.

Not that I was looking for any other reason than it was open to critique. 'Cause I was totally grossed out. Totally.

Especially about the port wine stain that fanned out across his chest like a sex flush, not that I knew what that was back then, but I'm not writing this back then, I'm writing it now.[111]

"Did you have a nice shower?" he asked, looking down his slender nose.

"That's an inappropriate question, Burt." It was too.

His lip curled and eyes steadily examined my face for some sign I might—what—be as slutty as my mother? Be receptive to his come-hither glances?

[111] So just shut up.

Fat chance.

"It's all in your perspective, I suppose." He withdrew into the shadows of the hall, the bathroom light refracting off the mirror and lighting his eyes up like a mask. I slipped past, but slowly, there was no way Friendly would think he intimidated me in the least. Now if he'd grabbed my ass, or pushed me back into the room, I wouldn't have felt too smart.

I listened for the door to close, for a slim piece of wood to separate us before I closed my own door and slipped the chair from my writing desk up under the knob. If that incident had been an isolated thing, I might not have reacted the way I did.

But the glances were too frequent, as was the "accidental" brushing up against me in the halls, kitchen, entryway—anywhere small, really. It didn't take a psychiatrist to diagnose Burt's sex addiction, the business cards were proof enough. I mean, really, where does one even get swinger cards?

I found the tangle of extension cords in one of the boxes of Christmas decorations, just under the handmade felt tree skirt with a patchwork of quilted letters spelling out "Santa's a Corporate Whore." The ball of wire was like a tumor, growing every year with my mother's laziness. She'd simply toss a new cord into the mix and inexplicably, like socks making a run for it through the dryer vent, they seemed to magically entwine themselves.

Like a miracle, only irritating as hell.

Wrestling with the knots took a good week. After I freed a cord, I'd run it down the hall, see how far it would go, then pull it back before anyone could see what I was doing. We had a plush enough carpet that I was able to tuck the cord under the molding without it being noticeable. It took four of them, end to end, to reach the bathroom. One more, almost reached the tub.

Do you see where I'm going with this?

Maybe you do and maybe you don't.

Unless you thought I was trying to kill the guy, then . . . yeah, you'd be right.

That last cord was a real bitch, like sailors had worked on it day and night under threat of the plank. And it had to be the exact one I needed, beige plastic. By the time I loosed it, my fingers were raw and purpled and ached like I'd been clinging to a ledge. But the effort brought the whole plan home.

The open end of the cord dangled a few inches above the floor of the tub. Burt never took baths so, I figured why bother hunting down another tan wire for what would essentially be overkill in the electrified drizzle of a shower. I stood to admire my handiwork.

I felt his breath bristle the hairs on the back of my neck and nearly jumped into the tub.

"Are you gonna take a bath or just stare at it?" he asked, trading places with me.

I was halfway down the hall and ready to plug in the cord when I realized Burt had upped the ante on his sexual harassment and left the bathroom door open a crack. The water gurgled and sputtered against the shower curtain and I couldn't resist peeking. Not to see him naked or anything; that would be gross. Just to see what he was up to.

What I saw was a glimmer of hope.

Burt stood at the counter, a ribbon of condoms trailing from his fist down the side of the cabinet. In his other hand, he pinched a sewing needle. One after another he pierced the centers of the rubbers, threading the metallic squares over the needle like an accordion bellows.

Somebody wanted kids.

Or a wife.

Or something else.

I shuffled back to my room and thought about it a bit as I sat on my bed and pulled at the carpet with my toes. But the more I thought, the more it escaped me. Why would Burt want to get Ethel pregnant? Assuming she still could get pregnant, that is? There'd certainly be no advantage to it. In fact, she hated kids—that part was obvious—and would probably abort.

Or at least, let's hope she would. I couldn't stomach to watch a sister or brother endure the trauma that was Ethel.

I decided I needed another perspective.

I glowered at the scrap of soy sauce–stained napkin the boy had pushed into my palm like it was a wad of dirty chewing gum. It was a phone number, obviously, with his name scraggled below in an ugly shaky cursive.

Geoffrey.

He didn't even have the decency to shorten it to Geoff, or spare me the pretention of the old English spelling. The effs sprawled across the note like pin-up girls. I was pretty sure I hated the kid, so it came as a bit of a surprise—even to me—when I poked the number into the phone.

His mother picked up on the second ring.

"Hello, Stanford residence?" Her voice was as cold and priggish as I'd remembered.

"Is Geoff at home?"

"He's at home, yes. But his name is Geoffrey." She paused, an audible sigh leaking out of her like gas. "Who's this?"

"Amanda."

"Well . . . Amanda. How do you know our Geoffrey?"

Jesus Christ, I thought. Was the bitch writing a book? I almost asked, too, but figured she'd hang up and immediately get in touch with the phone company to report me as a terrorist or some shit. Probably had the cops on speed dial or chained in her basement.

Mothers.

Downstairs, Ethel was having it out with the stove or the microwave or something. Her screams echoed through the bare halls, decidedly "décor-free" on the upper levels. Ethel went through periods and in those days, she had a subscription to *Architectural Digest* and minimalism suited her budget just fine. So you wouldn't find a painting or a color on any wall, unless it resulted from a shattered bottle of ketchup, thrown at a would-be suitor stupid enough to question Ethel's opinion. She had quite a few of those.

"I said, how do you know Geoffrey?"

"We met at school." Time to pull out the charm for the tight-ass. "He's told me so much about you I feel like I know you."

"Oh well, that's lovely to hear."

Hooked. I suppressed a giggle.

A soft scruff came through the phone. Mrs. Stanford must have been holding her hand over the receiver, politely, I was sure. If it had been the 50s she'd have removed her button earring and put it in a small china dish for safekeeping during the call. The dish, no doubt, sitting next to the Stanford family Bible, lovingly engraved and gilded and barely worn, an heir-loom. "Geoffrey, dear. You have a phone call."

"I know." His voice piping up creepily nearly si-multaneously.

"Oh. I see."

"You can hang up now." His voice cracked with sleep, or maybe the char of too much pot.

"That's fine, dear. Don't stay on the phone long, I've got your favorite meal tonight. Sloppy Joes." I imagined her staring blankly into her living room, eyes lighting on the glints of light reflecting off the plastic sofa cover, a bland smile plastered on her lips like a mannequin.

"Whatever," he said and we both listened for her phone to hang up.

I suddenly felt nauseous.[112] Why had I even dialed this kid? It's not like he possessed even an ounce of charisma. He wasn't even all that cute with his Luke Perry sideburns and those dimples could have been pockmarks for all I knew. It was unlikely he bathed, guys like that always have some hygiene issue. Probably stunk.

"I knew you'd call."

"Do you always listen in on phone calls? 'Cause I gotta say that's kind of creepy."

"You're right. It is."

"So you admit to being creepy."

"I do."

"Do you suppose it makes you mysterious and thus somehow magically desirable?"

---

[112] Suddenly isn't a word I use a lot, because I hate it. It implies an absence of forethought and poor planning. Bear in mind, I'm a teenager in this flashback. I appreciate your leeway.

"You tell me. You're the one that called."

I didn't like where this was headed. Now, back then I wasn't nearly the confident and forward Amanda you know (and love), but I was working on it. This guy had me beat in that department. Beat by a mile.

"I just figured I'd find out what you wanted."

"I suspect you know." I heard some banging around on his end, then a background assault of grunge. Screaming Trees, I thought, or Mother Love Bone, some amalgam of flannel-wearing second-string rockers with dirty guitars and even filthier hair. I countered with the Pixies. Velouria.

Take *that,* trend hopper.

"In fact, I *don't* know, smart ass. That's why I called."

"I figured maybe you wanted to meet up and maybe go to a movie or something." Something changed in his voice about halfway through the sentence, a slight quiver, like he'd brushed up against some wool and caught a shock.

Sounded like weakness to me. If Ethel was good for anything it was teaching how to spot prey. I had no choice, did I? I pounced.

"Was that your voice shaking just then?"

"Uh."

"Oh wow. Sounded like nerves for a moment."

Next comes the defensive posture. Like clockwork.

"No, it wasn't."

"Oh no, Geoffrey?" I think I pronounced it "Joffrey" and lingered on it, so he'd get my point.

"No."

"Okay then. Let's plan on a movie. But I get to pick, I'm not watching anything with Mel Gibson or Danny Glover, or buddies that save the day."

"Uh . . . okay." He'd traded up to Soundgarden. Chris

### *Battle for Musical Taste Supremacy*

*(90s Edition)*

*Alice in Chains • "Would?"*
*The Pixies • "Velouria"*
*Soundgarden • "Spoonman"*
*The Sugarcubes • "Motorcrash"*
*Mother Love Bone • "Crown of*
*Thorns"*
*Sister of Mercy • "This Corrosion"*
*Temple of the Dog • "Hunger Strike"*
*Bikini Kill • "Rebel Girl"*
*Nirvana • "Territorial Pissings"*
*The Dandy Warhols • "Not if*
*You Were the Last Junkie on Earth"*
*Pearl Jam • "Jeremy"*
*Portishead • "Sour Times"*
*Stone Temple Pilots • "Sex Type*
*Thing"*
*Radiohead • "Karma Police"*

Cornell may have been the only one of those Seattle guys that actually owned a bottle of shampoo, so I was almost hesitant to crank up The Sugarcubes and let Bjork massacre him with quirky vocals.

Almost.

"So, when's it going to be, lover?" I wished I could have reigned in that last word. My mother used it with nearly every man she ever met, like normal people use "sweetheart" to refer to all girls, or "slugger" for boys they hoped didn't end up wearing high heels and jizz on their blouses. For a moment, I thought he hadn't heard it. But the pause was just a few seconds too long.

"Lover?" he asked.

"Shut up and hang on. I'm going to get the newspaper."

"Well, we could skip the movie."

I let the phone drop on my nightstand the second he spoke, hoping it would cause a loud squelch on his end rather than just a squatty thud, though with my luck, I'd probably broken the phone. Ethel would put me through the ringer for a new one. I reached for it instinctively, checking for cracks and hazarded a pert blow into the mouthpiece. It echoed. A second later, Geoff sighed on the other end, but not the irritated kind. Bile rose in my throat.


Geoff slouched on a bench in front of the Orange Julius, one foot rocking back and forth on a crushed Coke can. The loud crinkling bought him all sorts of sneers from the blue-haired mall-walking set, who couldn't catch a break on their quiet pretzel eating. Not today. The boy wore a faded Nirvana tour shirt and some faded jeans, torn at the knees and tucked into a pair of scuffed Doc Marten boots. His hair fell in a touseled mangle of waves. When he spotted me he curled the sides behind his ears, smirked and kicked the can off into the main mall hallway, where it caught up in the plastic wheels of a stroller. The infuriated mother mouthed an exaggerated "Fuck you."

"Torturing passers-by?" I asked, sinking onto the bench beside him, but clearly leaving enough room for his attitudes.

He grinned, scooted a little closer to me. "One of my favorite pastimes."

"Listen." I threw him a bone and patted his shoulder. "I'm not gonna blow you or anything. What exactly are you expecting here?"

"Hey. You called me, remember? I was just thinking movie." He sucked at his teeth, much like Gil does now when he spots a tap.

"My intentions are just to pick your brain."

He scowled, followed a youngish mother of two as she led her jelly-smeared toddlers to the kid corral, her ass jiggling out from underneath a pair of Daisy Dukes like a couple of bald prison escapees.

"My mother just found out she's pregnant," he mumbled.

I cleared my throat. "Interesting you should say that. Remember that guy we were with at the teriyaki place?"

"Teppanyaki."

"Whatever."

"Yeah, I remember. He was pretty cool."

I rolled my eyes. "I'm going to pretend you just had a seizure and forget that you said that. Anyways. I caught him skewering his condoms in the bathroom."

"Weird."

"Yeah, he'd have to be crazy to want children with Ethel, the only reason for her to squeeze out another one would be to eat it."

Geoffrey chuckled a bit, eyes crinkling at the corner

in this odd way that made me laugh too. He reached over and put his arm around my shoulder, started leaning in.

I grabbed his hand and tossed his arm away. "Too soon."

He pouted.

"Now. There's no question I've got to get rid of the guy and, frankly, if my mother found out he was trying to implant her with his little Burt Friendlies, she'd yank out her own tubes."

"Well, then that's it," he said, licking the end of a cigarette and sticking it to his lower lip to dangle.

"What's it?"

"She's got to find out. Why don't you tell her?"

"She'd never believe me, she knows I hate him. I hate all her boyfriends. It's kind of a rule."

He shrugged his shoulders. "You're going to have to frame him."

I thought about it a moment and, as I'm me, came up with a hideous plot to expose Burt Friendly as the sick father fantasist he was and cause both pain and suffering to Ethel in the process. It was really a win-win situation.

So excited about the possibility of ridding my life of Burt Friendly, I leaned over and planted a kiss on Geoffrey's cheek. He blushed a bit and then threw his arms around me, pulling me back toward his lazily puckered lips.

"Ew, no. That was an accident."

"It felt on purpose to me. Look." He gestured to the bulge in his jeans. "You made me hard."

I balled up my hand into a fist, making like I'd punch him in the balls. "And I can make you soft."

His hands rushed to cover himself, even as he twisted away.

"So, I'm gonna need your help. It's not going to be easy or clean, but I'll make it worth your while." I was thinking of making out with him. But . . .

"If you fuck me."

"I'm not fucking you. I'm a virgin for Christ's sake. Can't you smell the purity?" I smirked. "It rolls off of me in fucking waves."

He snorted, licked his lips. "Yeah, I can."

"How about a handjob," I offered.

He glanced down at his crotch, domed and zipper exposed. "Blowjob."

"Deal."


We stopped by the little drug store by the food court—you know the one, prices jacked up on things like Pepto and Maxi-Pads, those items you inevitably forget until you're in a public place and start spraying out of one hole or another—and picked up the supplies: a Ball jar, a lightweight and clear plastic bowl, a bottle of syrup of ipecac and a key chain, the kind that looks like an "o" with a hinge that opens it up like a vise.

I put the plan into effect the following morning.

Ethel woke up promptly at 8:30, like clockwork—that way she could avoid me entirely as I'd have just left for school. Never one to be accused of being slovenly, she'd start her day with a brisk walk around the neighborhood, a tepid shower—her blood was ice-cold anyway—and close out the morning with a nice bowl of oatmeal with a quarter of a cup of half and half, no more, no less.

I wasn't sure how much ipecac would have the desired effect so I opted for half the bottle. I began hearing the complaints that very night.

"I think it's the stomach flu," Burt answered flatly.

"It's food poisoning. I'm certain."

The next morning was Saturday and so I had the distinct pleasure of being home to hear Ethel heaving her oatmeal into the toilet. I stood behind my bedroom door, ear to the wood veneer, and tried not to giggle.

By Sunday, the topic finally came up.

"Do you think it could be morning sickness?" Burt's tone was light and hopeful.

I made the corner of the open doorframe just in time to see my mother's head spin toward him, vomit flapping from her lips as she yelled. "It better not be!"

"Mother. I'll go get you a home pregnancy test. Don't worry about a thing." I crouched next to her and rubbed her back. It did quiver a bit from the unnatural sensation of tenderness between daughter and mother, but she acquiesced.

"Fine." She pushed away from the spattered toilet and glowered at Burt. "You. Stay away, at least till we figure this shit out."

I got on the phone to Geoffrey and gave him the prearranged code word, his idea. "Blowjob," I whispered into the receiver.

"I have it right here."

"Meet me in five minutes at Wilson Park." He paused a moment and then spoke again, suddenly breathless. "And wear something sexy."

"Shut up," I spat and hung up, forcing the paper bag with the home pregnancy test into my purse.

*　　*　　*

The "Cram Shack" sat atop a wooded hill in the forest on the far side of the park, appropriately "crammed" between a large boulder and an odd evergreen tree that mangled together in growth like a morbidly undivided set of conjoined Chinese twins. The piece of corrugated metal everyone used as a door was askew, so I knew Geoffrey was already inside. What I didn't know was that he'd already gotten started.

I peeked in the triangle-shaped gap and saw him leaned back on the dirty couch, rubbing his crotch through a dingy pair of camouflage pants.

"Whoa," I chided. "Hold on. We're not doing this now."

"If you want this pee we are." He held up a little baggie. "You know what I had to go through to collect it?"

"I can imagine, but I don't think we have the time." Even as I said the words, I could see in his face that, one, we'd have plenty of time, and, two, I wasn't as prepared as I let on.

I sat down beside him and slipped my hand over his thigh and across the front of his pants. There was definitely something hard in there, running just underneath the fabric like a vein under skin. I rubbed it a bit and he groaned, his head lolling on his shoulders.

I chewed at my lower lip and pulled my hand away. Geoffrey's hands fumbled for the button and zipper, which snagged halfway, forcing him to stand up and slip them down his hips.

"Are you gonna take those off?" I pointed at his boxers—reindeer frolicked on winter whites, Rudolph's nose sticking out farther than the rest as the boy's thing tented the fabric in precisely the right spot for some inappropriate and terribly unsexy animation.

"Yeah." He grinned uncomfortably and then closed his eyes as he slid the boxers down, reaching inside to free his erection over the band.·

It wasn't what I'd expected, just sort of tube-shaped and veiny, not big enough to be scary really, but at the same time, absolutely horrifying. It was smooth and the hair around it smelled like verbena or lavender or whatever old women like when they buy nice soap.

I looked up only once while I was doing it, not even sure I was doing it right, just sort of sucking and licking at it awkwardly. But Geoffrey's face explained everything, contorted in a grimace of both pain and panting pleasure, his breath shallow one moment and then gasping for air the next. When he came, his hips bucked and I pulled away.

That was for the best.

I would have never been able to figure out what to do with the junk that came out. Not back then, at least, it was just too weird a moment.

Geoff lay there a bit with his eyes closed and his penis soft against the top of his thigh. I stood above him and waited, not sure for what, or why I didn't just snatch up the bag with the Ball jar in it, which lay nearby atop a wire spool the kids used like a table. But I didn't.

When he opened his eyes they were wet with tears, but I think he was happy. I didn't ask.

"I'm going to get going." I reached for the bag and he nodded, pulling his pants up around him.

Geoffrey and I didn't go to the same school, or frequent the same places.

I never saw him again.

What I remembered about that day was the power I had over him.

\* \* \*

Back at the house, Ethel was finally coming to grips with her stomach and was apparently able to keep down water as she was guzzling it from the straw in a Big Gulp cup.

I followed her into the bathroom, hiding the small jar under my sleeve. "Here's the test. Says you just pee on it and then wait."

She handed me the strip of white plastic and walked out of the room. A bonus, since I was sure I'd have to somehow pour Mrs. Stanford's pee without Ethel seeing. I'd all but resigned myself to the idea of sopping my sleeve with urine in the process. But sometimes things turn out.

Just like the little plus sign on the test strip.

Ethel went crazy, screaming at Burt at the top of her lungs, while he deflected her blows and pledged his undying love. He even had a ring on hand to pop the question.

"You did this to me on purpose," she accused.

"Of course not, honey."

I cleared my throat loudly and played my final card.

And dropped the key ring of condoms—each one pierced through its center—into my mother's open hand.

# Amanda's
## *Très Importante*
# Authorial
# Acknowledgments

This book was a labor of love, and by labor, I do mean it was like forcing a fat baby out of my ass. A baby I'd never conceived if it weren't for Gil's prodding. So you have him to thank for all the fabulousness and pathos.

I should thank Johnny Birch, as this story never would have happened without his smarmy shenanigans, but I'm not going to. He should thank me. *American Minions* would have tanked, low-budget bullshit that it was. Now his name is associated with one of the most top-rated series ever. Thank you.

A thousand thank-yous to Scott for putting up with my dead ass. You really are a reason to keep pretending I'm alive.

I'd like to thank my readers.

Some of you get it. I mean really get it. The others

can just go on believing that their soy lattes with Splenda, SLOW-CHILDREN-AT-PLAY street signs, organic produce, and low-carbon footprints will save them from the inevitable. Sad.

We know it's not so horrible.

It's just more life.

I'm thankful for that, too.